THE
VANISHING

THE
VANISHING

Bentley Little

A SIGNET BOOK

SIGNET
Published by New American Library, a division of
Penguin Group (USA) Inc., 375 Hudson Street,
New York, New York 10014, USA
Penguin Group (Canada), 90 Eglinton Avenue East, Suite 700, Toronto,
Ontario M4P 2Y3, Canada (a division of Pearson Penguin Canada Inc.)
Penguin Books Ltd., 80 Strand, London WC2R 0RL, England
Penguin Ireland, 25 St. Stephen's Green, Dublin 2,
Ireland (a division of Penguin Books Ltd.)
Penguin Group (Australia), 250 Camberwell Road, Camberwell, Victoria 3124,
Australia (a division of Pearson Australia Group Pty. Ltd.)
Penguin Books India Pvt. Ltd., 11 Community Centre, Panchsheel Park,
New Delhi - 110 017, India
Penguin Group (NZ), 67 Apollo Drive, Rosedale, North Shore 0745,
Auckland, New Zealand (a division of Pearson New Zealand Ltd.)
Penguin Books (South Africa) (Pty.) Ltd., 24 Sturdee Avenue,
Rosebank, Johannesburg 2196, South Africa

Penguin Books Ltd., Registered Offices:
80 Strand, London WC2R 0RL, England

First published by Signet, an imprint of New American Library,
a division of Penguin Group (USA) Inc.

ISBN 978-0-7394-8575-0

Ⓓ REGISTERED TRADEMARK—MARCA REGISTRADA

Printed in the United States of America

PUBLISHER'S NOTE
This is a work of fiction. Names, characters, places, and incidents either are
the product of the author's imagination or are used fictitiously, and any resemblance to actual persons, living or dead, business establishments, events, or
locales is entirely coincidental.

The publisher does not have any control over and does not assume any
responsibility for author or third-party Web sites or their content.

This book is dedicated to all of my loyal readers, especially Lisa Allen and Paul Legerski. I know you're out there. And I appreciate it.

A special thanks to Lisa LaMunyon and Doug Lilley, who lent their names to this novel in order to raise money for Golden Hill Elementary School.

One

Another gorgeous day in paradise.

Well, it wasn't really that gorgeous. The sky was white with smog rather than a traditional clear blue, and outside the air-conditioned environment of his Lexus, the temperature was far too warm to be comfortable. And it wasn't really paradise. Just a few blocks down Sunset, transplanted pieces of used white trash, their dreams of stardom shattered, were either working as record store sales clerks, selling their bodies on the street or dealing drugs in their grim attempts to make ends meet.

But here in Victor Lowry's world, everything was fine. Tentative tourists were walking up the Rodeo Drive sidewalks with their usual mixture of bravado and nervousness, knowing they didn't belong but still prepared to aggressively defend their presence at the drop of a hat, while the matrons of Beverly Hills emerged from their gated homes on their way to multihour lunches with their friends and the young brides of older executives jogged along the winding roads pushing elaborately customized baby strollers.

Victor flew by them all, ignoring the speed limit as he swooped down the hill toward Wilshire and his office, CD player cranked up to earsplitting volume. Banners for the latest exhibition at the LA County Museum of

Art hung from streetlamps as he turned left off La Brea. His parents were donors and permanent members, and he'd gone to the museum practically once a week when he was a kid. But the exposure hadn't taken, and it had been years since he'd been inside the buildings. He felt guilty about that—but not guilty enough to actually start going. His interest was in pop culture not high culture, and the way he saw it, life was too short to go around feigning interest in subjects that didn't appeal to him . . . even if it would impress other people.

Like his dad.

Victor turned hard into the underground parking garage, waving his electronic passkey to open the gate and pulling into the space marked with his name. There was no reason for him to have his own office, really, but apparently his father wanted him to *pretend* that he was some sort of businessman, that he had skills and talents of his own and wasn't merely coasting through life on the coattails of his family.

Victor got into the garage elevator and pressed the button for fifteen.

The old man was one of those power-of-positive-thinking guys. He didn't seem to realize that it was luck more than anything else that had led to his prosperity, and he continued to believe that focus and determination accounted for his success. It was why he had called his son "Victor." He'd wanted to give him a name that *meant* something, that was descriptive of something to which he could aspire, and though Victor didn't really like his name, at least it *was* a name—as opposed to "Champion" and some of the other appellations that his dad had originally considered, all of which sounded like descriptions of racehorses.

The office had been a carrot, an attempt to woo him into a life of purpose and productivity. He even had his own secretary, Amy. And while Victor still didn't find the business world at all appealing, he felt obligated to put on the engaged-and-highly-motivated-son act and, at the very least, go through the motions. Because if he didn't make a go of it, Amy would be unemployed, as would several programmers who did not work out of his office but over whom he was in charge. He didn't want that on his conscience.

Slowly but surely, against his will, his dad was reeling him in.

Victor resented him for that.

The elevator arrived at the fifteenth floor, and he walked down the carpeted hallway past the mortgage company and the property management firm to the un-marked door that led to his office. Amy was typing something on her computer and she looked up when he entered. "Good morning, Mr. Lo—Victor," she cor-rected herself.

He smiled. "Good catch."

"Sorry. I'm still not used to the informality."

"That's what working for my dad'll do to you."

Amy held out a stack of mail. "Are you in today?"

"For the morning," he said. He walked past her desk into his private office, pretending to sort through the mail. Victor liked Amy, but he had a sneaking suspicion that part of her job was to keep tabs on him and report back to his dad. It was why, even after six months, the two of them were emotionally still at arm's length with each other, and why he spent most of his time away from her. Several times, he'd considered letting her know what his dad had told him, that despite her loyalty and hard work, she would be out on her ear should Victor screw up this opportunity. But he had the feeling that she would immediately tell the old man, who would feed her a reassuring lie, and then his relationships with both his father and his secretary would be more strained than they already were.

He threw the mail on his desk and stood next to the window, looking down at the traffic on Wilshire Boulevard. He shouldn't have come in today. He should have just called Amy, told her he was busy, and spent the day cruising around, having fun.

There was still the afternoon.

He flopped down into his chair, turned on his PC and then swiveled around in a circle while he waited for the computer to boot up. There wasn't really any work for him to do, but if he touched base with the programmers, had Amy send an update memo to their clients and answered his e-mail, it would look like he'd accomplished something today and he could bail, guilt free, after lunch.

Victor accessed his e-mail. There was the usual spam and assorted interbusiness correspondence, but jumping out at him was a message from his father, sent earlier this morning. He called it up, his stomach already tightening. Whenever his dad e-mailed him, it was always with some sort of "suggestion" that was really nothing more than veiled criticism of his job performance, a helpful reminder that he was not as smart or as successful as he should be.

Not this time, though.

Instead of words, streaming video appeared on his monitor, and the knot in Victor's stomach tightened even further as he watched, his dread growing as he viewed the unfolding images. A close-up of a growling dog's face pulled back to reveal that the dog's head was severed and sitting atop what looked like a wedding cake. The camera panned around, finding not only the animal's lifeless, bloody body on a white-sheeted bed, but a mutilated bride and groom lying on the bedroom floor, their faces shoved into matching dog bowls. Words appeared onscreen, white letters against a black background: THIS IS WHERE IT BEGINS.

Suddenly, two naked old people, an Asian man and a dark, possibly Hispanic, woman, were in what looked like an empty garage, dancing crazily on oil-stained cement, lunatic smiles held tight on their otherwise pain-racked faces.

The man's genitals had been hacked off.

The woman's breasts had been sliced from her chest.

Both were bleeding profusely from their wounds, the blood mixing with the dried oil on the garage floor and making a sickening sticky puddle. No audio accompanied the images, and the sight of the two old people in their grotesque dance seemed all the more frightening for the silence. It gave the scene, in a strange way, a documentary verisimilitude that sound would have lessened.

The dancing grew quicker, more jerky, as though the camera had sped up, and the entire scene spun, became blurry, segueing into an extreme close-up of a yellow plaque–covered tooth, which once again pulled back to show the growling mouth of the dead dog.

Victor stared at the blank screen, feeling more unnerved than he'd expected. He'd seen far worse things in horror movies, but the immediacy of the video and the sense that it was real, that it was a recording of actual events rather than a staged depiction of a fictional narrative, made it seem especially disconcerting to him.

And the fact that it had been sent to him by his dad?

That was the creepiest thing of all.

Of course, lately his old man had been talking about investing some of his money in a movie. A hard-core film fan, Victor was all in favor of the idea. He was well aware that in Hollywood, con artists routinely scammed wealthy businessmen out of millions of dollars with the promise of producer credits and lucrative back-end deals should their false projects get made. Indeed, his dad had been approached numerous times by filmmakers looking for private investors, and none of those movies had ever come to fruition. But recently, with all of the problems at the studios, a lot of legitimate directors had gone the indie route and were lining up their own financing. Victor himself had fielded calls from half a dozen big-name directors on his father's behalf, and his suggestion was to roll the dice.

Maybe, he thought, one of those filmmakers had submitted the video to his dad as an example of his work, and his father was merely passing it along to him for his opinion.

Why no explanation, though? Why no cover page?

The whole thing was disturbing.

What made it even more unsettling was that the dog looked familiar. And so, come to think of it, did the bedroom. And the garage. He had seen them before, but he could not for the life of him remember where. He thought hard, trying to place everything, but he kept drawing a blank.

He replayed the video once more and was again nagged by a sense of familiarity, although full recognition remained frustratingly out of reach.

The damn thing was even creepier on second viewing.

He'd never gotten the hang of the office's phone system, so he called out to Amy and asked her to give his dad a call and patch him through. A few moments later, she knocked on the doorframe and poked her head in. "I'm sorry. He's unavailable."

"Who'd you get? Tyler? Janeane?"

She shook her head. "He hasn't checked in today. No one knows where he is."

Victor thought of the e-mail. In the back of his mind was the vague thought that his dad might be in trouble, that there might be something wrong, but he dismissed that possibility almost immediately. There was nothing Tom Lowry couldn't talk or buy his way out of, and if there'd been any sort of medical emergency, he would have instantly found his way to the finest room in the finest hospital.

Maybe he was having an affair.

The idea made Victor smile. He couldn't imagine his straitlaced old man doing any such thing. Hell, he couldn't even imagine him with his mom.

"Well, try again later," he said. "I need to talk to him about something."

Amy nodded. "Okay."

But there was still no sign of his father at lunchtime when he left. He grabbed a couple of hotdogs from his favorite Farmers' Market stand and then went to Amoeba to look for new music. Hooking up with a few friends, he spent the rest of the afternoon just chilling, and forgot all about his dad.

There was a concert he wanted to see that night at the Wiltern—a retro pairing of Joe Jackson and Todd Rundgren, with the opening act Ethel to attract scenesters—and he scored some scalped tickets outside the venue after picking up Sharline at her apartment. They'd parted on bad terms last week after a very public fight at the SkyBar, but she seemed to have forgotten all about it—either that or she was so desperate to partake of some nightlife that she was willing to completely tamp down her true feelings—and when they had a couple of drinks at the bar across the street before going into the theater, everything seemed fine.

The concert itself was amazing, the performers exhibiting a virtuosity and breadth of styles that made him nostalgic for the eclecticism of the 1970s.

Not that he'd actually been around then.

Victor wished he *had* been born twenty years earlier, that he'd been a teenager or young adult in the seventies. He'd missed completely the artistic ambition of that decade, experiencing it only thirdhand, but he still found it compelling enough that he actively sought out music and movies from that period. As critics never seemed to tire of pointing out, even all these years later, there'd been overreaching, but Victor found that vastly preferable to the complacent mediocrity with which he'd grown up. Francis Ford Coppola, not content with his *Godfather* success, had striven for even greater heights with the vastly more ambitious *Apocalypse Now.* Woody Allen built upon *Annie Hall* with *Manhattan* and then the truly daring *Stardust Memories.* Rock groups like Emerson, Lake & Palmer and Renaissance incorporated symphonic textures in their music and toured with their own orchestras. Even hard rockers like KISS put out simultaneously released solo albums in which they followed their own muses.

What had happened to those sorts of aspirations? Why was everyone now content just to coast within the easy parameters of their abilities?

Why was he?

This always happened when he attended concerts he really enjoyed. He always ended up thinking about the unbridgeable gap between perfection and reality, between the way things ought to be and the way they really were.

He forced himself to clear his mind and concentrate only on the music.

Afterward, he took Sharline back to her apartment and did her quick and hard on the floor of the living room, finishing in her ass though he knew she didn't like it that way. "You bastard!" she yelled, slapping him as she pulled away and headed to the bathroom, one hand cupped between her legs. He smiled. It helped him get off, doing things to women they didn't like, and he supposed if he had a shrink that was one of the things they'd have to talk about. He felt good, happy, and he pulled up his pants, shouted good-bye and left before she came out, not really wanting to see her right now, not sure if he ever wanted to see her again.

It was late, after midnight. Beverly Hills was a city that went to bed early, where the sidewalks were rolled up by eight and whatever happened after dark happened behind tall walls and security gates, and he sped up the winding road toward home, the only car on the street. To his surprise, the gates to his family's house were wide open. He slowed down, in case one of his parents was on the way out, but the short drive was empty and both the Mercedes and the Jaguar were parked in front of the garage in their usual spots. Seemingly all the lights in the house were on because the windows were blazing. None of the shades or curtains had been drawn.

That was odd.

Victor pushed the button on his dashboard to close the gate and pulled to a stop next to the fountain.

The door to the house was open.

He cut the engine and got out of the car, looking around the upper drive, trying to see through the first-floor windows. He approached the entryway of the house and started up the porch steps, stopping at the top. He should have dialed 911 immediately, but he didn't want to look like a complete candyass in front of the police if it turned out to be nothing, so he poked his head in the foyer. "Dad?" he called.

"Back here, Vic!"

Alarm bells were going off in his head. The joyous, almost singsongy voice was nothing like his father's usual rumbling stentorian tones, and he could not recall the old man *ever* calling him "Vic."

He thought of this morning's e-mail. The streaming video.

Suddenly, he realized where he'd seen the dog before. And the bedroom. And the garage. It had been years since he'd seen them, but they belonged to the Jensons, their next-door neighbors.

This is where it begins.

"Vic!"

It was a game. It had to be. Or a trick. "What?" he called out.

"Come here!"

Call 911, his brain was telling him. *Dial 911.*

He walked through the foyer, through the living room, through the drawing room, down the east hall. All of the lights *were* on, and that was a red flag right there. His mom was a freak about conserving energy, and unless there were guests, she never left lights on in an empty room. Especially now, in the middle of the night, when both of his parents were usually fast asleep.

Victor realized for the first time that the house was silent. With all of the lights on, Lizzie and Jonnie, his mom's two Pomeranians, should be yapping up a storm.

Maybe his mom had left and taken them with her.

No. The Mercedes was still in the driveway.

"Vic!"

His dad was in the music room, and Victor made his way down the hallway toward the door. He slowed as he approached, not wanting to go right in, thinking he should check it out first, just in case.

Wise move.

The room looked like an abattoir. Blood was splattered over furniture, floor, wall, even the ceiling, in random bursts that reminded him of the paintings in an art exhibition his parents had dragged him to when he was ten. The Pomeranians had been slaughtered and gutted, their entrails flattened and ground into the once-white rug, their little heads smashed open, pieces of their furry bodies strewn about the room. His mom, or what was left of her, was lying on the piano bench, her eviscerated form draped over the seat like an empty rag doll. Her face had been peeled away and placed on a potted palm.

This is where it begins.

There were other bodies in the room as well, but he had no idea who they were or who they could be. Too many hands and feet littered the crimson carpet. The butchery had obviously been going on for some time, probably all day, and Victor stared in horror at the extent of the carnage. This was so far beyond anything he had seen in even the goriest slasher movie that his brain felt numb and heavy and slow, overloaded by the sight. The smell was overpowering, a terrible noxious stench unlike anything he had ever encountered before. The only reason he wasn't throwing up all over his shoes was because the numbness had engulfed all of his senses.

But that wasn't the worst thing.

No, the worst thing was in the far corner of the room. His dad.

Victor stared at his father. The old man was naked, his bare chest streaked with smears of blood, handprints visible in the thick crimson patina that covered his hairy skin, his arms so drenched with gore that they appeared to be skinned. Machete in hand, grinning crazily, his dad bounced from foot to bloody foot, his arousal evident in the large erection that bobbed with each jounce.

Only . . .

Only something was wrong. Very wrong. Victor's eyes were drawn to his father's midsection where, beneath the red wetness, the skin of his stomach looked white and slimy and wormlike. On the sides of his abdomen grew thick, coarse hair, and beneath the overlarge penis, where testicles should have been, was a rounded bony protrusion, like a rhino's horn with the point softened. He tried to remember whether or not he had ever seen his dad naked before. Surely he would have remembered

something this unusual, something this extreme—unless
it was new, unless it was the result of some bizarre disease or a plastic surgery effort that had gone horribly
awry.

No. He knew even as he thought it that that was not
the case. This was who his dad was. His father was hideously malformed and had no doubt been born this way.
Victor glanced automatically at his mother's limp, empty
body. She'd known all along that her husband was like
this.

How could she have brought a child into the world,
knowing it might inherit its father's genes?

Thank God he took after her.

His dad was still bouncing from foot to foot, but he
was moving forward as well, approaching Victor with the
machete extended and an excited gleam in his eye. "Hi,
Vic," he said in that singsongy voice. "Hi, Vic."

Whether or not his father had always been deformed,
he had not been psychotic. This was something new, and
Victor backed up, slowly reaching for his cell phone, not
wanting to make any sudden moves. He wondered where
the craziness had come from, whether it had been gradually building or had arrived full-blown. He didn't recall
any unusual behavior over the past few days. Glancing
down for a moment at the keypad of the phone, he
heard the wet slap of feet, saw a blur of red in his peripheral vision.

"Hi, Vic."

His father was standing right in front of him, grinning,
machete raised.

Victor tried to run.

And then his dad was upon him.

Tom Lowry didn't want to leave his lair, but when the
night passed and then the day and then another night
and another day with no one coming to visit him, no

new victims arriving, he decided to venture out of the room and out of the house.

The result was liberating.

He found a sparrow on the lawn, crushed it in his fingers, feeling the guts ooze between his knuckles. Then he ran through the overgrown bushes on the edge of the property, blade in hand, hopping the fence that led to the Akkads' lot next door, snaking along the perimeter of their property and sneaking into the next yard down the hill. A guard dog came after him, and he cut off the animal's head with one swipe, reveling in the blood as it gushed from the gaping wound. Before anyone could come out to investigate, he was gone, onto the next property, where he drank water from a birdbath and ate half a dozen mosquitoes. Branches slashed his buttocks, thorns scraped his erection, but he continued down the hill, house to house to house. In this way, he made it onto Sunset, slinking silently through the shadows, moving purposefully toward the lights of the strip.

And other people.

He was hacking up a girl in a Hamburger Hamlet parking lot when the police finally took him down.

Two

It had been nearly a decade since Brian Howells had been home, and what surprised him most as he headed up the Central Valley was that it had not grown the way Southern California had. If anything, the Valley seemed to have shrunk. There weren't miles of pink- and peach-colored Spanish-style tract homes and condos; there were no new golf courses or open-air malls. There were only dirty oleanders and eucalyptus trees lining a deteriorating too-narrow highway, and periodic clusters of old restaurants, trailer courts and industrial agriculture buildings that had been in use the last time he'd passed through here but were now abandoned. It was as if the already sparse population had constricted even further as ranching families went bankrupt and younger generations moved to the cities in the South.

Brian didn't care. There was something comforting about being in a place that was real, that wasn't always in the process of reinventing itself and expanding. He felt curiously reassured by the dying, dusty farm towns, and he was glad that he'd decided to make this trip home.

He drove past a peeling billboard advertising a local Ford dealership. He'd been living in Orange County ever since graduating from college, and though his mom had come down a few times to visit him, and they'd all spent holidays at his sister, Jillian's, house in San Diego, he had not been back to Bakersfield since winning the scholarship and leaving home the summer after high school. Part of it was logistics. Although he'd had two days off work each week, they'd rarely been consecutive, and even then he'd usually been on call. Not to mention the fact that he'd never trusted his crappy car enough to drive it out of Southern California. But now, after three years at the *Register* and two prestigious journalism awards, he'd been hired by the *Los Angeles Times.* There was a one-week gap between his last day at the *Register* and his first day at the *Times,* and he'd decided on the spur of the moment to rent a car, visit his mom and spend a few days with her. When he called his sister and told her, she'd offered to bring her family up as well, but he let her know politely that he wanted to do this alone. He needed to spend a little quality time with his mother.

Because the truth was, it hadn't been merely practical considerations that had kept him away from Bakersfield. That rationalization was legit as far as it went, and it made him feel better to think those were the only reasons, but in actuality he was the one who'd always insisted that they hold their get-togethers at Jillian's house, he was the one who'd invited his mom to come down and visit him whenever she tried to entice him back home, and he was the one who made his mother's few brief stays so physically uncomfortable that she couldn't wait to leave.

Was it his mom he'd been avoiding? His hometown? Or both? He wasn't sure. But he was determined to find out and to confront the problem head-on.

Bakersfield, as usual, was encased in smog, the series of concrete overpasses that bridged the sunken highway blurred by a haze of white. *Bakersfield has two seasons,* his sister liked to joke, *smog and fog.* There was more than a little truth to that, and as he pulled up the off-ramp and turned right, his eyes began to water, and he cranked up the air-conditioning.

His mom still lived in the old house. What used to be the field on the corner was now a vacant lot, and old man Murphy's chicken ranch across the street was gone, replaced with a cul-de-sac of unsold spec homes. Back in Southern California (or SoCal, as he was going to have to start calling it now that he was a *Times* staffer), his Bakersfield roots seemed cool. The town's connection to Buck Owens and Merle Haggard, both perennially hip among people who didn't actually listen to country music, gave him cultural cache. But in truth, the town was a dumpy lower-middle class community with gang graffiti spray painted on the sides of stucco houses and weedy yards enclosed by cinderblock fences. Downtown was a jumble of indistinguishable businesses interspersed with grimy gas stations and fast-food joints. He remembered now why he'd been so anxious to leave.

Still, it was nice to see his mom again, and over lemonade in the living room he caught her up on the details of events that he'd only outlined over the phone. Friends of hers who'd known him as a child dropped by, obviously invited by his mother and just as obviously warned to make sure their visits seemed casual and completely spontaneous. He didn't mind. It helped to have a buffer between him and his mom. He needed time to work up to the discussions he knew they had to have.

At night, after taking his mother out to dinner (she'd insisted on Denny's because she liked their chicken-fried steak, even though he'd tried his damnedest to get her to go to Souplantation or someplace even moderately healthy), they drove home the back way, past the Baptist church she used to drag him to when he was young. Like everything else in town, the chapel looked shabby, as though it hadn't been painted or fixed up in years, and

Brian found that depressing. He'd never liked church—particularly *that* church, where his ever-changing teenage hairstyles had been the object of ridicule and scorn from the tight-assed pastor—but, still, the sorry state of the building left him feeling melancholy. He wondered if his mom continued to attend services there. He didn't want to bring up the subject, because he knew it would lead to a lecture and an argument, but as they turned left beyond the edge of the church parking lot, his mom said, "Reverend Charles asked about you the other day."

"Really?" he said noncommittally.

"He knows you're a writer and thought you might help us out with our letter-writing campaign. The school board refused to allow science teachers in the district to talk about creationism *or* intelligent design. We're trying to get that changed."

"Mom . . ."

"Don't worry. I told him you wouldn't be interested."

"Okay, then."

"But it *is* important."

"Yeah, you're right. They should be teaching religion at school and leave that controversial stuff like science for parents to teach their kids at home."

"Don't you start blasphemin' with me."

He sighed. "I'm not, Mom."

"I didn't raise you to—"

"Let's just drop it, okay? I'm sorry."

"Well . . ." She mumbled to herself the rest of the way home, but he purposely didn't listen because he didn't want to take the bait. His mom had always been religious, but she'd never been nutty. He wasn't sure that was still true. He remembered when he was a teenager and his mom had first voiced the then-shocking opinion that she didn't believe in evolution. He'd asked why, if that were the case, people living closer to the equator were darker than people who lived in northern climes. Since, theoretically, everyone was descended from Adam—or, more correctly, Noah—didn't that imply that they had adapted to their environments and *evolved*? She'd laughed and said simply that God worked in mysterious ways.

He wasn't sure she would have the same reaction now. She seemed much more serious, much more set in her opinions these days. And disbelief in evolution was no longer just a fringe viewpoint. An antiintellectual, antiscience attitude now seemed to hold permanent sway over vast sections of the country.

The thought of that made him even more depressed.

He pulled into the dark driveway. He'd forgotten how black the night was away from metropolitan areas. "You should get a light with a motion detector out here, so it turns on when you come home."

"I never go out at night."

They walked up to the front porch in silence. Brian had the feeling that she was mad at him, and he marveled at how quickly the shared joy they'd felt at seeing each other had faded. He tried to think of something to say that would bridge the gap, but nothing came to mind, and as his mother slammed her purse down on the breakfront next to the door, he walked silently into the family room and turned on the television.

After several minutes in the kitchen, she joined him.

They sat in separate chairs, watching the news.

When a commercial came on for a new Dodge van, his mother shifted in her seat and turned toward him. "I got a letter from your father," she said.

Brian felt as though he'd been sucker punched in the gut. "What?"

"At least I think it's from him."

"Why didn't you tell me earlier? Why didn't you say anything?" He stared at her in disbelief, then took a deep breath, forcing himself to remain calm. No one in the family had heard from his father in more than twenty years. It wasn't one of those situations where a guy goes out for a carton of milk and never returns, but neither was it a typical separation, because, although his dad had informed his mom that he was leaving, he had not said where he was going. And once he had gone, it was as though he'd never existed. He'd never called or written or contacted the family in any way.

Until, apparently, now.

His mom sat there, unmoving, watching the television now that the news had come back on. A reporter was interviewing a health professional who was saying that America suffered from an obesity epidemic. Brian reached for the remote and turned off the TV. "Aren't you even going to show it to me?"

His mom sighed heavily. "I don't know what good it'll do. There's no return address on it or anything. There's no real information—"

"Jesus, Mom!"

"Okay, okay, I'll get it." She pushed herself out of the chair. "But no more swearing in my house. You understand?"

"Fine." He followed her into the dining room, where she opened a bureau drawer and withdrew a piece of paper that was wrinkled, folded and looked as though it had been rubbed in dirt. He took it from her, handling it gingerly, as though it were a priceless artifact. Dark brownish smudges that could have been bloody fingerprints were clumped in each corner and lined the right side of the page. But it was the writing itself that captured Brian's attention. For the rows of symbols that had been written on the paper resembled no alphabet he had ever seen. Drawn with some sort of charcoal pencil, they looked like a cross between primitive hieroglyphics and a child's random scrawls.

He looked up at his mom. *"This* is the letter?"

She nodded.

"How do you know it's from Dad?"

"I recognize his handwriting."

"Handwriting?" Brian rattled the paper. "This isn't even . . . It's not . . ." He shook his head. "It's a bunch of scribbles."

"It's from your father," she said firmly.

He stared at the dirty paper, trying to make sense of what he saw, trying to reconcile this incomprehensible mess with the neat, buttoned-down man he'd known as a child. On the top of the bureau, centered amid rows of framed family photographs, was a picture of his clean-cut father wearing a suit and tie—his preferred mode of dress—looking more like a businessman from the 1950s than a computer operator from the 1980s.

Brian recalled with perfect clarity the last time he had seen his dad. He'd been in junior high. It was a Wednesday afternoon in the fall, and he'd been sitting on the low block wall in front of the school office, a flat over-sized box filled with page dummies for the student newspaper on his lap. His dad was late. He was supposed to have come more than an hour before to take Brian to the printer, but he hadn't shown up, and in those pre–cell phone days there'd been no way for Brian to get ahold of his father.

So he'd waited.

And waited.

Finally, his dad's Subaru had pulled into the parking lot. Brian jumped off the wall, holding on to the box, grabbed his backpack from the ground at his feet and walked over to where his father had stopped the car. But instead of merely unlocking the passenger door, his dad turned off the engine, got out of the vehicle and walked around to where Brian stood at the curb. "Let's go for a walk," he said.

"Dad, the printer's expecting the pages! We're late

already! If I don't get them there in time, the paper's not going to come out!"

"Don't worry. We'll make it. I'll talk to the printer myself. Walk with me."

The two of them strolled past the front of the office toward the hulking domed gym. Brian was expecting some sort of lecture, or maybe another sex talk, but for a while his dad said nothing, merely walked along beside him, looking around at the school. Then they reached the gym, turned around, and out of nowhere his father said, "You're a good kid, Brian. You're a good boy."

Before he could come up with a response to this odd statement, his dad put an arm around his shoulder. Brian could not recall him ever doing such a thing before, and it felt more than a little uncomfortable. Even stranger was what his father said next: "I love you, Brian."

Looking back on it now, he knew that his dad had been saying good-bye, but at the time, he hadn't known *what* was going on. Not sure how to react, at that awkward early-teen stage where he was embarrassed by the very existence of his parents, Brian had moved away self-consciously, praying that none of his friends—or, even worse, his enemies—had seen the public display of affection. They'd walked to the car in silence, drove to the printer's and delivered the page dummies; then his father dropped him off at his friend Kenny's house.

By the time he got home, his dad was gone.

His mom had known ahead of time that he was leaving, and for years afterward Brian and his sister had been angry with her for keeping them out of the loop, for not allowing them a proper farewell. But over time, blame had shifted back where it belonged, to their father, as they both realized that their mother had been a victim as well, that *he* was the one who had torn apart the family.

Brian stared at the dirty sheet of paper in his hand,

trying to find some connection between the childishly scrawled symbols and an adult man's handwriting. "What was it sent in?" he asked his mom. "Did you save the envelope?"

"The envelope was blank. There was no return address. No, I didn't save it."

"Did you notice the postmark?"

"I'm not an idiot. Of course I looked. But there wasn't any, only some smudged lines, and I couldn't make out any of it. To tell you the truth, it looked almost as crazy as his letter."

"But you're sure it's from Dad?"

She nodded. "It's from your father."

None of this made any sense. Still holding the piece of paper, Brian went out to the family room and immediately called his sister. He told her what their mother had said, then described the letter itself, down to the fingerprints that could have been blood. Jillian demanded that he put their mom on the phone, and there ensued a heated discussion that ended with his mother crying and throwing the phone at him before rushing back to her bedroom.

"What did you say to her?" Brian asked his sister.

"The truth." Jillian took a deep breath. "So do you really think it's from Dad?"

He sighed. "I don't know *what* it is. I'm telling you, it's the strangest damn thing I've ever seen. If it *is* from Dad . . ." He trailed off, not sure where he was going with this, not sure he wanted to go anywhere.

They hung up soon after, Brian promising to FedEx a copy to her in the morning.

He walked back into the dining room and stood before the bureau, looking back and forth from the filthy piece of paper in his hand to the smiling, suited man in the photograph, trying to reconcile the two. The house was silent. He wondered if his mom was still crying, thought of going to her room and asking if she was all right, but then decided against it. She might know more than she was telling, and if he left her alone for a while, maybe she'd open up a bit more. Returning to the family room, he sat down, picked up the remote and flipped on the TV.

His mother did come out later, but she didn't want to talk about either the letter or his father, and when Brian started gently prying, she cut him off and ordered him to mind his own business.

This is *my business,* he wanted to say. *He's my dad.* But he let it slide. He was going to be here for several more days, he reasoned. There'd be time for this discussion later.

He kept the letter, putting it in his briefcase with the books and other papers he'd brought.

He slept that night in his old bed, in his old room.

And dreamed.

In the nightmare, he was walking down a winding yellow brick road, like Dorothy in *The Wizard of Oz.* On his left side was Los Angeles, on his right side was Bakersfield, but he couldn't go to either of them because the yellow brick road was encased in some type of glass, and the only thing he could do was continue forward. He walked for what seemed like hours. At the finish, he knew, was his father. But as the countryside flattened out ahead of him and he could see where the road ended, he stopped. Ahead was not the emerald city but a black mountain crawling with huge albino slugs.

From somewhere deep within the mountain, he heard a low, dull grunting.

And the piercing sound of his father's screams.

Three

Arlene was so jet-lagged that even though she'd dozed for more than half the flight from Paris, she still nodded off in the limo on the trip home. The driver had to stir her from sleep when they reached the front of the building, gently repeating her name over the intercom until she opened her eyes and informed him that she was awake.

Stephen, as usual, was gone, at work even on a Saturday, and she came home to an empty, silent apartment. It was just as well. The mere thought of meeting up with her husband, and all of the detailed discussion that would inevitably ensue, made her feel tired. James left her bags in the entryway, as instructed, and she closed and locked the door behind him, standing there for a few moments to depressurize. She needed a drink, Arlene decided finally, and she left her luggage in the middle of the floor, made her way to the bar and poured herself some gin. Stephen called a few minutes later, promising to be home by dinnertime, but she knew that "dinnertime" could mean anything between six and nine o'clock. She wondered idly if he was having an affair— then wondered if she cared.

She didn't want to unpack, but she did it anyway. If Stephen had had his way, she wouldn't have had to. A servant or housemaid would have unpacked for her. The whole idea of live-in help made her uncomfortable, though. Most of their friends had domestics, and they all told her how freeing it was, how liberating, how, unburdened by chores, they now had the time to do what they wanted to do. But this was her home, and the idea of sharing it with strangers made her feel ill at ease.

She unpacked, had another drink.

Afternoon became dusk, dusk became night. Arlene stood at the east window of the penthouse, looking over the lighted skyline of New York, the buildings like rectangular Christmas trees stretching in rows before her, the continuous line of cars on Park Avenue like little glowing ants between the trees.

This was about as far away from Marfa as it was possible to get.

She'd been thinking about that a lot lately, contrasting where she'd come from with where she was now. She wasn't quite sure why. It was something she'd have to bring up with Anna on her next appointment. The therapist was always saying that she was too disconnected from her past, that she lived only in the present, as though her life had begun the moment she'd met Stephen. In reality, the distance she'd traveled—socially, economically and emotionally—was probably the most interesting and important thing about her, was the reason why she was the person she was. Her grandmother had had a bit part in *Giant*, had been one of the background guests at the barbecue welcoming Elizabeth Taylor to Texas. That wasn't such a big deal in Marfa, where half the town had a *Giant* connection, but for years her family had lived off this fleeting brush with fame, and she lived today with a similarly superficial sense of self, allowing herself to be defined by her relationship to Stephen.

Stephen.

He'd been acting very odd lately, and Arlene supposed that was why she'd been examining her life, thinking about the past, wondering about the future. Even before her trip to Paris, he'd been behaving in a way that she could think of only as suspicious. And not suspicious in an ordinary way but in a weird way. A scary way. Not like someone who had committed adultery but like someone who had committed . . . murder.

Just thinking the thought, allowing it to breathe the air of her conscious mind, made Arlene feel lighter, less emotionally oppressed.

Murder.

She was not sure where that idea had come from or why it felt so right, but assigning a name to her suspicions, even one so horrible, made things seem more manageable somehow, made her feel almost relieved.

Because she'd been thinking it was something worse, hadn't she?

Arlene shivered, turned away from the window, faced the shadows of the darkened apartment. What could be worse than murder? She didn't know and she didn't want to know, but she had to admit that more than once when she was alone with her husband, she'd felt the presence of something she did not—and could not—understand.

She wondered now if it was why she'd gone to Paris in the first place, why she'd been so thankful that Stephen had not been here to greet her upon her return.

She'd have to tell Anna about that, too. The therapist would have a *lot* to say on that subject.

Stephen came home much earlier than Arlene expected, shortly before eight. She hadn't even started making dinner yet. Stephen suggested that they go out, maybe call up Kirk and have their son meet them at a restaurant, but Arlene begged off. She was tired from the trip, she said. And she was sick of eating out every meal.

"Me, too," Stephen said, laughing.

So he plopped himself on one of the chairs in the breakfast nook, and she described her trip to him as she chopped vegetables and readied dinner. She soon grew weary of talking, of answering endlessly detailed questions that for some bizarre reason seemed designed to trip her up and catch her in a lie (did he suspect *her* of having an affair?), and while they ate, she turned on the television. "I missed seeing American news," she explained. "I want to find out what's going on."

After eating, they did dishes together, just like in the old days, she rinsing them off while he put them in the dishwasher, CNN still on in the background.

Stephen snaked an arm around her waist, pulled her close to him, whispering in her ear. "Let's have a golden shower," he suggested.

She shook her head, tried to pull away.

"Come on."

"No."

"Come on."

"I'm tired. . . . I'm not in the mood. . . ."

"Please?"

Arlene gave in, as she always did, and she drank water until she had to pee, then stood above him in the sunken tub, bending over and spraying until he was completely soaked and his cock was as hard as a rock. She was aroused in spite of herself, and when he shoved his face between her legs and began licking her dripping crotch, she came. "Now," he ordered. She sat down on his erection to finish him off, and after a few quick, hard thrusts, they both climaxed together.

Afterward, in bed, she let her fingers trace the hard scales that ran down the center of his back and covered his spine. She rubbed the thick, coarse fur that grew on the sides of his stomach. He was embarrassed by these abnormalities—it was why he never swam or sunbathed in public—but she'd always loved the uniqueness of his body. Make no mistake, she was glad Kirk hadn't inherited his father's genetic anomalies, but for herself, the sight of that body was a complete turn-on. Even now, when everything else about him seemed so wrong, this still seemed right.

"I'm glad you're back," Stephen said, and the words seemed to possess a deeper meaning than they should have.

"Me, too," Arlene lied. "Me, too."

It was a muggy day in Manhattan, and Kirk spent most of it in his apartment, sitting in his desk chair listening to the stack of CDs he'd bought the day before. But by late afternoon, even he was tired of sitting on his ass. His mom had just returned from a two-week trip to France, and he'd promised to stop by and see her, so he took a shower, put on some clothes that his parents wouldn't find too offensive and made his way uptown to their building. He was happy to see his mother again. It was embarrassing to admit, but he'd missed her. *Mama's boy,* he chided himself.

His dad, on the other hand, was weird. *Creepy* was the word that sprang to mind, and Kirk wondered when that had happened. Like a lot of successful men, his father had never been a regular guy, had always been more than a little unusual, but within the parameters of his position he had always seemed to Kirk fairly normal. Lately, though, Kirk had been struck by how unnerving his dad's stare had become, how unnatural his minimal body movements seemed. He felt uncomfortable around his dad now. It wasn't an issue when the three of them were together, but he realized that he didn't like being alone with the old man, and he understood for the first time that that was why he hadn't seen his father when his mom was gone.

Not that his dad had noticed.

Or maybe he had noticed and was plotting revenge.

Revenge?

What kind of thinking was that?

Kirk was just glad that his mom was there.

He hung out for a while longer, but when his mother suggested that he stay for dinner, he used that as his opportunity to escape. "Sorry," he said. "I have plans."

"You knew your mother was coming home," his dad said sternly.

"I know, but it's—"

"Someone new?" his mom asked, barely concealing her delight at the prospect.

"Yeah," he lied.

His dad was still frowning, but his mom patted his arm. "You go," she said. "And have fun."

"I will," Kirk promised.

On the street, the doorman caught him a cab, and he stopped off at Nobu to see if anyone he knew was hanging out. Howard Stern was there, along with a few other celebrities, but no one he knew personally, so he had a quick drink and then went on to Mantissa, where he scanned the bar and then positioned himself next to a tall dark beauty who was either alone, abandoned or waiting for a friend. Before he could get up the nerve to speak to her, however, her date returned from the bathroom and the two of them wandered off in search of a table.

"At least when you strike out, you swing for the fences."

Kirk turned at the sound of the familiar voice. Waylon Jennings Bryant stood there grinning, holding up a bottle of expensive imported beer in salute. "I wouldn't kick her out of bed for eating crackers."

Kirk reddened. "I wasn't—"

"Don't apologize," his friend said. "I was paying you

a compliment. That's what I admire about you: your chutzpah, your moxie, your . . ."

"Balls?"

"I'm not going to admire your balls no matter how much you beg."

Kirk laughed. Out of all his friends, Waylon had the best sense of humor, or at least the one closest to his own. ("You have to have a sense of humor," Waylon always said, "when you're born to parents who made your *name* into a fucking joke.") Kirk leaned forward, looking at the red button pinned to his friend's jacket. "WWWD?" he read aloud. "What's that stand for?"

"What Would Whit Do?"

"Whit?"

"Whit Bissell."

Kirk shook his head to indicate his ignorance.

"Star of *The Time Tunnel*? He was in about a billion B movies. You'd recognize him if you saw him. Second only to Larry Hovis in the pantheon of greats."

That's another thing he liked about Waylon. He was even more into esoteric pop culture trivia than Kirk himself was.

As the two of them stood at the bar, talking, the room began to fill up. Kirk glanced at his watch and saw that it was already after seven. "I'm hungry," he said. "Want to grab a bite to eat?"

"Sure. Anywhere but here. Last time I was poisoned by the scallops. I swore I'd never eat here again."

"But—"

"Drink, yes. Eat, no. Come on. Let's roll."

They couldn't agree on where to go and ended up at a new Midtown restaurant that specialized in Mediterranean food and was owned by a chef who had a show on the Food Network.

Gwyneth Paltrow was holding court at a center table,

ostentatiously smoking, along with a bunch of her celebrity friends.

"Why do so many actors smoke?" Kirk wondered as they walked in.

Waylon shrugged. "Most of them aren't very well educated. So they're not as smart or well informed as the general population. It's the same reason so many of them become Republican politicians."

"Ronald Reagan," Kirk said quickly.

"Arnold Schwarzenegger," Waylon countered.

"Fred Thompson."

"Fred Grandy."

"Sonny Bono."

They went on with the competition, the names becoming more and more obscure, until finally Kirk gave up. "You win," he said.

Waylon grinned. "I always do."

They had no reservations and there were no tables available, but luckily Tina and her new fiancé, Brad, were there and seated near the wall. Tina waved them over, and Kirk explained their predicament. "Join us," she insisted.

Both Kirk and Waylon looked over at Brad for confirmation. They didn't know him as well as they did her and didn't want to intrude if this was supposed to be a romantic dinner for just the two of them.

Brad smiled, indicating the empty chairs. "Our dates stood us up," he said. "Have a seat."

Tina shook her head as Kirk and Waylon sat down. "April and Orlando. We've had these reservations for a week, and they called us five minutes ago, right after we sat down, and said they couldn't make it. I mean, how rude."

"A fight," Brad said.

Waylon laughed. "What else is new? Whenever I've

gone anyplace with them, they're either not speaking to each other or locking lips like two horned-out teenagers."

"They're very uncomfortable to be around," Kirk agreed.

Tina leaned forward. "Did you ever notice how his eyes start to *jiggle* when he gets mad? She'll say something that tees him off, and he'll still be smiling, still be talking to you, but his eyes will start to spaz out. They'll just jiggle real fast up and down. It's like a warning that he's about to blow."

"It's true," Brad said. "After she told me about that, I watched. And his eyes really do jiggle."

"Well! I can see why you'd want to go out to dinner with them," Waylon joked.

"Orlando's a strange guy." Brad took a sip of his water, raising a hand to get the waiter's attention.

"I expect to wake up one morning and read about him in the paper," Tina said. " 'Man Kills Wife and Self.' "

Brad and Waylon laughed.

"You think I'm joking, but I'm not."

A chill passed through Kirk. The feeling Tina said she got from Orlando was the same one he'd been experiencing around his father, only he had not been able to articulate it until now. He realized that it was not just the fact that his dad seemed so strange and creepy lately that disturbed him; it was an undercurrent of savageness he sensed there, an almost subliminal recognition that the potential for violence and atrocity lay just beneath his old man's outwardly placid surface.

Brad was still chuckling. "Why *did* we ask them out?"

"Because they're a couple," Tina said. "Because they're one of our few friends who actually have dates." She stared hard first at Waylon then Kirk.

Kirk shrugged. "That's just the way it is."

Waylon nodded. "As Bruce Hornsby once said."

"Do you think Nick Hornby likes Bruce Hornsby?"

"Doubtful. Bruce Hornsby doesn't have the right cool quotient. And Nick Hornby's an insufferable snob."

"Have you met him?" Kirk asked, surprised.

"No. But I can tell."

The conversation drifted away into gossip and trivialities, the way it always did when he, Waylon and Tina were in the same room, but beneath it all, Kirk still felt chilled. He kept seeing in his mind his dad's unnerving stare, his unnatural stillness—

MAN KILLS WIFE AND SELF

—and he couldn't help thinking that something terrible was going to happen.

Four

As a social worker in San Francisco for the past five years, Carrie Daniels had worked very hard on her professional demeanor, cultivating an all-purpose facial expression that conveyed concern and would suffice in nearly every situation in which she might find herself. Most important, she'd practiced being nonjudgmental, not allowing herself to show any sign of disapproval or disappointment to her clients.

But all of those efforts were being sorely tested right now.

For she had never seen anything like Juan Olivera. The boy sat on the floor of the small apartment's lone bedroom amid a jumble of torn newspapers and broken toys like an animal. She could see him through the sitting room doorway, looking out at her, and it was all she could do not to stare.

He had the face of a llama.

It was a genetic abnormality of some sort—although having just been assigned the case and meeting the family for the first time, Carrie did not know specifics and did not yet feel comfortable asking for any. The child had been hiding when she'd first arrived, either too shy or too wild to greet strangers, but gradually he had emerged from the shadows of the darkened bedroom to peer curiously out at her. He was dressed like an ordinary young boy, was not wearing a diaper or rags or sackcloth or anything, and despite the filth on the floor of the dirty bedroom, he was not confined in any way, was not shackled, caged or bound. What she found so disturbing was not the contrast between his average child's body and the monstrosity of his facial features, but the fact that his mother seemed not to notice or care, that she apparently accepted all of this as normal.

And the way he kept staring at her with his black ruminant eyes.

He scared her, and even as she talked to the boy's mother, her mind was racing, trying to figure out how such a thing could have happened, how an ordinary woman could give birth to such a . . . monster. Carrie hated herself for even thinking such a word, but it was the one that came to her mind. In her job, she was trained to deal with abuse, with poverty, with all of the ordinary social ills that befell people in the lower economic strata, but physical deformity was not really her purview.

She tried not to look at him.

But she kept stealing glances at the darkened bedroom.

The mother, Rosalia, was a beautiful woman: tall, thin, with perfectly formed features and smooth, unblemished skin. Were it not for the cast-off clothes she wore and the circumstances of her living conditions, she could have passed for a model or an actress. Her English, while not perfect, was delivered in a voice that was soft and clear, with a musical accent that paved over the fractured syntax. As she helped the woman fill out forms, Carrie wondered how such a beauty could have ended up an unmarried garment worker living in this overcrowded tenement.

Juan.

Of course. It was the only explanation that made

sense. Rosalia had probably been with someone and gotten pregnant, and when the father saw what the boy looked like, he'd bailed. This backstory wasn't in her file, but it seemed the most likely possibility, and though Carrie had developed an immunity from emotion over the past several years, she felt a sadness for both mother and son that she had not felt for any other clients.

She continued talking to Rosalia, keeping her eyes averted from Juan, looking at either the other woman's face or the stack of forms in her lap, not allowing herself to glance toward the doorway, though she wanted more than anything to do just that.

Rosalia had been turned down for medical treatment at one of the county's urgent care clinics, which was why she'd called Social Services, and Carrie had been sent over to deliver the bad news that Rosalia's meager health benefits had been slashed by the governor to finance tax cuts for his wealthy contributors. She'd been spending the past twenty minutes going over Rosalia's file, writing down additional information, looking for loopholes, trying in vain to find some way to get the woman's coverage reinstated or enroll her in an alternate program. Now that she thought about it, though, Carrie wondered if Juan's . . . *condition* . . . made the two of them eligible for some sort of disability benefits. She'd have to research that when she returned to the office.

Was there a tactful way to broach this subject, to ask about Juan's . . . deformity? Infirmity? Handicap? Affliction? Impairment?

She didn't even know what to call it.

No, Carrie decided. Best not to even bring up the idea of additional benefits until she knew for sure. She didn't want to give the woman false hope.

And she didn't want to talk to Rosalia about her son. Not yet. She wasn't ready.

Downtown, back at the office, she asked Sanchez, her supervisor, if he knew anything about the boy.

The bald man sighed heavily. "I knew this would come up."

"Well?" Carrie prodded after no explanation seemed forthcoming.

Sanchez leaned back in his chair, met her eyes for the first time. "Okay. I didn't hear this from Rosalia, so it's all secondhand, but I was told by Linda Yee, the woman who owns that building, that in order to get the money to come to America, Rosalia worked in a mule show, or I guess, a llama show, back in Mexico. She had sex with animals while people watched, and . . . and she got pregnant by one."

"That's impossible!" Carrie exploded. She felt her face redden. She was outraged that someone would even say such a thing. "First of all, I don't believe Rosalia would *ever* do anything like that." She thought of the woman's soft musical voice and gentle beauty. "I know I only just met her, but you can tell a lot about a person by talking to them, especially if they're the type of person who . . . if they're capable of . . . something like . . ." She shook her head disgustedly. "Second of all, that couldn't even happen. It's not physically possible. Whoever told you that's a liar."

Sanchez shrugged. "What's more likely: a genetic abnormality that makes a human face look like a llama's or a genetic abnormality that allows a human egg to be fertilized by llama sperm? Take your pick. I don't know, and I don't really care. All I'm concerned with is that we get them the assistance they need. These are the people who fall through the cracks. They don't apply for aid because they don't even know enough to know what they don't know. They're exactly the kind of family we should be helping, and it's up to us to steer them in the right direction and make sure they receive the proper support so that maybe, one day, they can lift themselves out of poverty."

"You're right," Carrie said. "You're right."

"Okay, then." He turned back to his paperwork.

"It's just—"

Sanchez looked up again.

"—that I feel so . . . helpless here. Because no matter how much time and effort we spend, no matter how much money we throw at the situation, that boy's always going to be . . . what he is."

"Yes. And sometimes you have to accept that that's how things are."

"But—"

"I know."

Carrie looked down at the case folder in her hand with its pertinent data about Juan Olivera that gave no clue at all to the real facts of the boy's existence. "What kind of a life do you think a child like that can have?" she asked.

"Not much of one," Sanchez admitted. His voice was kinder than usual, almost soft. "That's why you have to let this go."

But she couldn't.

The llama boy haunted her dreams.

In one particularly vivid nightmare, Carrie went to the Oliveras' apartment to meet with Rosalia and was sitting in a torn vinyl chair across from her when suddenly the lights went out. It was night, and a power outage must have affected the entire neighborhood because the streetlamps winked off and every light in the apartments across the street was out. Rosalia moaned chillingly, as though in fear for her life, and said something incomprehensible in Spanish, followed immediately by two words whispered in English: "He's coming." Carrie had no idea what that meant, but her body was suddenly covered in gooseflesh and she was filled with a feeling of blind panic. From somewhere within the pitch-black darkness came a raspy chuckle, a terrible, evil sound that made her think of horror-movie monsters. Her eyes were adjusting to the darkness. The moon was out, and by its indirect glow she could see Juan creeping out of the bedroom, into the sitting room, toward her. He was naked and walking on all fours, and his llama head rocked crazily from side to side as he advanced on her, still chuckling. Rosalia prayed in Spanish, her desperation obvious even through the language barrier. Juan opened his mouth, showing fangs . . .

And then Carrie awoke.

In another dream, Social Services had been contacted by the police. Rosalia had died of starvation, and Juan was alive only because he had eaten her legs. The decision as to what to do with the child had been left up to her, since she was his caseworker, and Carrie decided that as he seemed to be more animal than human, he was to be pawned off to a zoo or sold to a circus.

It was wrong of her to entertain such thoughts, though she obviously did, and she was embarrassed by her primitive reaction to the boy. She wanted to help him, wanted to ensure that he had as normal a childhood and as easy a life as possible. But that was an intellectual response. Emotionally, she was frightened of him. It still did not seem possible that such a person—

creature

—could exist, and her mind had a difficult time simply acknowledging the reality of his being. No matter how hard she tried, she could not reconcile her knowledge of biology with the boy she had seen in that apartment. *Is there a human brain behind those animal eyes?* she wondered. *Does he merely* resemble *a llama or is he* part *llama?*

What is he?

Carrie did her research. Rosalia and Juan were indeed

qualified to receive health coverage if Rosalia was willing to classify her son as handicapped, and Carrie returned to the tenement building on Thursday to discuss the situation. As before, the bedroom was dark, and also as before, there was no sign at first of Juan. She sat on the same torn couch she had the first time, speaking slowly and carefully so that Rosalia would be sure to understand, and explained the situation in detail, glancing every so often toward the darkened doorway, unable to help herself.

"No!" Rosalia insisted in her heavily accented English. "Juan es no handicap! He do everything all boy do!"

"I know," Carrie countered patiently, "but Juan *is* different, and if you just let me list him as handicapped—"

"No!" Rosalia shouted. "No es handicap!"

"I understand. But—"

"I say no!" She started to cry, and Carrie backed off. She felt frustrated in a way that she ordinarily did not, and though it was unethical, she wanted to simply fill out all of the forms herself and then tell Rosalia that the problem had been solved rather than try to convince the woman of the right course of action. She hazarded a glance toward the bedroom door. Juan had crept out from his hiding place once again and was sitting amid the torn newspaper, staring at her. Was there comprehension in those dark animal eyes? She couldn't tell, but she thought of her dreams and wondered what she would do if he suddenly started scurrying toward her on all fours.

"Just think about it," Carrie told Rosalia, packing up her papers. "I really don't see any other way for you and Juan to get medical coverage. Besides, this way, if something should happen to Juan, an accident or—"

"No," Rosalia said firmly, wiping away the last of her tears.

"Okay, okay." She took a deep breath. "If you need me, you still have my card, right?"

Rosalia nodded.

"Call me if you need help or even if you'd just like to talk, all right?"

"Thank you." The woman's voice was back to its usual soft tone, her pretty face no longer registering agitation.

Carrie got up to go, and before she did, took one last look at the boy in the bedroom. Juan was standing up now, digging through the right front pocket of his jeans and at that second, he seemed just like an ordinary kid wearing a mask. Then he looked up, and she saw his pointed ears prick up, saw his dark overlarge eyes focus on her, saw a long pink tongue reach between small teeth and lick slimy blackened lips. The sight chilled her to the bone. His face didn't look quite as much like a llama's from this angle. It looked more like that of a mutated wolf or some other animal that she couldn't quite place.

A monster, she thought, but pushed the idea out of her mind.

On her way back to the office, Carrie stopped off at a 7-Eleven for a Big Gulp. The afternoon was hot, her car had no air-conditioning, and after breathing the foul stale air of the Oliveras' dirty apartment, she needed something sweet, wet and cold to cleanse her mouth.

Carrie never read the tabloids. Even in line at the grocery store checkout, she usually glanced at the covers of the women's magazines, with their endless prescriptions for better sex, rather than waste her time with the outrageous inanities printed in the *Enquirer,* the *Star* and their ilk. For some reason, though, today as she stood behind a hirsute man buying beer and lottery tickets, Carrie bypassed *Cosmopolitan* and read the cover of the *Weekly Globe.* PROSTITUTE GIVES BIRTH TO RHINO

BOY! the headline screamed. Beneath that was a grainy photograph of a garishly dressed woman holding the hand of a small child with a hairless head and what did indeed appear to be a horn growing out from the spot where his nose should have been.

Carrie's stomach dropped. More than anything else, it was the grain that got to her, that granted the picture verisimilitude. Faked photos these days were usually much clearer than this. She recalled several years ago seeing a perfectly focused, perfectly composed picture of the president supposedly shaking hands with an alien. Something about both the graininess and the artless composition of this photo, however, made it look as though it had been taken by a hidden camera, without the consent of the subject, and to her that made it seem much more real.

Of course, she thought of Juan. There was no real physical similarity between Juan and the rhino boy, but the parallels were impossible to ignore.

The man in front of her finished scratching his lottery tickets, grabbed his bagged beer and walked away with a muttered, "Shit." Impulsively, Carrie grabbed the tabloid and popped it on the checkout counter next to her Big Gulp. Once in the car, she opened the paper, turning pages until she found the rhino boy article. Flanked by two more photos nearly identical to the one on the cover and obviously taken in sequence, the story was short and sketchy with very little hard information. The "prostitute," if that's really what she was, was identified only by her first name—Holly—and the city in which she lived— which just happened to be San Francisco.

Coincidence?

Carrie was beginning to think not.

The *Weekly Globe* was a national publication based in Minneapolis, but there was an address and phone number for a West Coast bureau listed in the staff box, and as soon as Carrie got back to the office, she called the number, got a receptionist on the line and asked to speak with Kent Daniels, the reporter who'd written the article.

"I'm sorry," the receptionist said in a pinched Ernestine voice, "but it is the policy of this publication not to give out the numbers of its contributors."

"I'm not asking for his home phone. Just transfer me to his desk or his voice mail."

"The *Weekly Globe* is one hundred percent freelance written," the woman said. "Mr. Daniels does not have a desk or a phone here."

"I just need to contact him," Carrie said, beginning to get frustrated. She paused, thinking of something. "I read his article on the rhino boy." Here she paused again, this time for dramatic effect. "I know someone else like that." She didn't elaborate, leading the woman to read between the lines that she might be calling in order to provide the reporter with a tip for a new story.

"I'm sorry," the receptionist repeated, "but it is the policy of this publication—"

"Forget it," Carrie said tiredly. She hung up the phone. She was not entirely convinced that the rhino boy was real, but the connection with Juan, as tentative as it might be, was enough to keep her going a little further.

She thought for a moment. A lot of prostitutes received some sort of assistance, particularly if they had children. She could pass around the photo and see if anyone recognized the woman, or even access records within the department and see if any Hollys were assigned to one of their caseworkers. Even if that angle didn't pan out, Social Services had numerous contacts within the police department. The two worked together frequently. She herself had good rapport with a sergeant who had recently referred to her a victim of domestic abuse. Someone somewhere was bound to be able to identify this woman and her child if they really existed.

She hit pay dirt almost immediately.

Jan Nguyen had counseled Holly a few years back. She, too, had seen the tabloid and had brought in the paper to show Sanchez. Carrie saw Jan and caught her before she could go into the supervisor's office. "I need to talk to you," she said.

Holly's real name was Elaine Peters, and she was indeed a prostitute who at that time had been working the park. When Jan had been counseling her, Holly had been pregnant, but then she'd called one day and said she'd had an abortion and found a new job and didn't need or want the state's help anymore. Jan suspected Holly's pimp was behind this, and she made several attempts to meet again with Holly, but all of her efforts were rebuffed, and she finally gave up, sucked back into the endless stream of cases that flowed through Social Services.

Carrie explained her interest in the case, told Jan about Rosalia and Juan, and said that she'd like to meet with Holly if she could.

Jan was by the book. She went to Sanchez first, showed the supervisor her copy of the tabloid and explained the situation. He gave her permission to contact Holly once again and allowed Carrie to tag along. "This is not Juan," he told Carrie, "but I understand your interest. I have to admit, I'm curious myself. Keep me up on what's going on."

"We will," she promised.

The phone number they had on file was no longer in service. Although Jan searched through the records using Holly's real name as well as various permutations of both her legal and street monikers, she came up with nothing. She was willing to wait, talk with some other caseworkers and come at this from another direction tomorrow, but Carrie wanted to act now, and Jan agreed to accompany her to the listed address.

Sanchez not only allowed them to take two hours but let them check a car out of the pool—an offer that shocked them both. Carrie quickly went to the bathroom while Jan printed out a map to the location, and after arranging for each of their calls to be covered, they were off.

Jan drove. It was a twenty-minute drive through some of the worst areas of the city, and Carrie was grateful that the other social worker was with her. Even after five years, she still didn't feel comfortable going into really rough neighborhoods alone.

And this neighborhood was rough.

She'd known it even before leaving the office, but it was confirmed when two police cars roared past them a few blocks from Holly's last-known address, sirens on, lights flashing, both coming to a screeching halt in the middle of the street, four officers jumping out, weapons drawn.

Jan quickly turned onto another street. "Maybe we should head back," she suggested. "We can come here tomorrow."

It was the logical thing to do. And, in the grand scheme of things, what difference did a day make? Still, Carrie felt a strong, almost compulsive need to continue on. "How close is Holly's place?"

"Two or three blocks."

"That's far enough away, isn't it? If we come from the side or the back and stay off that street?"

"There's no guarantee she still lives there. Or that she's even home."

Carrie held up the tabloid photo.

Jan sighed. "All right, you're right. I need to know, too."

They parked on the side of the three-story tenement

building, alongside graffiti that seemed to be a list of gang members' nicknames: *Shorty. Big Boy. Daddy. Cupid.* On the sidewalk, against the wall, a skinny black man lay in a fetal position, only the twitching of his feet indicating that he was still alive. From the distance came the sound of sirens and, closer in, gunfire.

Jan reached into her handbag before opening the car door. "Do you have pepper spray?"

Carrie nodded.

"Get it out." She locked the car and, armed, the two of them hurried past the twitching man, around the corner and into the building. The interior of the tenement house was, if possible, even worse than the exterior. Away from the public, taggers had felt free to cover every available inch of space with spray painted words and pictures. The unlit corridor smelled of stale urine and vomit. Huff bags, syringes and broken liquor bottles littered the floor.

"Holly lived upstairs," Jan said, walking slowly and holding the spray can of Mace in front of her. "On the second floor. The stairway's up ahead."

Carrie's heart was pounding. She had no desire to walk up any dark stairwell, and the rational part of her brain was telling her to turn tail and run. But there was nothing rational about the impulse that had brought her here, and the crazy desire to find the rhino boy overrode all arguments.

She remembered her dream of the blackout, heard in her mind Juan's raspy chuckle and the two English words whispered by Rosalia: *"He's coming."* The panic she felt now was eerily similar to the emotion she'd experienced in the nightmare, and she gripped her pepper spray more tightly as she and Jan approached the open stairwell. The two of them walked up the steps together. Shadows bathed the landing, and the strong, sickening stench of feces arose about them. Gagging, Carrie tried to breathe through her mouth, being careful where she stepped, although in the darkness she couldn't really see the stairs beneath her feet.

They reached the second floor without incident.

The hallway was dark, the building quiet.

Too quiet.

Carrie hadn't noticed it before, but the sounds of life usually heard in apartment buildings—crying babies, radios, televisions, arguments—were completely absent. Instead, an unnatural stillness seemed to have settled over the tenement house. They were in the center of the building, surrounded by dozens of rooms, yet it seemed as though they were all alone.

He's coming.

There was indeed a looming sense that someone—or *something*—was approaching, that if any people other than themselves *were* in the building, they were sitting in frightened silence behind closed, locked doors, desperately trying not to make a sound. As much as the threatening physical surroundings, it was this completely unfounded feeling that something big was on its way that made her pulse pound and struck terror in her heart. Carrie looked down the hallway, suddenly seized by the irrational conviction that if they could only get inside one of the apartments and out of the corridor, they would be safe.

He's coming.

She glanced over at Jan. The other social worker seemed, if not unconcerned for their safety, at least oblivious to this unseen threat, and Carrie forced herself to breathe deeply, calm down. She wasn't ordinarily an imaginative person, but something about Juan and the rhino boy and the entire situation set her nerves on edge and made her far more susceptible to illusory dangers than she usually was.

"Apartment 210," Jan said, and though her voice

wasn't loud, it sounded amplified in the stillness. She must have noticed it, too, because when she said, "It's right up here on the left," she whispered the words.

If there was a focal point to the silence, a still center about which the noiselessness spiraled, it was apartment number 210. Carrie had no idea what made her think such a thing, but as she stopped in front of the battered door, she was convinced that it was so. The two of them stood there for a moment, looking at each other, both of them nervous.

It was Jan who stepped forward and knocked on the door.

They waited several seconds, but there was no answer.

"Maybe she's not here," Carrie suggested. "Maybe she's on the street."

"Or strung out," Jan said hopefully.

But neither of them believed that, and as Jan turned the knob of the unlocked door and pushed against the peeling facade, Carrie prepared herself for what they might find inside.

It was a good thing she did.

The front room had been trashed. A coffee table was split in half, a mirror smashed, several wooden chairs broken, a television screen shattered, a crib crushed under the weight of an overturned couch. The lone window in the kitchenette was closed, and a suffocating stench permeated the air, a horrible, foul smell that was worse than rotting meat and worse than human waste but somehow incorporated both.

Blood was everywhere.

Jan was gagging, holding her hand over her nose and mouth, but Carrie had already taken out her cell phone and was calling 911. Even as she spoke to the dispatcher, explaining who they were and what they'd found, giving the address of Holly's apartment, Carrie was looking about the room, trying to find a body, searching for con-

crete information that she could provide the police. She
was surprised by how calm she was acting, but she
shouldn't have been. Under pressure, she inevitably
went into automatic mode. Her training took over, and
she was always able to handle any crisis that was thrown
at her. It was only later, when all was done, that the full
weight of what had occurred would sink in, and it was
then that she would collapse into a trembling heap of
gelatinous protoplasm.

The dispatcher informed her that officers were on
their way and told her to stay on the line, but Carrie
hung up on him. Hand still over her nose and mouth,
Jan was moving cautiously toward the bedroom and Carrie joined her. They were probably destroying evidence
with every footstep, but if Holly or her son were still
alive, they owed it to the two of them to try to help.

They reached the open doorway.

If the front room was bad, the bedroom was even
worse.

The bed was covered with blood and feathers. The
sheets had been torn, the mattress and pillows ripped
open, as though whoever had done this had been searching for something hidden and valuable. Carrie knew that
was not the case, though. In the same way that she'd
known she had to find Holly *today*, she was certain that
whoever had torn up the apartment had done so in order
to hide his real motive: killing the hooker and her son.

Holly herself, nude and spread-eagled, lay half on, half
off the bed, her belly slit open, its gruesome contents
piled next to her on the blood-soaked mattress. In her
mouth, the young woman's remaining teeth were red,
and one eye was swollen shut while the other was wide
open, giving the corpse an unnerving, deranged look.

Carrie's gaze focused on Holly's hanging hand, where
a white feather lay glued to the back of the woman's
index finger with congealed blood. It was an eerie imita-

tion of the artwork from a children's book of horror stories titled *More Tales to Tremble By*. Her uncle had given her the book for a birthday present, and as a young girl she had been terrified by the pictures on the cover, even going so far as to hide the book in her closet so she wouldn't see its spine on her bookshelf when she tried to fall asleep.

The feather fluttered in the breeze generated by Jan's passing, then loosened and fell to the floor, landing in a puddle of blood that immediately soaked the feather and turned it completely red.

It was obvious to both of them that Holly was dead, but Jan still placed a finger on the woman's carotid artery to check for a pulse. Her eyes met Carrie's and she shook her head, grimacing.

Carrie turned away, looking to the left at the sight she'd been avoiding since entering the bedroom. The *Weekly Globe* had not lied. There really was a rhino boy. Or there *had* been a rhino boy. For someone had cut off the child's head, tossing the small, broken body against the wall, where it lay slumped at an impossible angle on the side of the dresser, and placing the head atop the bureau, where dead eyes stared sightlessly over the room through slitted apertures in the rough gray face.

Carrie felt sick. She had no idea what had happened here or why, but the insane savagery of these murders and the lengths to which their perpetrator had gone in order to disguise his true intent made her think that this was far more than just an ordinary crime.

She wondered if Rosalia and Juan were in danger, too.

Already, she could hear sirens approaching. She wondered if the police who had been involved in the confrontation down the street had finished with their business and were now on their way here or whether an entirely new set of cops had been dispatched. It didn't matter. Either

way, someone was coming to the rescue. She felt a tremendous sense of relief and realized for the first time
just how frightened she was. The automatic sense of duty
that had kicked in was finally starting to slip, denial and
impassive detachment giving way to horror and emotional comprehension. Already her hands were starting
to tremble.

"Let's wait out in the hall," Jan said, her voice shaky.
"I can't take this anymore."

Carrie nodded, and the two of them made their way
carefully back out the way they'd come, maneuvering
through the apartment in an effort to cause as little con-
tamination to the crime scene as possible.

Crime scene?

Technically, Carrie supposed, that was correct, but the
description was far too prosaic. What had happened here
was much more than a mere crime, and to classify it as
such was to diminish it. This was something deeper,
more complex and far more frightening, and she did not
feel safe until the interviews were over and she and Jan
were out of the building, out of the neighborhood and
back at the office.

Five

The big story was still Tom Lowry. A week after his death, the Beverly Hills businessman's epic breakdown was still front-page news in Los Angeles, and Brian desperately wished he could get in on that action. Although he hadn't shared it with anyone, he had an angle on the story that no one else did: the crazy scrawls found in Lowry's journal and on the blood-spattered walls of his bedroom looked exactly like the "writing" on his father's letter. He had no idea what he could do with such information, but it was that connection much more than his traditional reporter's instinct that made him want—no, *need*—to investigate the murder spree.

He was the low man on the totem pole, however. Despite his awards, despite the fact that the *Times* had actively recruited and hired him, there were other reporters with more awards and, more important, greater seniority. Brian was going to have to prove himself before any editor trusted him with a plum assignment like the Lowry killings.

Right now, he was waiting for callbacks on three different stories, and he sat in the break room with a sports columnist, a couple of feature writers and an editorial assistant. All of them were reading various sections of today's paper. Ted Sprague, an entertainment reporter, walked in, got a cup of coffee from the machine and sat down next to Brian at the middle table. "So," he announced to the room, "what do you think is the best Charlie Brown cartoon? I'm conducting a little in-house survey."

"For what?" asked Mike Duskin, the columnist.

"For an article I'm doing."

"What's it about?"

"I'm not going to play games with you. Answer the question or not. I don't give a shit."

Mike laughed. "Okay, okay." He thought for a moment. "Has to be the Great Pumpkin."

"Why?"

"I don't know. It's the funniest. Has the best music."

"I vote for the Christmas one!" Steve Hernandez shouted out.

"I hate the Christmas one," Max Banks said. "Charlie Brown is such a fucking whiner."

Everyone laughed except Ted, who seemed on some level to be genuinely offended. "He's not a whiner," Ted said defensively. "He's just depressed because Christmas has become so commercialized."

"He's a loser and a whiner. Let's look at the facts, Jack. At the beginning, Charlie Brown pouts because he didn't get a Christmas card and no one likes him. So to cheer him up, Lucy makes him the director of the play, though he has absolutely no qualifications for the position. He becomes a complete megalomaniac, insisting that the most important thing is for everyone to pay attention to *him*, the director. When the other kids ignore him and have a little fun dancing, he throws a tantrum, slams his megaphone on the floor and bangs his head on the wooden arm of the chair. To placate him, Lucy sends him out to buy a Christmas tree, making a specific request for the kind of tree that would best serve the play. Charlie Brown completely disregards her instructions, thinking *he* knows better, and gets the wrong one. When everyone laughs at him, he cries that he doesn't understand the true meaning of Christmas. Linus explains it to him, and when everyone is feeling good and humble and a rapprochement is possible, Charlie Brown doesn't apologize or make up with the other kids—he takes his tree and walks out. On the way home, he steals one of Snoopy's ornaments to decorate his tree. When it's too heavy for the little tree and makes it bend over, he gives up, quits and runs away crying. Everyone else has to decorate it for him. After he sees what a good job they did, he finally agrees to sing with them. Like I said: a loser and a whiner."

"Yeah," Mike chimed in. "Besides, what kind of Christmas play combines the story of Jesus and some beauty contest about a Christmas queen? What's that about?"

"Aw, fuck you," Ted said, standing and picking up his coffee cup. "Poll's over."

Everyone laughed.

"Charlie Brown," Max said, nodding toward Ted's re-treating back.

Brian smiled. He was eating a Dave's Buttermilk Twizzle that he'd bought from one of the vending machines, washing it down with a too-small cup of uncarbonated Coke. *Breakfast of champions,* he used to tell his buddies at UC Brea, where a Twizzle and a Coke had been part of his daily ritual. But he must be getting old, because now the combination was starting to give him a slight stomachache, and he wished he'd chosen something else.

Returning to his cubicle, Brian called up the unpublished photos of the Lowry mansion on his computer and got out the Xerox of his father's letter. He wasn't sure why he'd been keeping this a secret, why he hadn't shared it with anyone, and it was getting harder and harder to convince himself that the reason was merely journalistic competitiveness.

Because everyone might think my dad had something to do with the slaughter.

Close, but no cigar.

Because I think my dad might have something to do with the slaughter.

Bingo.

For about the hundredth time, Brian stared at the Xerox with its smudged fingerprints and indecipherable scrawl. It looked to him as though a brain-damaged child had attempted to imitate ancient hieroglyphics while under severe time constraints. He found it almost impossible to reconcile the father he remembered with this chaotic, illegible scribbling. And the idea that his dad was involved in any way, shape or form with the carnage wrought by Tom Lowry was inconceivable to him. But despite his initial skepticism, he had no doubt that his mom was right, and there was no question in his mind that the letter she had given him was from his father.

His eyes looked to the photos on the screen, examining the ragged symbols scrawled in blood on the filthy walls of the Lowry mansion. The assumption everyone was working off was that the writing was nonsense, the random ravings of an unhinged mind. But Brian knew better. It was a language. What kind of language, he didn't know, and that's where he needed to start. His first step should be to find a linguistics expert and have him examine the letter, the journal and the bloody characters on the wall of Lowry's house.

"Brian?"

He turned in his swivel chair to see Wilson St. John, one of the *Times'* chief financial reporters, standing by the corner of his cubicle. Wilson had been assigned by the paper's managing editor to help Brian navigate the

confusing waters of the newsroom the first few days—
for no reason other than the fact that their desks were
in close proximity—and Brian found that although they
were an odd couple, he and the older man were surprisingly in sync in a lot of ways, especially journalistically.
The two of them had hit it off almost instantly.

"Hey, Wilson," Brian said. "How goes it?"

"I have a small favor to ask of you. Would you mind
accompanying me to my desk for a moment?"

"Sure. Hold on a sec." Brian turned over the Xerox
of his dad's letter and minimized the gruesome picture
on-screen—he didn't want any of the Lowry reporters
to think he was trying to horn in on their story—then
followed Wilson to his workstation two cubicles away.
The other man pushed his chair to the side, making
space enough for both of them to stand in front of his
neatly ordered desk.

Wilson pushed the speaker button on his phone console and pressed a series of numbers on the keypad.
"Listen to this message I received on my machine."

He pushed another button, and from the speaker
Brian heard a deep voice intone in a slow, carefully modulated voice: "I have been fucking her for more than a
day and my erection will not stop. Oh no, it will not
stop."

Wilson looked around, lowered his voice. "I think it's
Bill Devine, the CEO of Oklatex Oil."

"What?"

The other reporter nodded. "I'm working on a story
involving the merger with British Petroleum, and I've
talked to him half a dozen times. I'm pretty sure it's
his voice."

"When did you get this?"

"It was left last night around midnight. Eleven fifty-
seven, to be exact." He pressed the button again and
they listened to the message once more.

Brian looked at him, shaking his head. "That's really weird."

"To say the least." Wilson paused. "Are you busy?"

"Not at the moment. Why?"

"I'm scheduled to interview Devine in an hour. At his office in Century City. Would you like to accompany me?"

"Sure."

Wilson smiled. "To be honest, I'm afraid to go by myself. I'd take a photographer, but it's a financial piece and Jimmy won't let me have one. Your presence would be legitimate, however. You could write a sidebar, a feature on . . . on . . . well, you'll figure something out. Let me talk to Jimmy and see if it's all right."

Wilson walked into the editor's office while Brian stood there and waited. On top of the other reporter's desk he could see, next to the computer monitor and behind an old-fashioned pencil holder filled with pens arranged by color, a framed photograph of Wilson's family: a handsome older woman and a stunningly beautiful teenage girl. His eyes shifted to the phone console, and he thought about the voice mail he'd heard.

I have been fucking her for more than a day and my erection will not stop. Oh no, it will not stop.

It was the robotic, mechanistic delivery of the words that seemed so chilling. Wilson was right: "Weird" didn't cover it. The more he considered the message and its improbable source, the more Brian realized how completely insane the whole thing was.

Wilson emerged from the editor's office smiling. "You are doing a piece on the effect of the merger on Bill Devine's philanthropic efforts in LA." He held up a hand. "It's reaching, I know, so let us make haste and leave before Jimmy changes his mind."

They took Wilson's car, a two-year-old white Cadillac sedan, and on the way he filled Brian in on the details of the BP merger and his impressions of the man himself. Wilson had met with Devine twice previously and had spoken to him on the phone half a dozen times more in the service of different stories over the past few years, and his image of the CEO was of a fiercely intelligent, laser-focused, detail-oriented business savant who, like most men in his position, was wary and guarded with the press.

Which was why Wilson found the voice mail so disturbing.

"I wonder if he's just cracked under the pressure," Wilson speculated as he drove. "For all I know, he could be waiting for me in his office wearing a clown nose, with a spatula in one hand and a dildo in the other."

"Or a shotgun," Brian said softly.

"Exactly."

With two of them in the vehicle, they were able to take the freeway's carpool lane, and they arrived at the office building ten minutes early. Rather than wait for the appointed time, they decided to go straight up to Oklatex's headquarters on the top floor. "I doubt that he's even there," Wilson said as they entered the elevator in the lobby. "I would imagine that the message he left on my machine originated from his house."

"Then shouldn't you have called first to see if he was here?"

"Oh, no," the other reporter assured him, pressing the button for the fifteenth floor. "He could have canceled on me if he was here—which he has been known to do. I didn't want to give him that opportunity." Wilson smiled. "Besides, we might see something . . . newsworthy."

The elevator doors slid open. In front of them, a sculpture of freestanding metallic letters spelled out OKLATEX OIL. Brian had been expecting a corridor, but instead they were in a large, modern, expensively furnished space that seemed to take up the entire floor of the building. Green plants and skylights gave the room an open, airy appearance. Occasional segments of curved wall partitioned the floor into sections, but there were no cubicles, modular workstations, or even any individual offices that he could see.

Wilson had been there before and obviously knew where he was going, so Brian followed him past the OKLATEX OIL sculpture to a woman in the center of the room who sat typing on a computer keyboard behind a huge drawerless desk that appeared to be made of Plexiglas. "Hello," he said. "Wilson St. John, here to see Mr. Devine."

The woman looked up apologetically and not a little guiltily. "Oh, Mr. St. John," she said. "I'm sorry. I should have called you. Mr. Devine won't be able to make the meeting today. It's my fault. I should have let you know. If you'd like, I could reschedule you for another time. Would you like me to check his calendar for you?"

She was talking too fast, and they both caught it. Wilson shot Brian a look. "Did Mr. Devine say why he wasn't available?" he asked.

The secretary spoke guardedly. "I'm afraid I'm not at liberty to divulge such information."

"Well, can you tell me whether Mr. Devine has been in today?"

"I'm sorry, sir. Mr. Devine is a very busy and important man, and he doesn't want his whereabouts to be made public, as you might imagine. Let me just check his schedule and see if we can pencil you in . . .

Brian glanced around as the woman spoke, looking up at the domed skylight, down at the potted palm beside the secretary's desk. His gaze settled on a dirty piece of paper lying on top of a pile of business correspondence next to her computer. His heart started to pound. Even upside down, Brian could recognize the type of characters scrawled on the page. His mouth suddenly felt dry.

The secretary saw where his eyes were focused and quickly turned over the paper. Her face reddened with embarrassment, and she looked away from him, refusing to meet his gaze, keeping her focus on Wilson. Brian's heart was pounding so loud in his chest that he was afraid everyone in the room could hear it. "Where—" Nervously, he cleared his throat. "Where did you get that . . . letter?"

She pretended she didn't hear and asked Wilson if she could reschedule the meeting for next Monday.

"I'm sorry," he told her. "My deadline's today—"

Brian took a small step forward.

The secretary nearly jumped out of her chair. Her arm shot out, trying to cover the paper on top of the pile and accidentally knocked over the entire stack. Before the top page was engulfed by the falling batch of correspondence, Brian saw dark brown smudges—

bloody fingerprints

—and what looked like a cross between simple hieroglyphics and a child's scribble, drawn with some sort of charcoal pencil.

Just like on his dad's letter.

The woman glared at him. "Would you please leave?" she asked. "I'm very busy." Her eyes were angry, but her voice was frightened, and he understood that she was as lost as they were.

What he wanted to do was quiz the woman about what she *did* know, then go around the desk, grab the paper and take it with him. But instead he followed Wilson's lead, and the two of them retreated, saying good-bye and going back the way they'd come, down the elevator and out of the building. They walked across the parking lot toward the car. "If we were real reporters," Wilson said, "we would drive immediately to Devine's house and see what is going on there."

"Do you know where his house is?" Brian asked.

"No," Wilson admitted, "but with a little bit of research we could find out."

Brian looked at him. "*Are* we real reporters?"

The older man sighed. "Jimmy won't let us. We're on *his* time here, and I don't know about you, but I have a merger article due this afternoon."

Brian didn't really have a specific deadline today, but he was still on his probation period, and he knew how it would look if he spent the rest of the day gallivanting around the city with nothing to show for his efforts. Which is probably what would happen. His position was not secure enough that he could go on wild-goose chases *hoping* that something would come of it.

"Let's go back," Wilson said. "Maybe something else will occur to us in the meantime, and we can come at it from another angle."

Brian didn't tell Wilson about what he'd seen, about the letter. He wasn't quite sure why. Part of it was a proprietary interest in the information. Part of it was embarrassment about his dad's connection to all of this. Part of it was . . . something else.

They drove back to the *Times* building, speaking very little on the return trip. Wilson, no doubt, was thinking about his article, planning on how to write around the fact that he lacked a final interview with Bill Devine. But Brian was thinking about that letter. It was like a virus, this written language, popping up everywhere all of a sudden, corrupting everything with which it came into contact. What did it mean? he wondered. Was the secretary in on this? Could she read that letter? Did she know what those symbols meant? Was she able to communicate that way? Or was she like his mom, merely a confused recipient, trying to figure out what the hell was going on? Was Bill Devine going to end up like Tom Lowry, slaughtering his loved ones and going on some sort of murderous rampage?

Was his dad?

Brian pushed that thought from his mind.

There was too much to think about, and he didn't want to think about any of it. He glanced out the side window of the car but quickly readjusted his focus to look at the glove compartment in front of him.

There was graffiti on the cement wall adjoining the freeway.

And he didn't want to discover that any of it consisted of those strange scribbled symbols.

Once in the newspaper office, he and Wilson went their separate ways, Brian to the bathroom, Wilson to Jimmy's office to explain what had happened. But they were apart for only a moment. Brian was just sitting down at his desk, about to check his e-mail, when Wilson poked his head around the corner of the cubicle. "Come here," he said. The seriousness of his voice and the shortness of the command told Brian that something was up, and he followed the other reporter to his desk.

"I received a new message," Wilson said. "From Bill Devine." He said no more but handed the phone to Brian, pressing a button on the console.

Brian grew cold as he heard the by-now-familiar voice with its deep tone and robotic cadence.

"My cock is raw and red and bleeding. But my erection will not stop. Oh no, it will not stop."

Six

Kirk was awakened in the middle of the night by a wild pounding on the door of his apartment. The noise was so sudden and explosive that it startled him out of sleep, and for a brief disorienting second, he thought that a monster from his nightmare had invaded the real world and was coming for him. Then he recognized the sound for what it was and scrambled out of bed, pulling his robe on over his underwear and hurrying out to the front door.

He put his eye to the peephole to see who could be out there at this hour.

His dad.

Kirk's heart lurched in his chest. His father was standing in the well-lit corridor dressed in a tuxedo, as though he had just stopped by on his way home from an awards show. He stood there calmly, arms hanging passively at his sides, and there was no indication that he had been the one to beat so frantically on the door only a few seconds prior.

Kirk remembered what Tina had said about Orlando at the Mediterranean restaurant—*I expect to wake up one morning and read about him in the paper:* MAN KILLS WIFE AND SELF—and thought once again that the description applied just as well to his dad. More so, perhaps. For Orlando was merely horny, immature and a little too intense. His father was weird in a whole different way, a more primal and ultimately more unfathomable way. If Kirk had been the type of person to believe in aliens or nonsense like that, he might have suspected that his dad had been replaced by a pod person, so great was the change in his personality.

Only that wasn't really the truth. The truth was that the change was more organic than that and, as much as he hated to admit it, the seeds of this behavior had been there all along.

Kirk continued peering through the peephole at his father. The scariest thing was that he recognized the expression on his old man's features, that bland, blank look of utter vacuity. He'd seen it on his own face. Earlier this week, Diana had stayed over for a few days on her way to Milan for some fashion show or other. They'd had fun, as they always did. There would never be anything serious between them, but whenever they hooked up, it was a party.

Her second night there, though, he'd had a freaky dream, and in the dream he'd craved blood. He did not seem to be a vampire, not exactly, but he desired the taste of blood, and when Diana announced that her period had come, he'd ripped off her pants and panties, thrown her down on the bed and shoved his face in her crotch, lapping up the warm red liquid that was leaking from the soft opening between her legs.

He'd awakened with an erection and a mouth so dry that it made him cough.

In reality, Diana's period *had* come, and though he knew it was crazy, he'd carefully sneaked out of bed, crept to the bathroom and looked in the wastebasket, where he found a menstrual pad wrapped in toilet paper. Kirk withdrew the object, unrolled the toilet paper and gently touched his tongue to the red spot in the center of the pad. Gagging, nearly throwing up, he spit into the toilet and quickly downed a swig of Listerine to purge the sickening taste from his mouth. Disgusted with himself, he'd thrown everything back into the wastebasket, feeling ashamed and horrified and sickened.

Yet . . .

Yet he'd still retained something of the craving. The reality of blood had grossed him out, but the idea of it still held an allure.

Sealing up the bottle of Listerine, he'd looked at himself in the mirror.

And had seen that blank, vacant expression.

He'd made Diana leave in the morning, inventing a transparently false excuse that offended her enough to get her out but not so much that she'd never come back. Then he'd dumped all of the trash in the building's incinerator—to avoid temptation.

Something was wrong with him. He didn't know what it was, but he sensed that it was not something that could be cured by a psychiatrist. This was not the result of some childhood trauma or chemical imbalance. It went deeper than that. This was something inexplicable and inhuman that had recently manifested itself from God-knew-where. And was now a permanent part of him.

The same was true for his dad.

Tenfold.

His father held up both hands, ready to pound on the door once again, and Kirk announced, "Hold on a sec! I'm opening up!" He unlatched the dead bolt, the chain lock and the door lock, then opened the door, filled with a sense of dread, unsure of what might happen, prepared for anything.

His dad rushed in, the bland, blank expression gone, replaced by a look of fear and frantic worry that, if he had not known otherwise, Kirk would have sworn had been there all along. "Your mother's in the hospital! I just stopped by to pick you up on my way there! She's had some sort of hemorrhage, and the surgeons have to operate right away! Hurry up, get dressed and get your things together! Your mother needs you!''

Kirk did not believe him. About any of it. He did not believe his mom had had "some sort of hemorrhage," whatever that meant, and he did not believe she was in the hospital or that that was where his father intended to take him. He thought of the way the old man had stood there in the hallway, calm, placid, unmoving, and Kirk shivered with a cold that had nothing to do with temperature. But he got dressed and accompanied his dad anyway, both because he was afraid not to and because he had a sinking feeling in the pit of his stomach that something *had* happened to his mom—and that his father was the cause.

It was more uncomfortable than ever, being alone with his dad, and the two of them rode through Manhattan in silence. His father had actually driven here himself. That was a shock. Kirk had not even known that his dad *could* drive. Right there, his mental alarm bells should have been set off. As far as he knew, his old man always had a driver on call, and whatever the reason might be for the great and powerful Stephen Stewart to motor himself around the city in the middle of the night, it could not be good. Kirk glanced over at his father, who was staring straight ahead, face impassive. He could see a dark spot on the white tuxedo shirt, and although it looked black in the bluish glow of the dashboard lights, he found himself wondering if the spot was really red.

If it was blood.

His mom's blood.

They weren't going to any hospital. As if he'd needed any proof of that, his dad was driving in the wrong direction. He could be mistaken, but it looked to him as though the old man was heading home. Kirk stared out the windshield at the passing city, wishing he'd brought along some kind of weapon. Glancing again to his left, he saw that dark spot on the white shirt.

Blood.

He clenched his fists, wondering where they were going, wondering where his mom was, as the car rolled silently through the night.

Arlene lay on the hardwood floor, bruised, bloody and battered, unable to move, legs nailed down, broken arms lying uselessly at her sides. She had never before felt such agony—at one point she had passed out from the pain—but now she was simply numb, her senses over-whelmed and shut down by the brutality of the experi-ence. Stephen's sexual urges had been getting more deviant and dangerous for quite some time, but she still hadn't been prepared for tonight's assault, for the sav-agery of it.

For the incomprehensible strangeness of it.

She wondered where he was now, if he was planning on coming back. Her fear was that he'd gone for Kirk, that he intended somehow to harm their son.

Why the hell had she left Paris? She should have stayed there. A part of her had known it would come to this—fear was one of the reasons she'd taken the trip in the first place—but it was not something she'd wanted to acknowledge. Besides, she'd returned for her son. She'd missed him.

And, though she'd never admitted it until now, she'd been afraid for him.

She gagged, a wad of Stephen's fur caught in her throat, and she quickly turned her head to the side as she tried to spit it out, not wanting to choke in case she vomited. Even such limited movement caused the pain to flare up again, and a lightning flash of agony burst through the fog of numbness and shot through her body all the way to her crotch. Her bowels evacuated.

For the hundredth time, she tried to think of a way to get to the phone. If only she kept her cell phone on her person instead of leaving it in her purse. But of course that was impossible. She'd been asleep when he attacked her, when he'd yanked her off the bed and thrown her to the ground, screaming out his joy as he'd pissed on her face and stomped on her arms. There was no way she could have avoided any of it, and though she knew she was merely parroting the clichéd women's group mantra that she was the victim and was not at fault, it was true, and it gave her comfort to cling to such civilized bromides.

There was noise from downstairs.

Voices.

Stephen's and someone else's.

Kirk's?

Arlene tried to call out, tried to scream, but all her scraped throat could manage was a raspy wheeze. Her heart was racing, which only made the blood pump out of her faster. She felt it oozing from between her legs, seeping from the cuts and bites all over her body, in rhythm with the pulse pounding in her head. Arlene was under no illusions about her accomplishments as a mother. She knew she had always been far too self-absorbed to ever make a good parent. But despite whatever mistakes she had made, she loved Kirk, and it was her concern for him that enabled her to lift her head slightly an inch, two inches, three—and then let it fall to the floor. The sound of her skull hitting hardwood seemed deafening in her head, but she doubted that it was more than a muffled thump in the real world, so she struggled to do it again, hoping to lift her head higher this time and bring it down with more force, in order to make a louder noise. She needed to warn Kirk, needed to alert him to the fact that she was here so he wouldn't be caught off guard.

So Stephen wouldn't be able to kill him.

For she knew now that that was the plan. Stephen had left her alive only so she could watch her son die in front of her. This hadn't been just a sex thing. Not this time. It was something else entirely, and though she didn't understand it, she was pretty sure how it would end. Her only hope was to warn Kirk and pray that he would be able to fight off his father.

The voices grew closer. Footsteps sounded on the stairs, footsteps that were amplified through the wood of the floor. The voices were definitely Stephen's and Kirk's, and while she couldn't make out any words, she could hear the tone of each, and she knew from the stilted, awkward rhythm of their speech that both of them were wary, suspicious of each other.

There was hope yet.

A moment later, they walked through the door, and she saw instantly the look of shock and horror that engulfed Kirk's features. He turned and swung at his father, but Stephen was ready for him, and with a fiendish grin, he head butted his son and grabbed his groin, squeezing and yanking, eliciting from Kirk a shriek of pure primal pain.

Arlene closed her eyes, not wanting to see the rest. Beneath Kirk's cries, she recognized Stephen's familiar grunts of pleasure. She did not know what was happening, but she could guess, and when her son's tortured screams were abruptly cut off, she was filled with a horrible sense of relief. Warm liquid was seeping from beneath her closed eyelids, and she could not tell if it was blood or tears.

It ends this way, Arlene thought. She was filled with a bottomless bone-deep sadness. Here, at the last, where there was no deception, only truth, she could admit that the sadness was not for her son but for herself, for all the things she hadn't done and would never get to do, for all the possibilities that were now no longer possible. She thought back to her childhood in Marfa and wished she'd never left, wished she'd married Tully Daniels and had a big brood of kids and led a life of simple domesticity out there on the prairie. She hadn't become what she'd wanted to be, *who* she'd wanted to be. She'd ended up not an actress or a writer or even an astronaut, but a trophy wife, and if her dreams had to be thwarted, at least she should have been allowed to live longer, at least she shouldn't have had to die like this.

The pain returned, slicing through the numbness, a spike of agony that shot through her wounded body and caused her eyes to flash open. Something close to a scream erupted from her raw, raspy throat.

Stephen was standing above her, looking down. She could not tell what he had done to hurt her even further, but she saw that he had ripped off his tuxedo and was naked. Moonlight from the window glinted off his scales, and his tufts of fur looked like tribbles attached to the sides of his body. His cock was fully erect. Grinning, laughing, singing in some alien language, he began dancing, his feet stomping on her arms and legs, on her pelvis and her rib cage. She managed with great effort to close her eyes, and as the life ebbed out of her, she saw in her mind images of the past: the plains of Texas, brown weeds bending in the prairie wind; Marfa as it had looked in her childhood; and Kirk, as a baby, lying in his crib and cooing up at her, his toothless smile promising a future that had never come.

Seven

1844

James Marshall stood on the porch of his cabin looking
out at the barn and the field beyond. A small breeze
blew, causing dead leaves to dance through the swaying
forest of tall green grass, inspiring a crow to glide
through the sky instead of fly, black wings spread out as
it coasted on air. A chicken walked by, pecking fastidi-
ously at the dirt in front of the house, then flapped up,
squawking, as a stray gust fooled it into thinking it was
being attacked. His gaze alighted on the cows, placidly
standing by the fence that enclosed their meadow. He
had built this farm out of nothing, constructing the house
and outbuildings himself, using what little remained of
his money to buy seed that first year. In the time since,
he had made a life for himself here in Missouri, and
he'd become so successful at farming that he'd been able
to expand his endeavors and start a trading business.
That, too, had flourished, and he had done far better
here than he had ever foreseen.

He had always been a restless man, moving far and
often, continually chasing opportunity in search of a better life. But Marshall had found that better life here,
and he honestly thought that he had finally settled down,

that this would be it, that he would live out the rest of his days in the Platte Purchase—and happily so.

His eyes welled with tears as he looked out at his land, and he angrily wiped them away, embarrassed to be showing such feminine emotion. It was foolish to become attached to any one place, to allow sentimental feelings to form over what was, after all, just earth. But the truth was that he had put a lot of himself into this farm, a lot of thought and effort, toil and time, and if it had not been absolutely necessary to leave, he would have chosen to remain here until the day he died.

Two years.

That was all the time the physician had given him, and James had no doubt that the man was right. For the past five years, he had suffered unduly from fever and ague, maladies that refused to go away no matter what remedies he ingested. And he had tried them all. If there was to be any hope for him, he would have to leave these bottom lands, abandon his farm and his business and set off for healthier climes.

The thought saddened him. Not merely because of the hard work and energies that he had invested in this place, but because he had grown fond of the people as well. Farming was a lonely life, but trading was not, and he had many friends in Leavenworth as a result of his ventures. He would miss the fort and the community of settlers that surrounded it. There was even a woman he had been courting, Susan, whom he thought he might eventually marry, but that was no longer a possibility. She would not leave Missouri, and if he had any chance of living beyond the short time the doctor had allotted him, he could not stay.

He wondered how he would take his leave of her, and how he would say good-bye to his other friends, acquaintances and business associates. Parting was awkward for him. In the other places he had lived, the farewells had been difficult and had not always gone smoothly. More than one friend had been lost and more than one sweetheart had been hurt as a result of his ungraceful departures. He had no illusions that it would be different this time, and if there weren't so many threads to untangle, so many items to be sold off or settled, he would have slunk off during the night like a thief, taking the coward's way out. That was not possible, however, and Marshall tried not to think about what he was going to say to the people he knew as he calculated how much he could get for his cows and whether he would need an extra horse for the journey.

He had decided to go to California.

California.

Even the name seemed magical, conjuring up green hills, fertile valleys and virgin forests abundant with timber and game. It was country new and unspoiled, a place, it was said, where a man could live off the land with ease, where the deer knew nothing of rifles or hunters, where all manner of fruits and vegetables grew naturally and plentifully, where fish swam so slowly in their streams that they could be harvested by hand without aid of rod or net. Some of that, no doubt, was exaggeration, but if even a portion of it were true, Marshall would consider it a paradise.

It was also, he'd been told, a region whose climate might be able to cure his ills and restore him to health.

Might.

He was willing to take that chance, and if he could live out the rest of his days working outside like a man instead of confining himself to beds and darkened rooms, then any hardship would be worth it. Kicking at a chicken that was trying to peck his boot, he walked across the hardened dirt to the barn. The temperature dropped a good ten degrees as soon as he passed through the wide-open doorway. The mare and the gelding glanced up expectantly, and Marshall pitched hay into their stalls. He examined both carefully while they ate, still wondering whether he'd need an additional animal for the trip. The gelding simply consumed his food and allowed himself to be poked and prodded, but the mare was smarter and seemed to realize that there was something unusual going on. She paused in her eating and pushed against him, looking quizzical.

He ran a hand through the horse's mane, patted her neck. "We're going to California," he said.

It took less than two weeks to settle his affairs. He had never been one for procrastination, and once he had decided on a plan, he saw no reason to postpone its implementation. There was a wagon train leaving Leavenworth on the first of the month, and he made sure he was part of it. There was no telling when another might come through here, and he knew both from experience and from talking to other men at the fort that to head out alone, without the safety numbers provided, was a fool's errand. Plenty of corpses and broken wagons littered the way out West, and he wasn't about to join their ranks.

The quick disposal of his land and livestock and nonessential belongings did not mean, however, that he did not receive a more than fair price for his property and possessions. His trading skills stood him in good stead, and he came away from the days of negotiations with not only new horses and enough supplies to see him through a monthlong journey, but a tidy sum that would give him a grubstake and enable him to get along and perhaps begin a new trading business in California.

They left before dawn on a wet and rainy Saturday, a caravan of ten wagons and some forty people, including a handful of lone travelers like himself who carried all they owned on the backs of a few horses, oxen or mules. Despite the early hour and inclement weather, most of the community turned out to see them off, a double row of men, women and children lining the street, waving and cheering. It was an odd sight, but such an event was rare in Leavenworth, and Marshall understood the allure. Even he was caught up in the excitement, and as he looked down from horseback at the faces of Billy Treadwell and Sammy Johnson and some of the other boys running alongside the wagon train, yelling and shouting and jumping ecstatically, he knew that they would be replaying this moment in their games for the next two months. He scanned the crowd, searching for Susan, but either he'd passed her by already or she hadn't shown. He felt sad about that, but it was probably for the best. Seeing her would have put a damper on the day, would have forced him to think about the past rather than the future. Now he was free to concentrate on his new life ahead, with that burden out of the way.

Burden?

It was amazing how quickly he'd slipped off the shackles of polite society and rejoined the rough world of ramblers and rounders, mountain men and pioneers. This, he reflected, was what men were made for: traveling, seeking, exploring. It had been nice to be a part of a community, to put down roots, but heading out of the settlement toward unfamiliar territory with people he didn't even know, Marshall remembered the reason why he'd always been on the move before this, why he'd never been able to settle down in one place: excitement. The excitement of going someplace fresh, starting over from scratch, making a new life for himself. The uncertainty of the unknown had always appealed to him, and he had to admit that that was part of the allure of California. There was untamed land out West, wild land.

The weather might be good for the health of his body, but the wilderness was good for the health of his spirit, and for the first time he was genuinely glad to be leaving Missouri behind.

They passed by the last building in town, waving and shouting their good-byes to the cheering crowd, and the cheers continued long after they had stopped waving and had gone up the rise to catch the first rays of the rising sun on their backs.

The trek was long and arduous.

The Santa Fe Trail, they'd been told, was far too dangerous to travel upon. Indian attacks had decimated the last dozen parties who had set off on that route, and the disappearance of a military unit sent to quell the savages had struck fear into even the bravest pilgrim. The Oregon Trail was impassable due to continued extreme weather that had outlasted the season. But a new trail had been blazed West that took to a more central direction, and it was this course they had decided to take.

The first few days out of Leavenworth were fine. Marshall had hunted this far away from the fort before, as had a couple of the other men, and the landscape was essentially the same as that immediately surrounding the settlement. But after that, the scenery changed. The occasional village gave way to the occasional homestead and then to nothing. Woods thinned, the terrain grew rougher and rockier, and rolling hills were replaced by flat land broken up by rugged outcroppings of forbiddingly shaped boulders.

A week went by.

Two.

They'd been hunting and fishing along the way, gathering berries and digging up edible roots to supplement the flour, beans and dried meat they'd brought along.

Now, however, the game and birds were growing scarce, the streams less frequent and more often than not dry. Most of the time they had biscuits for breakfast, dried meat and beans for supper, both washed down with a small sip of warm water.

The land changed yet again, although this time the shift was more subtle and Marshall could not be sure when it actually happened. It almost seemed as though it had altered overnight, while they were asleep, but of course that was impossible. Whenever it had happened, the badlands were gone, replaced by a seemingly boundless plain that stretched in all directions as far as the eye could see, its monotonous sameness broken only by clusters of low mounds or hillocks. Their hope at first was that they'd have more luck finding food and water here, but if anything the plain proved even more barren than the rocky terrain that came before it.

Days passed.

Another week.

Beans and biscuits, beans and biscuits . . .

The animals were tired, more than a few travelers were ill, but still the pace continued unabated. Each day, it seemed, they started earlier and stopped later, spending less time resting though they needed it more than ever. Marshall understood the desire to press on, but to do so at the expense of the horses, the livestock and the people seemed at odds with the purpose of the journey and certainly with his own needs. Many of those about him felt the same, and he questioned Uriah Caldwell, the wagon master, about this unsuitable pace, but the man refused to give him a straight answer, promising only that the speed of travel would change soon, that once they reached the next river they would be able to slow down.

The plain was haunted, came gossip from the front of the wagon train. *That* was the real reason they were attempting to move through here so quickly, and while Marshall refused to believe in such nonsense, he did find this grassy region with its endless expanse of mounds and hillocks quite strange and more than a little unsettling. For one thing, the directions here were often wrong. They shifted and changed of their own accord, as if the plain itself were attempting to fool them, trap them, make them stay. Twice now, he had ridden to the front of the train to tell Caldwell that they had drifted off course and were heading north instead of west, only to find when he arrived that they had been moving in the right direction all along. He had no doubt that were he riding alone through these lands, he would find himself lost and confused, unable to escape, and would die here on this hellish plain.

There was also a nagging sense that they were not alone. Marshall had no idea how many others felt the same, because it was a thought he was too embarrassed to share. But for the past three nights he could have sworn that others were moving stealthily through the land surrounding them, hiding behind hillock and bush, scrambling about beneath the cover of darkness. Even in the daylight hours, it seemed to him that they were being spied upon, their progress carefully monitored. It wasn't Indians or other native savages that he suspected of watching them, nor other sojourners heading West, but . . . someone else.

Some*thing* else was more accurate, because his mind was possessed of the irrational idea that those who lived on this plain were not human. He was not even sure what he meant by that, but he had a lot of time to think on the trail, and no matter how he examined the situation, he could not conceive of any way that the watchers could be people.

They were there, though.

He knew it.

And still they pressed on.

Beans and biscuits . . .

They had not thought to encounter such a long stretch with no water or game. Dried meat was a luxury now, and water was rationed severely. Supplies were running low, particularly for some of the larger families, and if they didn't replenish their stocks soon, they would have to start slaughtering the animals—which would devastate most of the travelers, nearly all of whom had invested every cent they had in the world in what they were bringing along.

And then, water.

They were passing through an area of hillocks and saw, in the basin between two mounds, a pond. It was small and muddy, to be sure, but it was water and, judging by the bugs flying about it, fresh. Marshall happened to be riding near the front of the train and was one of the first to spot the watering hole. Late-afternoon sunlight glinted off its mottled surface, creating dancing shadows on the shallow slope surrounding it. Excitedly, he slowed his mount, but when he saw those before him continue on without pause, he rode up to the wagon master. "Uriah!" he called.

The other man turned slowly.

"Where are you going? There's water here, fresh water."

"No!" Caldwell stated flatly. His voice was firm, almost angry, and it was clear that he would brook no argument.

"The horses need water. All the animals do. Hell, *we* do."

"No!" Caldwell repeated. He glared at Marshall with something like hatred. Or fear.

Marshall looked over at some of the other men riding nearby, wondering why none of them were arguing, standing up for themselves.

"It's cursed!" Morgan James avowed, answering his unspoken question.

This was getting ridiculous. No matter how strange this plain might seem, here was a watering hole that could refresh the horses and even the other livestock that had been brought on this journey. To pass it by was a sin as far as he was concerned, and Marshall refused to succumb to the superstition that had apparently affected everyone else.

"I am watering my animals!" he announced loudly to anyone who would listen. He swung his mount around and rode back to grab the reins of his packhorses. George Johnson looked longingly at the pond and nodded his support, but most of the others pretended they had not heard, and all of them continued on without pause. Emily Smith, that pious shrew, even looked in the opposite direction, away from him, shielding the eyes of her young son from the sight of him dismounting and leading his animals to drink.

He was so angry that his face felt hot and his hands were shaking. It was all he could do not to curse his fellow travelers as they passed by with their poor bedraggled livestock. What was the matter with them? He understood that many people were very religious—living in this hard land made them so, gave them hope that their lives would improve after they were dead—and he, too, had felt the strangeness of this supposedly haunted plain, but for farmers and ranchers to let nebulous fears keep them from practical obligations like the care of their animals was idiotic. No, it was more than idiotic. It was wrong.

He felt proud, defiant, as he watered his horses, but the moment the end of the wagon train passed by—Clinton Haynes on his newly broken black stallion—the temperature seemed to drop, and though Marshall hated to admit it, he was frightened to be left alone here. Fear

changed to sadness as a gentle breeze, carrying scents of
long ago, tenderly touched his face. In what seemed like
an instant but had to have been the culmination of a
long, slow process, the sun disappeared behind the hillock, making the muddy water darker. He was filled with
a deep, intense melancholy. He had no idea what lay
behind these emotions or where they came from, but he
sensed that they were of this land, and he urged his
horses to drink faster, though he knew they could not
understand.

When the animals had had their fill, he pulled them
away, tied the reins together and mounted up. He'd considered replenishing one of his canteens, but the water
was too muddy for human consumption, and right now
he just wanted to get out of here.

He could no longer see the wagon train, but the tracks
were easy enough to follow. Besides, twilight was approaching. They had to make camp for the night, so they
couldn't be too far ahead.

Emerging from between the hillocks, he came out on
flat ground. There were patterns in the movement of the
meadow grass, waves created by the wind that spoke to
him on some level and reminded him of things of which
he did not want to be reminded.

Dark things.

He had been going west, but now he was going
south, and when he swung right to adjust, he suddenly
found himself facing north. The horses seemed confused, too, and he maintained a tight rein on his mount
as he kept toward the setting sun. The swaying grass
seemed more ominous now, the densely packed stalks
higher than they should be, the wind patterns creating
long black shadows that looked like figures darting left
and right.

As the sun went down in the east and night settled
over the plain, Marshall realized he was lost. He should

have caught up to the wagon train by now, should at least have been able to hear the others or see their campfire. But the only sounds that came to him on the wind were an odd wooden tapping and a persistent whisper that made him think of the voices of the dead.

He considered making camp but was filled with the certainty that if he did so, he would never catch up to the wagon train. He needed to keep on going until he found them again. Though it shamed him to admit it, Caldwell and the others had been right; he'd been wrong. He shouldn't have stopped to water his horses.

Fortunately, it was a bright night. The moon came out early and was bigger than it had any right to be, bathing the plain in a silvery-blue light. Ahead, on a slight rise, he saw a squarish shape that seemed completely incongruous in this land of flat ground and rounded mounds, and that almost certainly had to be man-made. It definitely did not look like anything they had seen for the past week, and his hope was that it was a building, a settler's house where he might get some directions and maybe something a little stronger than water to drink. He spurred his horses onward but slowed as he approached the structure. He could see from here that there were no pens or corrals, no animals of any kind. The place not only seemed empty but did not appear to be intended for habitation. Perhaps, he thought, it was a storehouse of some sort.

All three horses were still roped together and, dismounting, he tied the mare to a large rock. The building itself was a mud hut with a sod roof, although as he drew close, Marshall saw that what he'd taken for an exposed wooden beam on the east corner of the structure was actually a length of bone.

Human bone.

He did not believe it at first. Though the moon was large and low, full and brighter than he had ever seen it before, lunar light played tricks with shadows that sun-light never did, and even when his eyes confirmed that the object was indeed a bone, he continued to believe for several moments that it was the bone of an animal. An elk or buffalo that had died in the mud, perhaps. This close, however, he knew it for what it was, and the chill that passed through him made him shiver like a naked woman on a winter night. His instinct told him to turn tail and run, grab the horses and get away from here as quickly as he could, and it took every ounce of courage he had to disobey that impulse.

He forced himself to walk up to the hut and around it. There were no windows and no door, giving further credence to the possibility that this might be some sort of storehouse, and he wondered if there might be food in here, supplies. He understood that even if there were, the stores belonged to someone else, but he and the others on the wagon train were hurting, and he felt no qualms about appropriating some necessities for the trip.

He walked around the small building a second time, in case he'd missed an entrance. It was difficult to see on the far side, where the moonlight didn't shine, but he felt the walls as he passed by and found nothing but mud and straw. Back at the front of the hut, his eye continued being drawn to that bone. It looked like it was from the leg of an adult, but as far as he could tell there were no corresponding parts of the skeleton anywhere about. Maybe it really had been in the mud used for construction and its presence here was meaningless.

He didn't really think that, but Marshall would not allow himself to dwell on the subject. All of a sudden, it had become extremely important to him to find out what was inside the hut, and he made his way back to the horses, took his ax from one of the packs and brought it over to the building. The moon was higher now, its light brighter, and he could clearly see what he was doing.

He hefted the ax and swung it hard against the wall. The mud was thick, and while he didn't break through it, some of the hardened dirt crumbled. Marshall continued to swing, and by degrees the chip in the wall grew deeper, larger in circumference, until finally, in a single burst, it collapsed before him, creating an opening big enough for him to crawl through.

James Marshall was not a timid soul. No man alive could say that he lacked for courage. Yet he was afraid to poke his head through that hole in the wall, afraid to look into that darkness, afraid of what he might see. He backed away, retreating to the spot where he'd tied the horses, and with trembling fingers withdrew a match and a candle from one of the packs. Taking a deep breath, girding himself for whatever he should find, he lit the candle and, crouching down, still holding his ax, climbed through the opening he had made.

The flame of the candle combined with the moonlight streaming through the hole in the wall, illuminating nearly all of the space within. The hut was devoid of furniture, its single low-ceilinged room empty of everything save a large leather bag filled with human bones. The open bag sat in the far corner, framed by its own oversized shadow, its contents spilling onto the surrounding floor. He was afraid of that bag, frightened the same way he would be by a ghost or a demon, although such a reaction made no logical sense. In his mind was the notion that the sack was alive, an independent entity, that it did not belong to anyone, had not been made by anyone, that it had always been here and had seduced people into killing each other and depositing the bones of their conquered victims.

A small bone fell, clattering against the others on the hard dirt floor, and Marshall jumped, hitting his head on the low ceiling, clods of dirt crumbling into his hair. He was instantly ready to flee, but no further movement followed, and though his muscles remained coiled and tense, he decided that the bone had fallen naturally, as a result of being precariously balanced. He kept his eye on the bag, however, and as he did so a cold wind blew out the flame of his candle.

Only the wind did not come into the hut through the hole leading outside.

It came from the corner.

The interior was darker now by half. The bag seemed as black as its shadow, which had grown to engulf a third of the room, and the bones seemed to glow in the diffuse bluish light of the moon.

His perception of the sack shifted. No longer did it seem like the repository of vanquished enemies' bones. Instead, it seemed like the source of those bones, and in his mind he imagined them bubbling up from its depths like water from a spring then overflowing onto the floor.

Cold wind came again from the corner, pressing fetid air against his face, its force so strong that it pushed him back, causing him to trip and fall.

More bones dropped to the floor, their sound almost musical.

The wagon train had been right to move quickly through this land, and it was his own fault that he'd been seduced by the water and led into this trap. Marshall had never before been so frightened, and if he were allowed to live through this ordeal, he vowed to become a changed man. He attempted to stand, and once again a powerful wind blew from the corner (*the bag?*) and knocked him down. This time, the force felt less like propelled air and more like invisible skeletal fingers.

He took a deep breath before trying to get up. And then . . .

. . . it was morning.

It seemed to happen in an instant, the shift from night to day, but he knew that such a thing was impossible. Turning to look over his shoulder, he saw only harsh whiteness through the hole in the wall that led outside, the sun so bright after the dimness of night that it blurred his vision and made his eyes water. Standing up, he saw that although the bag was fully illuminated, its umbra frame gone, it had lost none of its threatening malevolence. A stray ray of sunshine highlighted a curved rib.

Marshall wondered if he had somehow been mesmerized. Although by what? The room? The walls? The bag? There was nothing here that could conceivably have put him in a trance. He had no memory of sleep, however, and no sense that time had passed. He had not even changed position while the shift occurred. The only difference he noted was a newfound belief—no, a *certainty*—that there were riches in California, treasures, unfound gold that was there for the taking. Such an idea was absurd to all but the most feebleminded. Whoever heard of an ordinary citizen finding gold? Or keeping it, for that matter. That was the province of governments and potentates. Nevertheless, the concept was embedded in his mind, impossible to ignore. When had the notion occurred to him, though? Or *had* it occurred to him? It did not feel like his own thought, and he considered that it might have been imposed on him through mesmerism or some other type of mind control.

He looked again at the sack of bones.

There was no wind blowing from the corner as he turned and ducked through the opening in the wall, exiting the way he had entered.

Outside, the plain was filled with multicolored flowers. They had sprung up in the meadow overnight and covered everything, even the hut, a rainbow of blossoms so thick that it was as though a blanket had been laid over the land. Marshall stared with wonder at the remarkable scene before him, overwhelmed by the beauty and mystery of the earth, aware for perhaps the first time, in a very profound way, of how little he and everyone else in this country actually knew of the world in which they lived. Outside of the cities and towns, in the vast open wilderness that comprised the bulk of the United States and its territories, were secrets undiscovered, wonders both dark and light that had yet to be experienced by civilized man.

A path wound through the flowers, a clearly defined trail that began at the hut and led West, away from the rising sun. At the bottom of the hillock, his horses, all of them, were peacefully nibbling at the flowers, seemingly content.

The feeling he'd had over the past several days that he was being watched, that sense that *others* were monitoring his progress, was gone. The menace that had hung over the plain was gone as well, buried perhaps under the flowers, and Marshall felt lighter, freer and more optimistic than he had since the beginning of this journey.

He gave the mud hut one last look, shivering as he saw the blackness within the jagged opening and thought of that leather bag filled with bones. He started down the gentle slope toward the horses. Would he tell anyone else what he had found? Would he describe to them the fearful darkness of the structure's windowless interior? Or would he pretend that none of it had happened?

He did not know. He would face that when he came to it.

Marshall reached the horses, untied the mare and mounted up. He glanced one final time at the small building atop the hillock, its squareness rounded by the soft layer of flowers that draped over its walls and roof, its muddy brownness hidden by the rainbow of blossoms, and started down the trail, following where it led.

He reached the others just before noon.

Eight

On Friday, Brian met with Dr. Lisa LaMunyon, professor of linguistics and recognized authority on written languages, in her office at UCLA. After talking on the phone the day before and detailing all of the questions he had, Brian had e-mailed Dr. LaMunyon scanned photos of his dad's letter and the messages scrawled at the murder sites. He'd expected to wait weeks for an answer, but to his surprise, the professor had called back early in the morning to set up a meeting. Although admitting that she had no real news, she still wanted to see Brian in person, and after filing a story on the mayor's reaction to the governor's response to the president's new immigration policy, Brian drove up the 405 freeway to UCLA.

Lisa LaMunyon was younger than Brian had expected. Although at first glance she looked more like a suburban mom than a tenured academic, the softness of her appearance did not diminish the intellectual confidence she projected. The professor rose from her chair enthusiastically when Brian knocked on the frame of her open office door. "Brian Howells?"

"Guilty."

Dr. LaMunyon motioned him in. "Thanks for coming. I appreciate it. I know you must be busy."

Brian glanced around the office. The professor not

only had the e-mailed photos of his father's letter and the blood-scrawled crime-scene messages showing on a computer monitor, but she had printed them out in various permutations, electronically cutting and pasting the figures and symbols to create new characters. The resulting pages were tacked onto a cork bulletin board that covered one wall.

"I see *you've* been busy, Dr. LaMunyon." Brian motioned toward the board.

"Yes indeed," the professor said eagerly. "And call me Lisa." She picked up a piece of paper from her desk, turning it over in her hands, looking at the printed symbols right-side up, sideways and upside down. "I cannot tell you how glad I am that you sent me all this. These writings are really remarkable. I can't make heads or tails out of them and can find no repeating pattern that would enable me to decipher these characters, but it's clear to me that this is indeed a shared form of communication, quite possibly a code or even, as you suggested, a language of some sort. The stylistic similarities between the symbols are just too pronounced to be entirely coincidental. Last year, I helped develop a computer program designed to analyze various forms of writing, but the computer is stymied as well. Whatever this is, it's unlike anything I've ever encountered. I plan on running it by a few of my colleagues, but to be honest, this is my field of expertise, not theirs, so I don't expect them to decipher any of it. I just want to show it to them. Fascinating."

Brian sighed. "I was hoping you'd come up with something."

"I'm sorry. I thought I made it clear over the phone that I hadn't—"

"Yeah, I know. It's just that that letter was from my dad, whom I haven't seen in some twenty years. And it looks just like what those killers wrote. In blood. So, as you can probably guess, I have a little bit of personal interest in this."

"I'm going to keep working, but it's challenging, to say the least. Do you know of any other linguists or cryptologists who are trying to decipher these messages? Someone with whom the police are working, perhaps?"

"No," Brian admitted. "I have no idea what's going on at that end. I noticed the similarities on my own and decided to find out what I could for a possible story—and for myself. When I asked around about linguistics experts, especially people who study written languages, your name came up, so I contacted you. If there's anyone else working on this, I don't know about it."

"I'm going to do my best," Dr. LaMunyon promised. Once more, she turned the paper in her hand before setting it down next to the monitor. "But, like I said, I have nothing so far." She called up a screen on her computer and, pointing with her pencil, began enumerating attributes of the symbols that she believed would eventually lead to a usable key. Brian asked a few obligatory questions, but it didn't seem to him that the professor was anywhere close to interpreting the writing.

"I have something I want to ask you," Dr. LaMunyon said. "About your profession. And I apologize in advance if it's rude."

"Go ahead," Brian told her. "Shoot."

"Why aren't there any real journalists anymore?"

Brian was about to give a glib, jokey response, but he sensed from the professor's demeanor that the woman was serious, that she genuinely desired an answer. Brian paused. *Why aren't there any real journalists anymore?* It was the sort of question he often asked himself, the sort of question that reporters frequently asked of each other—usually after several rounds of drinks—and it deserved an honest reply.

"I'm not speaking of you in particular," the professor

said quickly. "I'm not familiar with your work, and I'm sure you're an excellent reporter. But I mean in general. It just seems to me that most journalists don't do their job these days. They'll quote someone on one side of a story, then get a quote from someone else on the other side, print them both and pretend as though that's a balanced article. There's no attempt made to check the facts, to do a little research and determine which side is right. I'm not talking about opinions here. I mean articles on nuts-and-bolts subjects that have been settled for years and that have a verifiably correct answer—something I might put on one of my tests, that my students are supposed to know—and yet contemporary reporters act as though both points of view are equally legitimate. This really drives me crazy."

"Me, too," Brian said. "But, Dr.—"

"Lisa."

"Lisa. You didn't ask me to your office to discuss journalistic ethics. And everything else you told me we could have easily discussed over the phone. So I have a question for you: Why did you really invite me over here?"

The professor hesitated, and for a fleeting instant, Brian thought he saw an expression of fear on her features. "I guess . . ." Dr. LaMunyon looked embarrassed. "I guess I wanted to meet the son of the man who wrote that letter." She motioned toward the monitor.

Brian frowned.

"I know how that sounds," she admitted, raising a hand. "And after all my talk about the importance of science and facts, what I'm going to say next is going to seem completely crazy. But . . ." She took a deep breath. "I'm afraid of that language."

Brian wasn't sure he'd heard correctly. "What?"

"Those characters. There's something wrong with them or, more precisely, something wrong *about* them. Make no mistake; I intend to decipher those symbols, find out what they mean and discover everything I can about them. But—and I know this is going to sound insane—they scare me. They make me feel like I'm a little kid. When I'm studying them, I have to have the door open and the lights on. I get goose bumps. I start jumping at shadows. It's all in my imagination, of course, but I can't help feeling that the characters are the cause of it all, that they *make* me think of such things. Which makes this all the more intriguing and makes me want to decipher their meaning even more."

Brian was silent. He hadn't realized it until this very second, but he shared the professor's misgivings. Dr. LaMunyon had articulated perfectly a feeling that Brian had not known he'd had, and he understood that it was not merely their connection to his dad that disturbed him but something about the nature of the symbols themselves.

There was little to say after that. On the freeway, on the way back, he wondered if the two of them should have discussed things more, if he should have been more forthcoming about his own reactions. But that sort of touchy-feely sharing felt awkward and unnatural to him.

He would have to just wait and see if Dr. LaMunyon could translate that alien language.

Alien?

He pushed the thought from his mind. He wasn't even going to go there.

At the *Times*, a new assignment was waiting for him, an interview with a prominent Latino activist that was supposed to run next to his story on the mayor's immigration stance, and he was so busy the rest of the day that he didn't have time to think about anything else.

It was nearly nine o'clock before he arrived home, and as he walked into the silent, darkened condo, Brian decided that he needed to find someplace to live that was closer to work. Someplace in LA. With the assignments he'd been getting and traffic the way it was, it was rare that he got home before eight or eight thirty. Sometimes, like tonight, it was even later. And in the morning, he had to be on the road by six in order to get to the paper by eight, which meant that he had to get up at five. Basically, all he was doing was sleeping here, and thanks to his schedule, he wasn't even doing much of that.

Brian checked his answering machine while he got a beer out of the refrigerator. For the third day in a row, his mom had left a message asking him to call her back as soon as he got home. He felt guilty as he erased it. But he couldn't phone her now, he told himself. She was asleep already. He'd be waking her up. It would be better to call on the weekend, when they both had more time.

He was rationalizing.

The fact was, his reconciliation trip had turned out to be a disaster. Not just because of his dad's letter—although that was a big part of it—but because he and his mother simply did not get along. Alone together, in close quarters, they were like oil and water. It was what had kept him away from Bakersfield all these years, and any hope he'd had that things had changed in the intervening decade had died his first night there. As much as he tried not to offend her, and as much as she tried to overlook their differences, the two of them ended up insulting each other, hurting each other, fighting, and what should have been minor disagreements escalated into epic battles of will. She still treated him as though he were a rebellious teenager, which was exactly how he reacted to her, and that dynamic was not healthy for either of them.

And the fact was, she'd gotten worse since he'd left there.

Part of it was the religion. Church so dominated his

mother's life now that every single thought and opinion was refracted through that lens. But whose fault was that? He was down here in Los Angeles, his sister was in San Diego, his dad . . .

Where *was* his dad?

That was one of the things that gnawed at him. Brian had accepted almost immediately the idea that his father had written the letter, but *where* had he written it? The paper had been delivered by hand, so he had to have come to the house. That meant he was either staying in Bakersfield or living there. Of course, there was no guarantee that he was still around. He could have dropped the message off and continued on his merry way. But somehow Brian didn't think that was the case. As a reporter, he was supposed to base his opinions on facts not intuition, but more than one reporter's hunch had led directly to a Pulitzer prize, and right now his hunch was telling him that his dad was sticking close to the old house.

Was his mom in danger?

That was another thought that was never far from his mind, and it was a question for which he had no answer. For all he knew, his dad had been living only a few blocks away for the past twenty years and it was only chance that had kept his parents from meeting up again at the supermarket or the gas station. He didn't think so, though. He had the feeling that his father had been gone for all this time, that he'd been far away . . . and that he'd changed.

Changed how? Brian had no idea. But the idea that his dad had returned in order to deliver that letter and its indecipherable message seemed more than a little threatening.

He remembered what Dr. LaMunyon had said.

I'm afraid of that language.

He went over to his desk and opened the folder containing his father's letter, looking at the dirty, wrinkled page. It *was* scary. He didn't know how he could have missed that before. And, as always, those smudged—

bloody?

—fingerprints jumped out at him, this time making him wonder if violence wasn't behind their presence. In his mind's eye, he saw his dad, dressed all in rags now instead of a business suit, killing another raggedy man, then grabbing a piece of charcoal and paper and writing this message.

He wanted to phone Jillian and talk about it, tell her what had happened today with Dr. LaMunyon, but it was definitely too late to call. She'd forbidden anyone to phone the house after nine unless it was an emergency. She didn't want her daughter woken, for one thing, and as she explained, late-night calls scared the hell out of her; she always assumed that someone had died.

He looked at the paper for a moment longer, handling it softly, carefully, running a finger over the wrinkled ridges as though he might learn something about it through the sense of touch. He did this each time he picked up the letter, although he did not know why and an anal, logical part of his brain told him he was destroying evidence.

He put the letter away and turned on the television. It was on in the background, white noise, as he popped a Lean Cuisine into the microwave and sorted through today's mail. He ate in the kitchen while he scanned through both the *Times* and the *Register*, reading the articles of friends and colleagues to take his mind off his dad, his mom and the letter. After dumping the remains of his dinner in the garbage can and breaking out another can of beer, he walked out to the living room, where he switched the channel to a local station with ten o'clock news.

". . . Devine, founder and CEO of Oklatex Oil, had recently agreed to a merger with British Petroleum—"

Fumbling with the remote, Brian turned up the volume. In a small square to the right of the news anchor's head was a file photo of Bill Devine.

". . . His body was found in his office by an employee, and though sources say the billionaire apparently died from a self-inflicted gunshot wound, the investigation remains open and police have not ruled out foul play."

In an interview clip from last year, Devine was shown giving a speech to Oklatex shareholders. Brian recognized the deep intonation of the man, and the sound of it sent a chill through his bones. In his mind, he heard it on Wilson's answering machine, speaking those inexplicable words in a slow, carefully modulated voice.

My erection will not stop. Oh no, it will not stop . . .

"So?" Brian asked. "Does this qualify as an epidemic?" He and Wilson were looking over the wire-service photos of the Stewart murders.

"The tabloids will say so."

"What say we?"

"It *is* strange," Wilson admitted. "Two wealthy businessmen on opposite sides of the country go on murderous rampages? It's not exactly an everyday occurrence."

Ted Sprague walked by. "I hear Stephen Stewart made a killing in New York." He chuckled.

Brian hated puns. And he hated people who made puns. He remembered his uncle Frank, who'd always had a book called *People are Pun-ny* sitting in his bathroom next to the toilet. Uncle Frank had been an asshole. Just like Ted Sprague.

"You know," Wilson said, ignoring the entertainment reporter, "there are rumors that a couple other Fortune 500 heavy hitters may have a proclivity for violence. There've been situations that have been hushed up before—nothing to this extent, of course—but a couple of times the victims supposedly landed in the hospital."

"Where'd you hear this?"

"Finance is my beat."

"Do you think it's true?"

"Maybe. I'm pretty sure at least one of them is. I talked to the woman involved, after the fact, and while she wouldn't name names, everyone knew who she was seeing."

"Would I know who he was?"

"Yes, you would."

They looked again at the photos, most of them far too graphic ever to appear in a mainstream publication. The one Brian found most disturbing was of Arlene Stewart, the billionaire's wife. She'd been stomped to death after a host of other atrocities had been performed on her, and only her head remained intact, the open eyes making her face seem eerily alive above the shattered, bloody mess of the body below it.

Brian looked away. "And Stephen Stewart is still at large."

"Apparently so, although I don't see how that's possible. Someone so visible and publicly known . . ."

"Come on. With all the resources at his disposal, you don't think he could arrange to 'disappear' for a while?"

"Yes, I suppose so, but this isn't tax fraud or stock market manipulation. This is the biggest murder case in the United States right now. Every man, woman and child in this country has seen his face plastered all over TV, newspapers, magazines, the Internet. Unless he was able to smuggle himself offshore to a desert island, someone somewhere's bound to see him and call it in. I'm just amazed it hasn't happened already."

"If his son ever comes out of his coma, he might be able to shed some light on what happened."

There was a pause.

"What about Devine?" Brian asked.

Wilson sighed. "I knew you were going to bring that up. And, yes, before you ask, I was going to bring it up, too."

"So you think they're connected."

Wilson nodded.

"Any theories?" Brian asked.

"America's economic upper crust has become so in-bred that they're producing homicidal maniacs."

"Are you serious?"

Wilson smiled grimly. "No, of course not. But it just goes to show how difficult, if not downright impossible, it is to connect the dots in any meaningful way on a situation such as this. You do know how Bill Devine died, don't you?"

"Self-inflicted gunshot wound."

"*Wounds.* Plural. Do you know where they were?"

"No."

"He shot himself in the left leg. Then he shot himself in the right leg. Then he shot a hole in his left hand. Then he shot himself in the stomach. Finally, he shot himself in the head, putting the gun in his mouth and pointing upward, so the entire top half of his cranium was obliterated."

"Jesus."

"Now the question is: How could he do such a thing? How could he physically accomplish a suicide of that nature?"

"You don't think it was suicide?"

"I'm not saying that at all. What I'm saying is: How did he continue on after the first bullet and the second and the third? How did he stand the pain? And after he shot himself in the stomach . . . well, that should have finished him off. All the blood loss and organ damage. He should have been too weak to do anything but slump to the floor. And yet he still had both the strength and the presence of mind to shoot himself in the head." He paused. "That's why I think there's some sort of connection to the other killings. The extent of the carnage, whether directed inward or outward, seems to me to be of a kind. Combined with the similarities of the killers' backgrounds . . ." Wilson sighed. "It reminds me of a bad science fiction movie, where a virus that makes people commit violent acts is somehow transmitted from one person to another."

Brian was tempted to tell the other reporter about his father's letter, but instead he said, "Inbreeding doesn't sound that far-fetched after all, does it?"

"No," Wilson admitted. He pointed to one of the wire service photos, a shot not of the bodies but the crime scene itself: the Stewarts' bedroom. His finger traced the edge of the photograph, which seemed to be deliberately ringed by lushly growing houseplants. "I contributed to Devine's obit—background information, financial dealings, things of that nature—but McElvoy actually wrote the piece. Somehow he was able to get a statement from Devine's widow, to talk to her, not just recycle some prepared PR from the family publicist, and he told me that she said something strange. He didn't use it because it didn't make any sense and she was probably speaking from shock, but she said something about the plants growing wild and she couldn't stop them. The only reason that set off alarm bells was because when we went to see Devine at Oklatex, I noticed the plants in his office. Did you? They were huge."

Brian hadn't noticed, but now that he thought back on it, the office *had* had a lot of foliage. In fact, with all of the open space and skylights, it seemed purposely designed with such an environment in mind.

"Now look at this picture."

Brian glanced at the picture of the Stewarts' bedroom. Indeed, whether it was an artistic decision to frame the picture in such a manner or not, there was no arguing that the bedroom looked like a jungle.

"Tom Lowry's entire estate was overgrown with exotic plants."

"Is that supposed to mean something?"

"I don't know," Wilson admitted. "But if we're looking for things these situations have in common, we have to look at everything."

"But plants . . . ?"

"None of this makes any rational sense."

"Yet we still believe it."

Wilson nodded.

Ted Sprague walked past again. "Give it up, you two. Get to work."

"How's the Charlie Brown poll going?" Wilson asked.

Scowling, Ted held up a middle finger. Brian laughed.

Wilson walked over to his desk, motioning for Brian to follow. "There's a videotape," he said after a pause.

"Of the murders?"

"No. Not exactly. But . . ." Wilson trailed off. The expression on his face was one of uneasiness and apprehension. He withdrew a black unmarked VHS cassette from within a drawer. "It was Devine's. From his office. Someone at Oklatex slipped it to me. I'm not supposed to have it—"

"Who gave it to you? That secretary?"

"I'm not going to say. But I want you to look at it and tell me what you think. Take it into the conference room. There's a TV with a VCR already set up."

"What does—"

"Just watch it," Wilson said.

Apprehensive yet intrigued, Brian followed the other reporter's instruction. Closing and locking the conference room door behind him, he turned on the TV, popped the tape in the VCR and sat down to watch.

The video was in black and white. THIS IS WHERE IT

BEGINS, read a title card, and then the screen went dark. The camera pulled back, and the darkness was revealed to be the interior of a wound in the center of a dead man's chest. Although Brian was not exactly sure that it *was* a man. The figure's head and feet were blurred—only the midsection was in focus—and the shape of the head seemed grotesquely misshapen, too big and too irregular to be that of a human being. Then the scene switched, and he was looking at what at first appeared to be a forest but was soon revealed to be a bug's-eye view of an ordinary lawn. As the camera moved through the grass, the stalks came to look less like trees and more like people, although as far as he could tell there was no CGI trickery or special effects involved, merely a subtle shift in the viewing angle and the lighting. In the center of the screen, the stem of a plant swayed seductively, looking more like a woman than seemed possible, its reediness undulating like the body of an exotic dancer.

There was a split-second shot of a real exotic dancer. She was moving too fast to be clearly seen, go-going on some dark, grimy stage, but her blurred head seemed way too big, and there was something wrong with her arms.

Brian felt cold. The camera panned down the outside of a building, showing part of a neon sign on a concrete wall above a generic doorway, and then the screen was filled with a shiny black puddle that could have been oil, could have been blood. The final shot was a singularly unerotic close-up of a vaginal opening that somehow resembled the chest wound of the man at the beginning.

The video was silent, and, throughout, the only noise in the room was his own ragged breathing, the faint hiss of the air conditioner and the barely audible sound of the running VCR. The fact that there was no soundtrack to the horrific images creeped him out and somehow made the whole thing seem more real, as though the depicted events had not been intentionally staged for the camera's benefit but had merely been captured by someone in the right place at the right time.

Or wrong place at the wrong time.

For there was something so fundamentally disturbing about the video that Brian still remained in his seat, staring at the snowy screen even after it ended. He emerged from the conference room moments later, more shaken than he wanted to admit, and placed the cassette on Wilson's desk.

"Whoever made that," Brian said, "is one sick fuck."

Wilson stopped typing and looked up. "You'll get no argument from me."

"That building in there. I recognized that place," Brian said. "It's in Orange County. Santa Ana. A guy I know works there. He used to be a night custodian at the *Register.*"

"It doesn't seem to have any importance—"

"It's the only recognizable location in the video."

"You want to call your friend and ask him if he knows anything about it?"

Brian glanced at the clock. "They're not even open yet, I don't think. I'll stop by on my way home and see if I can talk to him. Or see if anyone else there knows anything about it."

Wilson took a deep breath. "What are we doing?" he asked.

Brian looked at him. "What do you mean?"

He motioned toward his computer. "I have actual articles on which I'm supposed to be working. I'm assuming you do as well."

"So?"

"So why are we involved here at all?"

"Because Bill Devine *got* you involved by leaving that message." Brian said nothing about his father's letter and his own involvement.

"At some point, we're going to have to tell the reporters who are really working on these stories what we're doing. And we should probably check in with an editor."

"Yeah," Brian agreed.

Wilson paused. His voice, when he spoke again, was pensive. "It's not just that this is a potentially great story. There's something else here. At least there is for me. It's like an itch in the back of my brain. I could try to say it's my reporter's instinct, but it's more personal than that. The truth is, I don't really care about writing the story. I just want to find out what is going on here. It seems . . . important somehow."

That was Brian's thought exactly, although he hadn't been able to put it into words.

"And," Wilson continued, "I'm not even sure that either of us could write an article about what's really going on here. Not unless we start getting into areas where we really don't want to go."

Brian nodded. He, too, had the nagging sense that "areas where we really don't want to go" was exactly where they *had* to go. There was no simple, rational explanation for everything that was going on. These killing sprees weren't crimes of passion or mob hits, Devine's suicide was not the result of depression over his love life or business, and his dad . . .

Where *did* his dad fit into all of this?

Brian thought of the video, the gaping wound in the dead—*thing's*—chest. He was frightened. He felt like Pandora, in a way, afraid to open the box but needing to know. This was deep, whatever it was, and there was no way for it to turn out any way but bad. Still, Wilson was right. It was like an itch. They had to press on.

"I have to get back to work," Brian said. "You're right. I *do* have articles to write."

"I'll make a copy of that tape for you," Wilson told him.

"And I'll stop by and see Manny on my way home."

Although he'd put in fifteen years sweeping up at the *Register,* Manny Ramirez was now one of the floor managers at Razzamatazz—what used to be called a strip joint but was now referred to as a "gentleman's club." Such businesses had gained legitimacy over the past decade, and instead of dateless trench-coated losers, their clientele now included hip twentysomething couples and groups of middle-aged professional men. It was why Manny said he'd had no qualms about taking this job. Hell, he told Brian, these days it was more of an embarrassment to work for a newspaper than a gentleman's club. And the pay here was better, too.

Still, there were drawbacks. The coating of respectability was only a thin veneer, and behind the scenes, life in the club was probably not much different than it had always been. He wasn't going to name names, but cocaine, physical abuse and alcoholism were all part of various dancers' lives. Two of them had kids. One was a part-time hooker. Some of the customers were a step above stalker. One of them *had* been a stalker and was now in police custody.

Manny sighed. "It's a lot tougher than sweeping up rat shit, gum wrappers and paper clips."

Brian held up the videotape.

"What's that?"

"I was hoping you could tell me. Another reporter got it and it's connected to . . . a big story." He wasn't sure how much he wanted to give away. "If you have a TV and a machine here, we can watch it. It's really short."

"Just tell me what happens."

"Well, nothing really happens. There's a dead guy's body and a dancer, although both of them look blurry and . . . creepy. There's some weird plants and a shot of this building. Oh, and the whole thing's in black and white. We're trying to find out who made it, and since it showed a dancer and the outside of Razzamatazz, I thought you might know something."

"Yeah, I know who made it. That rich dude that croaked. I saw him on TV the other night and said, 'That's him!' When he came in here, though, I thought he was just some ordinary asshole. We all did. No one knew who he was."

"Are you sure? You want to watch the video and see—"

"I don't need to watch it," Manny said. But something in his voice told Brian that he didn't *want* to watch it. That he was *afraid* to watch it.

"What happened?"

"We don't let people film in here or take pictures. For obvious reasons. But that butt-fuckin', mother-humpin', dick-lickin', dog-shittin', tit-tweakin', tater-twangin', tube-steakin' son of a bitch conned his way in. Said he was doing a documentary for HBO. Got carte blanche."

"Was there anyone else with him? A crew?"

Manny shook his head. "No. Just him with this little video camera. Thing is, he didn't want to tape the girls dancin'. I guess that made him seem more legit. He said he wanted backstage stuff, 'reality.' So when I saw him, he wasn't even tapin' anything. I was out on the floor, and I saw him every so often, but he just seemed to be wanderin' around, lookin' for sum'n to do. If it was up to me, he woulda been outta there. I didn't like the guy. But it wasn't my call."

Manny lit a cigarette. Nervously, Brian thought.

"As far as I knew, he didn't tape anything that night. So it's kind of a surprise to find out he did."

"It was just the building, like I said. And there's a dancer. But . . . I don't think she works here. You could see it for yourself—"

"No thanks." Again, Brian thought he sounded scared. "Is that where you got the tape? Was it his? The rich guy?"

Brian nodded.

"Thought so."

There seemed to be no more forthcoming. "Is that it?" Brian asked tentatively. "Is there anything else you can tell me?"

Manny smoked in silence for a moment before speaking. "We got a dancer here who stuffs animals." He rolled his eyes. "Don't ask. She's payin' her way through taxidermy school or some such shit. Anyway, she had a dead pigeon that she found outside the club and was keepin' on ice in the dressin' room 'til she got off that night."

"*That* night?"

"Yeah. Anyway, he wanted to see it. Didn't want to film it, just wanted to check it out. I wasn't there, but three other people were, and they all saw the same thing. The guy reached out to the bird and . . . touched it." Manny paused, took a deep drag off his cigarette. "It came back to life."

Brian shivered, feeling suddenly cold.

"It's still back there."

He looked toward the spot where Manny had gestured and saw a dark narrow hallway leading behind the raised stage. His senses felt heightened, as though he were in a nightmare, and the shadowed hallway seemed not only claustrophobic but threatening. He didn't want to go there. But he put one foot in front of the other and followed Manny past the stage, past a cluttered empty office to a shared dressing room.

"Girls won't be here for another hour," Manny said.

The lights were off, but even after he turned them on, the room remained dim. Brian supposed that if the round bulbs ringing the makeup mirrors were switched on, there might be enough illumination to see clearly, but Manny walked past the mirrors and directly to a sheet that had been hung between the walls and affixed to the ceiling with hooks, partitioning off the far side of the narrow room. He lifted the bottom of the sheet and held it up for Brian to pass under.

An open-topped Panasonic television box sat on the floor. "There," Manny said, pointing.

The bird was . . . puffy. It looked more like a chicken than a pigeon, and it moved in a lurching, disjointed, almost spasmodic manner, banging repeatedly against the opposite side of the box and flapping its oddly crimped wings. Its head was cocked at an upward angle, and there was a feral glint in its glassy eyes that chilled him to the bone.

"We don't know what to do. Everyone's afraid of it. No one wants to take care of it, but no one wants to kill it, either. If it *can* be killed. Again." He shook his head. "As far as I know, no one's fed it since it . . . came back. But here it is."

The bird staggered toward them, and Brian took an involuntary step back.

"Yeah," Manny said. "Creepy, ain't it?"

The creature craned its neck and cried out. The sound was grating, like nails on a chalkboard. At the same time, it reminded Brian of something he had heard before—although he could not immediately place it— and the familiarity of the noise made it seem that much scarier. The bird cried out again. Inside its beak, he saw what looked like gray splotchy mold.

"Jesus," Brian said.

"Yeah."

They watched the bird flounder around for another

moment or two; then Manny turned and went back under the sheet, holding it up again for Brian to follow.

"So why'd you give Devine so much access if you didn't know who he was?"

"That his name, Devine?"

"Bill Devine, yeah."

"Well, like I said, it wasn't my call. *I* didn't give him anything. That came from higher up."

"But why was he allowed to do whatever he wanted?"

Manny sighed. "We got scammed."

"How?"

"No one does shit here unless they get paid, right? I mean, rules of the fuckin' room. Well, this guy offers up big bucks. Five grand. On a Monday! That's nothin' to sneeze at. Even on a weekend that might fly. So he pays with a check, gives it to Willie, the bartender. Willie looks at the amount, makes sure it tabs up, puts it away. No one notices until later the way it's signed or who it's made out to."

Brian felt the cold creeping back.

"Fact is, we still don't know who it's made out to. Can't make head or tails out of that chicken scratching."

"Can I see it?" Brian asked.

"Sure. Well, not the real check. A copy of it. Owners have the real one."

"That's fine. I just want to see what it looks like."

Manny led him down the hallway and back out to the front of the club. Behind the bar, a Xerox was taped next to the register. He'd known ahead of time what he would see, but it was still a shock to spot that by-now familiar jumble of incoherent symbols and scribbles writ small on the preprinted lines of a Bank of America check.

I'm afraid of that language.

He wondered what Lisa LaMunyon would say about this. His eyes were drawn to the spot where the signer's address should have been printed, but he saw only a blacked-out square. Could the professor use the check as a key to decipher the writing? If the scrawls on the signature line corresponded to the letters in Devine's name, perhaps the code could be cracked.

"Do you think you could make me a copy of that?" he asked Manny.

"I don't know. I gotta check with my bosses. Somehow, I don't think they'll be too thrilled with the idea of a reporter lookin' into their business."

"I won't even mention the club," Brian said. "Just tell them I'm doing a story on Bill Devine. I only want it for that."

"This is about more than just that videotape, ain't it?"

"Yeah," Brian admitted.

"Does it have something to do with that rich fuck's death?"

"I don't know," he said honestly.

"What is it, then? What exactly are you lookin' for?"

"I don't know." Brian shook his head. "I don't know anything. Yet."

Nine

Carrie squirmed uncomfortably in her seat. On the stage of the San Francisco Opera House, ten musicians were performing a slow interminable piece titled "Ten Musicians" that had been written especially for this event by a supposedly famous composer.

How had she allowed Sanchez to talk her into this?

The benefit was for a good cause—helping the homeless—and a percentage of the money raised would go to their department for some much-needed improvements, but it really should have been the responsibility of Sanchez to represent their office here. Unfortunately, he, along with everyone else, seemed to have a life. She was the only one who was single and unencumbered, with no plans for the evening, so she'd gotten roped into attending the event. Sure the ticket was free, but parking wasn't—she'd had to shell out twelve dollars of her own money just to pull her ancient Celica into a spot in an underground garage that it would probably take her an hour to get out of—and she'd been forced to confront the fact that she'd gained weight when she put on her red evening gown and discovered that she no longer had the wiggle room she once had. The thong underwear that she used to wear as a matter of course now felt plain uncomfortable.

Which was probably why she couldn't seem to find a position in her seat that felt right.

Not for the first time, Carrie glanced down at the program in her hands, hoping to discover that the concert was further along than it was. No such luck. This was still only the fourth piece of music to be performed this evening. There were five more to go. Not to mention all the speeches between the music.

She felt awkward being here by herself. She wasn't one of those people who was comfortable attending social events alone. She didn't eat at restaurants by herself or go to movies unaccompanied, and she attended parties only if there were to be other singles in attendance. She realized with a start that it had been nearly two years since she and Matt had broken up. It didn't seem anywhere near that long—but it had been. And she hadn't been on a date since, not because she was in mourning or had sworn off men or anything but because she hadn't made the effort to get out and meet someone new. She'd just buried herself in her work.

How pathetic was that?

Sometimes she was glad that her parents were dead. She didn't have to explain herself to them or justify her life. She didn't have to be embarrassed or ashamed of who she was.

Although she *was* embarrassed. She *was* ashamed.

Why had she agreed to come here tonight? Why hadn't she lied and gotten out of it?

It had been a long day, she was tired, and the lengthy, quiet passages within the music acted on her like a soporific. It was only the discomfort of her clothing and the seat that kept her awake.

She thought about her job. She'd gotten to know Rosalia fairly well these past few weeks—social work inevitably accelerated the process of learning about a person—and the two of them were comfortable enough with each other that today she'd finally found the courage to ask about Juan. Unsurprisingly, the story Sanchez had told her about the llama show turned out not to be true. The real story was much more prosaic, although just as confusing. In her musical, heavily accented English, Rosalia said that soon after moving to the United States, she had been courted by a "very, very nice man," who was also "very, very important." She'd lived in a one-room apartment with six other young women at that time and had just started working as a waitress at a new Peruvian restaurant in the trendy section of town. He was a regular, apparently, and though one of her roommates warned her that he was not what he seemed, the roommate offered no proof to back up her assertion, and Rosalia put it down to jealousy.

The man was certainly charming. Polite and well spoken, he tipped lavishly, and when she made mistakes while serving—which happened far too often—he stuck up for her and made sure the owner knew that he considered her the restaurant's greatest asset. He started coming for lunch and dinner more and more often, eventually learning her schedule and making an effort to arrive shortly before her shift ended. He would take her out afterward for coffee or dessert, walk with her through the historic streets, and once he even took her to an expensive clothing store where he let her pick out the dress of her choice. He spoke Spanish, which meant they could communicate, and Rosalia found herself falling in love with him. Against her morals and better judgment, against her upbringing and the teachings of her church, she became involved in a physical relationship. She'd known at the time that it was wrong, but she had feelings for him . . . and they were going to get married . . . and . . . and . . . and . . .

So God had punished her by making Juan the way he was. He was her burden to bear, and after the restaurant had closed and she'd been unable to find another job, she understood that that was part of His punishment, too.

"What happened to . . . Juan's father?" Carrie probed gently. Even after all this time, a sense of honor had prevented Rosalia from giving the man's name.

Rosalia started to sob. "He leave."

"When he"—Carrie looked behind her, lowered her voice—"saw Juan?"

"No. When I get pregnant. I tell him and he disappear."

It turned out that she had no idea where he lived, that their trysts had always occurred in motel rooms or cars, and immediately Carrie's opinion of him shifted. Whereas she'd been imagining the kind, cultured, handsome man described by Rosalia, she now saw a cynical user, an exploiter of innocent immigrants.

Carrie had tried to get Rosalia to give her more information about the man, explaining that he was responsible for child support and that she was going to make sure that he did right by his son, but Rosalia clammed up and would say no more, bursting into tears once again and ordering Carrie to leave her apartment.

On the stage, "Ten Musicians" ended. There was no speech this time, thank God. Another piece simply started just as the applause started to taper off. "The Gate," according to the program. She tried to enjoy it, but the music seemed just as boring as its predecessor, and once again her mind wandered. She found herself thinking about Holly and her son—

Rhino Boy

—and the slaughter that had occurred in their slummy apartment. Even amid the heat of bodies in the crowded auditorium, her skin prickled with gooseflesh. As far as she knew, the police were nowhere on this. There were no suspects, no leads, and despite the assurances she'd

received, Carrie was not at all sure that they were working as hard as they could to solve the murders. After all,
the victims were only a hooker and her deformed son.

But Rhino Boy had been in the *Weekly Globe*. Press
attention always put pressure on the police. So maybe
they were trying their best.

Maybe the killer wasn't human.

He's coming.

Carrie pushed those thoughts away, tried to concentrate again on the music. Ever since that day in the
apartment, there'd been a nagging sensation in the back
of her mind that she'd done her damnedest to ignore, a
small voice telling her that Holly and her son—

and Rosalia and Juan?

—were connected to things that she could not hope
to understand. Deep things. Dark things. She'd assumed
that the feeling would fade over time, but it hadn't, and
the fear she'd experienced in that tenement building
could be called up at any time, as fresh and real as ever.

"The Gate" was mercifully short and ended just at
that moment. Applause took her mind off her reverie,
and the next performer, a former punk rocker from her
youth who was now a balding chubby folkie, not only
distracted her but kept her engaged. In fact, she remained interested and attentive for the remainder of
the program.

An announcement was made at the end of the show
that over $200,000 had been raised tonight for the cause,
and even Carrie stood and clapped for that astonishingly
good news.

The biggest benefactor by far was Lew Haskell, and
before the program began, he'd stood up to give a
speech about the importance of an involved citizenry
and how it was incumbent upon society's most fortunate
to give back to the community and help out those who
were less fortunate, especially in these days of seemingly

endless government budget cuts, when elected officials thought the Constitutional reference to "promote the general welfare" meant cutting services for the poor in order to cut taxes for the rich. "This is our country," he said. "We're all in this together." Carrie had been told in no uncertain terms that she was expected to meet with him, to convey the department's gratitude, and at the mixer afterward, she approached the philanthropist as he stood next to a pillar at the bottom of the sweeping stairway, drink in hand. He was talking to a well-known author who'd won every literary prize imaginable for a trilogy of novels set in frontier California that contained no punctuation of any kind. She'd tried to read one but had never been able to get through it, and she was inwardly pleased to discover that the writer was just as pompous and pretentious as she'd imagined him to be. She didn't feel guilty at all for hating his work.

Haskell's speech had been inspiring—as those things went—and she told him so in preface to thanking him for his generous contribution to the city's safety net, particularly the donations earmarked for Social Services. The author next to him smirked and made some sort of ironic comment, but Carrie ignored him and so did Haskell. In fact, her generic thank-you somehow turned into an honest-to-God conversation. The writer grew bored and drifted away, but Haskell spoke earnestly of transforming the way the poor were treated in America, and Carrie had to admit that she was impressed. Being in the trenches every day, she didn't exactly have the luxury of considering grand overviews, but she was glad that someone did, and she was glad that it was someone with sensibilities that paralleled her own. It made her feel more hopeful about the future, more optimistic.

Other people arrived, more important people, and though she wasn't exactly dismissed, Haskell's attention was drawn away from her, and after a polite interval

Carrie excused herself and got away. She grabbed a diet Sprite from the bar, was accidentally roped into a depressing conversation with a pair of community activists, then finally managed to sneak over to the elevators and escape.

Although most of the movers and shakers were still upstairs, a majority of the people who'd come to the benefit were already leaving, and getting out of the parking garage took just as long as she'd feared. Still, she wasn't in the mood to go home yet—besides, tomorrow was Saturday, and she could sleep in—so she drove by the arts district to check out some of the galleries.

Check out some of the galleries?

Who was she kidding? She wasn't a frequenter of art galleries. In fact, she hadn't been anywhere near this section of the city since she and Matt had broken up. The truth was that the only reason she was here now was because she'd seen an article in an alternative newspaper that said Matt had an installation displayed in one of the newer, hipper spaces. Did she want to see the installation? No.

Did she want to see Matt again?

Maybe.

She really *was* pathetic.

If it hadn't been for that stupid benefit, such an idea wouldn't even have occurred to her. She would be safely at home, ensconced in her bed, watching TV or catching up on her reading. But she was out and about, and Matt's presence was like a magnet. She was ashamed of herself, embarrassed, but powerless to resist. The ironic thing was, their relationship hadn't even been that great. And it hadn't lasted that long. But it *had* been her most recent relationship, and emotionally at least, that granted it an importance that perhaps it didn't deserve.

She lucked out and turned the corner onto Geary just as a powder-blue Mercedes pulled out of a prime park-

ing spot in front of the Landau Gallery. Carrie shoved
her Celica into the space before someone else could get
it and, after shutting off the engine, dug through her
purse, looking for quarters for the meter. She had a wad
of one-dollar bills, three dimes, four pennies and a
nickel—but no quarters. When had parking meters
stopped taking other coins? Who was the moron who'd
decided that the machines would accept only a single
denomination?

She finally found a quarter under the mat on the floor
of the passenger seat and got out, dropping it into the
meter. It gave her only fifteen minutes, but that should
be enough. After all, she wasn't going to hang out. She
was just going to take a quick peek and be on her way.

And she could always get change if need be.

The Lo Fi Gallery, where Matt's installation was on
display, was a block from the Landau, and Carrie walked
down the crowded sidewalk, her stomach tightening as
she approached. She knew she should turn around and
go home, but she couldn't. So instead, she slowed down,
looking in the windows of each shop and gallery she
passed, her steps getting smaller the closer she came to
the end of the block.

She looked at a boutique filled with primitive arts and
crafts from Central America. She pretended to examine
a group of metal sculptures made from pieces of old
cars.

And in one of the gallery windows she saw a wall-
sized photograph of . . .

Juan.

No, Carrie realized instantly. It wasn't really Juan.
And it wasn't the Rhino Boy either. But the child depicted in the photo suffered from the same sort of affliction that had disfigured both children—except that this
boy's face resembled a possum's. The picture could have
been doctored, she knew. One of the artists could have

combined two images to make some statement about . . . something. But, no, that wasn't the case. This was a photograph of a real child. The art was in the lighting and composition, not in any darkroom tricks.

She stared at the bristly face with its protuberant snout. Maybe there was an epidemic of birth defects out there, attributable to chemical exposure or some other environmental factor.

Stop it, she chided herself. She'd been searching for a rational, scientific explanation for all of this ever since the police had interviewed her at Holly's apartment, even though she knew good and well that rationality had nothing to do with the horrors she had seen. There was something else at work here, something that defied logic. She felt like Bill Pullman in *The Serpent and the Rainbow*, who'd discovered that beneath the political mess in Haiti was an older evil filled with voodoo spirits and magic.

Evil?

That was slightly melodramatic, wasn't it?

She thought of the Rhino Boy's head atop the dresser in that dingy bedroom.

Maybe not.

Carrie walked into the gallery to see if there were other photos of other children, hoping the artist was there so she could talk to him or her about the picture in the window. But of course no one was in the gallery save a smug and snotty young clerk. There *were* other photos, though, and Carrie walked slowly through the room, examining them all. Most were of the boy, showing him holding a lunchbox, playing on a swing set, riding a bike—heartbreaking juxtapositions of his grotesque physical appearance with the everyday realities of an ordinary childhood. The most disturbing shot was of the child with his mother, a young attractive Asian woman with all the accoutrements of the young and hip—

two-toned hair, pierced lip and nose, multiple tattoos—
and a look of sad resignation on her features that made
her seem far, far older than she was.

Although the clerk arrogantly refused to answer any
of the questions she put to him, the gallery's front table
contained photocopies of a review of the show from one
of the local alterna-papers, as well as a bio of the
photographer—John Mees. Carrie took one of each, intending to read them at home, and if possible, get in
touch with the man and see if she could find out more
about the boy in the photos. She left the gallery, un-
aware of how nervous and on edge she'd been until she
was once again out in the cool evening air. The sidewalk
was crowded with people, but still it felt more free and
open than the empty gallery.

She'd lost the desire to see either Matt or his work,
and instead of continuing on down the block, she turned
around and went back to her car, where she found that
the meter had already expired. Had she been gone that
long? It sure didn't feel like it. Luckily, there was no
ticket on her windshield, and she quickly got in, started
the engine and pulled out into traffic. Someone honked
at her from behind, but she ignored the jerk and made
a series of turns that allowed her to circle back the way
she had come.

On the way home, her anxiousness faded somewhat,
and she wished she *had* stopped by Matt's gallery. She
felt lonely and could have used a little companionship
tonight. He wouldn't have come through for her, though.
He didn't want her back; he'd moved on. And, knowing
him, he would have been rude and spiteful. He knew
exactly which buttons to push in order to hurt her, and
he would have pushed them with glee. Things had
worked out much better this way, now that she thought
about it, and she was glad that the two of them hadn't
reconnected.

Besides, she wouldn't have been able to concentrate on him or his art or anything. Not with those images from the gallery swirling through her mind.

And the images of Juan.

And the Rhino Boy.

Rhino Boy. She wished she knew that child's real name. It pained her to refer to him by his tabloid moniker, and she felt awful even thinking the phrase to herself.

It had been a long day, and once home, Carrie tiredly dumped her purse on the coffee table in the living room, got herself a drink of water from the kitchen, then trudged into the bathroom, where she changed out of her uncomfortable dress and scrubbed the makeup off her face before climbing into bed. She masturbated quickly and quietly, thinking of Matt, then pulled up her pajama bottoms, rolled onto her side and promptly fell asleep.

Ten

After the benefit, Haskell had his driver take him home. He glanced out the window as the limo purred through the city and across the bridge, smoked glass filtering out everything save the lights of the buildings. There'd been four or five women at the after party who would have gladly come with him—and Lord knows Suzonne wouldn't have given a shit if they had—but he felt tired this evening, and his body needed sleep more than sex.

Home when he was in California was a spectacular steel-and-glass structure in Marin, overlooking the bay. It was his newest house and also his favorite. His friend Frank Gehry had designed it, drawing the initial rough sketch on the back of an envelope—an envelope he now had framed and hanging in his office—and it had been featured in a host of architectural magazines as well as in a PBS special.

He was proud of the house, as he was proud of all of his houses, but he also genuinely liked it. He felt comfortable here. And it was perfectly suited to the special needs of his family.

Although upkeep was a bitch.

The limo pulled to a stop at the head of the circular driveway, and he let himself out, telling the driver to be in exactly the same spot at six in the morning; tomorrow was going to be a busy day. He watched the car cruise down the sloping drive to the garage, then turned to face the house and the bay beyond. Across the water, the lights of San Francisco twinkled in the fog, subdued and softened into something almost painterly.

Although it was not visible from here, the next estate over was empty and dark. He could tell because the glow he used to see over the stand of trees to the west had disappeared over two weeks ago. Word was that the estate was for sale, that the actor who'd bought it couldn't meet the mortgage payments and was trying to get out from under it before news of his financial situation spread.

Fame was so ephemeral. He remembered talking with his young secretary several years ago after hearing on the radio that the magician Doug Henning had died. He mentioned that he'd seen Henning perform in the late 1970s.

"Who is he?" she'd asked. "I've never heard of him."

He was shocked, and after that, he'd developed a small obsession, running by his secretary the names of minor celebrities from previous decades whenever they died or he came across them in print, checking to see if she recognized any of them. Louis Nye? No. Anthony Newly? No. Steve Allen? No. Godfrey Cambridge? No. Larry Hovis? No. Slappy White, Nipsey Russell, William Conrad, Charles Nelson Riley? No, no, no and no.

He realized that most of the people he'd grown up watching on TV had completely faded from the cultural landscape. It was a depressing discovery, although it taught him a lesson. In the celebrity-obsessed society of California, it was easy to ascribe a greater importance to fame than it actually deserved.

But fame was fleeting.

Money lasted.

Money and monuments.

Like this house.

He looked admiringly at the structure. It was a strange confluence of events that had created this wonderful building. If he had not wanted a house in the Bay Area, if he hadn't known Frank Gehry, hell, if they'd discussed the house on a different day, this edifice might not exist. At least not in the form it did now.

His gaze moved on to the surrounding grounds. The damn place was overgrown with vegetation. This was the fourth landscaping service he'd hired just this year, and it looked like he'd have to find yet another one. He'd explained to Gary Martinez, the owner of the business, how he wanted the property maintained, and the man had seemed to understand, but either he hadn't properly communicated with his employees or the landscapers who worked for him were incompetent. Whatever the reason, the area around the house looked like hell, and Haskell decided that tomorrow he would call Martinez on the carpet and tell him to shape up or ship out.

Or maybe he'd just fire his ass.

It depended on how he felt in the morning.

Haskell walked slowly across the cobblestone driveway and up the burnished marble steps to the front door. He considered ringing the bell and announcing his presence, but it was late.

He punched in the security code and opened the door.

As always, his mail was stacked neatly on a steel table designed to flow with the curved wall. An assistant had printed out a list of phone messages that had arrived for him during the day and had placed this sheet next to the pile of mail, weighing it down with a geometric hunk of translucent plastic. He picked up the sheet the same way he did each evening, scanning the phone numbers, struck by the realization that he had more daily contact with strangers than he did his own family.

The entry hall seemed empty and cold, the recessed

lights sterile rather than homey, and Haskell thought that maybe he *should* have brought someone back with him for the night. None of the Gucci-clad do-gooders who'd thrown themselves at him held any appeal, but he remembered a young San Francisco social worker from early in the evening who'd thanked him for his donation to the cause and who'd struck him as someone he wouldn't mind giving the high hard one. He didn't remember her name, but it would be easy enough to find out if he wanted.

Which he probably wouldn't by morning.

Still, the night was long and the thought of spending it alone left him feeling dispirited.

Of course, there was always Suzonne . . .

The smile on his face was not quite bitter, not quite amused, but some unclassifiable combination of the two.

He was too tired to even stop by his office to drop off the mail, so he left everything on the table and walked through the entry hall, past the unused guest wing, into the main corridor, loosening his tux as he proceeded through the house.

The building was not quiet. Howls were coming from the Quiet Room, and although they were faint, they could still be heard even through the soundproofing. The acoustics in this place really were amazing. He hummed to himself, trying not to hear the sounds, but the cries grew louder and wilder as he approached, and with the absence of any competing noise, they became impossible to ignore.

He strode up to the white door of the Quiet Room and flung open the viewing window.

"Shut up!" he yelled.

His . . . *son*—if that's what the creature leaping about the empty room could be called—stared at him with dull fury. As usual, he had ripped off his clothes. His grotesque member had been rubbed raw or shoved against something abrasive and was red and bleeding, but it was still erect, and Haskell was disgusted by the sight. Around him, the room was a mess, broken furniture thrown together in a pile at the center of the floor, primitive drawings scrawled on the walls with blood and excrement. Haskell thought of the one time, long ago, when his son had been allowed to play with another boy, the child of a housekeeper. There'd been a lot more blood then, and it had taken money and pull with friends of friends in the INS to keep that incident quiet.

The . . . *thing* in the room shrieked at him, leaping at the viewing window.

"Shut up!" Haskell screamed again, and slammed the window covering, locking it tight.

He stood there for a moment, unmoving, staring at the white door. Part of him *almost* understood the boy's behavior—and, in some way, envied it. It was a disconcerting realization, but many was the time he'd felt constricted by traditional modes of conduct, by the mores of society. Sometimes he longed to let loose, to give free rein to his wilder emotions, consequences be damned.

But of course he could not.

He moved down the corridor where the door to Suzonne's room was not only closed but locked. He knocked on the pale wood, politely at first then with more vigor, but she refused to respond. He kicked at the door, called her name but was met only with silence.

He *should* have brought someone home.

"You'll take it up the ass tomorrow!" he cried. "And you'll like it!"

He stormed over to his own room, slamming the door and yanking off his clothes before getting into bed naked. He lay there, staring upward into the darkness, feeling angry, wondering how it was that some people had the nerve to act on their impulses and others didn't, wondering what it would feel like to kill his wife and put his son out of his misery.

Thinking to himself that it would probably feel pretty good.

Eleven

1845

The wagon train split up near the Great Salt Lake. None too soon, as far as Marshall was concerned. They'd been through a lot on this trip, seen a lot, and for a fair portion of the journey, the travelers had been split into two camps: those who feared the land and saw biblical import in every minor bump in the road, and those like himself who understood that large portions of the West were undiscovered country and contained things that neither they nor, perhaps, any man had seen before. He imagined that it was similar to the first Englishmen to visit Africa and see lions, giraffes, elephants and those other great primitive beasts.

Although what they'd encountered along the trail made a trip to Africa seem like a walk to Grandmother's house.

After rejoining the wagon train following his experience with the hut—

the bag of bones

—he and the rest of the travelers had spent a blissful two days enjoying the water, shade and plentiful game of the woods beyond the plain. He'd told everyone what had happened—some of it. He'd left out the compression of time, that strange shift from night to morning.

And he hadn't said a single word about his odd conviction that there was wealth to be had in California. That knowledge he kept to himself. But he'd told them everything else about the doorless, windowless room and the human bones in the bag and in the walls. A few had not believed him, but of those who did, a goodly number came up with reasons for what he'd seen and experienced, telling him that what seemed so bizarre and unreal probably had a perfectly natural explanation.

Then they came across the burial ground.

It was a graveyard unlike any they had ever seen, not least for the fact that the graves had been big enough to accommodate giants. How could they know this, since there were no headstones and the burial plots had been exposed to the elements for so long that they had lost all shape or definition? Because one of the graves had been opened. The huge hole gaped before them like a foundation that had been dug for an unbuilt house, and footprints led away from the pit through the muddy soil, monstrous footprints that were not only four times the size of an ordinary man's but resembled those of neither animal nor human.

They had hurried away from that place, but questions remained in all of their heads, questions some of them posed at night when the campfires were low and the women and children had gone to sleep: Where had the giants come from, since there appeared to be no city or sign of encampment anywhere near the graveyard? And where had they gone? And how had the one giant come back to life and emerged from the grave?

" 'There were giants in those days,' " Morgan James said, quoting the Bible as if that explained everything.

Of course, it explained nothing, and they pushed their animals to the limit, trying to get as far from the graveyard as quickly as possible.

Then there'd been the Garden of Skulls.

It was what Marshall called it, though he'd never said so aloud. They'd discovered it shortly after passing through the burnt remnants of an Indian village. *Choctaw,* Uriah Caldwell had announced sagely, but none of them knew if that was true or not. What they did know was that the village had been decimated, the structures torched, even the surrounding fields set afire.

Beyond, past a stand of oak trees, they'd found the skulls.

It was a cold, gloomy day, but even if it had been hot and sunny with a bright cloudless sky, Marshall would have found the sight before them chilling. Skulls, hundreds of them, more than could have possibly belonged to residents of the Indian village, were arranged in various permutations within a walled area the size of a farmer's vegetable garden. Not all of them, he saw immediately, were human. Some were animal, some were . . . something else. Acting as a base for six baby skulls that had been fused together into a circle was a flat skeletal head as big as an elephant's with slitted eye sockets and sharp fangs longer than Marshall's fingers. Farther down was one with no discernible mouth and a single oversized eye.

All of the skulls were joined with other skulls to make shapes that reminded him of flowers or plants. It was what made him think of a garden, but the fact remained that they had not grown here. They had been taken from skeletons and brought to this place and manipulated into these unnatural configurations.

But by whom?

Or what?

Once more, they had fled, and there was no talk now about logical reasons or natural explanations. He and several other men, Uriah included, were willing to concede that there were things beyond their ken, that here in this new land they were encountering phenomena no civilized man had ever seen. But the religious among them took this to mean that God Himself was intervening on their journey, performing miracles, scourging the land of evil, and for the rest of the trip they had prayed and proselytized to the point where Alf Thomas raised his hands to the sky and yelled, "God, if you're up there, strike these assholes mute so I don't have to listen to their fucking voices anymore! Do . . . it . . . right . . . *now!*" When nothing happened, he turned to Emily Smith and her group of fanatics and said, "See? Either God is dead or He doesn't exist. Now shut the hell up!"

But of course they didn't.

Marshall had remained apart from all this, as he'd remained apart since the beginning of the journey. He, too, experienced hunger, fatigue, frustration and fear, but what saw him through was the confidence that there were riches in California, gold for the taking, that strange certainty that had come to him after his abbreviated night in the hut. In his mind, he remembered the flowers he had seen that morning, the rainbow of blossoms that had covered everything as far as the eye could see, and he knew that no matter what hardships they might encounter on the trail, he would make it through to California.

There'd been one other incident, an encounter so strange and inexplicable that even now he didn't know what to think of it. The wagon train had been traveling for well over a week, seeing nothing untoward, and for the first time in quite a spell, they were relaxed and at ease, the tension that had been pulling them apart nearly dissipated. They had crossed the Great Divide, and this milestone had buoyed their spirits, made them all more congenial, more willing to overlook their differences.

Then they'd passed through the Dark Woods.

They had seen this section of ground a day before from a ridge atop a low mountain pass. It had appeared burned and scarred, brown earth showing through while all around it the land remained green and fertile. Yet, coming upon the location, they discovered a savage overgrown forest, a spot of ground far more fecund than any they had yet encountered and with foliage the likes of which none of them had ever seen. There'd been bushes with tiny multicolored leaves that had grown naturally into the shapes of animals and people, grasses with gold stalks that did not bend in the breeze that blew through constantly and with edges that looked as sharp as razors. The trees, most of them, were taller than seemed possible, and their leaves and branches cut off the sky, shielding out the sun and creating a world of darkness below. A few others grew spindly and short, stunted and deformed, no doubt by the lack of light.

The wagon train had moved through slowly, warily, following a trail that seemed made for the passing of travelers but that Marshall could have sworn had not been in existence only moments previously. They'd been quiet, even the most talkative among them, even the children, and the animals had been subdued as well, as though sensing something amiss. At one point, he thought he'd seen something through the leaves, a squat dark figure darting away from them from bush to bush, and the shape of the figure had gnawed at his brain because he was sure he had seen it somewhere before.

Far more troubling were the whispers, sibilant sounds that came from nowhere and everywhere, that he couldn't understand but that seemed to be speaking directly to him.

Fortunately, the forest was small, lasting only a league, and once through it they again found themselves amid the ordinary greenery of the surrounding countryside, ensconced among plants they recognized with a bright sun in a clear blue sky above. All was right again.

It was then someone noticed that Emily Smith and her family were gone.

Uriah made everyone stop, and he rode quickly up and back the length of the caravan, counting wagons, looking for Emily and her husband. But it was true. They had not emerged from the forest. No one could quite understand how that was possible. Their wagon had been neither first nor last. It had been in the middle of the procession, but neither the Turners in front of them nor Jed Clayton behind claimed to have seen a thing.

Almost as one, they turned back to look at the wall of peculiar trees that marked the boundary of that mysterious place, and though no one said a thing, Marshall could tell that none of them were eager to retrace their steps and look for the Smiths. But it had to be done, and as much as he hated the woman, Marshall volunteered along with a few other single men and Uriah to undertake the search.

The woods seemed neither as dark nor as eerie as they had before. The noises were gone, as were any glimpses of hidden figures in the foliage. Unfortunately, Emily Smith and her husband were gone, too. They traversed the length of the woods along the same trail they'd traveled, then covered the opposite direction, crosswise, but to no avail. The Smiths, their wagon, their horses and their cow had completely disappeared.

They searched what felt like every square foot of the forest, and after several hours of this, the eight of them emerged from the western end of the strange wood and met up with the rest of the wagon train. None of them had any idea what to do next. They all felt guilty about leaving the Smiths behind, but they had done all they could to find the couple, and no one wanted to remain nearby with the coming of night. The decision was Uriah's to make, however, and the wagon master said they had to press on. Emily and her husband had food and supplies, and they could always catch up to the train.

If they were still alive.

"God will take care of them," Morgan James announced. "God will provide."

No one responded to that.

It was midafternoon, and the Dark Woods were no longer in sight by the time night fell, but the wagon train pressed on, not stopping before sunset as they usually did, not making camp for the evening until it was nearly midnight and the moon was high overhead.

It was Marshall and George who christened them the Dark Woods, and the name stuck, catching on even with the religious faction. Any agreement ended there, though, and for the remainder of the journey the travelers remained segregated and increasingly hostile to one another, Tyler Hamilton even going so far as to suggest that the "heathens" among them were responsible for the Smiths' disappearance. Rancorous confrontations had replaced normal conversation, and though no gun or knife fights had broken out, there'd been occasional fisticuffs, and Marshall thought that it was probably only a matter of time before conflicts escalated into violence.

So they parted ways after happening upon the well-worn tracks of the Mormon Trail and connecting with another wagon train a few miles up the route. The religious contingent headed west on the California Trail, claiming God would protect them from the winter, though they had been warned by fellow seekers that Donner Pass was inaccessible. The remainder headed northwest along the Oregon Trail, stopping for a few days of rest at Fort Hall before moving on.

Marshall felt as though a great weight had been lifted

from his shoulders, and the truth was that they seemed
to make much better time unencumbered by the dead
weight that was Morgan James and the other zealots.
They reached Oregon just before the change of seasons,
and he wintered there, working where and when he
could, living in a one-room cabin with George Johnson
and an ever-shifting group of hard-drinking not-so-hard-
working men who were biding their time until the cold
weather ended.

In the spring, he headed south on his own. As much
as he appreciated traveling with others and the security
it offered should they encounter Indians, he felt much
happier by himself. He didn't have to try and get along
with anyone; he didn't have to worry about offending
other people. He could be who he was and go where he
wanted without having to compromise.

He still had his horses, and he'd amassed a small grubstake over the winter that, added to what he already
had, allowed him a little extra bit of freedom. He had
no plan, really. He supposed he would make his way to
Sacramento or San Francisco, one of the towns, and talk
to people, try to get the lay of the land before deciding
where to go from there. George had given him a rough
map, copied from a friend who'd copied it from someone
else's hand-drawn directions, and though he had no idea
whether it was accurate, it was all he had to go on. He
figured it wasn't any worse than following the sun—his
original plan—so he made his way over streams, through
valleys, across deserts until he found himself in an area
that . . . spoke to him.

There was no other way to put it, and the fact that
these rugged foothills made him think of the mud hut
and the endless plain and the explosion of flowers—
though this region looked *nothing* like any of that—
caused him to realize that this was where he'd been
heading, this was where he'd been led.

Led by whom, though? God? He didn't believe in that. He now conceded that there were powers and entities beyond his understanding, but there was no proof that these powers had created men—the way the Bible said—or that they even *cared* about men. There was no indication that these entities were good, either. For all he knew, it was only man's mortal morality that stood in contrast to the evil of supernatural forces.

Riding the mare, leading the other horses and a pack mule behind, Marshall sauntered slowly through the shallow canyons of the foothills. Winter snow and rain had left the region green and lush, and between the outcroppings of rock and the occasional stands of trees grew oversized bushes with red branches, the likes of which he had never seen. This fertile land was so close to his initial conception of California that he found it hard to believe it was a real place. It was like heaven here, and he took off his hat and smiled into the warm dry sun, grateful to be alive.

It was early the next morning that he rode into an oak forest so beautiful it looked like a painting. He traveled along at a good clip, feeling unaccountably happy and energetic. He was still filled with the certainty that this area was his destination, this was where he belonged, and he left George's secondhand map folded in his saddlebag, navigating on instinct.

He had stopped to water the horses at a small brook when he thought he saw movement through the trees. Quickly but quietly, he grabbed his rifle. The dried elk he'd brought with him from Oregon had run out over a week ago, and other than a rabbit he'd caught two days back and a puny trout he'd speared in a stream higher up, he'd had no meat whatsoever. He'd been living on berries and biscuits and booze, and the thought that he might be able to bring down a buck or even a boar made him salivate and caused his stomach to rumble.

He approached slowly, cautiously, careful not to step on any dried leaves or twigs, not wanting to frighten the animal off. There was definitely something moving in a clearing up ahead—more than one, if he wasn't mistaken—and he could hear the muffled noises that the creatures were making.

Only . . .

Only the noises sounded like human voices.

Frowning, Marshall increased his pace, still moving quietly, until he reached the edge of the clearing. Ducking down behind a wall of brush, he peeked out through the leaves.

In the center of the meadow were two women, both completely naked and both kneeling in a patch of mud, posteriors up, each exposing her sex like an animal in heat. The one on the right, he saw now, was pissing, a yellow stream arcing behind her.

What was going on? The women obviously hadn't seen him, and he remained hidden behind the branches and bushes, sickened yet fascinated. The pissing woman started shouting something that sounded like a poem or a rhyme, and the small hairs on his arms and the back of his neck prickled.

Witchcraft, he thought, and though he had never believed in such mumbo jumbo, he had seen too much on the trail to completely discount anything. In fact, such an explanation seemed to him to be the only logical one. There was something ritualistic about the women's behavior, something that made him think they were appealing to a higher power or attempting to invoke unseen energies.

Now the other one was pissing, her stream shooting in a different direction. The first woman had placed her face in the mud, rubbing her cheeks in it, and Marshall grimaced in disgust as he realized how that dirt had probably gotten wet.

"Jack be nimble!" the second woman chanted. "Jack be quick! Take me with your dirty prick!"

He could hear her clearly, and there seemed to be desperation in her voice as well as determination. She was shouting to be heard, but by what or whom he could not guess. Involuntarily, he looked behind him, checking to make sure he was alone.

He was.

"They're not coming!" the first woman sobbed, bringing her head up.

"It doesn't happen every time," the other woman said consolingly. She pressed her own cheeks into the mud, as though resolved to complete the ritual no matter what.

"But I want a baby!"

A baby? Puzzlement changed into complete confusion, and Marshall emerged from the bushes, determined to discover what exactly was going on. "Hey!" he called out.

The women, startled and panicked, took one look at him and ran away screaming, dashing muddy and barefoot over the rough ground into the trees on the other side of the clearing. They did not stop to pick up their clothes because there were no clothes to pick up. They had arrived here naked, they ran away naked, and he thought that this was probably their natural state of dress. They were both fair of skin, but Marshall wondered if perhaps they weren't some new sort of savage indigenous to California. Not Indian or African but something new.

They'd spoken English, though.

There was no good explanation for what he had seen, nothing he could imagine that made any sense whatsoever. He considered following the women, but after all he'd experienced on the journey here, he thought that to do so might be dangerous. He was afraid of where they might lead him, and he quickly backtracked through the trees, retrieved his horses and deliberately set off in the opposite direction.

He hadn't known what to expect when he'd left Missouri for California, but there was no way he could have predicted any of the events that had befallen him. Marshall felt better, though, for having come. His health had improved greatly, and even the hardships of the trail had not diminished the positive physical effects of leaving the bottom lands and heading west. He had a new lease on life, and if that meant occasional encounters with things he could not explain, then so be it.

He rode south over a series of hills until he came to a well-worn rut that turned out to be a trail. Changing directions, he followed it until he saw signs of human encampment. There was an enclosed colony up ahead, and he wondered if it was Sutter's Fort. According to his map, that was still a day away, but the map had been wrong about almost everything so far, and he could think of nothing this could be *except* the fort.

Still, he approached slowly, unsure if he would be greeted as friend or foe.

He and his horses were spotted several yards away, and a sentry's shout asked him to identify himself.

"James W. Marshall!" he called out. "From Missouri!"

He was waved on and made his way into the fort, where he was greeted warmly by men and women alike. Dismounting, he shook hands and exchanged pleasantries before leading his animals to the stable next to the smithy. As he was instructing the stableboy on the care and feeding of his horses and his mule, Marshall was accosted by a rather stern-looking man dressed in black. "Do you by any chance do carpentry?" the man asked.

"I've been known to," Marshall allowed.

"We could use some help around the fort."

"If you're offering me work," Marshall said, "I'll take it."

The man held out his hand. "The name's Sutter," he said. "John Sutter."

Twelve

Andrew Bledsoe drove west on the interstate, ignoring the exaggeratedly loud conversation being conducted for his benefit in the rear of the van.

"Max's family has a DVD player."

"Shelley's has *two*. One in the front seat for her mom and one in the back for her."

"It sure makes trips a lot less boring."

The talk went on in this way for several more miles, but when Andrew didn't take the bait, Johnny asked him directly: "Dad, how come we can't get a DVD player for the van?"

"Because."

"Because why? Because we can't afford it?"

"That's right," he lied.

"Yes, we can."

He smiled, didn't respond. Of course they could afford one. But he didn't think it was good for the kids to have electronic stimulation every hour of the day, everywhere they went. So the rule in the car was no cell phones, no DVDs, no games, no iPods, no laptops, nothing but the car stereo and books. At the start of every vacation, they moaned and complained—as did Robin, to tell the truth—but he stuck to his guns, and after the first hundred miles or so they inevitably resigned themselves to the situation and settled into a comfortable routine.

That was what was wrong with families today. They didn't spend enough time together. Even when they were physically in each other's company, they were engaged in their own pursuits, emotionally cut off from one another, and it was sad to him that more parents didn't realize how important it was to be *with* their children.

Nothing was more meaningful than family time.

It was why Andrew enjoyed taking trips so much and why he liked driving. Kids in the back, Robin next to him, Dave Alvin on the CD player, the open road ahead . . . there was nothing finer. He enjoyed his work, he liked his home, but there was nothing on earth he loved more than traveling with his family.

There was a pall over the trip this time, though. Bill Fields, one of his friends from college, had been murdered by his own father, who had also slaughtered his stepmother and stepbrother before going on a shooting rampage in a mall, ultimately killing eight people before being shot himself by the police. Andrew had read about it in the paper, seen it on television, and the news had stunned him. He hadn't seen Bill in years—a trust-fund kid who'd been swept up into his father's business, he ran in different circles now—but back then they'd been close, double-dating, hanging out, going to clubs and concerts. Once they'd even taken a road trip together, driving from St. Paul to Phoenix in a crazy nonstop beer-fueled frenzy.

He missed those days, and though he loved his family and wouldn't trade his present life for the world, sometimes he wished that his college years could have lasted a little longer, that before settling down he could have had just a few more semesters of irresponsible freedom.

"We can so afford it," Alyssa said from the backseat. "He's lying."

"I know it," Johnny said.

"We should save up our own money, buy our own portable DVD player."

"That's a great idea!"

But they soon started bickering about what movies they would watch and that led to a discussion involving their disparate taste in television, music and pretty much everything under the sun. By the time they reached Windom they were no longer on speaking terms, and all the way to Omaha, they sat silently in the rear, reading their own books, communicating with each other only through their parents. A swim in the hotel pool before a Burger King dinner, though, put things right, and the two of them were once again happy campers.

They were on a trip to California's gold rush country. He thought it would be fun for the kids as well as educational, and it would be a nice time for him and Robin as well. He'd gotten the idea from an old Sunset guide to the region he'd picked up at a library buck-a-bag sale. He vaguely remembered taking a trip cross-country with his parents as a child, but as with so many of those vacations, the memories of it weren't clear, and he had the impression that for some reason things hadn't gone well—although that was true of most of the vacations they'd taken before the divorce.

By the time they finally reached Oak Draw, the small town that was to be their home base, they were all tired of traveling and were grateful to settle into their cabin, where they could unpack, relax and finally eat some home-cooked meals. Andrew had planned and booked several activities over the next week: a guided tour of some of the most important historical sites, a river-rafting trip, a gold-panning excursion. But there was also a lot of downtime built into this vacation, and he as much as any of them was looking forward to casual hikes and picnics and the ordinary sort of random exploration that usually ended up making family vacations memorable.

The cabin was not log but still rustic, and the kids were happy to find that it came equipped with satellite TV. With two bedrooms, a loft, a combination living room/kitchen and a bathroom with a claw-foot tub, it felt far more homey than the cramped hotel rooms of the past several nights. There was even a neighborhood of sorts: six other cabins, all arranged in a semicircle around a central lodge. The lodge, they were told when they first checked in, played host to different nature programs, and though Johnny and Alyssa complained that they wanted to stay in and watch *The Simpsons*, after dinner all four of them trekked down the dirt path to watch a slide show on predators of the Sierras.

In the daytime, the cabins had felt isolated, as though they were far out in the wilderness, but they were only a block off the town's main drag, and at night the lights of the business district were visible directly on the other side of a sparse line of planted ponderosas. In fact, the illumination from an adjacent miniature golf course lit their way as they marched single file up the dirt track to the lodge. From nearby came the sounds of music and crowds, and Andrew recalled seeing a fair or carnival set up on a vacant lot next to a grocery store.

Inside, the lodge was surprisingly crowded. They passed through the lobby into a large multipurpose room outfitted with wooden benches facing a raised stage and screen. A slide projector on a metal cart sat in the center of the room. Many of the attendees, it turned out, were camping on the grounds rather than staying in the cabins, and they sat next to a family from Nevada with an anal-retentive patriarch whose stated goal was to take his kids to the site of every major gold, copper or silver strike in the West by the time they graduated from high school.

After the presentation, they walked back to their cabin in the dark, accompanied part of the way by the family from Nevada. The dad was a real jerk, and Andrew was happy when they said their good-byes and walked down separate paths to their respective cabins. Tomorrow they were taking a guided tour by bus to the American River and Sutter's Mill and several other famous sites of the gold rush, so he told the kids to get ready for bed.

"It's only nine o'clock!" Johnny complained. "And we're on vacation!"

Andrew grinned. "Early to bed, early to rise, makes a man healthy, wealthy and wise."

"You can make us go to bed," Alyssa said. "But you can't make us sleep. I'm staying up until midnight."

"I hope the monsters don't get you."

"You better not scare me," Alyssa warned.

He cackled maniacally.

"Mom!"

"Don't scare the kids," Robin said.

"Now I'm staying up until one!" Alyssa announced.

But when he checked on her in her bedroom and on Johnny in the loft less than ten minutes later, they had both fallen fast asleep.

Robin lay in bed next to Andrew, staring up at the ceiling, her mouth still filled with the comforting, salty taste of his semen. The television was on, but he was dead asleep, breathing evenly, reassuringly, his body contorted into one of those awkward positions that he seemed to find the most comfortable for sleeping. She looked at him, touched his bristly cheek. *How did a summer turn into a lifetime?* she wondered. She'd met Andrew in college while working as a counselor at a camp for underprivileged kids in the summer between her freshman and sophomore years. He'd been a counselor there as well, and they'd connected almost immediately. For both of them it was supposed to have been just a summer fling, a little fun before school started again. But things had turned serious before the beginning of August, and by Labor Day they were exclusive. Now they had kids and a house, two cars, mutual funds and 401(k)s. That cute guy she'd seen at the end of the pier one Sunday afternoon teaching kids to dive was now the husband she had recently seen inducted with much civic fanfare into the St. Paul Silver Circle Club.

Time flew.

But in some ways . . . it didn't.

She took a deep breath, trying to quiet her nerves. Just because the present was here and the future was on its way didn't mean that the past was over and done with. Sometimes the past remained alive no matter what a person did to kill it off.

She got up carefully and began pacing around the bedroom. She should have told Andrew about what had happened to her, should have insisted that they vacation someplace else. It was eerie, in a way, how they'd ended up here. When Andrew had first suggested that they go to California, she'd said yes because she'd thought there was no way possible they'd end up anywhere near the spot where she and her classmates had gone all those years ago. What were the odds? Then, after he'd picked up that used guidebook, done some more research online and decided that it would be fun to tour the gold rush country, she still said okay because of course they'd go to Coloma or Sonoma or one of the historically important cities, not dumpy little out-of-the-way Oak Draw. By the time he informed her of the great deal they'd gotten on a cabin through an Internet hotel broker, it was too late to register any objections. And if she'd told him the whole story, it would have seemed like she'd been keeping secrets from him.

Which she had been.

She'd never told Andrew about the rape.

She'd never told anyone.

In her mind, they were monsters, the rapists. Not monsters as in horrible people, but monsters as in *monsters.* That couldn't be true, of course, but everything was all jumbled in her mind, and the only images she could conjure from that experience were horror-show creatures of fur and scales, with great bulging eyes and terrible pointed teeth. She'd been a child when it had happened, and obviously her brain had dealt with the trauma by converting it to a fantastical symbology. Still, the recollection seemed so real, so true, the faces of the beasts as clear to her as those in a photograph.

She tried to extract an authentic memory from the chaos of her perceptions, but no matter how hard she attempted to translate the events into a convincingly factual narrative, the scenario always remained the same: She was ten and on a weekend field trip. It was before Detroit and before Minneapolis, when they still lived in San Francisco. Along with her friends Maria and Holly and a bunch of other high achievers from their school, she took a bus to a camp near Oak Draw. Teachers were there, along with several parent chaperones, but her own mom and dad had been too busy or too disinterested to come.

The first night had been fine. But on the second day, she, Maria and Holly had decided to go for a hike instead of staying at the camp and making an art project. Although she wondered now how they could have been allowed to do such a thing. On a field trip, didn't everyone have to stay together? And why hadn't a teacher or parent come with them? It didn't make any sense.

But from here on in, nothing made any sense.

She remembered the three of them walking up a steep trail—

And then the monsters jumped out. They were vaguely humanoid—two arms, two legs, head and torso—but they were hairy and scaly, as though half fish and half bear. They didn't roar but whispered, and their faces were like something out of a horror movie. She saw vampire teeth and witches' noses, bloodred eyes and Peter Pan eyebrows, all of it configured in such a way that the totality gave an impression of pure unadulterated evil. A man's hands with scraggly fingernails reached out from a furry body and grabbed her arm.

This was the part that didn't seem to be in order. Her memories were clear but disjointed, and try as she may, she could not seem to put them into even a semblance of coherence. What she remembered was: watching a plant grow from a seedling to a bush; chanting nursery rhymes; painting Holly's face with mud; the pain of the actual act; folding clothes; the smell of flowers; crying; laughing; hot wind; screaming; rough hair; slimy skin; a hole in the ground.

Then they were headed back down the trail toward camp, dressed and cleaned up as though nothing had happened, nothing was wrong.

They'd never spoken of what had occurred. In fact, soon after that, the three of them began drifting apart. Although she hadn't put two and two together at the time, she realized now that it had been the memory of the attack they'd been trying to avoid—not each other—and it probably would have been better for them if they could have shared their feelings so they wouldn't have had to deal with the nightmare all by themselves.

Andrew stirred in his sleep, flopping over, and Robin stopped in midstride, catching a glimpse of herself in the mirror. She looked haggard and stressed, although whether that was due to her inner turmoil, the late hour or the bad light from the television she couldn't say. She certainly felt horrible, and she wondered if it might not be better to level with Andrew and tell him everything.

Did she really want to go through that, though? While they were on vacation? Did she want to put on a happy face for the kids and then rehash the worst trauma of her life ad infinitum? Because she knew Andrew, and she knew he would make her describe every little detail, relay every single thought, go over the episode with a fine-toothed comb until he was satisfied that they'd made some acceptable emotional progress. He wasn't a shrink, but he'd seen them on TV, and that, combined with his misguided belief that he was naturally empathic and had clear insights into the heart of every matter, made him feel as though it was his duty to dispense advice and set everyone right.

She loved him, but there were definitely certain aspects of his personality that she would change if she could.

No, confiding in Andrew was not an option. She would just have to grin and bear it.

Robin looked at herself in the mirror once again. There were women who'd gone through far worse than she had—men, too, for that matter. She could handle being here for a few days.

She went into the bathroom, got a drink out of the faucet, then turned off the television and returned to bed. It took a while for her to fall asleep, and when she did, she dreamed of a black mountain honeycombed with caves, where snakelike monsters with shiny white penis heads popped out and screamed at her, their voices those of Holly and Maria and herself.

Thirteen

"I'm glad you could come," Jillian said. "I . . . I didn't know what to do."

Brian walked into his mother's house and gave his sister a quick hug. He was dead tired. Jillian had called at the end of a long, grueling day that had capped a long, grueling week, and Friday traffic had ensured that he had not made it to Bakersfield until nearly midnight. She'd said it was an emergency, so he hadn't stopped off for dinner, and now he was tired *and* hungry.

"Mom's been out of her mind. I don't know what to believe and what not to believe. She seems to think Dad's come back and is, I don't know, *stalking* her. She said she's seen him a whole bunch of times and he's threatening, and . . . and she's just very scared." Jillian paused. "She got another one of those letters, too."

That perked him up. "Can I see it?"

"I think you should see Mom first, let her know you're here."

Brian looked at his watch. "She's still awake?"

"I don't think she's slept in days."

Their mother was at the kitchen table, reading the Bible. She looked awful. She was wearing torn pajamas and a bathrobe, her hair was wild and her face was puffy, her eyes as red as an alcoholic's after a particularly bad bender. He was shocked by her appearance but tried not to let it show. Just a few weeks ago, she'd been her usual prim and perfectly coiffed self; now she looked like a completely different person.

"Hi, Mom," he said.

She ignored him, kept reading.

"Jillian says Dad came back again." When she didn't respond, he continued. "Do you have any idea why? Do you think he wants something?"

She wasn't answering, but she'd heard him. He could tell by the way her finger was shaking as it underlined the Bible verses she was so intently reading. She was scared.

And that made him scared.

I'm afraid of that language.

Brian decided to leave it alone for a few moments. He was starving, for one thing, and he knew he'd be able to think better on a full stomach. He opened the refrigerator, taking out a carton of orange juice and a foil-covered plate that turned out to be fried chicken. "Where's Del?" he asked. He hadn't seen Jillian's husband when he'd arrived, but he knew she wouldn't have driven this far on her own.

His sister nodded toward the back of the house. "Asleep. It was a long trip."

Brian picked up a drumstick, slowly swiveling his neck to get the kinks out. "You're telling me."

"Sorry."

He waved her away. "Don't be." Biting into the drumstick, he poured himself a glass of orange juice. "Mom," he said. "What's going on? Why are you up this late?"

"He came home," she said, her voice hushed. "I saw him through the window."

"Did—"

"He comes home every night," she told him. "I hear him out there. I see him. He's *looking* for me."

There was such terrified conviction in his mother's

voice that goose bumps popped up on Brian's own bare arms. "What do you think he wants? Have you tried talking to him?"

"No!" she shouted, so loudly that it made Brian and Jillian jump. She grabbed her Bible and ran out of the kitchen.

"Now you see why I called you?" his sister asked.

Brian nodded tiredly. "Let me check out the letter," he told her.

While she went to get it, he finished eating the drumstick and quickly downed the glass of orange juice. He washed the grease off his hands, drying them thoroughly before touching the paper. As before, the page was dirty and smudged, filled with wild symbols and strange pictographic characters. But this time, there were letters of the alphabet mixed in as well, recognizable vowels and consonants. He had no evidence to back this up, only a gut instinct, but it looked to him as though whoever had written this—

his dad

—had been trying hard to send a message, had been attempting to break through the alien language that had been imposed upon him and communicate in English.

Brian sat down at the table and studied the characters on the page. They were not arranged in lines or any particular order, and he tried reading left-to-right, right-to-left, up, down, sideways, but could make no sense of any of it. "Do you know if it came in an envelope or anything?" he asked, looking up.

Jillian shook her head. "I have no idea."

He carried the paper carefully out to the living room and placed it between the pages of a *Good Housekeeping* magazine that he laid on an end table close to the door, where he'd be sure to see it on his way out of the house. After the situation with his mom was straightened out, he was going to take it to Dr. LaMunyon and see if the professor couldn't use it to help crack the code of that unfathomable language.

"I think we should call Reverend Charles in the morning," Jillian said. "Mom respects him. Maybe he can help us." She took a deep breath, and Brian could tell that she was very close to tears. "I just don't know what else to do."

He put his arm around her, held her tight. "We'll get through this."

"You think it's really Dad?"

He nodded slowly.

"Part of me hopes that it is and part of me hopes that it isn't, you know? I mean, I hope he's alive, and I want to see him again, of course. But . . . what would we say to him after all this time? 'Thanks for abandoning us'?"

"If he's the way Mom describes him, I don't think he'll be doing much talking."

She waved him away. "That's just Mom. She's having some kind of breakdown or something. It doesn't make any sense—"

"I believe it," he said.

"I don't. Just look around. The house is a mess, the yard's a jungle . . . Those weeds must be two feet high."

Brian's pulse raced. "What did you say?"

"I said the house is a mess—"

"No. What about the yard?"

"You'll see it for yourself in the morning. She must have fired the gardener and not hired anyone else. The place is a disaster." She sighed in exasperation. "My point is that I think she needs help. Mental help. I think we should talk to Reverend Charles, even though this is probably way out of his league. If he can't help, at least he might be able to direct us to someone who can."

But Brian was still thinking about the overgrown yard and Wilson's theory that abundant vegetation was another piece in the puzzle. Such an idea had seemed nonsensical at the time, but from this vantage point, it didn't seem quite so stupid.

"Hello!" Jillian said. "Earth to Brian. Are you even listening?"

"I am."

"And?"

"And I don't know that I agree with you that she needs mental help. But if she did, the last person I would go to is Reverend Charles. She sees far too much of him already, and I wouldn't be surprised if he was the one who got her worked up into this state. You saw her sitting there reading the Bible."

"She finds it comforting. You know, just because you don't believe in anything doesn't mean that other people can't."

"That's not what I'm saying."

"Then what *are* you saying?"

"Jesus, I feel like I'm talking to Mom."

Jillian glared at him. "Thanks a lot."

"You know that's not what I meant. Look, we're all under a lot of stress here. Let's try not to jump down each other's throats over every little misstep."

Jillian sighed. "You're right. I'm sorry."

"It's late. We're all tired. Why don't you go check on Mom, and if everything's okay, we'll go to bed, get some sleep, and see what things look like in the morning."

She started toward the hall, then stopped, turned around. "You really don't think she needs help?"

"I think she probably did see Dad."

Jillian nodded, said nothing, then turned away and headed down the hall.

Their mom had crashed and lay dead asleep on top of her still-made bed. Jillian tucked her in, then said good night to Brian and went into the guest bedroom, closing the door quietly so as not to wake her husband. Brian took a couple of sheets from the linen closet, pulled out the couch in the living room, made up the sofa bed and lay down in his clothes. He had never felt so tired, but he could not seem to fall asleep. He counted sheep up to five hundred, tried to think of nothing, forced himself to breathe in a sleep rhythm, but nothing worked.

Finally, after a frustrating hour, following a single chime from the grandfather clock that could have signaled one o'clock or could have meant one thirty, he dozed off.

He was awakened by the sound of howling from outside in the front yard. The cries were wild and Brian could not tell if they were of joy or anguish, but they sounded as though they came from wolves or coyotes. He quickly scrambled out of the sofa bed and over to the window. There was another element present in those cries, something familiar that made his flesh crawl and filled him with dread. Opening the curtain, he peered out. It had started to drizzle in the hours since he'd arrived, and a sheet of tiny raindrops was visible in the dim yellow light of the streetlamps.

There was something else visible as well, something dark and shadowy that sprang from the overgrown bushes on the right side of the yard and leaped behind the pecan tree before disappearing.

His father?

Pulse racing, Brian pressed his face against the glass, trying to determine where the figure had gone. Jillian was right. The yard was a veritable jungle, and he didn't know how he hadn't noticed that on his way in. What had been a well-manicured lawn offset by a few nicely trimmed shrubs and trees was now a chaotic mess of untamed vegetation.

From off to the left, the figure leaped out again, passing closely in front of the window, and for the first time, Brian got a good look at him.

It wasn't his dad.

It was Stephen Stewart.

The multimillionaire was naked and on all fours, bounding about like a wild animal. But that wasn't the craziest thing about him. No, it was his body itself that provided the biggest shock. For even in this weak, diffused light, Brian could see that Stewart was hideously deformed, his back shiny and segmented, almost wormlike, while thick tufts of hair grew abundantly from the sides of his stomach. He was behaving like a lunatic, running from one side of the yard to the other, and every so often he would leap into the air and howl with a soul-deep ferocity that scared the holy hell out of him.

His heart pounding insanely in his chest, remembering the gruesome photos he'd seen of Stewart's wife and son, Brian grabbed the phone and dialed 911.

There was a commotion in the hallway, and a second later Jillian rushed into the living room. "What is it?" she demanded, her voice frightened. Next to her, Del was wide-awake.

"I told you!" their mother screamed. She pushed through them and ran to the window, holding the curtains closed in her fist and peering out through a small open sliver.

Brian quickly explained to the police dispatcher what was happening and where, but when she asked him to remain on the line, he hung up and went over to his mother. She was shaking her head and muttering to herself. It sounded as though she were reciting a prayer.

"It's not him," he said gently. "It's not Dad."

"Of course it is!" she snapped. "Look at him!"

He peeked through the open slit. *Strange.* Now that it had been brought to his attention, he did notice a certain similarity. He had no idea why it now seemed so noticeable, but his mom was right. There was some aspect of the psychotic tycoon that reminded him of his father.

The drizzle stopped instantly, as though a spigot had been turned off, and now he could see even more clearly. Stewart was filthy, and while Brian couldn't be certain, he was pretty sure that there was blood as well as mud befouling the man. His eyes searched the yard for a body. Or a part of one.

The police arrived impossibly fast—there must have been a patrol car already in the neighborhood—and Brian went out to meet them. Shifting into reporter mode, he brought with him a notepad and pen to write down quotes and the name of each officer to whom he spoke. Two cops got out of the car, which had pulled to a stop in front of the house, and he immediately identified himself. "I'm the one who called. My name's Brian Howells. I'm a reporter for the *LA Times*. The man on the lawn is Stephen Stewart. He's wanted for—"

"I know who Stephen Stewart is," the older cop said, a trace of annoyance in his voice. "And, no offense, but I don't think—"

Stewart attacked.

None of them were prepared, and the older policeman went down under the millionaire's assault, involuntarily crying out as sharp fingernails raked across his cheek, drawing blood. Brian ran back to the safety of the house while the younger officer scrambled out of the way, fumbling with his holster as he attempted to pull out his sidearm. A second police car pulled up just at that moment, screeching to a sideways halt next to the first, but the two patrolmen inside must have been able to gauge the situation through the windshield because they emerged with batons drawn and rushed immediately into the melee.

Stewart fought like a wild beast, biting into the first cop's face, then jumping up and ripping at another's midsection with his long-nailed fingers. There were screams and blood, but with four cops on him, Stewart succumbed, and in a matter of moments he was on his stomach, eating grass, while his arms were being yanked up behind him and handcuffed.

Brian hurried back out. He wanted to talk to one of the officers and explain what had happened, but no one appeared to be in charge, and the older policeman who seemed to be sort of a natural leader was on the ground and out of commission, awaiting an ambulance while his partner administered emergency first aid.

Another patrol car arrived—someone must have had time to radio for help—and after quickly conferring with the cops already on the scene, one of them walked over carrying a notebook and pen. Brian flipped open his own notebook.

They were ready to listen to him now, and he explained that his mother had been receiving nocturnal visits from an intruder the past several nights, that she'd thought it was her long-estranged husband but that apparently it had been Stephen Stewart. He conveniently left out the part about the letters, hoping his mother and sister wouldn't mention them either, then told the cop that he was a reporter working on the Stewart story.

"Do you think that's why your family was targeted?" the policeman asked.

Brian shook his head. "No one knew I was working on the story. It's not possible."

"Then how do you explain the fact that Mr. Stewart traveled all the way across the country, eluding police along the way, to end up naked in your mother's yard?"

"I don't."

"Don't what?" The policeman frowned.

"I don't explain it. I have no idea what happened. I'm as confused as you are."

The man sighed. "Maybe we'll be able to get something out of him when we question him." He thanked

Brian for his time, then walked over to the house to talk with Jillian, Del and his mother.

None of the officers wanted to be quoted for attribution, but Brian did get their names and a promise that he would be the first reporter allowed to interview Ron MacNeill, the older officer who'd been mauled.

He watched the police cars and the ambulance drive away.

Stewart, Lowry, Devine, Fields. The list of rich men going off the deep end was growing (and they were all *men,* weren't they?). Stewart was the first to be captured alive, and Brian wondered if he might be able to shed a light on what was happening and why—*if* they could get him to talk.

If he *could* talk.

For what struck Brian most about Stewart was the utter wildness of the man, the complete lack of humanness he seemed to possess. It was not just the physical abnormality—which was odd enough—but his actions and the expressions on his face that seemed so frightening, that were so completely unlike anything he had ever seen. Brian had serious doubts that, in the state he was in, Stewart would even be able to formulate words, much less speak in coherent sentences.

Were they all like this? Had Bill Devine been this way at the end as well? He remembered the Oklatex owner's voice on the answering machine—

My erection will not stop. Oh no, it will not stop

—but he found it hard to reconcile such anarchic monstrousness with the controlled insanity of that message.

He tried to recall what he'd heard about Wesley Fields. Fields had been the most recent multimillionaire to freak out, and Brian had read about it in a wire service report before it hit the airwaves yesterday. The Midwest media mogul had murdered his son, stepson, wife and dog before going on a rampage and getting shot by police. As always, the details were horrific, and an unpublished AP photo showed the daughter's torso—minus legs, arms and head—sliced open and stuffed with apples. Fields' body had been naked when they'd found it. He'd been savagely mutilated by his own hand, and Brian could imagine him being as crazy and out of control as Stewart.

What about his own father?

Brian had been trying not to think along those lines, but it was the question behind everything, the fear that impelled him and made the subject of these murders and suicides so important to him, and as he walked past the overgrown bushes, back into the house with his mother and sister and Del, he could not help worrying that in some other yard, perhaps in some other town, his dad was jumping around naked and howling at the moon.

The Reverend Raymond Charles was awakened from a sound sleep by the conviction that he immediately had to go to his church—in order to protect it. Protect it from what, he did not know, but he dutifully got out of bed and began changing from his pajamas to his clothes.

He always obeyed his convictions. They didn't come as often these days as they used to, and when they did they usually led to nothing, but there was always a chance that it was the Lord speaking to him, and he could not afford to miss The Call when it came.

He glanced over at the alarm clock on his nightstand, not bemoaning the fact that it was two a.m., merely noting it. There was a tingling in his bones unlike anything he had ever felt before, and though he tried to remain humble, he could not help thinking that this was It. The Lord was finally speaking to him. Not just by proxy through the Bible, but directly.

The reverend drove purposefully over to the church,

his heart giving a little lurch when he saw that one of the inside lights was on. He *always* turned off everything before he locked up. He parked in his usual spot, his eyes on the soft glow that issued from within and illuminated the lighter colors in the two stained-glass windows flanking the door. He knew he should call the police— violent burglars could have broken into the church, for all he knew—but the same strong belief that had led him here in the middle of the night told him that this was not a secular matter and what was required of him now was to go inside the chapel himself and find out what was happening.

He felt no fear as he walked up to the door. As expected, it was unlocked, and he went inside, noticing instantly that there was someone sitting in one of the middle pews. The light that was on was the one above the pulpit, and it threw the figure into silhouette. "Hello!" the reverend called.

There was no answer.

The figure did not move.

Maybe the person was dead, he thought. Maybe whoever it was had been shot or stabbed and had come here to make peace with God.

But there were no drops of blood on the floor. And the door had been locked, the lights turned off, so the person had to have broken in.

"Hello!" he called again. "May I help you?"

The silhouette shifted in its seat but said nothing.

The reverend walked up the aisle, concerned but not afraid. Nothing appeared to have been stolen or vandalized. He himself had not been threatened or attacked. This wasn't an ordinary criminal. This was someone suffering a crisis of conscience, and it was his responsibility to show that person the Way.

He reached the center of the church and stopped, frowning at the figure in the pew, not sure he was seeing what he thought he was seeing. "George?" he said, squinting in the dim light. "George Howells?"

The man stared straight ahead blankly.

It was him, although Reverend Charles never would have made the connection had not Alice Howells been confiding her fears to him for the past week. The figure in the pew, hairy and filthy, dressed in rags, bore absolutely no resemblance to the clean-cut and meticulously groomed young family man he remembered from all those years ago. Privately, he had dismissed Alice's rantings as the delusions of an unbalanced woman. She was a good parishioner and could always be counted on to support the church's causes, but lately there'd been a whiff of fanaticism to her activism that made him slightly uncomfortable. So when she'd started telling him about the return of her husband, he'd taken it all with a grain of salt.

Obviously, though, she'd been telling the truth.

"George?" he said again.

There was no answer.

The reverend was suddenly afraid. He shouldn't have been. This was his church. And the house of the Lord. But fear followed no logic, and while he could tell himself that there was no place on earth that was safer or more comforting—and believe every bit of it—the fact remained that the dirty man frightened him. He said a quick prayer and took a step between the pews toward the hairy figure.

The head swiveled toward him.

And grinned.

He had never seen a smile so evil. Even in his dreams of hell, his mind had been unable to conjure a look such as that.

It was not God who had called him here tonight, he realized.

The light at the front of the chapel switched off.

They were not alone in the church. He saw movement in his peripheral vision. The slinking of shadows darker than the surrounding night. He held still, tried not to move or make noise. These beings were not human at all. They were monsters, demons, and they were here for him.

One by one, the windows of the chapel were shattered. Faint light from the city outside crept in at odd angles, throwing curious segments of the church's interior into relief. A stray ray of diluted blue shone upon a section of side wall, highlighting a confluence of boards that suddenly looked like a face. Refracted moonlight made the back of a pew resemble a coffin.

George Howells was gone, but there was movement all around, though he could see only suggestions of shapes, not the actual outlines of the monsters themselves. They were there, though, massing in the vestibule, blocking his exit, creeping up the side aisles, moving between the pews. He had no idea how many were there, but it felt like dozens, and their foul stench was overpowering in his nostrils.

A floor-shaking crash sounded from the front of the church as the mounted statue of the crucified Christ was dislodged from its perch and slammed down on the dais.

A car drove by on the street outside, its headlights shining through first one broken window then another, like a searchlight, as it passed the church. Now he could see one of the demons. It was coming toward him from the aisle on the right, a hideous thing of fur and scale, vaguely humanoid but with a mane of wild hair, ultralong arms and cloven hooves that hit the floor sounding like nails being pounded into the wood. Its mouth was impossibly wide, with too many teeth, and its red eyes glittered in the darkness.

Claws scraped along the backs of the pews as the monster approached.

The reverend looked around frantically for a way to escape. The church's front entrance was out of the question, but to the side of the pulpit was his office, and it had a door that led outside. If he could just get there, he might be able to run away and . . . and . . .

And what?

He could go to the police, but he doubted that bullets would stop these hell spawn. He could run to his fellow clergymen, but what could they do that he couldn't? His only hope was to simply hide and pray that God protected him by keeping those demons far, far away from him.

God wasn't protecting him now, though.

He didn't want to think about that. *Couldn't* think about that.

There was a whispery moan from behind him, followed by what sounded like a mocking human laugh.

George Howells.

The reverend ran. He knew every square inch of this church, could have navigated it blindfolded. Such familiarity served him well as he dashed for the office, maneuvering around pockets of darkness and the unknown horrors they hid, as well as the curiously methodical monsters moving toward him in the indirect light.

He reached the door to his office and—

It was locked.

The key was on the ring in his pocket, and if he had time he could have found it, but he did not. The demons were suddenly next to him, segmented bodies leaning toward him at impossible angles. There were just two of them, and when he glanced out at the pews and toward the rear of the chapel, he saw only George Howells standing in the doorway, grinning hugely. His mind had merely *thought* there'd been more, darkness and shadows exaggerating the threat and creating the illusion of creatures that were not there. He probably could have escaped, he realized; he probably could have gotten away.

A clawed hand grasped his shoulder, sharp nails sinking into his flesh.

There was no escaping now.

He was turned around to face the demon, and he closed his eyes to pray. There was no better place to die, he thought, than inside the house of the Lord.

Only he didn't die. Not right away. They played with him first. One of them was female, and it did things to him that were so wrong and evil that his soul cried out in torment even as his body responded with ecstasy.

The other was male, and it participated, too, humiliating him, debasing him before slowly tearing him apart.

And *then* he died.

Fourteen

Carrie stared at the massive bouquet of flowers sitting in a crystal vase on top of her desk. Jan, Donna and Lateeka stood nearby, curious yet patient, waiting for her to open the tiny envelope and find out who had sent the obviously very expensive array. She was sure they would have checked themselves, but the small envelope accompanying the flowers had been sealed shut.

Carrie put down her purse and briefcase. "What is this?"

"You tell us," Lateeka said, grinning.

"It arrived about ten minutes ago," Jan explained.

Matt? Carrie wondered. She picked up the small envelope and opened it. Inside was a card with a picture of red flowers on the cover. On the blank space within, written in a sloppy, unfamiliar hand totally unlike Matt's mannered calligraphy, was a message: "Dear Ms. Daniels, I enjoyed meeting you Saturday night. I was wondering if we could continue our conversation sometime. Please give me a call."

It was signed "Lew" and was followed by a phone number.

She frowned. "I don't know any Lew."

"Oh my God," Donna said. "*Saturday night? Lew?* I bet it's Lew Haskell!"

"No," Carrie protested, but even as she denied it, she knew that was exactly who it was.

"It is!" Lateeka said, reading her face.

"Oh my God," Donna repeated. "You must have made some impression on him."

Carrie sat down, stunned. "I don't see how. I talked to him for a little while, thanked him like Alex told me to, but . . ." Her voice trailed away. Already she was remembering their conversation and the way they'd instantly hit it off. But he was married, wasn't he? The man couldn't be hitting on her. Not this publicly. This had to be legitimate, business-related.

But then why the flowers?

"Well?" Lateeka asked. "Are you going to call him?"

"I don't know."

"That's a 'yes,' " Donna said.

"I . . . don't . . . know," she repeated more forcefully.

Sanchez poked his head out of his office. "Ladies?" he said. "Don't we have some work to do around here?" He nodded at the huge display of flowers. "And let's find a more convenient place for those."

Carrie picked up the vase, looking around for a spot in the office where she could store them until it was time to go home. The other three grudgingly returned to their desks, but not before Donna tapped her on the shoulder. "It's the best way to meet people," she said sincerely. "Through work. That's how I met my husband." She glanced around, to make sure Sanchez wasn't in view. "Call him."

As it happened, he called her. She was out on a case at the time—interviewing a seventeen-year-old girl who'd been pretending to be the mother of her ten-year-old sister so the two of them would not be split up and sent to foster homes after their parents had abandoned them—but she got his voice mail when she returned.

The tone was light, casual, but the fact that he had called at all meant that he was serious about getting together. He was an important man, a busy man, and if he had taken time out of his day to contact her—*twice!*—then obviously he really wanted to meet with her.

For the next half hour, she tried to write her report on the abandoned sisters, but her gaze kept straying from the computer screen to the miniature envelope that had come with the flowers and now sat propped against her cat cup. Finally, she took out the little card and called the phone number. To her surprise, there was no assistant to go through, no secretary. Lew Haskell himself answered, and she could tell from the change in his voice when he found out it was her that he was happy she had called.

They spoke very briefly. He was about to go to a meeting, and she wasn't supposed to be using her line for personal calls, so they acknowledged their conversation on Saturday night, said a few words of mutual appreciation and made an appointment to get together for dinner that evening.

Carrie hung up the phone to discover Jan, Donna and Lateeka standing very close by while they pretended to engage in other business.

Donna grinned. "We couldn't help overhearing."

"A date?" Jan said. "Tonight?"

"It's not a date."

"You're going out to dinner," she pointed out.

"But he's married," Carrie said. "Isn't he?"

"That's a slippery slope," Lateeka warned. "Don't go there."

"I'm not going anywhere."

"It's about time," Donna whispered. "I'm happy for you."

Carrie reddened. Was it that obvious? Was her lack

of a social life actually discussed and speculated about by her coworkers? "It's not a date," she protested. "It's just a . . . meeting." Still, the rest of the day seemed long, and she found that she was looking forward to this evening far more than was probably appropriate.

There was a crisis in the late afternoon. She was checking in with Rosalia, just a quick call to let her know the status of her various applications, but the woman was in such distress that her English was nearly indecipherable, and the only information Carrie could get out of her was that she was going to move right away, somewhere where no one would be able to find her.

"Listen to me, Rosalia," Carrie said carefully. "I've been working really hard on your case, and I think we have a very good chance of getting coverage for your medical expenses. But if you drop from sight or change your address or exhibit any behavior that tags you as unreliable, all that will be lost. Do you understand?"

It was clear from the panicked jumble of English and Spanish that she didn't understand.

"Don't go anywhere. Don't do anything," Carrie told her. "I'm coming over."

"Okay," Rosalia agreed, and hung up the phone.

Carrie considered bringing along someone who was fluent in Spanish, but she knew that Rosalia would close down in the presence of an unfamiliar person. Even if she couldn't understand everything Rosalia said, it was still better for Carrie to go it alone and try to muddle through. The two of them had developed a sort of rapport, and she was counting on that to see them through whatever had arisen.

Carrie reached across her desk, opened the tiny envelope once again, got out the card and called Lew Haskell. He answered on the second ring. "Hello, Carrie."

"Hello. Mr. Haskell—"

"Lew," he said. "Call me Lew."

"Okay, Lew, I—" She frowned. "How did you know it was me?"

"Caller ID. Who else would be calling me from Social Services?"

"Right. Anyway, I just wanted to tell you that I have to cancel tonight."

He sounded genuinely disappointed. "What happened? Second thoughts?"

"No," she said. "Nothing like that. It's one of my clients. She has a . . . problem that I need to address right away, and I doubt that I'll be able to get away before six. By the time I go home and change—"

"I'll wait."

"No, really."

"You don't even have to go home. Why don't I just pick you up at your office?"

Carrie looked down at her unfashionable jeans and plain cotton blouse. "I don't think that's such a good idea."

"We'll play it by ear. Give me a call at this number when you're through, and if I can't convince you to relax and unwind a little after a hard day's work, well then we'll call it a night and reschedule. How about it?"

She really did want to see him. And if everything went smoothly, there was no reason she couldn't be ready to go by seven o'clock. "Okay," she agreed. "But I have to leave now. I'll call you later."

"I'll be waiting."

He's married, she told herself as she gathered Rosalia's case file. But maybe he wasn't *happily* married, maybe he and his wife were separated, maybe . . .

Rosalia had calmed down quite a bit by the time Carrie arrived at the Oliveras' apartment. She had started to pack a suitcase, but she hadn't finished, and Carrie considered that a good sign. At the moment, she was sitting on the faded sofa, watching a judge show on her little black-and-white television, Juan cuddling next to her.

After all these visits, she should have been used to Juan, or at least not shocked every time she saw him. But as usual, the inscrutable expression on his animal face caused her heart to beat faster, the skin on the back of her neck to prickle, and for a few brief seconds she was back in the abattoir of Holly's apartment, staring at the Rhino Boy's head on top of the bureau.

She concentrated on Rosalia, not looking at her son. "Now, Rosalia, tell me what's the matter. I'll do anything I can to—"

"I see him!"

Carrie frowned. "You saw him? Saw who?"

"Him!"

An idea occurred to her. "Juan's father?"

Rosalia nodded vigorously. "He see me, too! And he shake his fist like this." She demonstrated. "He is after me!"

"Wait a minute. Slow down. First of all, where did this happen? And when?"

"It happen today, this afternoon, by bus stop. I see him across the street. Only because other people there he leave me alone. But he shake his fist at me!" Her pretty features were contorted in an expression of anguish. Next to her on the couch, Juan was sitting up straight, but Carrie did not look at his face.

"Listen to me," Carrie said. "Did he come after you? Did he try to follow you?"

"No."

"Does he know where you live or where you work?"

"I do not think so."

"Then you have nothing to worry about."

Carrie spent the next half hour convincing Rosalia that she was safe and that it was in her best interests to remain where she was. In the back of her mind, she was not at all sure that her reassurances were true. In fact, she was possessed of a completely unfounded belief that Rosalia and Juan were in grave danger—

Rhino Boy

—but at least if they remained where they were, she would be able to keep an eye on them, look out for them. If they took off and disappeared, they would be completely on their own, and Carrie suspected that that would be far more dangerous.

She was finally able to extract a promise from Rosalia that everything would remain as is for now, and she returned to the office much earlier than expected. Calling Lew Haskell, she asked him what his plan was for tonight. He seemed caught off guard. "Well . . . I thought we'd have a nice dinner and then . . . see where the evening leads from there." He sounded suddenly embarrassed. "I like to keep my options open. I mean," he said quickly, "there are a lot of other places we could go after dinner . . ."

"I understand," she said, laughing. "Why don't you tell me where you'd like to eat, and I'll meet you there at, say, six thirty?"

"But I thought I'd pick you up."

"I'd rather drive myself and meet you," she said. "If that's all right."

There was a slight pause. "Sure. Of course. Whatever you want would be fine." He gave her the name of an expensive Italian restaurant downtown, asked her if she needed directions, and when she said she didn't, he told her he'd see her there.

Carrie hung up the phone, not quite sure why she hadn't agreed to let him pick her up with his car or his limo or whatever he'd had planned. Part of it, she supposed, was her natural pessimism and paranoia—after all this time out of the trenches, she needed a quick escape route handy—but part of it was probably the nebulous nature of this "date." Was he married or wasn't he? Was this a business meeting, a friendly get-together or a romantic evening?

There were too many variables, too much unknown. She needed to maintain control.

And she was probably just a teensy weensy bit embarrassed by the shabbiness of her rental house.

"I heard about your big date," Sanchez said, coming out of his office. "Congratulations."

The office was nearly empty, and Carrie reddened. This was definitely a conversation she did not want to have. "Thanks," she said.

The supervisor grinned. "I knew if I could just get you out and about, get you to stop moping alone at home, that you would once again rejoin the human race."

"I'm not *that* pathetic," she protested.

He looked at her, one eyebrow raised, Spock style.

"Okay, maybe I am."

Sanchez clapped a friendly hand on her shoulder. "Have fun. And if you come to work tomorrow wearing the same clothes you're wearing today, I will not only understand but I will be very proud of you."

"You *are* aware of the department's policy on sexual harassment, aren't you?"

"Joking," he said, holding his hands up innocently. "Joking."

Marcello's was one of those old-school restaurants with dim lighting, dark wood and red upholstered booths. Haskell—*Lew*—had gotten there first, and immediately upon entering, the maître d' led Carrie to a nearby table. It was neither hidden in a corner nor on public display. She didn't know what, if anything, to make of that, so she simply smiled, said hello and slipped easily into the booth.

He reached across the table and put his hands on hers. "I'm so glad you could make it."

She pulled her hands away, deciding to get it all out in the open before anything started. "Is this a date?" she asked.

"I certainly hope so."

"I thought you were married," she said carefully.

"No. That's just what we tell the press in order to keep away the bloodsuckers." He smiled easily. "It's amazing how attractive a single man with money suddenly becomes."

She blushed. "That's not why I . . . I mean, I'm not . . ."

He laughed. "No need to explain. But I'm single, this is a date, and as far as I'm concerned, we're at the beginning of a beautiful evening."

"Okay, then," she said, smiling. "Okay."

A waiter came, they ordered drinks, the drinks were delivered and the waiter promised to return for their dinner order. "Give us some time," Lew requested.

He was as easy to talk to in the restaurant as he had been at the fund-raiser, and it wasn't until the waiter returned a discreet fifteen minutes later that Carrie realized neither of them had bothered to look at the menu. She quickly opened hers and scanned the fish and pasta dishes while Lew made inquiries about the specials of the day and their specific ingredients. It sounded as though he had allergies, and she looked at him quizzically.

"I eat only organic," he explained, and though she herself was a fast-food devotee, she liked that. It showed a commitment to principle that she found admirable and that no doubt manifested itself in other aspects of his life.

She ordered chicken marsala while he ordered a capellini pomodoro with whole wheat pasta.

Carrie was dying to ask him about his work, his life, the whole rarefied world in which he lived—all of the things that her coworkers would quiz her about tomorrow. But he seemed more interested in *her* work, and he asked intelligent, probing questions about her job, the department, and the economically disadvantaged people with whom they worked. She'd never talked shop with Matt and ordinarily didn't enjoy discussing the ins and outs of social work—it was too emotionally draining—but sharing the details of her day with Lew made her feel energized and alive. Excited. He had the money and power to get things done, to turn ideas into action, and she knew that talking over problems with him could lead to solutions.

She understood for the first time why people said that power was the ultimate aphrodisiac. It was heady stuff, being with someone who shared her views and possessed the means to act on them.

The food came, they ate, but they might as well have been dining at McDonald's for all the attention she paid her meal. They talked about race and poverty, and she admitted that most of her clients were from Latin America and that many of them barely spoke English. Defensively, she said that she received great satisfaction from helping people from other countries establish a foothold in the United States. She braced herself, expecting to hear an antiimmigrant speech. She got a lot of tirades on that subject these days. They all did.

But Lew surprised her.

"People don't realize it," he said, "but America needs a constant influx of immigrants to remain economically healthy." He smiled. "I know what you're thinking, and as an employer, of course, I appreciate the cheap labor. But from a historical perspective, political boundaries are a recent invention. For thousands of years, large groups of people have migrated according to shifting weather patterns or fluctuations in food supply or encroaching enemies. Essentially, they went where the jobs were. The same is true today. And for Americans to get so worked up over men and women who are merely trying to work is ridiculous."

She said nothing as he continued on, merely watched him. Lew was older than she was by a good ten . . . fifteen . . . maybe even twenty years. She had never before dated a man more than three years her senior and had never had any respect for younger women who went out with rich older men. But she found herself attracted to him.

By the time they left the restaurant it was late. He wanted to extend the evening by going to some nightspot or other, but she was tired and told him she had to work tomorrow. There was a moment of awkwardness on the sidewalk outside, when he leaned forward to kiss her and she inadvertently stepped backward and away from him at the same time. But then she moved forward and into place, and the two of them merged together. She pulled away feeling slightly light-headed and more than a little aroused.

She was glad that she'd driven herself.

They made a date for Saturday. The whole day. It was a big step for her, but she felt proud of herself for taking it. Either they would have a wonderful time together and end the day far closer than they were now—or they would tire of each other and their mutual interest would disappear like smoke in the air. It was all or nothing. She'd either soar or fall flat on her face.

But that was what had been missing from her life: risk.

And it felt good to be taking that gamble, to lay herself on the line after the years she'd spent in emotional hibernation.

They kissed again, a shorter, more casual good-bye; then Lew's limo pulled up to the curb, and a driver got out to open the door for him. "Are you sure you don't want a ride?" he asked. "I could send someone back for your car."

She waved him away. "No, thank you. I'll see you Saturday."

He smiled brightly. "Saturday it is." He got into the car and waved good-bye before the driver closed the door. Seconds after the limo had pulled into traffic, a valet arrived with her own worn Celica—an incongruous combination if she ever saw one. Taking her keys from the uniformed young man, she was grateful that her car had not been brought out before Lew's.

She didn't know how much she was supposed to tip, so, embarrassed, she took two dollars out of her purse, handed them to the valet, quickly got inside the car and drove off.

She analyzed the evening all the way home, going over what she'd said, what he'd said, trying to determine if she'd made any serious faux pas.

Things had gone very well, Carrie finally decided.

The telephone was ringing as she opened the front door. She quickly closed and locked it, and ran over to answer the phone, dropping her keys somewhere along the way. *It's him!* she thought, and like a giddy schoolgirl prayed that the ringing wouldn't stop before she got there.

She picked up the phone. "Hello?"

"*Baa,*" bleated a faint inhuman voice.

Her breath caught in her throat.

"*Baa.*"

It reminded her of the sound a llama might make. "Juan?" she said.

There was a click and a dial tone.

Carrie hung up the phone slowly. Rosalia did not have her home phone number. None of her clients did. She thought of Holly's blood-splattered apartment, the white feather glued to the back of the hooker's hanging hand with congealed blood, the head of her son—

Rhino Boy

—placed upon the top of the bureau in the bedroom.

She double-checked the locks on the front door, made sure that the back door was locked and that all of the windows were closed. The euphoria she'd felt had fled, and instead of thinking about her date, she kept hearing that bleating animal sound, thinking of Juan and the Rhino Boy and Holly's apartment and blood, lots of blood.

After changing into her pajamas, she got into bed and stared at the phone next to the nightstand, willing it to ring, willing Lew to call her.

But he didn't.

Fifteen

1848

James Marshall arrived home dirty, tired and sore, with only a jackrabbit to show for his efforts. Above the ridge, the sun was setting, and the sky was bluish purple in the east, a brilliant orange in the west. Here in the shadow of the ridge, it was already night, and as he dismounted all he could see of the cabin was a square black smudge against a background of pointed pine tree silhouettes.

He'd been out since dawn, staking a new claim and building a makeshift sluice that he could carry across the hills from one location to another. Around noon, between the claims, his horse had been spooked by a small bobcat and thrown him. He'd spent the better part of the afternoon looking for the damn animal, then the rest of the daylight hours hunting dinner. It had been another in a long line of fruitless days, and Marshall was beginning to wonder if maybe those geology experts down at the bureau office were right. Maybe there wasn't any gold here. Maybe he should pull up stakes and head to Colorado along with everyone else.

But he remembered the knowledge that had come to him on the trail—

the bag of bones

—and the certainty that there was treasure awaiting him here in the West. He could not quit this country. Besides, he'd invested too much time and energy here in California to give up now. And maybe this new claim would pan out. It was situated at the bottom of a rocky hill, and the soil looked right. He'd even found traces of rose quartz in the rubble near the bank of the creek.

He strung up the rabbit on the porch so Pike couldn't get at it. Feeling too tired to skin the animal, he kicked the door open, walked into the house, lit the lantern and slumped down onto his pallet. The dog ran around outside, barking, chasing imaginary enemies. Tomorrow he had to go back and oversee construction of the mill. Sutter had entrusted him to manage the project as he saw fit, and as the location was some fifty miles northeast of the fort on a section of the American River, he'd been taking the opportunity to do some scouting of his own in the surrounding mountains, using his cabin as a base. But half of the workers were Indians and all of them were drunks, and they needed much more supervision than he'd hoped. Although he'd gone over the plans with the men again and again, even going so far as to assign to individuals simple repetitive tasks that could not easily be ruined but collectively would contribute to completion of the mill, he still spent most of his time at the site correcting the mistakes of others.

He'd told Sutter to hire carpenters, men who could understand the job and do it well, but the captain was too cheap and instead saddled him with this worthless crew of incompetents.

Marshall glanced out the window at the small sliver of sky visible to him from this angle. The first star was out, a pinpoint of white light too weak to provide any illumination. He was hungry but too tired to get up and make supper, too tired even to go to the cupboard and take out the biscuit tin.

He lay back on the pallet and closed his eyes, thinking he would just take a quick nap and eat afterward, once he'd rested.

He was awakened by the sound of mewling.

The cries were strange, eerie, and made him think of babies and kittens, though ones that were oversized and deformed and crawling about in the wilderness at night.

Marshall sat up, the mewling close by and coming to him through the open window, sounding somehow *slimy,* though that did not make any sense. Where was Pike? he wondered. The dog barked at every stray lizard that scuttled within a hundred yards of the cabin. He should have been barking up a storm.

But there was no Pike.

Only the mewling.

Marshall had lived in this section of California for nigh on three years, and he had never been afraid here until now. He'd slept with spiders, awakened next to wolves, bathed with snakes. He had even had a chunk of his left arm ripped out by an angry bear before he'd built the cabin. But he had not experienced the deep paralyzing fear that he felt right at this moment.

Not since the trail.

He was suddenly aware of how far away from the fort he was, how far away from people.

Marshall walked across the cabin, lit a match and turned up the flame on the lamp. "Pike!" he called.

No answer.

He looked out the window at the blackness of night. "Pike!"

Only the mewling.

He realized now what bothered him the most about those whiny high-pitched cries. They weren't cacophonous, overlapping the way such noises usually did. There were deliberate pauses, calls and responses. The creatures making the sounds were communicating with each other. Talking.

He was afraid to leave the cabin and go outside, but he knew he must. Pike was more than just an animal; he was his friend, and Marshall could not just sit indoors and hide when the dog might be in danger. He owed it to Pike to find out what, if anything, was wrong.

Marshall picked up his rifle and lit another lantern, leaving the first one on the table and carrying the other outside with him. The lamp threw a circle of light around him as he walked. Although he could still hear the mewling, it was fainter than it had been, and he wondered if his presence had scared the creatures away.

He checked the ground for footprints as he walked, or spoor, but either the lantern did not provide enough illumination or the creatures had not ventured this close.

Why did he keep thinking of them as *creatures*?

Because he knew they weren't human and didn't think they were animal. He kept remembering the wagon train's journey through the Dark Woods, the squat, dark figure he'd seen darting from bush to bush, the whispers that he couldn't understand but that seemed to be speaking directly to him.

"Pike!" he called. "Pike!"

The mewling had stopped now. Or was too far away for him to hear.

"Pike!"

The dog's body was lying in the dirt path on the south side of the cabin, a dark shape on the light ground. He saw it first in the periphery of his lantern circle, a vague silhouette, but he knew immediately what it was.

Marshall moved closer. "Pike?" he whispered. The dog did not stir, and when he got near enough to see details, he understood why. The animal's head had been ripped off, and large talons or claws had rent the body, leaving it a terrible mess of blood and fur. The head itself was nowhere to be seen, and Marshall looked away, both sickened and scared, searching for the glint of predatory eyes in the darkness surrounding him.

He shifted the lantern and rifle in his hands, making the gun easier to shoot should he need to do so.

A fly buzzed by his ear. He looked up involuntarily, his eyes following its ascent . . . and he saw Pike's head. It had been speared to a branch of the tree a foot or two above him. Dead white dog eyes stared unseeingly into his own, the bloody tongue hanging between parted canine teeth. More flies hovered about, their buzzing suddenly loud in the night stillness.

Marshall backed up, nausea and terror alternating their demands within him.

He returned quickly to the cabin, leaving both lanterns on, and spent the rest of the night in a chair, his back against a wall, holding the loaded shotgun in his lap.

As expected, the workers had not accomplished the tasks he had set out for them, and Marshall spent the next week overseeing the men and ordering them to fix the mistakes they'd made, all the while doing the work of ten men himself, trying like hell to finish the mill on schedule. If before he would have felt anxious spending so much time away from his claims and not searching for gold, he was now thankful to be around other men, grateful for their company. He'd told no one what had happened, and when High Jim asked about Pike, Marshall said absently that he was probably around somewhere.

The days were short, the nights were long, and it was those long nights that gave him the most trouble. He could handle the work, *needed* the work, and the more jobs he had to do during daylight hours, the happier he was. It was his goal to tire himself out so that he could sleep through the night.

It was a goal that remained unmet.

There was music and drinking among the men, loud talk and life. But the coming of darkness served to accentuate how far they were from either fort or town, how small their encampment was against this vast wild land. He woke up several times each night, and often at those odd hours he heard noises in the distance that he could neither explain nor identify: strange whistling in the hills, harsh cries in the canyons, grumbles and growls that blended with the sounds of the river but were not of it.

And the mewling.

Did the others hear those noises? If so, they didn't mention it.

He didn't either.

The weather was cold, as it always was in January around these parts, but that didn't keep Marshall from checking the millrace each morning to see how much the water had deepened the channel overnight. Mud and gravel inevitably accumulated toward the bottom of the race, and he usually waded in to clear it out.

On the Monday after his return, exactly ten days since he had found Pike's mutilated body—

the dog's head speared to a tree branch

—Marshall was inspecting the millrace when something in the debris at the lower end of the watercourse caught his eye. Frowning, he crouched down in the water and sorted through the rocky silt until his fingers found what his eyes had seen. Slowly he stood, holding the rounded shiny nuggets up against the light of the rising sun. His heart was pounding, his pulse racing.

"Gold," he said reverently.

Sixteen

The trail wasn't steep, but it did wind up the slope at a grade that left them all sweaty and slightly breathless. The kids, of course, complained all the way, but Robin told them it was good exercise. "Cardio," she said.

"Oh boy," Johnny responded sarcastically.

Yesterday they'd taken a tour of some of the more famous gold rush sites, a bus driving them from Oak Draw to Coloma to Placerville, the knowledgeable guide walking them through Sutter's Mill and telling stories of the forty-niners that made early California come to life. The kids had enjoyed that outing, but today's hike was meeting with much less enthusiasm.

"There's not even a pool when we get back," Johnny said. "There's nothing to look forward to."

"You can take a cool shower in the cabin, then sit on the porch and contemplate nature," Andrew told him.

"Or read a book," Robin suggested mischievously.

"Great."

"Are we going to go to another lecture tonight?" Alyssa complained.

Andrew grinned at her, raising his eyebrows villainously. "You know we are."

Both kids groaned loudly.

Andrew laughed. "How about we get some ice cream

after this, then check out our guidebook and see where to go from there?"

"Better," Johnny admitted.

They continued up the trail. Robin was not sure what the altitude was here, but it was more than she was used to, and the air seemed deprived of oxygen. It was hard to breathe. She'd been hoping for a panoramic view of the countryside once they reached the top of the ridge. Below them, through the trees, they could kind of see the town and a portion of the highway, but otherwise there were only more trees and higher hills. It seemed impossible for a person to get his or her bearings up here, to even know in what direction they were heading, and Robin thought that it would be very easy to get lost.

She wondered where the camp had been. Or where it still was.

Does Two Forks Camp still exist?

The thought made her uneasy.

"Hey, check it out!" Johnny said, running ahead. He pointed toward another, smaller, more primitive path branching out from the one they were on now.

"Stay on the marked trail!" Robin ordered.

"Mom!"

Andrew looked down the side path. "It's flat here. Let's go down this way for a while and see where it leads, do a little exploring."

"Yeah!" Johnny said.

"That's how people end up on the news," Robin told them. She pretended to read a headline: " 'Novice Hikers Trapped in Canyon.' "

"Ten minutes," Andrew promised. "Five minutes there, five minutes back. What can happen?"

"Mountain lions, bears, cliffs . . ." she rattled off.

"It'll be fun."

She looked down the narrow, primitive path. It *was*

flat, and it seemed to wind through the golden grass and occasional trees toward nothing in particular.

"All right," she said, giving in. "But five minutes each way. That's it. And stay together!" she called as Johnny sprinted ahead.

"What's that?" Alyssa asked.

Robin's eyes were still on Johnny, who was reluctantly walking back toward them, and she turned to look where her daughter was pointing. Lying by the side of the trail, beneath the branches of a scraggly bush, was a dead cat. It had obviously been someone's pet because there was a red collar around its neck, but it was so thin and emaciated that it had to have been living out in the wild for quite some time. Black with white paws and a white head, it must have been a very beautiful animal, but now its matted fur was covered with dirt and leaves, flies scrambled over the ring of dried blood where the cat's missing tail should have been, and a line of ants marched across the ground into its nostrils and open mouth.

"Don't look at it," Robin told Alyssa, turning her daughter's head away.

"Gross!" Johnny exclaimed.

"Come on," Andrew said. "Keep walking."

The novelty of the new path wore off very quickly, and even before the five minutes were up, Johnny and Alyssa were dragging their feet and complaining about the sameness of the scenery, suggesting that they turn around and head back. Andrew looked at his watch. "Two minutes to go!" he announced cheerfully.

Robin looked off to the left and saw, between the pine trees, something square and tan. Frowning, she walked forward a few steps until a ponderosa in the foreground was no longer blocking the object. It was, she saw, a small adobe hut with neither doors nor windows.

She knew that hut.

She hadn't remembered it before, but she recognized it now.

The past came back in a rush.

She, Holly and Maria had been walking up a steep trail—*this trail?*—and the monsters had jumped out, grabbing them, pulling them off the path, whispering in their ears, terrible sounds that made no sense but whose meaning they understood nevertheless. The three of them had been not dragged but carried over the ground to this hut. As now, there'd been no doors or windows, only solid adobe wall. She couldn't recall what had happened in between—once again there were only those specific memories, disjointed and out of time: chanting nursery rhymes; folding her own clothes, the growing plant, painting Holly's face with mud, Maria screaming, the smell of flowers, rough hair and slimy skin, laughing, crying, pain, a hole in the ground—but she knew they had somehow ended up inside the hut.

It had been dark.

There'd been bones on the floor.

Once more, her memory failed her, and her next recollection was of the three of them walking back down the trail toward camp, dressed and cleaned up, though still feeling sore and dirty . . . down there.

"Is something wrong?" Andrew asked. He was frowning at her, and she saw now that the kids were gathered around as well, worried expressions on their faces.

She tried to smile. "No, it's nothing, I'm fine."

But this time she was not at all sure that her mind was compensating for the horror of the rape by recasting the rapists as monsters. As insane as it sounded, she thought that maybe their attackers really *had* been monsters. She looked over at the hut, feeling cold.

"Hey, what's that little house?" Johnny said, stepping off the path.

Robin grabbed his arm, yanking him back. "Stay away from there!"

"Ow!" he cried.

"What's going on?" Andrew said.

"We're turning around," Robin told him.

"I just wanted to check out that little house, and she went crazy!"

"That's weird," Alyssa said. "There're no windows."

"Maybe they're on the other side," Andrew suggested.

"We're going back!" Robin yelled.

All three of them looked at her.

"Now!" she screamed.

Back at the cabin, she told Andrew everything. She left nothing out, though she could see from the expression on his face that he didn't believe half of it. He believed the rape, though, and for the moment that was good enough. She had his sympathy and, through that, his allegiance. He'd go along with whatever rules and regulations she imposed on the family this trip, no matter how wacky they might seem.

"Why aren't the kids back yet?" she asked suddenly.

"They're just over at the lodge."

"We told them they could buy postcards. They should've been back by now."

Andrew put his hands on her shoulders. "They'll be okay."

"You don't know that! Haven't you heard a word I've said?"

"That was twenty years ago," he reassured her. "I understand why you're concerned for them, but they're on the grounds, only a couple of yards away in the gift shop . . ."

"You don't understand!"

"Robin," he said seriously, looking deep into her eyes. "You're overreacting because of what happened to you. Eventually, we're going to have to talk this through, the two of us. But for now we're on vacation, probably our only trip out here, and for the children's sake, we should try to make it a fun one."

Intellectually, she knew he was right—though she was dreading that "talk" he wanted to have—but she still felt frightened. Not for herself so much but for Johnny and Alyssa. She would have to make a concerted effort to behave as though everything were normal, to not see boogeymen behind every bush. Oak Draw was a minefield, and as far as she was concerned, there was potential danger in every step. The sooner this vacation ended, the better.

Alyssa ran up the porch steps and into the cabin seconds before Johnny. "We got the postcards! Did you bring the address book? I don't know anyone's address!"

"Yes I did, honey," Robin said, and her voice was calmer and much more normal than she'd expected it to be.

Johnny saw how close they were standing. "Gross. You guys aren't doing any sex stuff, are you?"

"No," Andrew said, pulling away from her. "And you watch what you say."

"I know what sex is," Alyssa announced.

"That's fine. But we don't have to talk about it," Robin said. She turned away. "I'm thirsty. Anyone else want some iced tea?"

Andrew barbecued hamburgers for dinner—they'd bought ground beef and buns from the market in town, taken extra condiment packets from the fast-food joint where they'd had lunch—and afterward he and Robin sat out on the porch, watching the kids run around the tall wispy meadow grass that grew in the open space between the cabins and the lodge. The kids had been joined by the children of the guy from Nevada, as well as two boys and a girl from town. All seven children were playing freeze tag, and Andrew smiled down at them as he saw how much fun they were having.

Robin sat next to him, quiet and subdued.

Tomorrow, they were supposed to pan for gold. It was strictly a tourist thing to do. A guy dressed up like a forty-niner would lead them and a group of other vacationers to a selected spot on a local stream, demonstrate a few panning techniques, then let them see what they could turn up. But Robin didn't want to go. She was afraid to go into the countryside, scared to venture past the boundary of the town.

He understood her apprehension. But he didn't feel it. And though he told himself that if he had known the details ahead of time they never would have come, he wasn't sure that was true. Because he almost felt more at home here than he did at home. This land and these communities inspired within him a calmness, a serenity he had not known before. It was something that had translated itself to him through the black-and-white photos in that old Sunset guidebook, something that had grown stronger when he'd started researching the gold country online. But he hadn't realized until they'd arrived, until they'd moved into the cabin and spent a full day here, just how much he would love Northern California, just how fully in tune with this land he was.

How to explain that to Robin, though, with her traumatic memories of the past?

He wasn't even going to try.

Andrew reached between their two chairs, grabbed her hand and held it. "Are you all right?" he asked, looking at her.

She nodded, attempting a smile. "I'm fine," she said.

The kids came in a little while later, when the sun started going down, and the whole family watched an old Godzilla movie before going to bed. Andrew didn't know whether it was the altitude or the excitement, but they seemed to go to sleep a lot earlier here than they did back home. This was the third night in a row that they were all in bed well before ten.

He fell asleep almost the instant his head hit the pillow and woke up in the middle of the night to go to the bathroom, groggily feeling his way out of the bed and across the bedroom to the hall, where the light from the bathroom illuminated his way. He was vaguely aware of a noise outside, and he thought it sounded like a cat, but he didn't care enough to check.

On his way back to the bedroom a few moments later, he definitely heard a cat's meow. It was coming from somewhere nearby, but sound was hard to pinpoint at night. Just as a cricket outside the house could sound through an open window as though it was in the room, the cat, too, sounded closer than it probably was.

"Meow."

He pulled aside the curtain and looked out the bedroom window, but saw nothing outside.

"Meow. Meow. Meow."

It sounded even closer than before. He was surprised it hadn't awakened Robin, Johnny or Alyssa.

"Meow. Meow. Meow. Meow."

Now the cat was getting annoying. If this didn't let up, he wouldn't be able to fall back asleep. He padded out to the living room and looked through the front window. The porch light was on, and by its glow he could see a cat sitting in the middle of the dirt walkway that led to their cabin. He tapped on the glass of the window, making shooing motions with his hands, trying to scare it away, but the animal either didn't see him or didn't care.

"Meow. Meow. Meow. Meow."

Andrew looked up at the railing of the loft to make sure Johnny wasn't awake, then carefully opened the front door, stepping onto the porch. "Shoo!" he whispered, advancing toward the edge. "Get out of here!"

"Meow."

He stopped suddenly, a strange feeling fluttering in the pit of his stomach. He knew that cat. He recognized it. It was the one they had seen on the side of the trail. If the white paws and head had not been enough of a giveaway, its red collar, and the dried blood clumped around where its tail should have been, let him know that this was the same animal that earlier today had been decomposing in the hills above town.

He took an involuntary step backward.

The animal lurched up the path toward the cabin as though it were drunk or disoriented.

"Meow."

Maybe this was a dream.

No. Even as he thought that, he knew that it wasn't. He glanced back into the cabin to make sure that neither Robin nor the kids had awakened. They hadn't. Amid all the horror, he felt relief. The overriding thought in his mind was: *Robin can't see this.*

Glancing around the porch, Andrew looked for a weapon but saw nothing he could use. He remembered earlier in the day seeing a rake or a hoe or something leaning against the side of the cabin. Some sort of gardening implement with a long wooden handle. Moving quickly, he dashed down the steps and around the corner of the cabin. Sure enough, there was an upside down hoe angled against the wall between the windows, and he grabbed it, hurrying back.

In the few seconds he'd been gone, the cat had lurched farther up the path and was almost to the porch steps. Several other animals had also found their way to the area in front of the cabin: birds and mice, a rabbit, even a bobcat. All of them were moving in the same strange jerking way as the cat, and he assumed that they, too, had been resurrected from the dead.

Resurrected.

What the hell was going on here?

He didn't have time to think about that now. Grasping the handle of the hoe as firmly as he could, Andrew lifted the blade high above his head and brought it down hard on the back of the cat, cleaving it in two. No blood gushed out of the animal; the halves simply fell where they were, dry organs spilling from the ragged openings on both sides. If he'd thought such action would frighten away the others, he was out of luck. The remaining creatures hopped, danced and staggered toward him, their motions awkward and unnatural, and he swung the hoe like a scythe, mowing them down. None of them tried to fight back or get away—even the bobcat remained passively in place as the hoe sliced into its head—and in a matter of moments the area in front of the cabin was littered with the dismembered corpses of nearly a dozen small animals.

Andrew was breathing heavily, and he couldn't believe he hadn't cried out as he'd attacked the—

resurrected

—creatures. But he hadn't, and now all was silent. No one had been awakened from their sleep by the noise, and the only lights on were the porch lights in front of the cabins.

Now he just had to find some way to dispose of the bodies.

He could dig a hole, but that would take forever. He could dump them in a garbage can, but they would be found. The best solution, he decided, was to gather the hacked up pieces and throw them behind the trees at the edge of the property. If he was lucky, a bear, mountain lion or some other wild animal would eat them.

He needed something with which to pick up the body

parts. Moving quietly, he reentered the cabin, closing the door softly and listening for any sound. All was still. There were garbage sacks under the kitchen sink, and he took the whole box. Once more, he looked up at the loft before going outside, but Johnny remained asleep.

He had neither gloves nor shovel, so Andrew put his hands in one of the black plastic bags and used it as a buffer as he picked up the pieces of dead animal and dropped them into another sack. He grabbed the cat's head first and dropped it in, followed by the ragged feline body. The garbage sack started to get heavy well before he had cleaned up the entire mess. He didn't want the bag to break on him, spilling everything out, so he carried what he had over to the line of trees to the east, behind the cabins and out of sight of the campground. He turned over the garbage sack behind a bush. Furry heads and torsos, paws and tails spilled onto the ground, though it was so dark here that it was difficult to differentiate between the body parts. There was a slight breeze, and the sack itself he threw into the grass, hoping it would blow away somewhere.

Then he went back and did it all again.

Finally he was done, and he leaned the hoe against the wall where he'd found it, sneaked back inside, closed the front door, put the box of remaining garbage sacks under the sink and quietly washed his hands with cleanser. Twice.

He crept back into the bedroom, trying to make as little noise as possible.

Robin, thank God, was still dozing peacefully.

He got back into bed, his body wet with sweat, his muscles jumpy from both exertion and fear. He had no idea what time it was, but it had to have been getting close to morning, and he tried to think up legitimate reasons to explain his physical condition should Robin wake before the perspiration dried from his skin and the tension eased from his muscles. Breathing deeply and evenly, closing his eyes, Andrew attempted to fall asleep. He tried not to think of what had just happened, what he'd just done. He tried not to think of anything.

He had almost succeeded in nodding off when he heard a low, familiar noise.

His eyes snapped open. No, it couldn't be. He must have been dreaming, his mind in that nether state between wakefulness and sleep.

But it came again.

He was wide-awake now, and the sweat felt cold on his skin, like ice water, as he heard the familiar low cry.

"Meow."

Seventeen

"Good work," Wilson said admiringly, holding up the newspaper. Brian's article on Stewart's capture was above the fold, not in the coveted upper-right position, but still centered and accompanying a large eye-grabbing photo of a clearly deranged Stephen Stewart being led shackled and jumpsuited to his arraignment.

"Thanks," Brian told him. Wilson was the first person to offer congratulations, although Brian understood why no one else had. Even though they were essentially partners on this story, he was not sure he would have been as magnanimous if the shoe were on the other foot. Something about the competitive nature of the journalistic temperament forbade camaraderie.

"You know the minister Stewart killed?" Brian said. "He's the one at the church my mom goes to." Brian had already come clean about his father and the letters when he'd called Wilson from Bakersfield.

"That's . . . very . . . interesting," Wilson said slowly. "Isn't it?"

"Keep it down over there," Ted Sprague said, poking his head over the side of the cubicle. "Some of us are trying to work here."

"On another poll about cartoons?" Wilson asked drolly.

"Very funny."

"Did you see my article?" Brian said with as much innocence as he could muster. "Jimmy told me that it's been picked up by over twenty other newspapers nationwide."

"Fuck you," Ted said.

Brian laughed.

Mike Duskin walked by. "Hey," the columnist said, clapping an arm around Brian's shoulder. "Nice piece."

"Fuck you, too!" Ted called out.

"Jealousy is a bitter fruit," Mike said.

"I'm not sure I would call Ted a *bitter* fruit," Wilson mused.

"I'm not gay, and I'm not even going to dignify that with a response!"

"You just responded," Brian pointed out.

"Go to hell. I'm going back to work."

"It really was a good article," Mike said.

"Thanks," Brian told him. "I appreciate it."

"We'll talk later." Wilson started back toward his desk. He poked his head in Ted's cubicle. "Away from prying ears," he said loudly.

Brian spent the rest of the morning on a follow-up to last week's immigration article, and met up with Wilson for an early lunch. They were the only ones in the break room, and Wilson commandeered the large table in the center, opening his brown paper sack and pulling out a sandwich while Brian scanned the vending machines for something edible. He finally settled on a potato burrito and a Coke, and brought them back to the table.

"So what is the connection between your family and Stephen Stewart?"

Brian sighed. "That's what I'd like to know."

"You think there is one?"

"No."

"And yet after killing his wife and putting his kid in

a coma, murdering several other locals in an inexplicable frenzy, he traveled all the way across the country and ended up prancing naked around your mother's front yard. Your mother who's been receiving letters from her missing husband that match the messages scrawled in blood at the murder scenes."

"And whose minister Stewart killed," Brian said glumly.

"Your family's hip deep in this, my boy. Have you thought about getting some sort of protection for your mother? Or getting her out of Bakersfield for a while?"

"My sister and her husband are staying with her."

"Do you think that's enough?"

Brian thought of his mother's overgrown yard and remembered what Wilson had said about Devine's wildly flourishing plants. He recalled the photo of Stewart's bedroom with its junglelike vegetation, and the fact that Tom Lowry's entire estate had been overtaken by exotic foliage.

"No," he said, standing. "I don't. Excuse me. I'll be right back." Leaving his untouched burrito and drink, Brian hurried over to the newsroom and his desk to call his mom. As he'd hoped, his sister answered. It took a lot of convincing to get her to agree to take their mother with her back to San Diego. He couldn't really tell her why—the reason was crazy and there were far too many gaps in the story to make any of it believable—but he was eventually able to get across both his fear and a sense of urgency, and she finally agreed to bring their mother home with her.

"It'll be good for her to get out of here anyway," Jillian conceded. "Especially after what happened to Reverend Charles. *If* I can get her to go," she added.

"*Get* her to go," Brian said. "Now."

He returned to the break room feeling a little better.

His burrito was cold, and he popped it in the microwave.
Wilson had finished his sandwich and was eating an
apple. "How'd it go?"

"My sister's bringing her back to San Diego with her."

"Good."

Brian popped open the microwave and brought his
food back to the table.

"You know," Wilson said between bites, "an epidemic
of murders and suicides among our financial elite has
happened before."

Brian unwrapped his burrito. "How did you find this
out?"

"I did a little background research. As good reporters
are wont to do."

He reddened. "Point taken."

Wilson smiled. "That *wasn't* my point . . . but it's still
a good one. Anyway, this is not the first time this has
happened. It may be the first time that it has occurred
to such an extent, over such a broad geographical area
and within so short a time, but there was a pattern already. I counted eighteen very rich men who either went
on public killing sprees or murdered their immediate
friends and family in the past hundred years or so.
Eleven of them ended in suicide. What I find most intriguing, however, is that prior to this, almost all of the
killings took place in California, the majority of *those* in
San Francisco. The one exception appears to have been
Otis Compson, who lived in Atlanta. But he was a recent
transplant—his family came from Sacramento."

"That's interesting," Brian said. "But does it mean
anything? Conspiracy theorists have built a multimillion
dollar industry out of coincidences and half-truths. Have
you read any of that September eleventh numerology
crap? There are nine letters in September, there are
eleven letters in Afghanistan . . . None of it means
anything."

"Maybe not," Wilson said.

"But that's what a good reporter does," Brian filled in for him.

"Exactly."

"What do you think?"

Wilson took another bite of his apple and chewed thoughtfully for a moment. "I'm not sure what I think." He looked over at Brian. "But I'm open to ideas."

"Well, my family's certainly not rich."

"Was it ever?"

"Not to my knowledge."

Wilson swallowed. "I suppose what I think is that we have a California-based phenomenon that causes heretofore sane and sensible individuals to go on murderous killing sprees and/or commit suicide in unusually violent ways. It's accompanied by unusual plant growth and primarily afflicts the wealthy." He looked at Brian. "Although perhaps not exclusively. And," he added, "it's been occurring on and off for well over a century."

"Where does that leave us?"

"Without a paddle, I suppose." Wilson paused. "But I do believe the fact that its rate has increased, that we're getting all of this happening at once now, has some sort of significance. It's like the pot's about to boil. We're in the right place at the right time, and if we just knew what we were looking for, if we only had a little more information, we might . . ."

"Might what?"

"That I don't know. Prevent more murders?"

Brian was silent for a moment. "Do you think Stewart's . . . deformity, I guess you'd call it, has anything to do with anything? I did tell you about that, right? The hair and the slimy skin?"

"Indeed you did, although I noticed that you kept it out of your article."

"Peripheral."

"Maybe."

Brian looked at him.

Wilson shrugged. "At this point, anything's up for grabs."

"I just wish I could find my dad."

"Have you thought about involving the police, telling them what you know, explaining that he's missing?"

"He's been missing for twenty years. And what do I know? Only what my mom told me."

"But you have those letters."

"And I believe they're from him. But there's no way to prove it." Brian took a sip of his Coke and sighed. "So what's the next step? Wait until someone else dies and we get a phone message or a videotape?"

"As a financial journalist, I have one overriding motto: Follow the money. It works for almost everything. Since, with the possible exception of your father, everyone involved with this story seems to be someone from my beat, I suggest we do exactly that. Maybe what all these men have in common can be ascertained from looking into their financial dealings and backgrounds. My hunch is that we will find connections we did not know were there."

"That's not a bad idea," Brian said.

"Thank you."

Brian tossed his wadded-up burrito wrapper into the trash can. Or tried to. He missed by about a foot and was about to pick it up and try again when his cell phone rang.

It was Jillian. His sister was uncharacteristically tongue-tied, and Brian got a queasy feeling in the pit of his stomach. "Mom?" he asked quickly. "Is it Mom?"

"No," she said, but there was a long pause after that, and for several seconds he thought his phone had dropped the call.

"Hello?" he prodded. "Jill?"

"I just finished talking to the police. They matched the prints at the church. It wasn't Stewart who killed Reverend Charles," she said. "It was Dad."

He was almost getting used to the drive.

Brian sped up the Grapevine, stopping for coffee at a McDonald's in Gorman before heading down the highway into the Central Valley. Wilson had offered to come with him, but Brian didn't really want company. This part of the story was his own. It was personal, and he didn't want to share it with anyone else.

The small towns flew by, the abandoned buildings and trailer courts, the fields, the orchards. He'd driven this route more in the past week than in the past decade, and he was actually starting to recognize some of the landmarks along this narrow stretch of highway.

Once in Bakersfield, he drove immediately to the police station, where he asked for Captain Disch, whom he'd interviewed extensively for the article. "Why didn't you just call?" the captain said after the desk clerk had led Brian back to his office. "I could've told you we have no idea where your father is."

"I figured that. But . . ." Brian took a deep breath. "Do you have any other information on him? I assume you've done some type of background check. Do you have any idea where he lives, where he works . . . what he's been doing for the past twenty-some years? I don't know if my sister told you, but my dad abandoned us. I haven't seen him since I was a kid."

Disch nodded. "She told us the whole story. And of course we did a background check. Or tried to. But the thing of it is, your father's off the grid. We have nothing on him more recent than the mid-eighties, when he abandoned your family. I have two men working on it, and I'm sure we'll eventually dig up something, but for now we're flying blind. In fact, I was kind of hoping *you* could help *us*. It's obvious he's here somewhere in the Bakersfield area. Do you know of any friends he might be staying with, places he might go, bars or restaurants where he might hang out? Is there anything you remember from your childhood, anything at all, that you could tell us about him, that might give us a clue to his whereabouts?"

Brian thought back, seriously trying to recall information about his dad that might be of help, but all of his memories were from a kid's perspective and involved his mom, his sister or himself. He knew nothing about his dad in relation to the real world; everything he remembered had to do with their family. He agreed to meet with a couple of detectives, however, to see what they could get out of him, and though he answered all of their questions, nothing jogged his memory, and he was unable to provide any new information.

"You have my cell number," he told Disch before he left. "Call me if you learn anything. *Anything.*"

The captain nodded soberly. "I will. And, for what it's worth, I'm sorry. I know how tough all of this must be on you."

"Thanks," Brian said.

He drove to his mom's house.

He pulled to a stop in the driveway. It was evening. The house was dark, and the yard seemed even more overgrown than before, though he didn't see how that was possible. He got out of the car and looked around carefully. Was his dad here somewhere, hiding? There were plenty of bushes to conceal him, plenty of spots where he could be lurking.

What would his dad look like now? Brian wondered. He'd probably be gray, perhaps bald, and there'd be lines etched on his face that represented all of the years spent away. Thinking of his dad as an old man was almost as difficult as thinking about him as a murderer,

Brian realized. He didn't want to consider either option. He wished that his father had never shown up again and had left him with only untainted memories.

He got out of the car and walked slowly up to the front of the house, alert for any signs of movement, listening for stray sounds. Opening the door with his key, Brian stepped inside and turned on the living room light. Rather than dispelling the darkness, it only pushed it back to the hallway and the kitchen, making those areas seem even blacker by contrast. He was suddenly filled with the absurd conviction that he was not alone in the house, and he called out, "Hey!" in the toughest voice he could muster. "Who's there?"

Silence greeted his query, and rather than moving slowly and cautiously through each room, Brian decided to take the bull by the horns and ran quickly through the house, flipping on each light as he passed, ready at any second to either jump away from danger or defend himself. He was alone, thankfully, and once the place was completely illuminated, he immediately set about to search every room. He didn't know what he was looking for, but he figured he'd know it when he found it.

Or maybe he wouldn't find anything.

He was prepared for that, too. But he felt the need to be here, to explore the house and inspect his mom's belongings in order to find out whatever he could about his dad.

Before rifling through closets and cupboards, drawers and dressers, Brian gave the room a quick once-over to make sure there was nothing he had missed. He'd been so concerned with trying to find an intruder that he hadn't really paid attention to the contents of the individual rooms, and he walked from his mom's sewing room to the hall bathroom to the master bedroom—

And stopped.

For lying in the middle of the flowered bedspread was

a torn and dirty scrap of paper. It was easy to miss. The dull tan cast of the old paper matched almost exactly the hue of the background between the colored flowers, making it blend in. But he saw it now, and with tightly held breath Brian walked across the room to the bed.

He picked it up, turned it over. There was a message written on the opposite side in what appeared to be charcoal. *STOP ME*, the message said. The letters were written crudely, as though by a child.

Or someone who was just remembering how to write after an absence of many years.

Yes, Brian thought. That was exactly what the shaky letters looked like, and he recalled the previous message, with its random vowels and consonants that seemed to be trying to break through the straitjacket of the alien language. It was as if his dad were gradually regaining his faculties, coming up from the bottom of some mental well and slowly remembering life in the real world.

STOP ME.

Brian's chest tightened as he reread the message. It was the plea of a tortured serial killer, and the shred of doubt to which he'd been clinging had vanished the second he saw those words. His dad was not an unwilling accomplice or someone who had been in the wrong place at the wrong time. He was a murderer, responsible for the death of Reverend Charles and God knew who else.

But *was* his father really responsible? Brian wondered. The fact that these bloody rampages seemed to be spreading like a plague across the land and that nearly all of them seemed to be accompanied by messages written in the same alien language indicated that there was something bigger at work here. His father was undoubtedly a killer, but he was also a victim, and whatever person or power or virus was making him do this was ultimately accountable.

Brian still continued his search through the house,

going through all of the cupboards and drawers, but he found nothing, and an examination of the front, back and side yards similarly yielded no results, although if he returned in daylight he still might conceivably find something. Locking up the house, he knew what he had to do, but first he stopped off at a twenty-four-hour Kinko's and made a copy of his father's message.

Then he drove to the police station and gave the original to the cops.

Wilson St. John arrived home after dark, an event that to his chagrin was becoming all too common. One of the things he'd always liked about the financial beat was that, for the most part, it allowed him to keep banker's hours. But looking into these murders and suicides was time consuming.

Consuming.

That was a perfect word for it. Because investigating this . . . situation was quickly becoming an obsession with him—if it wasn't already—eating up not only his work hours but his personal time. He was sorely tempted to call Brian on his cell phone and find out what he'd learned, but Rona was probably mad that he was late for dinner. As she had every right to be.

Bringing work home after coming back at such an hour would be adding insult to injury.

Besides, Brian would call him if he found out anything important.

Wilson opened the front door and walked inside. "I'm home!" he called. He didn't wait for an answer but tossed his newspaper on the coffee table and sat down on the couch to take off his shoes. He smelled what he thought was spinach quiche. Not one of his favorites, but coming home this late, he didn't dare complain. He stood up and walked through the dining room into the kitchen. "So—" he began.

And stopped.

The kitchen was empty. The oven door was open, and cold quiche sat untouched on the tiled counter. Rona could be in the bathroom. Or helping Julie with her homework. But the house seemed too quiet. And Rona never left the oven door open, never left food out.

Something was wrong.

"Rona?" he called. "Julie?"

Where *were* his wife and daughter?

The lights went out.

They went off all at once, every light in the house. *It could be the circuit breaker,* Wilson thought, but that was just wishful thinking. Feeling his way through the darkness, he stumbled past the refrigerator into the hall. He wanted to call Rona's and Julie's names, but he was afraid. He didn't know who—*what*—was out there, or where, and he needed to be careful. He followed the hallway wall until his hand reached the open space of Julie's bedroom doorway. He was drenched with fear sweat, and he didn't know whether to whisper her name, go silently into the room or keep walking on down the hall.

"Your daughter's here. I killed her."

The voice, wild and crazy sounding, came at him from somewhere deep within Julie's bedroom. Fear was shoved aside by anger, and Wilson stepped through the doorway. "Julie!" he called.

There was a soft click, and a red dot of light in the darkness.

Someone was videotaping this.

"Julie!" He stumbled forward blindly, hands extended, dimly aware that the red light of the video camera was moving around him, behind him. He nearly tripped over something pillowlike on the floor but quickly caught himself and grabbed a corner of the bedpost.

It was wet.

The lights flipped on.

The pillowlike thing on the floor was Rona's body. She was curled into a fetal position, her clothes shredded, and the skin of her arms and legs had been sliced open and peeled away. Julie's body lay on the bed, savagely eviscerated. The tendons of her face had been slashed, and her mouth was stretched out in a grotesque parody of a smile. His hand was covered with her blood.

Wilson heard screaming, terrible cries unlike anything his ears had ever before experienced, and it took him a moment to realize that they were coming from him.

The walls, he saw through the haze of his anguish, were covered with symbols scrawled in blood, the primitive scrawls and squiggles that he recognized from the other murder scenes and from Brian's letters. There was no sign of the person with the video camera, but he caught a glimpse of movement in the dresser mirror and turned around to see what it was.

The man who emerged from the hall was naked and horribly deformed. Parts of his body had scales instead of skin, and there were ridges along his hairy back that resembled those of a stegosaurus.

He was also a Silicon Valley entrepreneur who last year had spent millions of dollars on an unsuccessful run for governor.

Wilson recognized him immediately. Arthur Fawcett.

Fawcett was laughing, a low, steady Renfieldian laugh that threatened never to stop. At some point, Wilson had quit screaming, and now he just stood there mute and drained as the cackling millionaire advanced on him. The man's hands looked normal, but his scaly feet had nails like needles. With one quick flip, Fawcett was walking on his hands, his legs in the air, not sticking straight up but moving around, seemingly just as agile as a monkey. His head was near the ground, but his face was still looking at Wilson and laughing that endless laugh, his feet jabbing and thrusting, the needlelike nails swishing through the air.

Wilson stood in place, not running away, not trying to defend himself, his mind numbed into immobility by the horror of what he'd seen.

The five nails of Fawcett's right foot lashed out and struck the side of his face, opening up parallel gashes that sliced off his ear, cut through his cheek and caused his head to whip hard to the right. Wilson found himself staring at his daughter's naked eviscerated body. "Julie," he breathed.

And then the nails of Fawcett's left foot severed the arteries in his neck.

Eighteen

She'd bought new underwear.

Carrie hadn't said a word about it to anyone, was pretending even to herself that it was just a coincidence, that it didn't mean anything. But the fact remained that Friday night she had braved the after-work traffic and made a special trip to the mall, where she'd looked through all three department stores and five specialty shops—including Victoria's Secret—before buying herself sheer black lace panties and a matching bra that cost as much as all of her other lingerie combined.

And of course she was wearing both today.

Just in case?

She didn't know.

Maybe.

So far, the day had been going well. Extremely well. Lew had picked her up from home in a chauffeur-driven limo shortly after breakfast, and they'd spent the morning touring a piece of land that he had donated to the city for a park. A planner for the city met them there, as well as an urban landscaper and playground designer Lew had hired to map out the park.

For lunch, they went to Alioto's, one of those places she'd always heard about but had somehow never gotten around to visiting. "Touristy but fun," Lew told her. She didn't find it at all touristy, but she didn't tell him that, not wanting to reveal herself for the rube she was. Lew, of course, made a point of ordering organic food off the menu.

If on their first date they had purposefully kept the conversation superficial and work related, intellectual not emotional, they talked more personally this time, about who they were, about things that mattered. He seemed to find it hard to believe that she wasn't seeing anybody.

"You mean to tell me there's no special someone?" he teased.

She shook her head. "Not for a long time. *Too* long."

"And you're not even dating?"

"No."

"The old Freddy Fender situation."

Carrie looked at him, puzzled.

"Wasted days and wasted nights?"

She shook her head, still confused.

"Never mind. It's an old song. Anyway, I guess the next question is: Why?"

So she told him about Matt, revealing much more than she intended, more than enough to scare off anyone who wasn't seriously interested.

But he wasn't scared off.

After a leisurely meal, the limo drove them to Marin, to Lew's estate, which was the most amazing place she'd ever seen outside of a movie. The driver parked at the head of a circular driveway that appeared to be made of unpolished marble. Through the front windshield was a massive house of burnished steel and darkened glass that looked more like a museum or a theater than a home. Exotic trees and flowering plants grew in abundance, some neatly trimmed, others germinating wildly, creating a controlled chaos that perfectly complemented the smooth lines of the building.

They got out of the car, and Lew pointed to the left.

The view was breathtaking, a stunning panorama with the bay in the foreground, and the Golden Gate Bridge and San Francisco visible in the distance. She was pretty sure she'd seen the same vantage point in a movie before. "Beautiful, isn't it?" he said. "You should see it at night."

Was that a hint? She examined his face for clues, but his expression gave nothing away.

He put his left arm around her shoulder and with the right gestured expansively about them. "Ready for the tour?"

She nodded happily.

"Let's walk off that lunch," he suggested. "I'll take you around the grounds, show you the cactus garden, the Japanese garden, the duck pond. One of my interests, you know, is sustainable farming. I have quite a bit of land here, and a few years ago I decided to dedicate a portion of it to growing organic fruits and vegetables, enough to provide for myself and my entire staff. I can afford to buy food, of course, but I think it's important for a man in my position to set an example. As our population grows, it becomes more incumbent upon each of us to leave a smaller footprint on the planet."

He continued talking as they walked down a cobblestone path that led through the veritable jungle that grew on the side of the house. There was indeed a duck pond surrounded by cattails, fed by a stream whose waters flowed under a Japanese-style bridge farther up the hill. Beyond the bridge were a host of Asian plants and trees, as well as a suiseki rock garden. After that, the path forked. Lew started toward the trail on the left, which obviously led to the cactus garden—Carrie could see the century plants and exotic succulents from here—but she stopped him, pointing to the right. "What's that building?" she asked. "A barn?"

"Yes!" he said excitedly. "I'm glad you asked. I was

going to take you to it later, but we might as well go there now. That's where I get my milk."

"Oh, you have cows?"

Lew shook his head. "It isn't natural for humans to drink the milk of cows or goats or other *species*. It's disgusting when you think about it, stealing the lactation from a female animal that was intended for its offspring and feeding it to people." He leaned closer, and Carrie saw a fervency in his face that made her feel uncomfortable. "That's why I collect my own milk here on the property. Fresh. Organic. Come on, I'll show you."

She didn't want to go. All of a sudden, the wonderful day she'd been having seemed to evaporate, leaving behind unease, uncertainty, and the definite sense that something was wrong, that the day had gone far off the rails. It was the same feeling she'd had when entering Holly's tenement, an almost psychic sensation, more felt than thought, and some primitive instinctual part of her was telling her to run, flee, get as far away from here as quickly as possible.

But, passively, she went along with him, allowing Lew to lead her up the path, over a small grassy area to the building, which, this close, did not resemble a barn at all but looked more like a hospital annex. As opposed to the ostentatious showcase that was the house, it was clearly designed to be as unobtrusive as possible, and Carrie realized that it could not be seen from the driveway or from any point that might be visible by guests or visitors not already walking along the path through the grounds.

It was purposely hidden.

Her inner alarm was working overtime, but still she accompanied Lew as he slid open the oversized metal door of the building and led her inside, flipping on the lights as he did so.

The interior of the structure was a single room filled

with row after row of wooden holding pens no more than three feet long by two feet wide. Crammed into those pens were dozens upon dozens of women. Naked women, all of them on their hands and knees in straw fouled by their own waste. Industrial-strength breast pumps were attached to each, and intertwining hoses led to a central storage tank made of gleaming steel. All of the women were dark, and Carrie remembered what Lew had said about hiring immigrants.

At least he's not a racist, she thought, and the quip, so wildly inappropriate, helped ground her, kept her tethered to the real world in the face of this insanity.

The woman in the pen closest to where they stood looked over at them with dull, lifeless eyes. Carrie would have thought she was drugged, but Lew's insistence on having everything organic pretty much ruled that out. No, it was hopelessness that had dulled those features, hopelessness and despair, and Carrie observed the same slack, zoned-out expression on each of the women she saw as Lew held her hand tightly and walked proudly up the wide aisle between the pens.

He seemed completely oblivious to the suffering women around him, but Carrie wasn't, and she grew more and more horrified as she saw how *many* women were here, as she saw their hanging breasts pulsate with the suctioning force of the pumps.

Her feelings must have been visible in her expression because he squeezed her hand gently, reassuringly. "I know what you're thinking, but these women aren't here against their will. They work for me. I hired them to do this. It's the same basic concept as a wet nurse, only I've devised a way to harvest the milk and make it available to more than just one child." He gestured around the huge open room. "Our operation is laid out in this way because, physically and ergonomically, it makes more sense."

She nodded silently, not trusting herself to do anything else. These women had not been *hired*. This wasn't their *job*. One look at their faces and the physical condition of their pens told her that they were prisoners being held captive against their will. She imagined that most of them were undocumented workers who had been captured and whose absences would not be reported.

"Human beings are supposed to drink the milk of human beings," he declared, and the fervency was back in his voice. "Not *animals*. It is my hope that in the future we will be able to completely do away with traditional farms and ranches where milk is extracted from *beasts* and replace them with co-ops where we pump the milk from *women*."

They had reached the steel storage tank, on which had been stenciled the words: ORGANIC MILK. An array of pipes and valves ringed the bottom of the tank, and one clear tube led to a freestanding metal box that looked like a water cooler without the bottle at the top. From a dispenser on the side of the box, Lew took a paper cup. He placed it under a spigot, pressed a button, and milk flowed through the clear tube, squirting out of the spigot into the cup. He drank the contents, closing his eyes in satisfaction. "Fresh. Still warm. There's nothing finer."

He filled another cup, offering it to her. "Try it. It's delicious."

Carrie backed up, feeling sick. Her impulse was to run away screaming, but she looked at Lew and at the women all penned up like cattle and knew that if she tried to do so she might end up like them. Not only was Haskell rich enough to do what he wanted and get away with it, but his craziness was not of the ranting and raving variety. It was like that of the Nazis—methodical, systematic, organized. She needed to play along with him, find some way to ease out of this situation, get away and then call the police. Her cell phone was in her purse. If she could just find a way to grab a few moments of privacy . . .

The bathroom!

Carrie shook her head, made a motion of pushing away the cup. "I'm not feeling quite right," she said. She frowned, feigning stomach cramps. "Is there a restroom I could use?"

He looked honestly concerned. "Sure," he said. "There's none in here, of course, but outside, around the side of the building, for the employees . . ."

Her brain tuned out everything that followed. *The employees.* That meant that others knew about this, that he had helpers. It also meant, as if she'd needed more proof, that the women confined in the pens were *not* employees.

Lew led her outside, and it was not until she was once again in the open, breathing fresh air, that she realized how fetid the stench had been inside the building. "Over here," he said, walking around the corner, and pointed to what looked almost like an attached outhouse.

"Thank you," Carrie told him and quickly went inside, locking the door behind her. It was not an outhouse but a fully functional restroom, and she turned on the faucet to cover all sounds. Dialing 911, she breathlessly explained to the dispatcher who answered that she was at Lew Haskell's estate and that on his property he was holding women in captivity. The male voice on the other end of the line sounded skeptical but dutifully asked the address of her location. "I don't know!" she said with something like panic, and quickly lowered her voice. "But it's in Marin . . . It's Lew Haskell's place. It's big. You can find it."

"And you say there are women being held on the property against their will?"

"*I'm* being held against my—" she said. And shut off

the phone. She breathed deeply. Maybe if they thought she was in physical danger they might make an effort to send someone out.

Or not.

The thought chilled her. What could she do if no one came, if she was stuck here with him by herself? In a movie, of course, the heroine would make a weapon out of found objects and fight her way free, but this was not a movie and she'd never been in a physical altercation in her life. She wouldn't know *how* to attack Lew.

She'd been in here for too long already, and as crazy as it might be, she found that embarrassing. She quickly hid the phone in her purse, shut off the water and walked back outside.

"Are you okay?" Lew asked, concerned.

She waved him away. "I'm fine," she said. "But maybe we should start walking back."

From far off came a familiar noise, growing closer by the second.

Lew frowned. "What's that?" he asked. "Sounds like sirens."

"I don't know," Carrie lied, feeling grateful. She took his hand. "Let's go find out."

There was even more about him on the news.

She had thought that, after everything she'd been through, everything she'd seen, it was impossible for her to be shocked. But the extent of Lew Haskell's depravity was truly overwhelming. It frightened her to think how close she had come to being plunged into all of that. What would have happened if they'd continued to date, if the relationship had gotten serious? Would she have eventually ended up in a secret room somewhere, shackled to the wall and periodically tortured?

He had a son, a mentally ill and hideously deformed teenager whose existence had never been revealed, who didn't even have a birth certificate and who'd been locked up in a secret room for his entire life. He had a wife, too, whom he'd kept imprisoned within her bedroom. She was near death, starved and dehydrated, and authorities were not sure she would live, let alone be able to tell them anything about what had happened on the estate.

Carrie had a nightmare that night that Lew Haskell had purchased her, buying her from the Department of Social Services, who apparently held title to her life. She was a mail-order bride, and in the middle of that hellish barn, with hundreds of dirty women having their breasts pumped for milk, he put a ring on her finger and shackles on her wrists and bent her over, taking her hard from behind. She stood up straight, sobbing from the pain and humiliation, and with a sickening squelch, a baby flopped out from between her legs and landed on the ground. It had a horn like a rhino, claws like a lobster, cloven hooves like a goat and a snout like a pig. "Mama!" it screamed at her in the voice of a crow.

She spent Sunday inside. Alone. Most of it in bed.

On Monday she went to work early, carrying with her a copy of the *San Francisco Chronicle* so she could read it at her desk. Even after taking up half of Sunday's front page, Lew Haskell was still the main story in today's paper, and a photo of him looking completely deranged anchored the two related articles surrounding it. Photos of the wife and child had not been released to the press, but she called Dave Washington, her source at the police department, and he said that she could come over and see them. Sanchez okayed it, and she went over to the PD, where Dave had three folders spread out on a large table in an unused conference room. He opened the first one, which was stacked several inches high with photos. "These are the women who were being held captive," he said.

Carrie looked at the top photo. The Hispanic woman staring into the camera was standing against a white wall and dressed in what looked like a hospital gown, but her face was blank, her eyes dead, as though she were still on her hands and knees, hooked up to the pump in Lew's industrialized barn.

Carrie closed the folder, not wanting to see any more of the pictures, more disturbed by the image than she would have thought.

"This," Dave said, moving on to the next one, "is the wife."

Carrie sorted through the photos slowly, shocked anew by the appalling condition in which Lew had left his spouse. For evidence, she had been photographed exactly as they had found her, tied with rough hemp to a brass bed in her bedroom, an all-white chamber that resembled Ann-Margret's in *Tommy*. Her cheeks were cadaverously sunken, her ribs and collarbone visibly protruding and giving her a skeletal appearance. Her eyes were closed, her mouth open, lips thin and white and covered with scabs. Subsequent photos showed close-ups of the bruises and abrasions on various parts of her body, as well as protuberant joints and bones that offered further proof of her lethal malnourishment.

Carrie put the pictures away, unable to endure more.

"And the son," Dave said, flipping open the cover of the final folder.

The boy had the face of a lizard.

Carrie sucked in her breath, the fear rising within her. Lew's son had brownish scaly skin, bugeyes, two nostril slits instead of a nose, and a lipless mouth that wrapped much too far around the sides of his elongated head.

But that was not all. He had been naked when they'd found him, so that was the way he'd been photographed, and she could see a band of catlike fur ringing his mid-section, as well as a short pointed tail protruding from just above his buttocks. His erect penis was scraped raw and bloody, as though it had been rubbed against a cheese grater. He looked almost demonic, and though that was a terrible thing to think, it was the conclusion to which anyone looking at the photo would have come.

She thought of Juan and the Rhino Boy and that unknown kid in the photograph at the art gallery. A horrible suspicion entered her mind. Thanking Dave for letting her view the pictures, she returned to the office, where she told Sanchez that she was going to see Rosalia. She didn't need to stop by the Oliveras' apartment as part of her job—in fact, she had half a dozen more urgent cases waiting on her desk right at this moment—but there was something she had to know for herself.

"Why don't you take a few personal days," Sanchez suggested. "I'll make sure your cases are covered."

"That's okay," she told him.

"You've been through a lot. A few days off might—"

"I'm fine," she said.

After calling first to make sure Rosalia was home, she drove to the Oliveras' place. As always, Juan was hiding in the shadows of the bedroom, and as always, Carrie was glad. She declined Rosalia's offer to sit down on the ratty couch and instead showed the other woman the newspaper she had brought with her. "This man," she said, pointing to the photo of Lew Haskell. "Is he Juan's father?"

Rosalia turned away, obviously upset. She moved across the room, not speaking until she was standing next to the wall, facing away from Carrie and the newspaper. "No," she said.

"Take another look."

"No!" It was practically a shout.

"Rosalia," Carrie said gently. She walked over to the other woman, acutely aware of Juan's eyes watching her from the bedroom. "This man is in jail now. He cannot harm you." She laid a light hand on Rosalia's shoulder. "Be honest now. Tell me: Is this Juan's father?"

"*Sí,*" Rosalia said, agitated. "That is him." She still wouldn't look at either Carrie or the newspaper, and when Carrie moved around in front of her, she saw that Rosalia was crying.

Carrie comforted her, putting down the newspaper and putting her arms around Rosalia, but her mind was racing. Lew had not only fathered that deformed child he had hidden away in his mansion, but he had also impregnated Rosalia and had probably paid for sessions with Holly and gotten *her* pregnant. As well as whoever was the mother of that boy in the photograph and God knew how many others.

What if she and Lew had had sex?

Carrie refused to think about that.

Rosalia was aware of none of this, though she deserved to know all. The trouble was, Carrie didn't know where to start. She led Rosalia to the couch, sitting next to her, and after Rosalia stopped crying, Carrie explained as straightforwardly as possible how Lew had been holding immigrant women captive and how he had imprisoned his wife and son within their house. His son, she said delicately, had a face that looked like a lizard's.

"Juan es not only one?" Rosalia asked, wiping her eyes.

Carrie shook her head.

This was not her responsibility. The best thing she could do was go to someone in authority and tell them the whole story.

She did not want to violate Rosalia's privacy and confidence, but Holly and her son were dead, and the photo of the boy who looked like a possum was on public display in an art gallery. John Mees was the photographer's name, she remembered. She'd intended to track him down but hadn't gotten around to it.

When she returned to the office, she called Dave at the PD and told him all she knew, leaving out Rosalia and Juan. He seemed decidedly underwhelmed but promised to pass on the information to the officers involved in the case. She then went into Sanchez's office, closed the door and told her supervisor *everything*. He listened patiently, then calmly advised her to take a few days off. She had plenty of vacation and sick days.

"You don't understand," she said. "This guy has not only imprisoned immigrant women in a crazy attempt to farm organic human milk, he's also fathered these . . . children. And the police don't seem to care about that." She ran a hand through her hair. "Maybe that's not illegal, but not paying child support is, and since that's our department, I think we should get involved. This guy's a monster."

"This *guy*," Sanchez said evenly, "is rich. And powerful. So forgive me if I don't leap to prejudgment and assume he's guilty until proven innocent. What's more, it would be unethical, not to mention against department policy, for you to divulge privileged information about one of your clients."

She met his eyes. "You don't believe me? You think I'm lying?"

He looked away. "That's not the point."

"It *is* the point!" She slammed her hand on his desk so hard it hurt. "It's exactly the point!"

"Let's stop right here before we both say something we might regret. I'm not going to put you on leave at this point, but my suggestion is for you to give yourself a couple of days and think things through." He stood. "Now please leave my office. This conversation is over."

Carrie walked out feeling frustrated. She didn't know what to do with the knowledge she had, but it seemed to her that she had to do *something*. The tabloids would jump at the information, but she didn't want to go to them. Besides causing her problems at work and possibly getting her fired, it wouldn't be fair to Rosalia or Juan or any of the other children.

She sat down at her desk, nodded politely at the sympathetic comments of her coworkers, turned on her computer and tried to work.

And then the phone rang.

Nineteen

James Marshall called for another glass. He was already drunk, but he wanted to be drunker. The bartender, a squat ugly man with the personality of a rattlesnake, slammed the whiskey on the bar next to him, scowling, and held out his hand for payment. Marshall flipped two coins at the man, making sure one fell on the ground so the bastard would have to scramble around in the dirt to pick it up.

The truth was, those coins were pretty damn close to his last—which was one of the reasons he wanted to stay liquored up. When he'd come to California believing— no, *knowing*—that he would discover gold, he had assumed that he would get rich from it, that he'd been granted this special knowledge in order to benefit. But he was like Moses, leading people to the promised land yet unable to enter it himself. Marshall smiled bitterly. Wouldn't Morgan James and Emily Smith and all of those religious lunatics appreciate the irony of that!

What *had* happened to Emily Smith's family? he wondered.

Sutter had not profited from the discovery of gold either. It had taken a monumental number of bad decisions on both their parts to be so completely excluded from enjoying the wealth that was now flowing to every opportunist and ne'er-do-well who made his way West, yet that was exactly what had occurred. Sutter, as always, had plans and schemes on which he was working, attempts he was going to make to claim what he saw as his rightful due, but Marshall had all but given up the idea of making a fortune in gold.

In fact, now, he wasn't sure he *wanted* any gold.

Not after what he'd heard.

One story had come to him through the fort. A trio of greenhorns from back East had made their way to Coloma and had set off to live in one of the camps, bartering their animals and supplies for positions, filled with the cocky certainty that in a month they would be rolling in money and able to buy whatever they wanted. A week later, two of the men were dead and the lone survivor had a tale to tell that no one believed.

Marshall wouldn't have believed it either—if he had not experienced what he had.

The broken man who returned to the fort was dirty, bloody and barefoot, his clothes little more than tattered rags hanging from his bony frame. He was sobbing and incoherent. It was two days before he was able to tell anyone what had happened, and even when he did, everyone thought that his mind had been addled by whatever experience had befallen him and his comrades.

Everyone except Marshall.

The man's name was Jake, and he said that two days out, they'd been attacked in the night by creatures neither beast nor man. The three of them had been sleeping under the stars near the Sacramento River when they'd been awakened by the sound of something big crashing through the underbrush. "Bear!" one of them whispered, but it was the last thing he ever said because he was set upon by creatures that seemed shiny and slimy in the moonlight, creatures a head or two taller than a man, with tails and horns and claws unlike anything Jake had ever seen.

Jake had taken off through the trees, stumbling over roots and branches, his arms scraped by thorns as he ran away from the slaughter. Behind him, his other partner, also trying to flee, was caught. His screams rent the night.

Jake reached the river, splashed into it, was carried downstream, and spent the next several days and nights lost and wandering, in constant fear, trying to find his way back to the fort or a camp or someplace where there were people. Shortly before he reached the fort, in the middle of the day, he ran across one of the creatures. It was sleeping in a hollow, curled up, looking more like a giant snake than anything else. But it must have heard Jake or smelled him, because it woke up, stood to its full height and stared at him.

It was not snakelike at all. Its skin was slimy and white, like a worm's, but there were arms and legs, strange horns and protrusions of bone, a forked tail like a devil's, and patches of filthy hair all over. The head was huge, the face like something out of a nightmare.

He was terrified. But what seemed odd was that the creature appeared to be frightened as well. It kept looking behind and to the sides of him, as though searching for others. He had been doing the same, but when it became clear that it was only the creature and himself, that no one or nothing else was around, he began to back up slowly.

That was when the creature attacked. It didn't try to kill him as the others had his companions. Instead it tried to . . . mate with him. It became clear almost instantly that the creature was female, and despite its size and horrifying appearance, its touch was gentle, almost womanly.

Jake would reveal no more about that part. He would

only say that he managed to escape and finally find the fort, where they had found him, bloody and sobbing, half out of his mind from what he'd seen and experienced.

Another story Marshall had heard in a bar, and in its quiet way, it was even more disturbing. This one concerned two brothers who had found gold, who had struck it rich up past Helltown and were looking to move on to more productive diggings now that their first claim was running dry. They'd traced a creek backward into the high country via increasingly smaller tributaries, until the water disappeared entirely and there were no more forks to follow. A day of pickaxing had told them all they needed to know about the rocks here, and they decided to try their luck downriver instead of up. Attempting to return the way they'd come, the brothers had gotten lost, and after traipsing around for days through the unfamiliar terrain, sometimes walking in circles, sometimes making progress toward who-knew-where, they happened upon a strange verdant region teeming with oversized plants and trees unlike any they had ever seen that were growing in the shadow of a black mountain. The mountain was the same color as the iron filings that always accompanied panned or sluiced gold, and the brothers decided to scout the area and see if it might yield riches.

But it wasn't gold they found at the Black Mountain.

It was monsters.

When they finally returned to Helltown, they told of an entire community of horrific creatures that hoarded bones and used them in building homes, that ate the skeletons for sustenance while the rotting carcasses that had housed the bones lay wet and stinking in the heat. Creatures more beast than man, more devil than beast, that had only to look at bushes to make them grow or touch eggs to make them hatch.

There were people there as well, they said, and while

some of them were clearly being held captive, others seemed to be collaborators and acted as willing slaves.

Of course, this was a story Marshall heard in a bar, one that had probably been told and retold until there was no truth left in it. But there still seemed to him a reality about it, and he believed every word. California was filling up fast, but there was still a lot of unknown territory, empty spaces and places people knew nothing about, and judging by the long journey out here, many of them probably housed horrors that none of them could even imagine.

Marshall finished his whiskey, debated with himself whether or not to order another, then decided to save his money for tomorrow, when he'd need it. He was drunk enough now for sleep, and he stumbled off his stool and staggered out of the bar. From somewhere came the sound of fiddle music and laughter. From farther away: gunfire. Working hard to remain upright, weaving so badly that he felt dizzy, he headed out of the camp.

He tried to make it back to his cabin, but he must not have succeeded, because when he awoke the sun was up and he was lying in a tent made from animal skins. He heard voices outside, Indian voices, and he emerged from the tent squinting against the sun, his head pounding and his back aching. He attempted to stand straight, but the pain was too much, and he remained hunched over as he made his way through the Indian village. There was a pale face visible among all the dark ones, and Marshall headed toward it.

Doug Lilley, one of the few men from the mill who had not deserted to find his own treasure, was squatting next to a campfire, pushing coals with a stick as he waited for coffee to boil. He looked up as Marshall approached and grinned, revealing a newly missing tooth. "I was wonderin' when you was gunna wake up."

Marshall squatted down next to him. "I need some of that," he said.

Lilley cackled. "I bet you do." He nodded at the Indians. "You's lucky they took you in instead a lettin' the animals have at you where you fell."

"I don't remember," Marshall said.

"They respeck you," Lilley told him. "Cuz you never took no gold."

Marshall snorted. "People so stupid they respect failure." He shook his head.

"Tha's not why—"

"Yeah," Marshall said. "I know."

He glanced over at one of the older men, who nodded solemnly. Two younger men passed by, grinning at him.

He knew their opinion. The Indians believed that the gold was cursed, and though he'd never admit it to another man, Marshall was starting to think it was true. It belonged to a demon, the Indians said, and the demon would punish all who tried to steal its bounty. Sutter and the other men laughed this off as superstition, but Marshall recalled how he had first learned of this gold—

the bag of bones

—long before anyone had even entertained the thought that it might exist, and to him the concept of demon treasure made a lot of sense. At least as much sense as anything else.

And it explained the tragedies that were starting to befall some of the miners.

"Y'know," Lilley said. "I ain't never believed in God." He dropped his voice. "But these Indian gods? They scare me."

It was as if he could read Marshall's mind.

"I—" Marshall began.

There was a sudden commotion at the entrance to the village. An Indian man moved falteringly into sight, naked, the skin of his chest and legs torn and bloody, half of his scalp gone. He was carrying in his hand the head of a dog, and with each step he wailed loudly in pain and anguish.

Marshall stood, looking over at the older man with whom he'd earlier made eye contact.

"Roo-sha," the Indian said fearfully.

At first he thought the man meant "Russian," because there were quite a few Russians coming into California from Oregon, but the word was repeated, echoed through the gathering crowd, and Marshall quickly realized that this was another word, an Indian word, and that it meant some sort of monster or demon with which they were all familiar.

No one made any effort to help the man as he lurched farther into the center of the village. In fact, the growing crowd parted before him, as if by touching him they risked death. He seemed to grow weaker and weaker as he walked, and finally he fell to his knees, remaining there for a moment, looking up at his fellow villagers as the blood poured down his face, before he collapsed unmoving in the dirt.

The dog's head rolled away from him. It was alive, Marshall saw now. Its eyes were blinking, and its broken jaw was moving, trying to work, though no sound emerged from the mouth.

He thought of Pike.

The villagers were talking quickly and quietly among themselves. Whatever was out there, whatever lived in the mountain passes and secret canyons of this land, was known to the Indians, and they feared it. They were probably thinking of ways to appease it.

No one made any effort to help the man who lay bleeding in the dirt.

No one touched the still-moving dog's head.

Marshall grabbed the arm of a young man walking by. "What's happening?" he asked. His query was met with a blank stare, so he tried asking again in the Indian's language. He knew a little of it and managed to make himself understood, but the response he received was a jumble of unconnected nonsensical assertions.

The dying man was unclean because he had been attacked by a demon. If his body was not burned and his ashes scattered within a day, bad luck would befall the village and everyone in it would die. There was a race of demons. They were of the land and had been here long before the people came. They lived in the wilderness, away from man, and they didn't like humankind. Just as plants grew better in shit and filth, nourished by waste, so too these creatures—

Roo-sha

—thrived on death, disease and rot. From this, they brought forth new life.

And yet, they weren't plants. Nor were they animals. They were demons, magical beings of great power.

And they owned the gold.

Marshall wasn't sure how much of this he believed. His head was still aching and throbbing from last night, and there were gaps in translation that his mind had filled but could very well be wrong. And yet . . .

And yet none of the contradictions in the Indian's description seemed contradictory to him. Marshall thought of the flowers that had bloomed overnight in the plain surrounding that hellish hut on the trail. Behind the mysteries of this land, there seemed to him a single truth, and though he did not understand it, he believed in it.

The entire village, it seemed, had gathered around the unmoving body of the man and the head of the dog with its rolling eyes and snapping mouth. Several of the men were chanting something Marshall could not quite make out, and a naked man wearing a large colorful headdress was dancing wildly about, screaming and throwing dirt on the man's body and the dog's head.

Doug Lilley spoke in a low, taut voice. "Les get outta here," he said. "I don' like this."

Marshall nodded, and the two of them retreated down a trail toward the camp.

"Where you goin'?" Lilley asked after they'd gone a ways.

Marshall shrugged. "Sutter don't need me back until tomorrow, so I'm a free man."

"Me too. Wanna buy me a drink?"

"We'll see what happens."

They walked along for a while in silence. "You ever hear of those demons before?" Marshall asked finally. "Ever hear any stories about them from white people?"

"Oh yeah." Lilley nodded. "They're here."

"Here?"

Lilley looked up into the hills surrounding them. "Cain't tell where they be. But this their land. We just trespass on't. Least, thas how it use ta be. I guess it's gettin' t'be ours now. There's more of us'n there is of them."

"You believe all that horseshit about it being their gold and all? You think they can do magic?"

Lilley thought for a moment. "Yeah," he said.

"Did you ever . . . see anything?"

Lilley nodded.

"What?"

"You want me t'show you?"

Marshall was incredulous. "You know where they are?"

"Not exackly. But I can show you some'n."

"You ever tell Sutter this?"

"Oh, Sutter knows. He was the one what discovered 'em first."

Marshall stopped walking.

"Oh yeah. Afore you came, afore most a these men started a comin', this place was difernt. Ever wonder why there ain't more women at the fort? There was. Squaws and Mexicans, sure, but some of the men brought their own wives. Or daughters." He gestured toward the river, visible through the trees and, by implication, the fort beyond. "Where are they, huh? Where you think they are?"

"I don't know," Marshall admitted.

"Sutter sent them away. Because they *consorted*."

Marshall shook his head. "I don't understand. What does that mean?"

"I'll show you. Up at First Camp."

"First Camp? I was just there last week."

"You're Sutter's man. They would'n tell you."

"Then why should you?"

"The Indians think you're safe."

"Because I have no gold."

Doug Lilley shrugged and smiled, revealing missing teeth.

Marshall's horse was back at the cabin. Lilley had lost his in a card game, so Marshall lent him a mule, and the two of them took the trail east toward First Camp. It was midafternoon and they could smell the smoke from the camp and hear the sounds of shouting men and falling rocks when Lilley hopped off the mule to get his bearings. He walked around in a circle, then pointed through the ponderosas to their right. "This way," he said. "An' if we don' find a box canyon soon, we turn back."

Sure enough, the ground rose before them, and they rode between two ridges into a narrow gorge that opened out to reveal a small community of tents and windowless shacks situated around a large pond fed by what appeared to be a seasonal waterfall. "Ho!" Lilley called. His voice echoed off the rock walls, bounced back, but no one came out to greet them, and Marshall realized that as new as the tents and shacks looked, the community had turned ghost.

He didn't like that.

"Where is everyone?" Marshall asked.

He was hoping Lilley would say they were off working a vein or a Long Tom or even blasting a hillside—his own pet peeve in these gold-fevered days—but the other man shook his head. "Don't know. I can guess, though."

"What—"

"This way," Lilley said. "Come."

They got off their mounts and walked around the edge of the pond to the first shack, ducking under the low sill of the doorway to get inside. It took their eyes a moment to adjust, and in that moment Marshall was brought back to the mud hut on the plain. Now, as then, he found himself in a single windowless room, and his body was filled with tension, his mind with unease.

Now he could see.

The dead woman lay on a pile of leaves against the back wall. The child, if that's what it was, crawled blind through the dirt, mewling like a kitten, its segmented body moving in staggered stages, at opposing angles. There was no face that he recognized, only a blank section of skin above an open gash of a mouth, all of it surrounded by a lion's mane of coarse black hair.

"They was all afraid of it," Lilley said, and his voice was quiet, soft, almost reverent. "Last time I come." He looked at the body of the woman. It was black with rot but for some reason did not smell. The only thing visible in the darkness of her face was the whiteness of teeth. "She was one of 'em what *consorted*, and this come of it. She died givin' birth." He pointed to the . . . child crawling awkwardly about the dirt. "They was all afraid t' touch it. Even th' midwife what help her. They jus' lef' it here, hopin' it'd die. But it dint. Now, I guess, they's all gone."

Marshall had been thinking the same thing. Why *hadn't* it died? How had it survived? Apparently, it just spent all day and night crawling around this single-room shack. What did it eat? He glanced over at the mother, trying to determine whether any bites had been taken out of her, but the skin of the body was so black and rotted it was impossible to tell. Maybe it didn't *have* to eat, he thought.

Lilley's voice grew even quieter. "Her name was Alma. I knowed her back at th' fort. We was almost . . ." His voice trailed off into nothing.

Maybe the father came back periodically to feed it.

Marshall ducked under the sill to get outside and away from the closeness of the shack, breathing deeply as he hit the fresh air. He looked up at the rock walls nervously. There was only one way out of this canyon. It was an easy place to get trapped. He glanced across the pond, grateful to see that their mounts were still in place and unmolested. "Let's go!" he called out to Lilley. His voice echoed in a way he did not like.

The other man emerged from the shack, and the two of them walked back around the side of the pond in silence. Marshall stared at the ground as he walked. He saw now why the tents and shacks had sprung up here in this place. There was gold for the taking, actual nuggets lying in the sandy soil by the edge of the water. One the size of a bullet sat atop a flat piece of sandstone. Another, equally large, was surrounded by shimmering gold dust that could be easily panned by even the most incompetent prospector. He had not noticed any of this on the way in, yet now that he was looking, he saw that gold was everywhere. He slowed his pace, measuring and comparing the pieces he spotted, but while he could not take his eyes off the shiny metal, he refused to touch it.

He reached his horse and mounted it. Lilley got on the mule.

The two of them started back the way they'd come, neither turning for one last glance at the encampment. Or the shack.

"Lot of gold there," Marshall noted a few minutes later.

"You take any of it?"

He shook his head. "No."

"Wise choice," Lilley said as they rode out of the canyon.

Twenty

"That looks like the cat we saw when we were hiking," Alyssa said. "The dead one. I bet it's his brother. Or sister."

"Yeah," Andrew said thickly, not trusting himself to speak.

They were unloading the ice chest and backpacks from the van, and the cat stood on the side of the parking lot staring at them. At *him*. It was the same cat. He could tell not only by the white paws, white head, red collar, and dried blood where its tail should have been, but by the long scar that bisected its body—at precisely the point where his hoe had cleaved the animal in two. Its second death had made it look even more disturbing than before, if that was possible. The animal's fur was still matted and bloody, but there was more dirt now, and the head and upper torso were slightly off center, as though the two halves of the body had not fused together properly.

He stared at the creature, thinking of that old wives' tale about nine lives.

"It looks like the same one to me," Johnny said, peering at it.

"You and your sister pick up the handles on that ice chest and carry it back to the cabin," Andrew told him.

The kids obliged. Robin was already in the cabin, and

he waited until Johnny and Alyssa were out of sight before running over to the cat and stomping his foot in an effort to scare it away.

The animal did not budge.

Glancing quickly around, praying that no one was watching, Andrew hauled off and kicked the cat. He did not merely push it with his foot but drew his leg all the way back and booted the creature as hard as he could. It skittered head over heels across the ground . . . but then landed on its feet several yards away.

And stared at him.

"Meow," it said.

Overhead, a bird fluttered by, its flight as erratic and drunken as Woodstock's. He saw it in his peripheral vision, but even without looking at it directly, he knew that it was one of those he'd killed and dumped at the edge of the wood. Glancing one last time at the unmoving cat—

"Meow"

—Andrew picked up the remaining backpack, closed and locked the van door, and headed toward the cabin. He resisted the urge to turn around.

They'd gone on a rafting trip, but it hadn't been fun. The day was chilly and overcast, the river guide hostile and unfriendly. Johnny and Alyssa had fought. None of them had enjoyed the experience.

On the way back, they'd passed a carnival set up in a vacant lot in the middle of town between the grocery store and a Shell gas station. SUMMER FAIR read the banner strung over the street.

"Hey, let's check it out!" Johnny said excitedly.

"No," Robin told him. "We're going back to the cabin. I need to take a shower and wash this crud off me."

So here they were.

At least the sky had cleared a little, the uniform ceiling of gray that had been hovering over the area since dawn breaking up into smaller combinations of differentiated clouds, allowing shafts of sunlight to beam down on the town and forest.

"Meow."

Andrew turned at the sound of the cat's voice, expecting to see it following him along the path to the cabin. But though the cry had been clear, the animal was nowhere to be seen and he hurried on.

They put away their supplies. The kids from Nevada were playing in the meadow, throwing a Frisbee, and he told Johnny and Alyssa that they could play, too, as long as they stayed within sight of the cabin. The two ran off, and Andrew helped Robin unload the plastic cooler. He dumped the melted ice water off the side of the porch, looking around all the while. He felt like an Edgar Allan Poe character. All he could think about was the cat. In his mind, he was trying to come up with ways to dispatch the animal once again. But every scenario that came to him ended in discovery.

"I think we should go home," Robin said. She hadn't spoken since the kids had left, and her voice startled him.

"Why?"

"You know why. Besides, what more is there to see here? Or do? Why don't we start back and spend the extra time sightseeing along the way? We could check out Yosemite or the redwoods or even make a detour to the Grand Canyon."

He didn't answer. She was right. There was no real reason to stay and plenty of reasons to leave early.

But he didn't want to.

It was an irrational position and not one that he totally understood. Despite the resurrected animals and Robin's history here, he really enjoyed being in gold rush country, but that didn't explain his firm tether to the place.

For it was not just a vague connection he felt but a concrete attachment that stubbornly refused to acknowledge either logic or reality. From the beginning, it felt as though he'd been *called* here, and while he did not know how or why, he wanted to stay around and discover how this played out.

That was wrong, he knew. He was a husband and a father, and his first priority should be his family. There was definitely something about this trip that did not seem safe, that was totally at odds with his duties as a spouse and a parent, but he felt all of this at a remove, as though he were underwater and hearing the muffled sound of voices from the surface.

He'd been thinking a lot about Bill Fields on this trip. He hadn't thought of Bill for years, and though it was only the notoriety of his murder that had placed him back in Andrew's mind, the fact remained that there seemed to be some sort of link between his old friend and the feelings he had for this part of California. It was not something intellectual but instinctual, a below-the-radar recognition that there were connections between seemingly unrelated aspects of his life. A six degrees kind of thing.

He had no idea what it meant.

There was a pounding of feet up the steps and onto the porch. "Mom! Dad!" Johnny called, the screen door slamming shut behind him.

"What is it?" Andrew said.

"Are we doing anything today?"

"We went on a rafting trip. And—"

"No, I mean later," Johnny said.

"Why?" Robin asked suspiciously.

"Alyssa and I want to go to the fair."

Robin was already shaking her head.

"Terry and Claire's parents said they can go."

"Only if we come with you," Robin said firmly.

Andrew saw the look of shame and embarrassment that crossed his son's face, a look he remembered well from his own teenage years. He felt sorry for the boy, but he agreed with Robin. That cat—

"Meow"

—was still out there, along with God knew what else, and it frightened him to the core of his being to think of his children encountering one of those resurrected animals. He could easily imagine the creatures attacking his children, making them pay for what their father had done, and that was something he could not allow to happen.

"But Tony, Dexter and Pam are going to be there! They're the ones that invited us!"

"And who are Tony, Dexter and Pam?" Robin asked.

"Those kids from town we played with yesterday."

"No," Andrew said.

Johnny looked at him. "Dad . . ."

In his mind he saw a line of dead animals advancing toward his children while zombie birds zoomed in from the sky. "We don't know those kids. Besides, you can go to a fair or carnival or amusement park anytime. Better ones than this. We're here to learn about gold rush country and enjoy the sights of California."

"From our room? We're just going to sit inside until it's time for bed."

"I said no," Andrew told him.

Johnny left the cabin much more slowly and considerably more discouraged than when he'd arrived.

"Let's go home," Robin said again. "Let's get out of here."

"No," Andrew said. "Not yet."

Yet? Why had he said that? It made it sound as though he was waiting for someone or expecting something to happen.

Maybe, he thought, he was.

They had sandwiches for dinner. Robin hadn't been in the mood to cook anything elaborate, and he didn't feel like driving to the store to get more charcoal for the barbecue, so they made do with what they had. The kids didn't seem to care. Johnny's earlier disappointment had disappeared, and he and his sister chatted happily through the meal, retroactively making even the rafting trip fun.

It was the kids' turn to do the dishes, but afterward they came out on the porch where he and Robin were watching the sunset. The sky in the west had turned bright orange as the sun started to drop slowly behind the hills.

"Can we go to the lodge with Terry and Claire?" Johnny asked. "They're having a slide show about volcanoes."

"That sounds fun," Andrew said. "We'll all go."

Johnny looked crestfallen. "Dad . . ."

"This *is* supposed to be a family vacation."

"But Terry and Claire get to go by themselves! And Claire's the same age as Alyssa and Terry's younger than me! Couldn't you just hang out with their parents and let us go to the slide show?"

The last thing he wanted to do was "hang out" with Terry and Claire's parents. But he understood his son's desire for independence, his need to do things on his own. He glanced across the meadow at the lodge, which was clearly visible from the porch.

"It's more fun without you," Alyssa said bluntly.

Andrew had to laugh, although Robin didn't even crack a smile.

"It's still light out," Johnny said, and there was a note of pleading in his voice.

"All right. You can go," Andrew said gently. "But

you have to stay with your sister and both of you have to come back right after the talk ends. Right after. Do you understand me?"

"But, Dad . . ."

"Then no."

"Okay! I'm sorry! I won't complain!"

"Andrew," Robin said grimly.

"They'll be all right," he reassured her. "It's only the lodge." But he thought of the cat sitting somewhere in the path on the way to the lodge and already regretted his decision.

"Thanks, Dad!" Johnny said, grabbing his sister's hand and running down the steps as if afraid he might change his mind. "I'll watch Alyssa! Don't worry!"

"Andrew . . ." Robin said.

He knew how she felt. He felt the same way. But he forced himself to smile at her. "They'll be fine," he told her.

Robin watched them speed down the path through the meadow. They were both getting so big. Even Alyssa. A lot of the women she knew missed the days when their children were babies. She didn't. What she missed were the preschool years, when the kids were old enough to talk but everything was new to them, everything was exciting, everything was fun. Those days had been almost too hectic at the time for her to enjoy them, but she looked upon them now as the happiest of her life.

If it were up to her, the two of them would have remained four forever.

But time passed, kids grew up, and as much as she hated and feared Oak Draw, she was at least grateful to have the opportunity on this trip to spend time with Johnny and Alyssa. For most of her workaholic friends, family vacations were distant memories—they generally grabbed a three-day weekend here or there when they could, often *without* the children—and Robin knew how lucky she was that the four of them did so many things together.

But she *did* hate Oak Draw.

And she feared it.

For the second night in a row, she'd had the same dream. Or nightmare. She was still not sure how to classify it. She had been walking down a yellow-brick road, as in *The Wizard of Oz*. Only it was really a pathway lined with bars of gold, not yellow bricks, and it ended not at an emerald city but at a black mountain. There were monsters crawling all over the mountain, the same sorts of monsters who had raped her and her friends, and wherever they crawled they left behind trails of rapidly growing grass.

Andrew walked back inside the cabin, bringing her with him, and closed the door behind them. He wanted to have some quick sex before the kids came back. She didn't know what had gotten into him on this trip. He seemed to want it all the time now, despite what had happened to her here—

Because of it?

—and though she kept turning him down, he kept putting on the pressure. "Pull your pants down and bend over," he told her. "I'll do it really fast."

"No," she said.

He pulled down his own pants, and she saw his erection. "Just suck it then."

"No!" Robin went into the bathroom, closed and locked the door, and stood there looking at herself in the mirror. She was shaking, though she was not quite sure why. She wasn't afraid of her husband, and while she was angry with him, it was not to such an extent that it would cause such a physical reaction. She held a hand sideways in front of her face, watching it tremble.

What was the matter with her?

It was nothing; it was everything. It was this place, and she wondered why Andrew was so dead set on staying here no matter what. He was not usually so inflexible, particularly when it involved things that were important to her.

But he seemed different on this trip, more tense, more secretive, and she wished she knew how to talk to him and break down those barriers. Since coming clean herself, she'd been feeling extremely vulnerable, and she wished her honesty had been met with a similar openness on his part, but exactly the opposite had occurred. They'd become more wary with each other, more distant, although she knew of no reason why that should be the case.

She wanted this vacation to be over. She just wanted to go back home.

Robin waited in the bathroom a few moments longer, until she'd stopped shaking and could at least pretend that everything was back to normal. Then she unlocked the door and walked out. Andrew was in the kitchen area with his back to her, but his pants were around his knees, and she strode over to where he stood, intending to find out exactly what was going on.

He had masturbated into the sink, and she grimaced as she caught him washing a gob of semen down the drain. He pulled up his pants, embarrassed.

"What is wrong with you?" she asked.

"I don't know," he said. "I . . ." He shook his head. "I don't know."

Through the open window came the meowing of a cat, and Andrew's face turned pale. She shivered, too, thinking of that dead cat they'd seen on the trail—

near the spot

—and its doppelgänger who'd been hanging around the cabins today. She wasn't sure why Andrew seemed so afraid of the cat's meow, but he did, and some of that fear transferred to her.

He chose not to talk about it, however, and she chose not to ask him about it, and the two of them pretended he had not done what he'd done in the sink. Sometimes denial worked, and it did in this instance. They retired to the couch, turning on the television. *Lost in America* was on one of the movie channels—a comedy Andrew had raved about but that she'd never seen—and they settled in to watch it, snuggling together as though nothing were the matter and they were home alone.

The film was as funny as Andrew had promised, and at several points they were both laughing out loud, but somewhere in the middle of the movie she became aware that Johnny and Alyssa had not returned. They'd been gone a long time, and Robin glanced over at the clock on the mantel above the fireplace. It had been slightly over an hour since they'd left, and while the slide show on Sierra predators that they'd seen their first night had lasted this long and it was more than possible that tonight's talk was still going on, she felt nervous. It was dark outside and . . . something . . . didn't seem right.

Andrew must have sensed it too, or perhaps she communicated it to him through her body language. Either way, he sat up and said, "Do you think we should check on the kids?"

"Yes," she replied with an exhaled sigh of relief. She'd thought she was going to have to talk him into it.

"I don't like the thought of them walking back alone in the dark."

"Me neither," Robin said. "Let's go."

She shut off the TV, he grabbed a flashlight, and they walked over to the lodge. In the meadow, chirping crickets silenced as they approached, though others farther away continued to sing. Above the noises of nature, Robin heard an oddly pitched voice singing something that reminded her of a children's nursery rhyme or Mother Goose song. She couldn't quite place it, but the sound of that voice carried on the slight night breeze caused a shiver to run down her spine.

She reached for Andrew's hand, held it tight.

The lodge was open, its windows well-lit, but inside the building seemed curiously empty. Robin glanced into the big room where the previous presentations had been held and saw no screen set up, no chairs. Andrew walked directly up to the counter, where an older woman in a faded granny dress was reading a paperback romance novel. "Excuse me," he said. "Our son and daughter came with friends of theirs to your slide show . . ."

The woman frowned. "There was no slide show this evening."

Robin's heart was racing. "But our son and daughter are here?"

"No," the woman said slowly, shaking her head. "I don't believe anyone's come in here tonight at all."

"Mind if we look around?" Andrew asked, but he was already doing so.

"Go right ahead," the woman said.

Robin and Andrew went into the big room, checked the bathrooms and the coat closet, even went upstairs and looked at the balcony, but the lodge was empty.

"Thank you," Andrew said to the woman as the two of them headed out the door. Once out in the night, they looked around at the partially visible lights of the various cabins, arranged in a rough semicircle around the edge of the meadow and between the black silhouetted trees. Crickets were chirping, bats were squeaking, the underbrush was rustling, but wafting through the air, on the breeze, was that tune again, lilting, familiar, childish.

She listened to it for a moment.

Now she recognized the song.

Oh, dear! What can the matter be?
Dear, dear! What can the matter be?
Oh dear! What can the matter be?
Johnny's so long at the fair.

"Andrew!" she cried. But he had heard it, too, and it must have set off the same alarm bells in his head that it had in hers, because he was grabbing her hand and rushing toward the parking lot.

Johnny's so long at the fair.

They fairly flew over the rough ground, the beam of the flashlight leading the way, and though that horrid cat sat in the center of the parking lot, meowing incessantly, they ignored it. Andrew clicked open the doors with the remote attached to his key, and they got in quickly. "He's going to be in so much trouble," Andrew said grimly as he swung the van around and sped out of the parking lot, but there was as much fear in his voice as anger, and Robin said nothing as they headed toward the highway and town.

The fair was crowded. The small pay lot was full, vehicles were parked solidly along both sides of the highway for nearly the entire length of town, and the driveways of the other local businesses were staked with signs that read NO FAIR PARKING and PARKING FOR CUSTOMERS ONLY. Heedless, Andrew pulled into the lot of a dentist's office, locked the car after they hopped out, and the two of them sped over to Oak Draw's Summer Fair.

They didn't know where to start. Throngs of people were milling about, buying fried food and waiting in lines for carnival rides. Johnny and Alyssa could have been anywhere. Holding hands so they wouldn't get separated, the two of them went up and down the midway, through the crowd, looking for black T-shirts like Johnny's or red blouses like Alyssa's, distracted by the sight of every child or teenager who passed by.

"Did they have any money?" Robin asked.

"I don't know," Andrew admitted. "I don't think so."

She looked around at the rides and attractions, searching for one that Johnny and Alyssa might like to go on. Not the thrill rides. They were both too cautious. Not the merry-go-round. Too babyish. The mirror maze, maybe?

The fun house.

Yes. If they were on a ride, it was that one. As if on cue, she heard music above the noise of the crowd, the talking, screaming, laughing, crying crowd. It was a tape of a calliope over tinny speakers, and it was the song that had brought them here, though there was no voice singing the words.

> *Oh, dear! What can the matter be?*
> *Johnny's so long at the fair.*

It was coming from the fun house, and Robin yanked Andrew's arm, pulling him through the squash of people to the far end of the midway.

The facade of the fun house loomed before them with its gaudy colors and giant mirror-eyed clown head. A lifetime of moviegoing had made the sight seem automatically creepy, but there was something genuinely threatening about it, too, and Robin pointed. "I think they're in there."

Andrew nodded, not needing an explanation. "Wait out front here," he said, "in case they come out or come by. I'll see if they're inside."

A dwarf sat on a stool in front of the moving stairs that led up to the entrance of the attraction, collecting tickets. "Did you see a boy and a girl come through here?" Andrew began.

"Two tickets."

"I think my kids are in there," Andrew explained. "I just want to—"

The dwarf held out a small, chubby hand. "Two tickets."

Robin could see the look of exasperation on her husband's face. "How much are they?" he asked.

"Buy them from the ticket booth." The little man pointed toward the front of the fair.

"I just want to look inside and see if my kids are there," Andrew said. "I'll give you two dollars."

"Five," the dwarf countered.

Andrew opened his wallet, handed over a five-dollar bill and quickly dashed inside the fun house. Robin waited and watched while he appeared and disappeared at the various windows and open ports in the two-story facade, the maddening music seeming to grow even louder.

The dwarf grinned at her, wiggling his tongue lasciviously.

Moments later, Andrew emerged, shaking his head. He hurried over. "They're not there."

It seemed hard to breathe. She imagined the two of them kidnapped by some psycho, held in a basement, tied up in the trunk of a car, left for dead in the forest.

Where the hell were they?

She looked over the throngs of standing, walking, jostling people, and suddenly she couldn't help herself.

She began to cry.

Johnny and Alyssa followed the path to the lodge . . . then walked around the side of the building and took another path that led to town.

It was the path Tony, Dexter and Pam had taken yesterday, and it led to the parking lot of the Tastee Freez. From there, they walked out to the sidewalk and down the street to the fair.

It was wrong of them to have lied to their parents, and Johnny was not even sure why they had done so. Terry and Claire were safely in their cabin watching TV, and he didn't even know if there *was* a slide show tonight in the lodge or, if so, what it was about. But he'd wanted to go to the fair.

He'd wanted to see Tony, Dexter and Pam again.

Tony, Dexter and Pam *had* invited them to the fair, and when they'd asked, Johnny had made it seem as though meeting there would be no problem. He wanted the other kids to think he and Alyssa were cool, and she'd played along with him. Terry and Claire hadn't even been invited, and that made him feel even better, even more privileged, even more determined to make sure they went.

There was no sign of Tony, but Dexter and Pam were waiting, as promised, in front of the mirror maze, leaning against a concave looking glass and blocking anyone else from seeing themselves in it. Pam was his age, but Dexter was a year or two older, and he looked around the fair disdainfully. "This place sucks," he said.

"Yeah," Johnny agreed, trying to be cool. He, too, casually leaned back against a mirror, saying nothing for several moments, pretending to be nonchalant. "We could go to the Place," he said, as though the idea had just occurred to him.

"I have a better idea," Dexter told them. "Let's make fun of old people."

Johnny was disappointed but tried not to let it show. The truth was that ever since the town kids had told them about the Place yesterday, it was all he could think about. They'd been playing freeze tag, all of them, in the open area between the cabins and the lodge, and when they'd paused to rest, Dexter had said, "You know what's even more fun than this? Going to the Place."

"What's the Place?" Johnny finally asked.

Pam chuckled in a sly adult way that made him feel tingly all over. Dexter and Tony grinned. "It's something we do around here for fun." Dexter gestured around at the trees and hills and town. "You may not've noticed, but this ain't exactly the center of the universe. I don't know where you all are from, but I'm pretty damn sure it's bigger than this town. You probably got movie theaters and malls, places to go, things to do. Out here . . . well, we can either hang with tourists like you or go to the Place."

"What is the Place?" Johnny repeated.

"It's a place. Where grown-ups go. Our parents might even go there, too, but that's kind of gross to think about."

"What is it?"

Pam chuckled knowingly again.

"We have a secret spot. Where we can watch." Dexter looked up into the sky. "It can't be daytime. It has to be dark. Night. And then you wait and usually someone'll go there. A man and a woman most of the time but sometimes just a man or just a woman. They have to be *naked*."

"What happens then?"

"They have to invite one of *them*. Not invite exactly, but lure them out from the woods, the wilderness, wherever they hide, wherever they live. And if one of *them* does come out, they can do whatever they want."

"Who is *them*?"

"That's part of it. You don't know until they come."

"Are they other grown-ups?" Terry asked, worried.

Dexter leaned forward. "They're not *people*," he whispered.

They'd broken up after that: Terry and Claire running back to their parents like the wimps they were; Tony, Dexter and Pam heading back down the path toward town. But before they left, Dexter invited Johnny and

Alyssa to hang out with them at the fair the following night. Johnny promised that they'd be there.

He'd dreamed that night of the Place, and in his dream he and Pam had hidden together behind some bushes while they watched a woman take off all her clothes until she was completely naked and he could see everything.

Now the four of them stood staring at those who passed by the mirror house. Groups of kids like themselves. Couples. Families.

"I don't want to make fun of old people," Pam told Dexter. "*I* want to go to the Place." She looked significantly at Johnny.

"Okay," Dexter agreed. He pointed at Alyssa. "But she has to come, too."

"No," Johnny said firmly. He didn't want Alyssa involved in any of this.

"I'm big enough to decide for myself," his sister told him. "Besides, what am I going to do, wait around here by myself until I get kidnapped?"

She had a point.

"If you can do it, I can do it," she said defiantly.

That made him uncomfortable. She shouldn't be here, he thought. He shouldn't have brought her along in the first place. He was beginning to think that *he* shouldn't have come either. All of a sudden, an evening lounging around the cabin watching TV didn't seem so bad.

"Come on," Dexter said. "I know the way."

With Pam practically dancing behind him, Dexter led them around the back of the fun house at the end of the midway and across a field of dried grass toward a line of trees. The town was very narrow here, like one of those in an old Western movie. There was no depth to it. No streets or homes or buildings lay behind the empty lot where the fair had set up, and immediately after passing the fun house they were in open country, noise and lights and life behind them.

The woods ahead looked dark.

He wasn't going to let Alyssa see anything, Johnny decided. He was going to make her look the other way. If Dexter tried to push, they would just leave.

Why didn't they leave right now? Why were they even following Dexter and Pam?

Because he wanted to see the Place.

Pam was singing something as she danced, though it was not a song he recognized.

If they went too far into the woods, he and Alyssa were going to turn around. Johnny did not want to get too removed from civilization. But to his surprise, they stopped just inside the line of trees. If someone from the fair had trained a spotlight in this direction, the four of them could probably be seen.

"This is the Place," Dexter said.

Johnny glanced about. Moonlight filtered downward through the trees, and light from the fair and the town seeped in behind them, granting sparse illumination to the area in which they found themselves. It was enough to show him that the clearing where they stood was overgrown with lush vegetation. It was like an oasis, he marveled. The bushes were huge and full, the grass tall, completely unlike what he'd seen elsewhere around Oak Draw.

There were animals here as well, small woodland creatures like squirrels and chipmunks, robins and rabbits. Only they weren't behaving the way normal animals did. They seemed more like characters from cartoons in the way they sat still in a semicircle around the side of the clearing, chittering, chirping . . . and watching.

"This way," Dexter said. He led them around the side of a particularly large bush. Behind it and under the branches was an indentation in the ground, what looked like almost a small room within the huge bush itself, where they could sit or even stand and watch whatever went on in the clearing. "We'll wait," he announced.

They didn't have to wait long.

Shortly afterward, a couple entered the clearing from a slightly different direction than they had come, looking furtively about as though afraid of being caught. They said nothing but merely looked at each other for several moments . . . and then started to remove their clothes.

"They're going to pee over there," Dexter whispered. "It brings *them* out."

The woman's shirt and pants were already off, and she was squatting in the dirt where he pointed, urinating.

"Let's go," Alyssa whimpered, tugging on his arm. Now she sounded scared.

"In a few minutes," he promised. Part of him wanted to leave, too, but part of him wanted to stay and see what happened. He hazarded a glance at the woman. She had picked up a handful of mud from between her legs and was rubbing it on her buttocks. "And everywhere that big cock went, this Sue was sure to go," she said in a singsongy voice.

"They like rhymes," Dexter whispered. "Nasty ones."

The man was taking off his clothes. Johnny definitely did not want his sister to see this.

Alyssa gripped his hand tighter. "Let's go." Her voice was barely audible.

The man was totally naked now. He put his hands on his hips, facing away from them, and started chanting. "My dick is here. It took a whiz. Eat it! Eat it! Here it is!"

All was suddenly quiet. Everything had gone silent, as though a soundproof bubble had descended over the woods. The noises of the fair, the town and the highway were gone, and only the sounds *they* made were audible.

Johnny heard the crunching of leaves, the panting of breath, the slap of mud being applied to skin.

Either the moon had grown brighter or his eyes had adjusted, but he saw now that the cute little animals on the side of the clearing were dead. Only . . .

Some of them were moving.

A rabbit thumped its foot. A squirrel wiggled its tail. A bird twitched its wing.

The rabbit's face had rotted away. The squirrel's eyes were missing. The bird's stomach had been ripped open.

The sounds of the outside world were still missing, but from the trees came a sharp whistle, followed by a whooshing windlike noise. The branches of bushes began whipping back and forth as though in anticipation of the arrival of something *big*.

"Run," Johnny whispered to his sister, and he grabbed her hand. Before Dexter or Pam could stop them, they were out of the bush and dashing across a small section of the clearing, then back the way they had come. He hazarded a glance over his shoulder as they broke the line of trees and started across the open field toward the lights and noise of the fair. He saw the woman on her hands and knees, with something slimy and sort of human approaching her from behind. Where the man had been stood a creature that looked like Bigfoot, although a tree blocked part of its body.

Then they were running and not looking back, keeping their eyes on the prize as they dashed desperately toward the fair and the town. They ran around the side of the fun house, the final attraction on the midway, and back into the mix of townspeople and tourists, grateful for the music, the voices, the lights. He thought of Dexter and Pam behind the bush, watching those summoned creatures enter the dark clearing.

"Johnny!"

He jumped at the sound of the voice, startled.

"Alyssa!"

Their parents were in front of the fun house and hurrying over. He saw wild relief on his mom's face and, on top of that, bone-deep anger. His dad, too, looked at once relieved *and* ready to beat them both.

"Where were you?" "You could've been kidnapped or killed!" "I told you you couldn't go!" "What got into you?" "What in the world were you thinking?"

They were both talking over each other, shouting so loudly that other fairgoers were turning to stare, and though Johnny was dreading the punishment to come, he was absurdly thankful that his parents cared so much, that they were both there for him and Alyssa.

His mom grabbed his shoulders "Where were you?" she demanded, her eyes boring into his.

"No place," Johnny said, looking away.

"What were you doing?"

"Nothing," he said. He glanced toward his sister, met her eyes.

She stared back at him stoically, then nodded imperceptibly. "Nothing," she agreed.

Twenty-one

Brian passed by Wilson's cubicle, paused for a second to stare at the empty chair and dark computer monitor, then continued on to his own workstation. He was pretty sure his friend was dead, but the not knowing kept everything in limbo. That made it harder in some ways but easier in others, for while he remained in a constant state of tension, waiting for confirmation, he was at least spared the pain of grieving. Because as long as he didn't know for certain, his emotions were reined in—and that was exactly what he needed right now.

The important thing was to remain focused.

It was getting harder, though. The police had found blood all over Wilson's house, and though investigators speculated that the two distinct types belonged not to him but to his wife and daughter, nothing could be proved and theories abounded. Many had a murderous Wilson at the center, though Brian gave absolutely no credence to any of those.

In his mind, a psychotic millionaire was behind it all, probably someone Wilson had covered for the paper, probably someone he'd known.

The man had slaughtered Wilson's family.

And killed him as well.

But Brian didn't know that, and right now he didn't *want* to know.

He sat down at his desk, sorting through the notes and messages that had accumulated since yesterday. Earlier in the week, he had scanned and sent copies of both new letters to Dr. LaMunyon—the one his mom had been sent and the one he'd found in the house—but he had not yet heard back from the linguistics professor. He was about to call UCLA and see what was going on when the phone on his desk rang. According to the blinking light on the console, it was from the managing editor, and he quickly picked up. "Hello. Brian Howells. Newsroom," he said, answering in the officially sanctioned manner that he was supposed to use all the time but didn't.

James Bieber—Jimmy—asked him to come directly to his office, and Brian picked up a notebook and pen and hurried immediately to the other side of the newsroom. He knocked on the wall next to the open office door.

"Come in," Jimmy said brusquely. He motioned for Brian to sit down in the chair opposite his and tossed a paper-clipped sheaf of papers across the desk.

Brian picked it up.

"I assume you've heard about Lew Haskell up in the Bay Area. Another rich lunatic. Not violent so far as we know, but he'd been abusing his wife and son, was arrested for human trafficking among other offenses. It's all there. Public records, wire service story, local articles." Jimmy leaned forward. "I know you and St. John were sniffing around this story—"

Brian looked up in surprise, but Jimmy waved him away.

"Nothing stays secret in this building. And I think you're on the right track. No one's connecting these, but I want us to. We're the ones who are going to figure out the jigsaw; we're going to draw the map for everyone else. But until then, we need to keep up with everything that's going on. To that end, I want us to have the best, most thorough, most well-written coverage of each and every incident. So we need to talk to that woman. The one who was dating him, the one who turned him in."

Brian cleared his throat. "I'm not really assigned to that."

"You are now."

"But—"

"It's your story," the editor said. "Go with it."

Brian nodded. He couldn't believe his luck. But in the world of journalism, fortunes changed overnight. One mistake, and you were Dan Rather, out on your ass. One big break, and you were Bob Woodward, perpetual icon. He was sure he was making enemies in the newsroom over this. He wasn't exactly a rookie, but he was new to the *Times*, and some of the reporters who'd been here longer probably resented his quick rise through the ranks. Brian knew that *he* would, were the shoe on the other foot.

He only wished that Wilson were here, too. It was his story as much as Brian's.

But he was dead.

Probably.

Had he been killed because he was investigating these murders?

It seemed likely, and Brian found himself wondering if he was targeted, too. And by whom. And why.

It was the scope of it all that seemed so daunting. All of those rich men? Over all those years? And his dad as well? There was no common thread, no dots he could connect. And yet it was epic, quite possibly the biggest, most important story he would ever work on in his life.

And he didn't know what the hell it was.

Jimmy explained in detail exactly what kind of coverage he expected, and spelled out the travel logistics. Airline tickets and lodging costs had already been preapproved, and once he made contact with the woman—Carrie

Daniels—and set up a meeting, all he had to do was make reservations, grab a photographer from the pool and be at LAX by the proper time.

Everything went smoothly, and by eleven Brian was on his way to San Francisco, photographer in tow, feeling like the Hollywood conception of a reporter. Warren Beatty in *The Parallax View*. Robert Walden on *Lou Grant*. Hell, Michael Keaton in *The Paper*. It was a good feeling, a powerful feeling, and for a brief period of time it actually distracted him from the impossible immensity of his task.

Carrie Daniels had agreed to meet him at a coffeehouse downtown at one o'clock, and since he arrived over a half hour early and hadn't eaten anything all morning save a small bag of peanuts on the plane, he decided to order lunch. Merritt, the photographer, was a good guy, laid-back, easy to hang with, and Brian charged his lunch to the account as well. Both of them sat outside in the brisk cool air, eating gourmet sandwiches, drinking lattes, laughing at the thought of their colleagues sitting in the windowless *Times* newsroom or scurrying around hot, smoggy Los Angeles in search of stories.

"Thank you for picking me," Merritt said. "I thought I'd be spending the day taking photos of angry commuters for an article on the bus strike."

"I was supposed to be *writing* that bus strike article." Brian grinned. "Instead, we both got a free trip to San Fran. There is a God."

"Not only that. If I can get into Haskell's farm or whatever it is and get some shots of those milking booths, that's a career maker."

Carrie arrived shortly after. She seemed nervous, and after introductions were made, Merritt excused himself and said he had some street shots to take. "Call me on my cell when you're ready," he told Brian. "I'll be out and about, building up my portfolio."

Brian nodded. Not only was Merritt a good photographer, but he knew how to read a situation. Indeed, after he'd gone, Carrie seemed to visibly relax.

If, in the future, he had his choice of photographers, Brian decided, Merritt was going to be his go-to guy.

She ordered an iced tea, and they started off with small talk. He broke the ice, casually discussing how lucky he was to have been chosen for this assignment, how coming to San Francisco made him feel like a school kid on a field trip. She talked a bit about her job, he described how he'd only recently been hired at the *Times,* and when he felt that the pump had been primed enough, he took out his notebook and turned on his tape recorder. "I guess we should get started," he said.

Carrie nodded. "All right."

"So tell me what happened," Brian began. "In your own words. Start with how you met Lew Haskell and how you came to be invited to his house."

She'd probably told this story to the police ad nauseam, but that may have helped her hone her account, because the description she gave Brian was thorough, complete and left almost nothing out. On the phone, he had explained to her that he was doing a news article and possibly a feature story on Lew Haskell and would use her for background information. A lot of subjects got scared off when they found out they would be quoted publicly, which was why his initial approach had been so soft, but Carrie exhibited no such qualms, and when he broached the idea of using her as a primary source, since she was the one who had discovered what was going on at Haskell's estate, she was fine with it.

Indeed, her descriptions seemed almost *too* personal as she recounted her feelings and reactions while Haskell had led her on a tour of the property.

It was a hard story to believe, but even if there hadn't been so much supporting evidence, even if Carrie had been unable to prove that what she'd seen was real, Brian would have bought it. Too many other incidents had led him here. And Carrie was an extremely credible witness. He was deeply impressed by the way she not only observed everything around her as it occurred but remembered the tiniest details. "You would've made a great reporter," he said.

"If I had the ability to write." She tried to smile but was obviously still thinking about the captive women she had found in the barn.

"So what happened after the police came?" he asked gently.

She shrugged. "I showed them the . . . pens. They took Lew into custody, then searched the rest of the property. That's when they found his wife and son being held prisoner in the house. I didn't see it at the time—I was interviewed and then taken home—but I saw the photos afterward." She shook her head. "It was horrifying."

"I can imagine."

Carrie looked at him. "You said on the phone that you thought this was connected to those other millionaires who went crazy."

"Well . . ." he hemmed.

"I do, too. Can I talk to you off the record?"

"Of course."

She looked at him skeptically.

He turned off his tape recorder and held up his hands in a gesture of surrender. "I realize that you have no reason to believe me. You don't know me from Adam, and I could be a complete slimeball who's lying through his teeth."

She laughed.

"But I'm not. And I swear, if you tell me something off the record, it stays off the record."

She looked into his eyes for a moment, as though to gauge his trustworthiness, then nodded. "This may be something you know about already. I have no idea. But I talked to an acquaintance of mine—a source, I guess you'd say—who's a policeman, and he told me something that I haven't seen in any of the papers, that they're keeping quiet." She paused.

"What is it?"

"Off the record, right?"

"Of course."

"Tom Lowry, Bill Devine, Stephen Stewart, Wesley Fields and even Lew are all . . . physically deformed."

Excitement rose within him, the excitement of a reporter on the verge of cracking a story, and an ambitious part of him wished that he had not agreed to keep this off the record, although as soon as he thought of his father, that impulse fled instantly. "How?" he asked.

"This is going to sound crazy, I know. But they all seem to have animal characteristics. Fur, horns, tails, snakeskin."

"I saw Stephen Stewart," Brian said. "I was the one who found him. He was naked at the time. And you're right. He *was* like that. There was something wrong with him. But he didn't remind me of an animal. It was more like . . ." If she could be honest, he could be honest. "A monster."

"Lew's son is even worse than he is. More . . . devolved, I guess. He has another son as well, an illegitimate one named Juan Olivera, one of my cases. Juan has the face of a llama. And I have reason to believe that Haskell has other illegitimate children here in the Bay Area who also have the faces of animals—or *had*. At least one of them's dead.

"Although," she mused, "since they all have the faces of *different* animals, maybe Lew isn't the father of all of them. Maybe there are other men like this living around here."

"So it's like whatever's causing this problem intensifies with the children," Brian said. "Or maybe it skips generations. Or it's just the luck of the DNA draw."

"I don't know." Carrie leaned forward over the table. "But Social Services maintains records of children with birth defects. I think we can use that to track them down."

"Them?" Brian said.

"The fathers. Whoever—whatever—they may be."

Whatever.

It felt reassuring to hear that word. Validation of his own thoughts by someone with whom he had no connection lent a legitimacy to his half-baked ideas and theories and gave him more confidence that he was on the right track. Taking a deep breath, he told her everything, explaining about his dad's decades-old disappearance and his mysterious letters written in the same language as the scrawled messages found at the murder sites; the killing of Reverend Charles; Bill Devine's creepy voice mail message; the videotape and the resurrected bird; Wilson's strange disappearance. Halfway through, Merritt called from down the street. He was getting restless and wanted to know how things were going, if he could come back.

"Almost done," Brian promised. "Give me another ten."

Carrie was looking at him as he clicked off the cell phone.

"What?" he asked. "What are you thinking?"

She shook her head, as though trying to clear it. "I never thought when I agreed to this interview that I'd be drawn into such a vast . . . conspiracy isn't the right word, but you know what I mean. I didn't think this was so *big*."

"Do you now?"

"Of course."

"Good."

"So what do we do next?" she asked.

Brian thought of what Wilson had said: *Follow the money.* If they could only keep tabs on all of the nation's richest men, perhaps they could prevent further murders and atrocities from being committed. Although that still wouldn't bring them any closer to understanding what these people were or why these things were happening.

"Do you have to go back to work?" he asked.

She smiled wryly. "It's been suggested that I take some time off and relax after all I've been through."

"Take the time off," Brian said. "And help me."

"Help you do what?"

"Find out what's going on."

"Where do we start?" she said.

Carrie didn't trust her car, so they took Brian's rental and drove to Haskell's compound in Marin. The place was spectacular, although the disconnect between the beauty of the location and the horror that had occurred there was profound.

Merritt was not allowed past the gates with the three cameras strung around his neck, but a combination of fast talking, Brian's press pass, and Carrie's role in apprehending Haskell got the two of them on the grounds. "You can't go in any of the buildings," warned the officer guarding the gate. "I'm doing this as a favor, so you'd better follow the rules. We have men stationed at the house, the garage and all peripheral buildings. You won't be able to get in. But I'll give you a half hour on the property."

"Thank you," Carrie said.

"Write a good story," the officer told Brian. "We have more than enough to put this guy away, but some public outrage wouldn't hurt.

"You can go, too," he said to Merritt. "But you'll have to lose the cameras. Policy."

"That's okay," the photographer said. "I'll wait."

Brian and Carrie walked up the drive, and she showed him where the limo had parked, then took him exactly where Haskell had taken her.

He tried to keep the tone casual, though his questions were anything but. "Why do you think Haskell picked you? Or any of those other women? Rosita?"

"Rosalia."

"Do you think he *sensed* something about you? Were you in the right place at the right time, or was there something specific that he was looking for and found in you?"

"I don't know," she admitted.

Brian glanced around at the overgrown vegetation. "This always happens, too. It's like a side effect. Wherever these guys live, it's always a jungle. The plants go crazy around them. Even inside plants." He took a deep breath. "Even my mom's yard."

Carrie had told him the story already, but it was different being here, actually seeing where everything was, the physical layout of the place, and she described again how she had first seen the barn from far away, then took him up the same path she had walked with Haskell.

Despite what they'd been told, there was no guard in front of the barn—maybe he'd gone for a bathroom break—and they took advantage of the opportunity to duck under the yellow tape and walk through the open doors into the building. Carrie tensed up the second they passed through the threshold, and though it was empty, he too felt a sense of dread as they stood at the edge of the giant room, as he saw all of the small wooden pens and the huge central milking machine with its hoses hanging down like the tentacles of a dead octopus.

He wished Merritt could have come in with them and taken photographs. This was one of those a-picture-is-worth-a-thousand-words situations, and he knew that nothing he could write would have the impact of a good shot of those empty mazelike pens in this vast over-sized room.

There was a sudden noise behind them, and both Brian and Carrie whirled around, startled.

"Hey," Merritt said, grinning.

Brian looked at him in astonishment. "How did you get in here?"

"It's amazing what a lecture on first amendment rights and a ten-dollar bill will get you."

"Ten dollars?" Carrie said.

"I guess you should pay your cops better up here."

She shook her head. "I don't believe it."

"You have good instincts." Merritt grinned. "I fol-lowed the edge of the property and hopped a fence. The things we do for art." He held one of the cameras to his eye and started focusing. "I'd better do this fast." There was a series of quick-fire clicks and an accompanying whirring. "Wow," he said. "This is hard to believe."

"You should've seen it when the women were here."

"How many altogether?"

"I think they counted fifty-two."

"Jesus," Merritt breathed.

Brian's cell phone rang, its jaunty little tune com-pletely at odds with the grimness of the scene before them. He looked at the number.

It was the paper.

Jimmy.

He was about to answer when a harsh authoritarian voice shouted, "Hey! What are you doing in there?"

All three of them turned to see a uniformed policeman striding through the doorway toward them.

"You are not authorized to enter the structure!" the officer stated.

"I'm out of here," Merritt said. "Distract him. I have to protect the stash." He patted his cameras.

"Got it," Brian told him. He started toward the cop, hands raised like a surrendering criminal. "Sorry, Officer!" he called. "My name's Brian Howells. I'm from the *Los Angeles Times*. This is Carrie Daniels. She's the one who made the 911 call."

"I just wanted to show him what happened where," Carrie said right next to him. "I didn't know this area was restricted."

"Don't give me that. The structure's cordoned off. You had to duck under the tape to get in."

Merritt ducked under the tape and got out.

"Hey! Where's he going?"

The photographer was around the corner and gone.

"I don't know," Brian lied. "He's not with us."

The policeman grabbed his arm roughly. "You're coming with me."

"You sure you want to do this?" Brian said. "I have your department's permission to be here, and I'm working on an article for the largest newspaper in the western half of the United States." He squinted at the man's badge. "Officer Neth."

The cop let him go. "Okay. But you're coming with me to the gate. We need to get this straightened out."

After a discussion that turned into an argument, he and Carrie were kicked out. They picked up Merritt down the road apiece. He was walking away from Haskell's estate, and he grinned when he saw them, sticking out a hitchhiking thumb.

"Oh! I almost forgot," Brian said. He pulled out his cell phone and accessed his voice mail while the photographer got into the car.

Jimmy's message was simple, direct and to the point.

"Kirk Stewart came out of his coma. He's talking."

Twenty-two

1849

Marshall hadn't told Sutter about the ghost camp in the canyon. He hadn't told anyone, though he still had nightmares about the dead woman and her monster baby. Doug Lilley had drifted away somewhere, no one seemed to know where, and that was probably for the best. With him around as a reminder, Marshall would have been constantly thinking about what he'd seen, would have quite likely gone back to the canyon and drunkenly spilled the beans to someone, causing a mini-rush. Whatever happened as a result of the cursed gold would be on his head.

Cursed gold?

Yes. That's what he believed.

Sutter was still making a living off the fort and everything that had stood him in good stead all these years, but it killed him that the parade of easy wealth was passing him by, that every Johnny-come-lately and his brother could dip a pan in the water and end up rich while he remained mired in boring traditional mercantilism. Marshall had been angry at that as well. He was the one who had *discovered* the damn gold! He was the one who'd known about it in advance! But now he was glad that he'd never struck it rich. There was a price to pay for that gold, and though such a thought might be mumbled about in a bar after many, many drinks or whispered late at night around a wilderness campfire, it was not something that was ever mentioned by sober, civilized people.

The mill still wasn't finished. Everyone wanted to work for himself in the gold fields rather than have a normal job, so it was hard to hire these days. Marshall doubted the project would ever be completed, though that was not an opinion he shared with Sutter.

Right now, Sutter was trying to scout a spot for a new general store, and Marshall and a few old hands from the fort were coming along to give their opinions on how difficult it would be to actually construct the store as well as keep it stocked. It was Sutter's contention that a wilderness store stocked with dried foodstuffs and mining supplies would make a fortune because the men would be willing to pay more if they didn't have to go all the way to a town. It was a good idea, Marshall thought, and he hoped for his friend's sake that the store was a success. The man deserved to have some good luck thrown his way. Hell, they all did.

Right now, they were exploring a deer path alongside a tributary of the Bear River. New camps had been popping up in this section of the Sierras for the past few months, and if Sutter could find a centralized location that was easily accessible to all, he stood to inherit the lion's share of the miners' business. Marshall appraised the ease of travel along this route, decided that if they could hire some Indians, the path might be widened enough for oxcart use.

They made camp for the evening in a stand of trees close enough to the water that they could hear the burble of the creek but far enough that they wouldn't end up in the soup should they get up in the middle of the night to take a piss. Marshall laid out his bedroll between Sutter's and Matthew Taylor's. Time was when he would've been out on his own, as far away from the other men as possible. Nothing ruined a good night in the wilderness like the snoring, farting and sleep talking of a bunch of filthy drunken men who'd been on the trail since dawn.

But these days, as far as he was concerned, there was no such thing as a *good* night in the wilderness.

Pike.

Given his druthers, Marshall would spend every night for the rest of his life in a house or a cabin, preferably in a town. His days of enjoying the solitude of open country were over.

That night, Sutter and the other men stayed up drinking and lying about their hunting prowess and female conquests. Marshall tried to go to sleep early, feigning tiredness, hoping to doze off while the others were still up and about, but he ended up tossing and turning, and his eyes were still wide open when Sutter, the last of the others to fall asleep, finally nodded off for good.

Sutter had been acting odd the past few days. Ostensibly, he'd been working on the plans for this store, even going so far as to consider expanding it into a new fort, but despite his stated intentions and the seriousness of this scouting expedition, he'd seemed distracted a lot of the time. And he'd brought along some heavy extra equipment—like a bear trap—that served no useful purpose and made Marshall wonder if there wasn't some other unspoken reason for this trip.

He didn't like the bear trap.

Marshall finally dozed, but his sleep was light and fitful, a succession of dreams that, unfortunately, he remembered each time he awoke. In one, hordes of monster babies like the one in the canyon were swarming over a hill made out of garbage and shit. In another, a creature with the arms of an ape, the skin of a lizard and the tail of a devil was raping the corpse of Emily Smith, which lay sprawled over a mossy log. Emily's corpse was smiling.

When he finally woke up in the morning for good, it was not to the crow of a rooster or the smell of coffee, but to the wild cries of John Sutter, who was absent from his sleeping spot and off somewhere in the woods. The sun had not yet arisen, dawn was only a faint lightening of the sky above the hills to the east, and Marshall saw that the rest of their party had been jolted awake as well.

"What the hell?" muttered Matthew.

Goose, Jameson and Big Reese were putting on boots and grabbing rifles as quickly as their groggy minds and unwilling bodies allowed.

"Hurry up!" Sutter yelled. "I need help *now!*"

The five of them ran toward the sound of his voice, Marshall in the lead. They found Sutter several yards from camp, next to the spot where they'd made their shit hole and dumped the bones from their meal in order to keep animals away.

Only this wasn't an animal that Sutter had caught in his bear trap.

Marshall felt his heart lurch up to his throat when he saw the creature whose leg was clamped in the iron jaws. It wasn't human, whatever it was. *Monster* was the first thought that came to him, and he recalled the baby and the dead woman, his dreams of the night before. Its body had two arms and two legs, but there the resemblance to a person ended. For it was well over eight feet tall, and its skin was slimy and shiny, like that of a fish or a worm. Around the middle was a band of thick fur that resembled a belt. On the shoulders were two wicked-looking horns, and protruding from the right side underneath the armpits was what looked like a double row of rose thorns. Its head was too small for its body and was topped by several strands of bloodred hair, each as thick as a finger. Two beady eyes peered out from under a bulging brow, and in place of the nose was a leathery nub bisected by a single slit. The mouth, wide open, was filled with several rows of sharp, tiny teeth.

There was something vaguely arousing about the beast, however, and though he was sickened by this thought, Marshall couldn't help but be stirred by the sight of the naked creature. It was female, that much was clear. Oversized pudenda spread out pink between the hairless thighs, and *three* breasts were aligned across the broad chest, each made from that slimy skin but with large womanly nipples that stuck straight out.

They consorted, Doug Lilley had said, and for the first time, Marshall could understand how such a thing might occur. He tried to imagine what *he* would do if he came across a human mating with such a creature, and he understood now why Sutter had banished all offenders from the fort.

Except it was only the women he'd banished, wasn't it? The ones who had coupled with the male versions of this monster. If any men had been caught fornicating with creatures like this, they had not been cast out, and Marshall thought of how Sutter had brought his bear trap on this trip and wondered what exactly had been the man's ultimate goal.

"Come on!" Sutter cried, holding on to a jerking arm. "I need help!"

The creature was howling like a dying dog, although it had been silent only seconds before. It thrashed about crazily, threatening to rip its leg off at the ankle. In the predawn light, the blood dripping down the leg and from the jaws of the trap looked thin and watery. Marshall, Matthew and Big Reese helped Sutter grab the thing's arms, holding tight, while Goose ran back for some rope.

The skin felt spongy and rough at the same time, not nearly as slick and slimy as it looked.

The creature continued to howl.

"Maybe it's calling for help," Big Reese said. "Maybe it's calling its friends."

"Keep an eye out!" Sutter ordered Jameson.

Goose returned with the rope, and while Marshall and the others continued to hold its arms, he and Jameson hog-tied it. They pushed it over, onto the ground, then jumped back. It had stopped howling but was rolling over, back and forth, the chains of the trap rattling. Marshall found himself staring at the alternating views of buttocks and vagina.

"So what now?" Jameson asked.

"We'll keep it," Sutter said, wiping the sweat from his red face with a dirty kerchief.

"And do what with it?" Marshall asked. The only possible use he could see for such a creature would be to sell it to a circus.

"I don't know yet," Sutter admitted.

"These things been killing miners and animals," Matthew said. "Hell, they's even taken some of our women, the men ones have. I say we hang it."

"Maybe we could use it to attract others," Big Reese opined. "Like bait. Maybe we could clear the whole area of 'em!"

Marshall pulled Sutter off to the side while the others debated. "You might be able to fool them, but you can't fool me. You didn't just happen to catch one of those things. You were looking for one. That's the whole reason we're out here, isn't it?"

Sutter looked at him, saying nothing.

"I've known you for a while now, John. I know how you think. I know how you act."

"Yes!" he hissed. "I wanted to trap one!"

"What the hell for?"

Sutter turned away, didn't answer, but as he walked back toward the other men, Marshall saw him surreptitiously press down on the lap of his pants.

Bringing the creature back to the fort had been hard. They'd waited it out, knowing it would eventually pass out or fall asleep, and when it did they tied it up even tighter to make sure it could not escape, put a gag over its mouth, and pried the trap off its ankle.

They carried it on a pole, like a dead deer, taking turns as they retraced their route, always on the alert for anything out of the ordinary, aware that at any moment other creatures might emerge from a canyon or copse in an effort to save their companion and slaughter all the humans. It was a long tension-filled journey, and the nights they spent with the creature were the worst Marshall had ever experienced. They took turns guarding it, so that they could all get a little sleep, but the truth was that none of them were relaxed enough to slumber. Marshall took first shift each evening, and as he sat watching the monster his blood ran cold.

And hot.

For just as every time he looked into its beady eyes he saw an evil alien unfathomability, each time his gaze moved lower on the creature's body, he felt an unwelcome stirring in his loins. Was he imagining things or did the monster try to raise its hips higher when he looked at it? Was there an attempt to part those bound legs and display its sex?

They hadn't fed the thing, had been afraid to even remove the gag. Not that they knew what it ate anyway.

People?

But it hadn't seemed to grow any weaker or lighter, it hadn't had to excrete waste and from what he could tell it didn't exhibit any signs of hunger. He thought of that half-demon baby in the canyon that had been left there to starve yet hadn't starved.

Maybe they lived on air or sunshine. Like plants.

Its eyes glittered in the light of the campfire, as dark as the night, and while Marshall watched it, it watched him. There was a calculating shrewdness in its gaze that frightened him, and he knew that deep within its brain it was planning, plotting. If it had been up to him, they would have killed the creature and burned its body.

It was no wonder that even when his shift was over, he couldn't fall asleep.

By the time they reached the fort, all of them were irritable, exhausted and practically at each other's throats. Sutter and Jameson had ridden ahead the day before in order to set up a location where the captive creature could be housed, and obviously the word had spread. A large crowd came out to greet them, including the squaw Matthew had married, but they were quiet when they actually saw the monster, shocked into silence by the site of this strange being tied to a pole like an ordinary hunting prize. Matthew's wife said some words in her language that sounded like a prayer but that none of them understood before running quickly back into the fort, but the rest of them merely stepped aside in order to make a wider berth for the travelers' passage.

Sutter, Jameson and some of the other men had cleaned out an unused storage room and equipped the windowless chamber with an extra padlock for the door as well as leg irons and chains bolted to the heaviest beams in the wall. They would have used the brig, but Teagarden James was already locked up there, and Sutter wasn't sure how long a space would be needed for the creature. He still had not decided what to do with it.

Or so he claimed.

Marshall was not sure he believed that.

He wasn't actually involved in the incarceration of the

beast. Once they returned to the fort, Sutter had others take over. It was just as well. He was tired, as were the rest of the men who'd accompanied Sutter on his expedition. It was Marshall's shift, he'd been one of those carrying the pole on the last leg of the journey, and he gratefully handed over his burden to Graham Arthur, who at least looked as though he'd had a decent night's sleep within the past week.

He watched the men carry the bound and gagged creature across the open courtyard, the other residents and visitors to the fort following at a safe distance.

Is this one of the demons the Indians are so afraid of? he wondered. Judging by the reaction of Matthew's wife, the answer was yes, but Marshall found it hard to ascribe to this captured beast the sorts of powers that demons were supposed to have.

He was still afraid of it, though, wasn't he?

Yes, he had to admit, he was.

He spent the next day in bed. He was more than just tired. He was exhausted. But he still needed a trigger to fall asleep, and he pulled out an old bottle of whiskey from the cubby where he'd hidden it and polished it off in a few eye-watering minutes. That put him out, and he slept straight through for the next twenty hours or so, his sleep undisturbed by dreams.

When he awoke, it was night and his cabin was dark, the great swaths of stars in the moonless sky visible through his window failing to provide even a smidgen of usable light. He sat up coughing, his head pounding with each hack, his mouth tasting like dog shit. He reached around on the floor for his bottle and held it upside down over his open mouth, a few leftover drops falling onto his tongue. Rather than getting rid of the taste, they intensified it, and he stood unsteadily and made his way to the table, where he fumbled with the matches and lit his lantern. There was a half-eaten box of crackers next to the lantern, and he grabbed a few and ate them, grateful for the salty flavor that spread through his mouth.

It must have been very late at night or very early in the morning because on the other side of the garden, the fort was nearly silent.

Nearly.

Marshall moved closer to the window and stood there. Watching. Listening. There were no lights or signs of movement, but from this spot he could hear the creature and the noise it made. The mewling. He thought of Pike, and an icy chill slid down his back and into his arms.

He could have gone back to bed and waited for morning, but he had never been a coward and had seen too much since leaving Missouri to be scared away by anything. Picking up his lantern, he walked out of the cabin and over to the fort, where Sutter, Matthew, Big Reese and Whit Fields were standing near the livery.

"Good," Sutter said. "You're up."

"Yeah," Marshall grunted.

A lot of them were up, and the courtyard continued to fill with men as more and more of them were awakened by that mewling and felt compelled to investigate. The cries seemed to grow louder and softer in a recognizable rhythm.

"What do you think's going on?" Marshall asked. "You think it's trying to call for help?"

"I think it's in heat," Sutter said. "Come with me." He led the way across the courtyard to the storage room where it was being held. Drawing forth a ring of keys, he unfastened both padlocks and pulled open the heavy door. With nearly all of the men carrying lanterns, the dark room was clearly illuminated, their jostling throwing strange jittery shadows on the walls and ceiling.

Marshall was next to Sutter, in the lead, and he saw that the monster was chained to the rear wall but not like a prisoner. Instead, the captain had had his men shackle the creature so that it was on its back, arms and legs spread out.

The thing looked at them and made that terrible mewling noise, but now it sounded . . . enticing.

Marshall's gaze went from its face to its breasts to its oversized sex.

"Let's fuck it," Sutter said, and there was a gleam in his eye that Marshall didn't like.

"No," he said, grimacing, but he wasn't nearly as offended as he let on, and a voice inside was saying, *Yes, yes.*

Matthew was already pulling down his pants and pushing past them, his penis erect and ready. "Hell, they's taken our women. We might's well take theirs."

The men were lining up. The mood had changed, and whatever nervousness and fear had drawn them out from their beds and into the courtyard had shifted and hardened into a greedy and lustful sense of entitlement. Matthew was already on top of the creature, and both he and it were moaning as their intertwined bodies moved up and down. He finished, then pulled out, pushing himself off and staggering backward. "Oh my God," he breathed. "I ain't never felt nuthin' like that before. Jesus Christ. No wonder . . ." He shook his head numbly.

Grinning, excited, Sutter stepped up to have his turn, but the night air was shattered by a scream of pain and fear that came from somewhere outside and all of the men swung awkwardly around, their lanterns crashing into each other.

Matthew had just finished pulling up his pants, and he turned white, the color draining from his face. "Tha's Nina!" He shoved his way through the crowd like a wild man, pushing everyone aside. Marshall and the others butted heads and elbowed ribs as they tried to scrabble their way out into the open air.

The fort had been breached.

They saw it instantly. Monsters were throwing themselves against doors, climbing stairs, stalking horses. It had been so long since Indians had been considered a threat that the fort had not been entirely closed, none of the lookout posts had been manned, and Marshall cursed the complacency that had allowed them to become so lax—although he knew that the guilt and remorse Sutter was feeling at this moment completely dwarfed his own.

The captain was shouting orders, sounding the alarm, calling on everyone who was still in their quarters to come out with weapons and defend the fort.

Marshall and Jameson sprinted together toward the armory along with a host of other men who weren't at the moment armed. The monsters were all around, in every direction. He counted at least five of them, but it felt as though there were a lot more. They didn't all look the same. Some were hairier than others, some slimier, some with horns and tails, others with body parts that had no names. But they were of the same ilk—

demon

—and he had no doubt that it was the creature's mewling cries that had called her kind to the fort.

The armory was locked, but Sutter was right behind them with the key, and he opened the heavy door, all of them rushing in at once, grabbing rifles, pistols, swords, whatever they could lay their hands on. Marshall ended up with a rifle, and somebody shoved some shells into his hand as he made his way back outside. Looking around, assessing the situation, he saw now where the initial screams had come from.

It was Matthew's wife. She was bent over a bench on

the far side of the fort, and one of the monsters was behind her, grunting with pleasure as it plunged its enormous organ deep inside. She had stopped screaming by now, and blood erupted from between her slack open lips in time to the rhythmic thrusts.

Matthew was right there. He always had a pistol at his side, day or night, and he slapped leather so fast that Marshall could hardly see it, his hand coming up and pointing the weapon at the monster in a single move.

He shot it.

What spewed from the bullet hole was not blood but something black and thinner, like dirty water.

Then the others were shooting, the best among them staking out positions that allowed them maximum coverage, and the creatures started to fall. One with horns and a forked tail tumbled from a turret, its body riddled with bullet holes. Another, loping across the open center of the fort, was thrown backward by the force of the blasts aimed at its chest.

Marshall returned to the storage room, poking his head in the doorway. The men were gone, but the shackled creature grinned at him and cackled, its laugh an eerie hiss that seemed low and quiet but somehow carried above the clamorous chaos outside. He went inside the room and in the light of a left-behind lantern saw satisfaction in those beady, calculating eyes, derision in the upturned corners of that cackling toothy mouth. Before Sutter returned to tell him he couldn't do it, Marshall raised his rifle and shot the monster full in the face. That watery black liquid sprayed out from the shattered mass of flesh and skull, soaking the wall and floor, and after a few quick convulsions, the creature lay still.

Marshall stepped outside. As quickly as it had started, it was all over. There was still a lot of shouting and screaming going on—Sutter was ordering all lookouts manned to make sure they weren't still under attack—

but amid the clamor and commotion it was clear that the monsters had all been killed. Their freakish bodies lay in twisted heaps all about the fort, and a quick count told Marshall that his initial estimate had been right. There were only five of them. Why had it seemed as though there were many more?

Sutter explained something to Goose, then hurried over to the storage room. Marshall stepped aside to let him pass. The captain emerged a moment later with a stunned, devastated look on his face.

"So they can be killed," Marshall said to him.

Sutter looked at him, nodded.

"That's good to know."

Twenty-three

Kirk woke up again, his mouth so dry that he felt like gagging, but before he could even croak out a request for water, someone was carefully putting a straw to his lips. He drew in the cool, refreshing liquid, feeling it smooth over the harsh roughness of his throat. Gradually, his vision adjusted to the brightness of the hospital room and he made out the machines and monitors, the utilitarian furnishings and pastel wall decorations.

Waylon, Tina and Brad were there, Tina and Brad seated on the small square love seat, Waylon perched uncomfortably in an atrociously designed chair. Earlier, Monica, April, Orlando and Sal had been sitting by his bedside, but he hadn't wanted to talk to them and so had pretended to be asleep, waiting them out, knowing that with their short attention spans he was certain to outlast them. He had. This time, though, he smiled at his friends and used the push button control at his fingertips to raise the back of the bed as far as he could. He was not allowed to move to a sitting position, but he was able to better see the room in front of him.

There were cards and flowers, get-well gifts galore on the dresser beneath the wall-mounted television. In front of everything, standing astride a tiny sleigh, was a toy figure that had obviously been given to him by Waylon, a little man in blue snow clothes with a curly brownish red beard. Kirk grinned. "Poontang Cornelius!"

Waylon nodded. "Crouton Pornelius himself."

It was an old private joke: purposely getting the *Rudolph* character's name wrong and seeing who would pick up on it. Both Tina and Brad did. "*Yukon* Cornelius," they corrected, almost in unison.

Waylon nodded, grinned at Kirk. "Good catch."

Kirk leaned against the pillow. It was nice to be back, though in truth he didn't feel as if he'd really been gone. In his mind, it had been only a few hours since his father had brought him home—where his mom had been tortured and his dad had tried to kill him. It had been weeks, though, and according to Waylon, his dad had been arrested several days ago in California, although Waylon didn't know if he was still there or if he'd been extradited back to New York.

Kirk knew he was flying on some serious painkillers. His body remembered the agony suffered at the hands of his father, and the casts and bandages testified that the injuries had been major, but at the moment there was only a light numbness that made every part of his body feel just like every other. He could blink his eyes and nod, speak and drink, move his fingers and toes, but all of that was at a remove, as though his brain were telling a robot what to do. He'd asked the nurse how long it would be before he was out and about, but she dodged the question and went to get a doctor, who told him he was looking at another week in the hospital and six months of physical therapy.

"It's going to be tough, too," the doctor had warned. "Recovery is not for the fainthearted."

Kirk looked at his friends, tried to smile. "So what's going on in the real world? Not *news*. Clubs and concerts. Feuds. Fights. Gossip. Fluff."

"Well . . ." Tina said. "Word is that Shelli's looking to get back with you. She misses you terribly and realizes she made a huge mistake and feels just *awful* about everything that's happened to you. Of course, the fact that you've been in the papers nonstop—on the front page no less—has absolutely *no* bearing on her sudden interest in rekindling an old flame."

They all laughed.

"Huston's insanely jealous over all the sympathy and publicity you're getting, so he's letting the world know that *he's* suffered, too. He's revealed to all and sundry that his late great father molested him as a child and that he's been hiding this dark secret all these years, struggling alone and in silence."

"Anal?" Waylon asked. "Did his dad get anal off him?"

"I hope so," Brad said, grinning.

It was starting to hurt when he laughed, and Kirk wondered if it was time to receive more medication.

A nurse stepped into the room. "Excuse me, Mr. Stewart. There's another reporter on the line. He's from the *Los Angeles Times*—"

"Oh shit," Waylon said.

"No reporters," Kirk told the nurse.

"I didn't think so." She smiled sweetly at him. "Thank you, Mr. Stewart."

Kirk sighed heavily. "That's like the tenth one who's called me. It's why the calls are going through the nurse's station now instead of coming directly here. Let them handle it. I'm supposed to be recuperating."

"It's going to get worse before it gets better," Tina warned. "You're the talk of the town."

"Hold out for Diane Sawyer," Waylon suggested. *"PrimeTime."*

The nurse returned moments later. "I'm sorry to bother you again, Mr. Stewart. But that reporter asked me to give this to you." She handed him a piece of paper.

"What is it?"

"Some questions. He said they're not for an article," she added quickly. "They're just questions you should be asking yourself. He said your situation is not unique, that this has happened to other people, and there are things you need to know."

Kirk nodded at her. "Thank you," he said. He scanned the list of questions she'd written down: *Do you or your father have any unusual physical characteristics? Do plants or flowers grow wildly around your house or the place where you live? Are you able to read the bloody symbols scrawled on the wall where you were attacked and your mother was killed?*

He glanced up from the paper, eyes suddenly misty at the thought of his mother. He had been repressing all memories of her, thinking about her only in bits and pieces and only from times of his childhood, not wanting to remember the last time he had seen her. That last question had jogged his memory, however, and though he hadn't recalled it until now, it seemed to him that there *had* been some sort of writing on the walls of the trashed apartment, except that in his mind they had resembled Egyptian hieroglyphics.

He looked at his friends. "Is there—" He swallowed hard, willing the tears not to rise. "Is there a picture of my parents' apartment . . . where this . . . happened?"

Tina frowned. Her voice was cautious. "Are you talking about crime-scene photos? Of you?"

And your mother? he knew she was thinking, but she didn't say it.

"No. There should be some sort of writing on the wall." He took a deep breath. "Maybe in blood. But they'll be symbols, like hieroglyphics or something. I need to see a picture of that."

"My laptop's in the car," Brad said. "I might be able to pull up something on there. Do you want me to go get it?"

"That'd be great," Kirk said tiredly. He smiled, closing his eyes for a second, but it must have been more than a second, because when he opened them, Brad, Tina and Waylon were all clustered around Brad's laptop.

"You're up," Brad said simply.

"Yeah." He glanced at the clock but couldn't remember what time it had been, so he didn't know how long he'd been out.

"I can't access anything here in the hospital—it screws up the machines—so I checked it out in the parking lot and saved what I found. Look at this." Brad brought the laptop up to the bed and adjusted the screen until it was visible from Kirk's angle.

He didn't know where it had come from, but it was a photo of his parents' living room wall. The Chagall that had been hanging there was gone, and in its place what looked like a child's scribbles mixed with words written in an alien alphabet had been inscribed in red. Bloody handprints that had to have been his father's were pressed onto the wall below and to the right of the strange symbols, probably where he had supported himself while writing.

Oddly enough, it was the placement of the handprints and the image of his dad leaning awkwardly against the wall in order to write that made him suddenly miss his father. The two of them had not been close, and his conception of the old man now and forever was as an inhuman monster, but he realized nonetheless that he would miss him.

Tears were threatening again, and Kirk looked at the photo, concentrating on those scribbled hieroglyphic symbols. He found that he *was* actually able to read that writing, though he had never seen it before in his life. He spoke the words aloud, saying them slowly, and everyone in the room stared at him in shock.

"What . . . was . . . *that*?" Tina asked.

"I was reading those words."

"You were screaming like a wild animal."

"I was—"

"Screaming," Brad said.

He looked at Waylon, who nodded. "I didn't know human vocal cords could make those sounds."

He would have thought his friends were joking were it not for the circumstances—and for the fact that the expressions on their faces looked genuinely horrified.

"Let me do it again," he said.

"Shoot," Waylon told him.

He spoke even slower this time, and in the middle of the sentence two nurses ran in with looks of concern on their faces. "What is it?" the first one demanded. "What's wrong?"

Tina was plugging her ears and grimacing.

Brad pulled away the laptop.

To Kirk, the words he'd spoken sounded perfectly natural. Not English, certainly, but another language, one not nearly as loud and cacophonous as the reaction of the others made it seem.

He didn't finish the sentence. "Nothing," he told the nurses. "Everything's okay."

"Then why were you screaming like that?"

"I . . . I don't know." He couldn't come up with a believable explanation.

"Maybe we need to adjust the dosages of your medications. I'll call Dr.—"

"I'm fine," he assured them. "Just . . . let me talk to my friends. If I need anything, I'll ring you."

"Are you sure you're—" the first nurse began.

"I'm fine."

The nurses retreated reluctantly. The second they were out of the room, Waylon closed the door behind them. "Check it out," he said, pointing.

The plants that well-wishers had left in his room had grown. No, *were* growing. Even as they watched, a rosebud opened into a flower and a fern frond uncoiled to its full extension.

"It happened when you screamed like that."

"When I read those words?"

"Yeah."

"Keep the door closed," he told Waylon. He remembered one of the words he'd said, and he tried to whisper it, but he could tell from the reaction on Tina's face that either he did not succeed or else the sounds required to make that word were so harsh and unpleasant that it made no difference at what volume he spoke. He watched the flowers, and before his eyes they became brighter in color, doubled in size, grew offshoots.

"Open the door," he told Waylon. He pressed the call button to summon a nurse. One came running.

"What is it, Mr. Stewart? Is everything all right?"

He nodded, trying to keep the quaver out of his voice. "Let me talk to that guy from the *Los Angeles Times.*"

Twenty-four

Merritt left for LA on an early-morning flight. He needed to print the photos he'd taken and also head back for a Rolling Stones concert that he wanted to shoot—and attend.

Seconds after he'd gone, Brian's cell phone rang.

It was Carrie, and he was about to ask when he should stop by and pick her up—their plan was to spend the day visiting with Haskell's illegitimate children, one of whom she knew and another who had been identified—but she didn't let him say anything other than "Hello."

"Turn on your TV! CNN," she ordered. "Quick!"

He did, dropping the phone as he fumbled with the remote, but the only thing on was a commercial for some sort of allergy drug.

He picked up the phone again. "It's a commercial," he said.

"Shit. You missed it."

"Missed what?"

He heard the frightened intake of her breath over the phone. "They did a story on something weird that happened here in Northern California. I don't know what made me think it was connected. I guess the fact that it involved plants and you said growing vegetation was one of the signs. But . . ."

"What was it?" Brian asked.

"An area of clear-cut forest sold off in the last decade
to timber companies. Fifty square miles of it." There
was that sucking in of breath again. "It's grown back.
All of it. Overnight."

Merritt shouldn't have left, Brian thought. He'd probably love to get a shot of this. But it wasn't exclusive,
was all over the TV news channels, and he'd probably
have more fun at the Stones concert anyway.

The chartered helicopter flew over acre after acre,
mile after mile of dense green forest. It was the same
thing he'd seen on CNN after that commercial break,
and on every news channel and major network since
then, but familiarity with the sight did not lessen its impact. If anything, seeing it in person brought home to
him how simultaneously real and flat-out impossible this
was. Of course, if he hadn't seen those "before" shots,
he never would have known how great the difference
was between yesterday and today.

The terrain below did not look like California. No,
this looked more like a South American rain forest. Instead of oak and ponderosa growing amid dried grasses
and hardy drought-resistant bushes, there were leafy um-
brellalike trees that formed an almost unbroken blanket
of bright green over the land. Here and there, through
the binoculars, equally lush and dense underbrush could
be seen in the few open spaces visible between the trees.
Far off, in each direction, small black specks that looked
like birds but were actually the helicopters of various
networks and news organizations flew through the sky.

The noise in the copter was deafening, the *chop-chop-
chop* of the rotors giving rhythm to the roar of the wind.

"Is there anyplace you can set us down?" Brian
shouted.

The pilot shook his head.

"I thought that was the point of a helicopter! I thought you could set it down anywhere!"

"I need a clear space!" the pilot called back.

Brian peered once more through the binoculars, searching for an open meadow or field, but every square inch of ground appeared to be covered with some sort of vegetation. Whether this was connected to the story he was pursuing or not, the event was truly astounding, and he was glad that he had come. Gut feeling told him that it *was* connected—he got the same creepy feeling from the overnight reforestation that he'd gotten from seeing Stephen Stewart leap around his mom's yard in the moonlight—but he could not for the life of him figure out how. The only idea he could come up with was that a millionaire or billionaire had bought up this land and was building a house or compound down there, with the regeneration of all the trees occurring as a freakish side effect. It was why he wanted to set down and look about the new forest, to see if he could find a sign that such a project was being built, but it didn't look as though that was about to happen.

Maybe he could rent a Jeep or something and drive in there.

And explore some fifty square miles? That was looking for a needle in a haystack. Who knew how long it would take?

Brian continued to scan the land below. He thought he saw movement for a quick second—a dark shadow skulking through the forest, visible briefly in the space between two trees—but then the helicopter had passed on and he lost it.

In his phone call, Kirk Stewart had told him that he had spoken the words scrawled on the wall of his parents' apartment and that had triggered plant growth in his room. He could read the words and say them in their original language, but for some reason his brain could not translate them to English, so it was impossible to know what they meant. It seemed clear, however, that they were magic words, part of some sort of spell, and Brian wondered if something like that wasn't involved here.

Magic words?

Spell?

How quickly a person's vocabulary and worldview changed when confronted with evidence of the unexplainable.

The helicopter flew back and forth over the regrown forest, from end to end. The boundaries were clear, straight, almost as though they were lines that had been drawn on a map, and the artificiality of that brought home to him even more the unnaturalness of it all.

The eeriness.

Carrie sat next to him, looking through her own pair of binoculars, not saying a word, although whether that was because she was frightened or because it was so hard to hear through all of the noise he could not say.

The pilot finally decided to land in a field on the edge of the trees, and the helicopter set down near a small duck pond. They waited until the blades had stopped turning, then stepped out onto solid ground. From this vantage point, the trees looked huge, almost the size of redwoods, and their trunks merged with the thick leafy bushes that grew between them to form a continuous wall of vegetation that seemed purposefully designed to keep out intruders. It was an intimidating sight and one that gave Brian pause.

"None of this was here yesterday," the pilot marveled.

"No," Carrie said.

"It's like being in a goddamn science fiction movie."

Brian took a step forward, looking for a path into the forest, not wanting to *touch* any of the trees or underbrush. He could blaze his own trail, push aside bushes and make his way into the woods, but something told him that those leaves and branches would be slimy and abhorrent to him. Listening carefully, he tried to determine whether any noises were coming from within the forest, but he could hear nothing, only a lack of sound so complete that it seemed deliberately imposed.

"Okay, boys and girls. Let's get out of here." The pilot's expression had darkened.

"Why?" Brian asked.

"What is it?" Carrie said.

He was striding back toward the copter. "Radiation. I should've thought of it sooner. I should never have landed."

"We don't know—" Brian began.

"We don't know anything. All we know is that this sprung up overnight. We don't know what caused it, we don't know what kind of energy it involves or whether it's giving off harmful radiation. Better safe than sorry. We're out of here."

He couldn't argue with that, and Brian followed Carrie and the pilot back to the helicopter where, moments after strapping themselves in, they took off.

They landed at the helipad back in San Francisco just after noon. They said good-bye to the pilot, who was planning to take an immediate shower and advised them to do the same, and walked out to the parking lot where Brian's rental car waited. Carrie had brought a disposable camera with her on the trip, and she'd used up all the film, though it was impossible to tell how well any of them would turn out. She was planning to take it to an instant photo shop and see what she had.

"I have to write an article," Brian said. "I've been wasting the paper's money gallivanting across California with nothing to show for it—not a good thing to do with all the budget cuts we're facing—so I need to talk to someone from the forest service, maybe a botanist from a prestigious university or something, and then write a piece and file it. Are you sure your cop friend can't get me an interview with Haskell?"

Carrie nodded. "I'm sure."

"Then do you think you can still arrange a meeting with those children and their mothers this afternoon?"

"Sure," she said. "But I don't know how much you'll learn from it."

"I don't either, but we might turn something up." He paused. "It also might not be such a bad idea if we both did take a shower. Just in case."

"I was thinking the same thing."

"Okay, then. Where and when do you want to meet?"

"I'll call you. I'll drop off the film, go home, shower, see what kind of meeting I can set up with Juan and Rosalia, and the other boy and his mom, then give you a call."

He nodded. "Sounds good."

"You know," Carrie said, "we're not any closer to figuring out what Lew and his kind actually are than we were when we started."

"I know," he admitted. "That's why I want to talk to those children and their mothers."

"I do have another idea," Carrie told him. "What are you doing tonight?"

"Whatever your idea is."

She laughed. "Okay," she said. "It's a long shot . . ."

"Long shots are my life," he told her.

"Write your article then. I'll call you."

Rosalia did not want to talk to any reporters, and Carrie didn't push her. As much as she wanted to help Brian and get to the bottom of everything that was going on, her first responsibility was to the Oliveras, and she understood completely Rosalia's feelings and promised that she wouldn't let anyone harass her.

Joy Sing was not her client, however, and since the woman had already signed a release allowing John Mees to photograph her son Austin and display the pictures publicly, Carrie had no qualms about trying to convince the woman to tell her story to Brian. She explained to Joy about her own involvement with Lew, and said that by coming forward they were making it easier for others who might be out there.

The big surprise was that Austin was a twin. Lew had fathered *two* boys by Joy, although the other child—and their sister—seemed perfectly normal. Only Austin had been born with . . . abnormalities.

Maybe that information could be helpful.

Following the directions Carrie had written down, Brian drove them in the rental car to Chinatown, where they paid to park in a lot and then walked to one of the newer apartment houses.

Like Rosalia, Joy was a single mother, but unlike Rosalia, she had a good job managing a boutique and lived in a loft in the trendy part of town. Her own widowed mother babysat the boys while she was at work during the day, and though it was clear that the old woman deeply disapproved of her daughter's lifestyle, it was also obvious that a sense of obligation made her willing to watch the children. It was at her apartment that they were all to meet, and when Carrie and Brian arrived, the door to the apartment was open and the two women were arguing loudly in Cantonese.

Joy looked just as she had in the photographs: young, pierced and tattooed, with a look of sadness etched permanently onto her otherwise pretty features. Austin was even more hypnotically grotesque than he had appeared in the photos. His possum face had a tactile reality that could not be conveyed through two-dimensional media. Carrie had never really seen Juan in direct light, not like this, and the sight of the boy standing before them made her realize on a nuts-and-bolts level just how fundamentally alien these children really were.

She cursed Lew and all of the other men like him for what they had inflicted on their children.

A thought suddenly occurred to her: What had *their* fathers been like?

Or their mothers?

Her gaze shifted to the other boy. *The normal one.* Maybe she'd been right in her initial speculation with Brian. Maybe whatever caused this affliction was random, or the result of a recessive gene that popped up only once every couple of generations.

Joy's mother had retreated to her bedroom and quietly closed the door. Joy bade them sit on the covered couch. She herself sat in a reclining chair, the two boys sitting on the chair's arms.

"How old are they?" Carrie asked.

"Six," she said.

Brian had not been able to take his eyes off Austin. "Can he talk?" Brian asked Joy. "I don't mean to offend you," he added quickly. "I just need to know, from a practical standpoint, whether . . ." He seemed to realize that he was only digging himself a deeper hole and let the thought trail off, unfinished.

"He doesn't have human vocal cords," Joy said, and Carrie could tell from the look on the woman's face how much it pained her to say those words.

"I can talk," the other boy said shyly.

Carrie smiled at him. "And what's your name?"

"Wyatt. Wyatt Sing."

"Nice to meet you, Wyatt," she told him.

Brian didn't seem to know where to begin. It was clear that he had a lot of questions he wanted to ask, but it was just as obvious that he didn't feel comfortable doing so in front of the kids. Carrie glanced around the apartment, saw a small rabbit-eared television set on a little table at one end of the narrow kitchen. The grandmother probably watched it while she cooked.

"Let's watch cartoons," Carrie suggested. She looked over at Joy. "Can we watch cartoons?"

The young woman nodded tiredly. Wyatt hopped off the chair arm and led the way into the kitchen, turning on the TV. Austin remained next to his mother.

"He doesn't watch cartoons," Wyatt explained. "He doesn't understand them."

Her heart went out to the boy. To both boys, really, but to Wyatt the most. He was the one who understood what was going on, he was the one who would be hurt by the taunts of other children, and he was the one whose life would always be lived in the shadow of his brother's because families inevitably organized themselves around major illnesses or handicaps.

The two of them leaned against opposite kitchen cupboards, watching *Yu-Gi-Oh!* while Brian spoke quietly and began asking questions.

After the interview, they walked downstairs and down the street, not speaking until they had almost reached the parking lot. Carrie looked over her shoulder to make sure Joy and her children weren't anywhere behind them. "So did you learn anything?"

"Not really," Brian admitted. "She wasn't that forthcoming about her relationship with Haskell—understandably—and nothing she told me about her son was really new, but seeing those two brothers together did get me thinking about the reason all this is happening. If my dad is . . . one of them . . . how come I'm not? How come Wyatt's not? How come my *sister's* not? Is it genetic?"

"It seems to be," Carrie said.

"That's the thing," he said eagerly. "A lot of the incidents that have occurred, that we're investigating, are, for want of a better term, supernatural. Is there a gene that controls that? Haskell and Stewart are both alive and locked up. They can be studied, tests run . . ." He shook his head. "I was sitting there talking to Joy Sing, and all of a sudden I was just kind of overwhelmed by the realization that this is something really big. We've stumbled onto history here."

Carrie smiled. "Yeah. I guess." She didn't understand his sudden enthusiasm, but it was nice to see, and it sure beat the frightened feeling of being completely at the mercy of malevolent fates that had been her constant companion since Lew had taken her into the barn to see his revolutionary milking process.

"So what's the plan for this evening?" he asked as they reached the car. "What's the big idea?"

"We're going to a book signing," she said.

She'd read about it several days ago in one of the alterna-papers she'd picked up to read at lunch. A name in the weekly events calendar had jumped out at her, and she'd remembered back in college attending a signing at the bookstore on campus, a hippie-ish shop more City Lights than Little Professor's. A suspense writer named Phillip Emmons had been there promoting his latest novel, and the guy she'd been dating at the time had dragged her to the signing, which to her surprise, had been more crowded than the John Sayles lecture she'd attended the week before.

Emmons was a weird guy. Between books, apparently, he traveled the country as some type of ghost hunter, folklorist and amateur parapsychologist, and it was these subjects more than his new novel that people had come to hear about. Question after question had to do with supernatural experiences the questioners claimed to have had, and Emmons was able to address each one authoritatively, even bringing in some of his own experiences to serve as examples when he made a point. Although at the time she'd been defiantly a nonbeliever, she'd still gotten a little spooked by some of his stories, and it was an evening she'd never forgotten.

Now Emmons was speaking in San Francisco as part of a Writer's Block series. She'd registered that fact and forgotten it, but something had jogged her memory when they'd been on the helicopter and although it was a long shot, she figured Emmons might have some idea of what was going on or, at the very least, might be able to point them in the right direction in their research.

"Who is it?" Brian asked. "And, if I may be so presumptuous, why?"

"His name's Phillip Emmons, and he writes sort of mystery/suspense novels. Although that's not why we're going to see him. He's also an expert on the occult, the supernatural, Bigfoot, UFOs, all the stuff that's right up our alley."

"Lay it on me, Scully."

"If there's anyone who might have background information on all this, it's him."

"Where and when?"

"The Hartford Theater, seven o'clock. We should probably be there early to make sure we can get tickets." She looked at her watch. "There's a Subway across the street from the theater. I suggest we get our tickets first, then grab something to eat and line up."

"Okay."

As she'd expected, the place was crowded, but they got there early enough that they were able to score seats in the center of the auditorium. Although Emmons was ostensibly there to talk about writing, the interviewer, a professor from UCSF, soon got off topic and onto the paranormal, and there the rest of the conversation stayed. Most of the audience questions concerned the supernatural as well, although a few wannabe writers asked about specific books, then casually followed up by asking if Emmons had any advice on how *they* could break into publishing.

One person actually brought up the overnight reforestation of the clear-cut land—how could someone not? It was all over the news—and what Carrie found interesting was the way he glossed over the question. Every other query put to him was met with thoughtful, detailed discussion, but he seemed to have nothing to say about the regenerated trees. She looked to her left and caught Brian's eye. He'd noticed, too.

After the talk, there was a signing in the lobby, and the two of them hung back, waiting for everyone else to ask their questions, say their piece or get their books autographed. When the last fan finished—a disheveled, overweight man who'd brought along a shopping bag filled with both hardcovers and paperbacks—Carrie and Brian stepped up to the author's table.

She let Brian do the talking. "Excuse me, Mr. Emmons?" he said. "My name's Brian Howells and I'm a reporter for the *Los Angeles Times*. I was wondering if I could ask you a few questions."

The writer seemed singularly uninterested. He nodded distractedly as he slipped his coat off the back of the chair.

"This is Carrie Daniels. She—"

The change in his demeanor was instantaneous. "Carrie Daniels? The one who discovered Lew Haskell's double life?"

"Y-yes," she said, surprised.

He stood, hand extended. "I'm very glad to meet you."

"That's one of the things we want to talk to you about," Brian said. "There's been an epidemic of murders, suicides and just generally strange behavior among a lot of very rich families lately. And it's not the first time. This has happened before."

Emmons had stopped fiddling with his jacket. "Go on. I'm listening."

This was not the time to hold back, so Brian told him everything. His father's letters. The phone messages on Wilson's answering machine. The resurrected bird. The growth of plants. The killing of his mother's pastor, apparently by his father. His encounter with Stephen Stewart. Details of the killings. Wilson's disappearance. Everything.

Carrie had heard it before, but laid out like this, logically, chronologically, made the connections between everything seem less tenuous, more real, and brought home to her just how epic the situation was.

She told him about her experience with Lew.

Emmons, it turned out, kept an apartment in San Francisco, though his primary residence was in Arizona, and after saying his good-byes to the Writer's Block officials and the volunteers who'd staffed the event, he led the two of them back to his place.

It looked like the apartment of a writer. The walls of the sitting room were lined with bookcases, the occasional open space filled with exotic artwork. There was an old-school stereo system set up before a single over-stuffed chair, and dowdy furniture that seemed to be an afterthought was arranged indifferently around these essentials. Upon close inspection, Carrie noted that nearly all of the volumes on the shelves were reference books, many of them extremely old.

"I brought you here to show you something," Emmons told them. "Wait here a moment. I'll be right back." He retreated into one of the bedrooms.

"Look at this," Brian said, pointing.

Next to a bound set of *Man, Myth and Magic*, Carrie saw a thick book with gold embossed lettering: *George Washington: A Cannibal's Story*.

Before she could say anything, Emmons had returned. "I want you to read this." He handed them a Xerox copy of what looked like an old manuscript written with quill and ink. "It's by Meriwether Lewis, part of the censored Lewis and Clark diaries. A friend of mine who works for the Smithsonian got it to me. Read this part here." He pointed.

Carrie squinted at the smudged archaic lettering while Brian read the words aloud. "We Encountered yet another One by the Bank of the River. Our Guides Knew of It and Bade Us stay away, yet We Watcht as It had Its way with a Woman of the Tribe. Its Organ be of exceptional Size and admirable Shape, though That alone could not Account for the Hold It Had upon the Woman. Afterward, the Sand on which They Lay Bloomed with Flowers that Had Not been There previously."

Brian stopped reading, and the two of them looked over at Emmons.

"There were many encounters with these beings, not only by Lewis and Clark, but by other explorers and settlers who lived at the edge of the wilderness. In many accounts, people report that they traveled or lived in packs, and both males and females mated freely with humans.

"They also killed many individuals in particularly brutal ways."

"You think this is what's happening now?" Brian asked.

"I think they live among us, yes. Disguised, perhaps. Adapted. I've thought so for some time, although it has never been more than a hunch, and there has never been any proof or even indication that this is the case. Until now. I must commend you not only on your investigative skills and your tenacity but on your boldness of thought. It is not everyone who would have seen these facts and come to such a conclusion."

"Wilson," Brian said.

"What?"

"It was mostly his doing. He was the one who put most of it together." He paused. "And I think they killed him for it."

"That could very well be. It would not be in their best interest to be found out."

Carrie's pulse accelerated. "Maybe we're next."

"Maybe," Emmons agreed. "But Lew Haskell didn't harm you." He looked at Brian. "And you've been jetting about California, stirring things up for some time after your friend's disappearance and nothing's happened. My guess is, you're safe."

"My dad," Brian said softly.

"That could be the reason. But in this business, we don't look a gift horse in the mouth. Now, you said that all of the men involved in the murders were deformed, had animal characteristics. It's what made me think of these creatures. Because the beings Lewis and Clark and others wrote about were also described as having snakeskin or wormskin, as well as devil tails and other varying attributes. There are a lot of contradictory stories. The historical record is like that. But, as you saw, there's also the flowers, the plants. That, too, ties in with what you've said."

"Yeah." Brian nodded. "So what else do you know about these . . . whatever they are?"

"Some Native Americans thought of them as demons."

"What do you think?" Brian asked.

"I don't know. I'm not saying I disbelieve in demons, but I'm not sure these things fit the qualifications. Although," he added, "bringing back a forest overnight is pretty major."

"No kidding," Carrie said.

"It seems, from everything I've read, that they *spoke* to certain people. Not 'spoke' like we're speaking, not in words, but to particular individuals who were somehow receptive, they called to them, enticed them to leave their villages or their settlements and . . . that part's not very clear. Maybe they ended up slaves; maybe they ended up food."

She thought of Brian's father, and she could tell from the expression on his face that he was thinking the same thing.

Emmons said it aloud. "When you told me about your dad, that's the first thing that occurred to me. It would explain to some extent the anomalies."

"You think he's *working* for them?"

Emmons shrugged. "Do you think he's *one* of them?"

Carrie could tell that he didn't know what to think, and she wondered if she would be dealing with things this well if one of her parents had somehow been at the center of a horror like this. She probably would have been a basket case, and she admired Brian's ability to remain focused with this emotional tornado spiraling destructively all around him.

"They also seemed to have a propensity for recording their atrocities," the writer said, "be it through cave paintings or carvings or—"

"Videotapes?" Brian said. "Or messages scrawled in blood?"

"Perhaps."

"But if this *is* what our millionaires are," Brian wondered, "why are they murdering their families and going on killing sprees? What's the point of that?"

"I don't know. And I have to admit that the fact that this has happened before, that other rich men went on earlier rampages is news to me. I never noticed that or picked up on it in any of my studies. Again, I commend you."

"Still Wilson," Brian said. "And did I mention that all of those other killers were from California?"

"Interesting."

"Yes, it is," Brian said. "But what does it mean?"

"That I can't tell you," Emmons admitted.

"You said those . . . things that Lewis and Clark encountered killed people in very brutal ways," Carrie stated.

"That is true. But from what I can determine, they slaughtered invaders in order to preserve and defend the vanishing wilderness in which they lived. It was a protective measure. Which I suppose ties in with the regrowth of the forest. How it relates to Stephen Stewart and Bill Devine and all the rest . . . ?" He shrugged. "It's anyone's guess."

Brian handed back the Xeroxed paper. "The question is, what do we do about it? What *can* we do about it?"

Emmons shook his head. "History is silent on that subject. This is one of those stories that exist in the margins, that I've put together myself from scraps of information collected here and there. Like I said, some of the Native American tribes had stories of demons that seemed to jibe pretty closely with what the settlers and explorers wrote about, but to my knowledge there were no prescriptions for exorcising or getting rid of those demons. And none of the pioneers mentioned anything about killing these beings."

"So what do we do?"

"I don't know."

"Who does?" Carrie asked.

He sighed. "I honestly have no idea."

"Then that's . . . it?" Brian asked.

"I'm afraid so. I've given you all the help I can. I

mean, I can provide you with other texts, point you toward other descriptions, but you have the gist of it, and unless you're planning to write a thesis, you probably don't need that many background details."

"I'm writing an article," Brian said.

"Are you?"

That seemed to stop him.

"Forgive me for saying so, but this quest seems personal to me. And I seriously doubt that the *Los Angeles Times* or any reputable newspaper is going to publish an article linking murderous millionaires to early American demons unless concrete proof is not only corroborated by witnesses with the impeachability of the Pope but captured live on film as well. And speaking as someone who's been around the block on this a couple of times, that doesn't happen."

"*The Weekly Globe* would print it," Carrie said.

"My point exactly."

"Then maybe I won't write an article," Brian said. "Or I won't write *that* article. But I need to know."

"I do, too," Carrie said.

"So, are you in with us?"

Emmons shook his head. "I'm more of an armchair detective. Besides, there's something else I'm working on, something else I need to do." He looked from Carrie to Brian. "What's *your* next move?"

If they had a plan, Brian hadn't told her what it was, and she turned to him for an answer to the question. But he was already looking at her.

Both of them shrugged. "I don't know," Brian said.

"One bit of advice?"

Brian nodded. "Sure," he said.

"Be careful," Emmons said grimly. "Be very, very careful."

Twenty-five

Another hike.

The last of their vacation?

It was supposed to be, but Andrew wasn't sure. Despite the fact that they were scheduled to head home the day after tomorrow and he and Robin both had to be back to work on Monday, he seemed unable to entertain the idea of leaving. There was still so much to do here.

Although when he tried to think about it logically, he did not know *what* exactly there *was* to do.

Robin, of course, wanted to leave yesterday. She'd grown more and more uncomfortable here even as he had come to feel more and more at home. Their scare at the fair notwithstanding, this had been a wonderful trip, and he wished it could last forever.

Alyssa grabbed his hand as they started up a steep section of trail. "I'm tired," she whined. "I want a piggyback ride."

"You're too big for that now," he told her. "Just keep walking. We're almost at the top."

Last night, he'd had a dream that he'd met a beautiful, sexy woman on a hilltop above Oak Draw. Only she wasn't exactly a woman. And probably, by conventional standards, she would not be considered beautiful. But there was something incredibly erotic about the way she

looked, the way she stood, the way she moved—
everything about her—and he'd awakened with an erection so powerful and close to the edge that it had taken
only a slight shift of position to send him spurting into
his underwear.

He didn't want to admit it, but that was probably the
reason he'd wanted to come up here this morning.

They were hiking up a different trail this time, heading
in the direction opposite the town. Robin had stated
flatly that she would not go on another hike. He'd understood why, and that was fine, but she'd glared at him as
though that should be reason enough for *him* not to
want to hike either. She was already mad at him for the
mess he'd made in the bed—some of the stickiness had
gotten on her nightgown and hardened on her thigh after
he'd fallen back asleep and rolled over—but he wasn't
about to let his vacation be ruined by her hang-ups, and
he'd told her pleasantly that he'd take the kids and she
could lounge around and catch up on some of her summer reading.

They reached the top of the hill. It was not flat, as
the crest of the other hill had been, but rocky, wedges
of broken stone that looked like the ruined walls of
some ancient civilization winding about the irregular
ground. Once again, though, there was another path, an
offshoot, and once again it either led to or passed by an
adobe hut that could be seen peeking out from between
boulders. He didn't want to go that way—not with the
kids—so they continued hiking straight, toward a stand
of tall pines that towered over the rough rock forma-
tions.

The trail ran alongside a granite wall, through an
opening in the stone, next to a protruding rock shelf. It
really did look like an eroded fort or the ruins of a
city, and Johnny suddenly stopped, pointing. "Look!" he
said excitedly.

There were strange, almost hieroglyphic symbols displayed on several boulders that lined their path. They'd been carved into the rock but had then been traced over with white paint that was now chipped and faded. Andrew bent down to examine the symbols. He didn't recognize them, had no idea what they meant or how they had gotten here or who had made them, but he suddenly wanted to learn them, wanted to be able to read them, write them. He stood, looked around, glanced back at where that adobe hut was, though it couldn't be seen from this vantage point. Something here seemed to be calling to him, and he wished the kids had stayed with Robin at the cabin, wished he had come here alone.

Ahead, through the trees, he saw movement and caught a glimpse of something white and shiny that resembled wormskin and for some reason reminded him of the woman in his dream.

"Dad?" Alyssa said, tapping him on the shoulder.

He tried to press down on his erection before standing, hoping neither of the kids would notice. "What is it?" he asked.

"Could we go back? I don't like it here."

Glancing over, he saw the same look of worry on his son's face. "Sure," he said. He stole a quick glance at the trees, but whatever had been there was gone. "Let's turn around."

They spent the afternoon touring a winery a couple of miles up the highway from Oak Draw and then a small volcanic tunnel misleadingly called Gargantuan Caverns.

After dinner, Andrew walked onto the porch alone. Robin was doing the dishes and the kids were watching television. Outside, the night was silent, the cicadas that had been buzzing earlier in the day now quiet, last night's cricket symphony nowhere to be heard. It seemed darker than usual, and Andrew realized that that was

because two of the other cabins were dark. The middle
of the week was never as crowded as the ends, and he
assumed that some of their neighbors of the past few
days had moved on while their replacements had not yet
arrived. He breathed deeply, smelling pine, smiling. He
liked the feeling of being alone here.

And then he saw the cat.

It was standing on the path in front of the cabin, looking up at him, and the way the moonlight fell upon its
face made it look as though its eye sockets were empty.

Maybe they were.

The animal *was* dead.

Whatever fear or dread he had felt before was gone,
and looking at the cat he felt as though he were com-
muning with an old friend.

An old friend he had tried to kill.

Even this seemed comfortable, natural, and he
stepped off the porch and walked slowly toward the cat,
petting hand extended. "Hey," he said softly. "Hey, little guy."

And then he found himself walking down the path,
around the side of the cabin and into the trees. It was
dark, but somehow he didn't stumble, didn't trip on any
of the rocks or pinecones that littered the rough, uneven
ground. He hadn't told Robin or the kids where he was
going, hadn't even told them that he *was* going. He simply followed the dead cat into the forest and up the hill,
heading toward . . . toward . . .

Toward that adobe hut at the top.

He hadn't realized that was his goal, but he understood now that it had been in the back of his mind at
least since seeing its complement on the other trail this
morning. Robin's violent reaction to the structure had
also piqued his interest. Unfazed by altitude since it no
longer breathed, the dead cat moved in its jerky awkward way up the trail. Along the way, he saw writing on

rocks that he hadn't noticed before, and the strange childish symbols seemed to glow in the moonlight.

Then they were at the flat top of the ridge, moving onto the side trail, past the spot where he had first seen the cat's body, through the gently swaying grass, toward the stand of ponderosas that housed the adobe hut. He lost the cat somewhere along the way, but it didn't matter. He was where he was supposed to be, and he reached the dark entrance of the small building and, after a quick moment's hesitation, walked inside.

He could see, somehow, though there was no source of light. Andrew was not sure what he'd expected to find within the adobe structure, but the floor of the single room was dirt, the walls unadorned and there was no furniture. In one corner was a carefully tended tree with bright red leaves that came up to the height of his stomach and had about it the precise configuration of a bonsai. Behind the tree, making it easier to see and stacked against the angled meeting of the two walls, was a pile of white bones that he did not look at too carefully but that he knew were of human origin.

There was a hole in the center of the floor that smelled of sewage, and he was compelled to walk forward and peer into its depths. What he found was a shaft dropping down farther than he could see, lined with mosses and plant stalks that swayed seductively in an unseen wind and made him think of Middle Eastern belly dancers. The sight was hypnotic, and he stared into it for quite some time before finally pulling himself dreamily away. He felt light-headed, almost drunk, and he realized that he had no idea how long he'd been standing there. His legs felt prickly, as though they'd fallen asleep, and his eyes burned, as though he'd been staring for a while without blinking.

He suddenly felt the need to get out of this room. There was another doorway (*or was it the same one?*

His sense of direction and sense of time both seemed to have deserted him), and he walked out to find himself on another path that led through the trees to yet another adobe hut. Pressing onward, he saw another hut beyond that . . . and another beyond that. They stretched in a crazy line through woods that did not look like the woods he remembered seeing up here, past mounds of moss as big as men, and he had the disorienting feeling that he'd traveled a lot farther than he thought he had.

The path he was on was no longer dirt but had grown soft, and he looked down to see a ribbon of lush grass winding through a verdant forest toward a collection of adobe buildings built at the foot of a black mountain. At the head of the path, just before the entrance to this village, he saw a whitish shape that shimmied in the moonlight like those belly-dancing plants in the hole. He rushed forward, excited but not sure exactly why.

Then he figured out why.

It was the woman of his dream. Or the female *creature* of his dream. She was beckoning him, calling him with her dance. The lust he felt for her—

it

—reminded him of the way he'd first felt when he and Robin were dating, a passionate desire that had been reawakened since they'd come up here, although with her memories of this place Robin had obviously not been in the same sort of mood. He was fully erect, and though that made it difficult to run, he continued to hurry forward, needing to reach her yet not knowing what would happen when he did so.

She was not alone, he saw as he drew closer. There were others just like her, walking around naked, and it was only the fact that many of them were male that made him slow his pace.

Come, she danced. *Come.*

Now he was looking at the scene before him more objectively, his critical faculties breaking through the haze in which they'd been shrouded since his encounter with the hole in the hut. What he saw was impossible, though he accepted it unquestioningly. He had stumbled upon—or been led to—a community of these creatures. They were of a kind but not identical, and he saw fur and scales, horns and tails. Their homes had bones visibly embedded in the adobe, and rotting carcasses lay on the ground between them.

He understood that these were the type of beings that had assaulted Robin and her friends all those years ago, and he wondered if that had been the reason for his attraction to her in the first place, if on some subliminal level he had sensed that taint—and wanted her for it.

He told himself that was crazy thinking, but as outrageous as it sounded on the face of it, he could not dismiss such an idea out of hand. Particularly when he considered his own reaction to the revelation of her attack. Rather than cutting the vacation short the way she wanted and being concerned with the feelings this was dredging up for her, he had insisted that they remain and had even contemplated staying longer.

Not only that, but his desire for her had intensified.

He felt guilty, but the guilt turned to disgust as he saw a large male—nine feet tall if it was an inch—hold a small skull in its hand and bite into the cranium as though it were a cracker.

The woman—

creature

monster

—of his dreams continued to dance for him, trying to seduce him. She had only one breast but it was perfectly formed and centered pleasingly in the center of her chest, jiggling slightly as she swayed sensuously from left to right. She thrust her hips forward, moving in and out of the moonlight and shadows, exposing the exaggerated attributes of her vulva, her shiny tail slithering seductively between her legs.

He wanted to jump on her, wanted to rip off his clothes and taste her, touch her, take her. But he resisted, and as the minutes passed, the come-hither expression on her face was replaced with something that more resembled puzzlement. It was clear that she was not used to rejection, and his ability to withstand the temptation even though every fiber of his being longed to be intimately joined with her, made him feel powerful, gave him strength.

He could not see as well as he had only a few seconds previously. The moonlight seemed dimmer. Shadows appeared darker, and there were more of them. From within one of those shadows came a man who made his way past the milling creatures, around the dancing seductress and up the grass-carpeted path, a human being like himself wearing only dirty, raggedy clothes. He seemed uncomfortable and ill at ease, and he stood in front of Andrew for several long moments as if unsure of what to do.

Or as though he was waiting for instructions.

That was more like it, and even as Andrew's brain articulated the thought, the filthy man attempted a smile and held out his hand to be shaken, like a parody of a bad salesman. Andrew did not shake it, and the hand slowly dropped back to the man's side.

"Who are you?" Andrew asked. "What are you doing here?"

"I . . . am . . . here . . . for . . . her." He spoke slowly, and his speech was thick and awkward, as though he hadn't spoken English in a long, long time. At the word "her," he absently reached down to touch his penis, and Andrew saw that while it was hard, it was also bruised and scraped, red and bloodied.

This man, too, he understood, was in the thrall of one of the females.

In love?

Andrew was not sure he'd put it that way, but it was clear that the desire had become obsessive, so much so that the man had turned his back on human beings and civilization and had come out here to the wilderness to live with these . . . whatever they were.

Wasn't that what he was doing, too?

No, Andrew realized, and for the first time since arriving in California he knew for certain that he did not belong here, this was not for him. He might have been called, but he did not have to answer.

More than anything else in the world, he wanted to see Robin and the kids right now, wanted to be with them, wanted to be traveling east on that highway home.

"We . . . can . . . help . . . them," the man said in that maddeningly slow, dumb voice.

"Help them do what?"

The man's mouth hung open and his eyes moved up as his brain searched for the word. Frustrated, he shook his head.

"I'm not helping anyone do anything," Andrew said. "I'm going—" *Home,* he'd planned to say, but just at that second soft hands reached around from behind him, one snaking around his neck, one cupping his crotch. The fingers, white and slimy as they were, knew what they were doing and even through the thick material of his jeans manipulated him expertly. He tried to pull away, but she was stronger than he was—and part of him did not want to pull away.

"You . . . help . . . or . . ." The man made a high-pitched whistling noise that sounded like something made by a ceramic flute, and the sound was echoed by the beings all around them.

He could guess what that meant, and to his mind the chuckling that followed confirmed it.

If he were a religious man, he would have prayed.

But he was not.

So instead he cried.

Twenty-six

1850

John Sutter was not the man he had been.

Neither, Marshall supposed, was he.

The two of them had not had a falling out—not exactly—but the friendship was strained between them. If it could even be called a friendship anymore. "Business partner" was probably the most accurate description of their relationship, but even that implied more contact than they had with each other these days. For the most part, Sutter attended to affairs in Coloma and around the fort, while he saw to things farther afield, and the less they had to see of each other the better.

He'd been gone for two months this time, although one of the reasons was a freak spring snowstorm that had kept the high-line trail impassable for nearly a week. He'd even made it to San Francisco, and he'd found it relaxing to be in a real city, to be away from the wilderness and among the monuments of men. On the way back, he found himself thinking that there was probably a lot of carpentry work to be found in such a growing city, and he decided that the next time he was out that way, he would try to look for a job and leave the diggings behind permanently.

He didn't have the stomach anymore for a life in the wild.

His party arrived at the fort, and he sensed the difference immediately. It was nothing concrete, nothing he could point to with any specificity, but no one came out to greet them, and the few people they saw were surly and preoccupied. The buildings themselves seemed shabby and untended, and while there weren't weeds actually growing in the gravel of the courtyard, they would not have been out of place. Life at the fort had changed, and Marshall wondered if that was merely because he'd been absent for a while or if Sutter's previously iron grip had faltered.

There were quite a few unfamiliar faces at the various posts. He knew the men who'd returned with him and recognized a few people here and there, but for the most part Sutter seemed to have replaced most of his dependable old hands with newer workers whom Marshall couldn't identify and who did not look particularly trustworthy.

The captain was not in his office, but Marshall and Claude Lake, his second in command on the trip, gave an abbreviated report and a stack of invoices and paperwork to the rather belligerent young man who was manning the office, telling him to make sure that Sutter knew they were back. Claude went for a drink with the others, but Marshall was tired and said that he just wanted to go back to his place and catch up on some much-needed sleep. On the way, he walked by the storage room where he had shot the female creature—

Let's fuck it

—but he passed by without even trying to open the door and look inside, his muscles tense and knotted.

His own cabin had remained untouched, but there was another cabin being built nearby, in view of his side window, and he realized that although this was his home, it did not *feel* like home to him anymore. He had some money saved up, not a lot but enough, and he decided that rather than wait until his next journey to San Francisco, he would collect his pay from Sutter and start looking for a new situation immediately.

He was through with this.

Marshall found an old whiskey bottle, downed its contents, then slept soundly through the rest of the day and well into the night, undisturbed by dreams.

It was the tapping on his door that woke him up. "Hold on!" he called, groggily getting out of bed and stumbling toward the door to unlatch it.

He wasn't sure how long the tapping had been going on, but it was low, not loud, and he sensed that it must have been sounding for quite some time in order for its percussive rhythm to capture his attention in his sleep. And it was *tapping*, not *knocking*, a light, continuous rapping on the wood that he should have realized instantly was far too even and far too consistent to have been made by any person. But he was still sleepy, was at the door already, and he unlatched and opened it.

A crow had been making the noise, its beak pecking on the door, and the big black bird stood in the dirt in front of the cabin looking up at him.

Its right wing was gone and that entire half of its body was featherless and bloody.

Marshall was suddenly wide-awake. The crow had been shot and should be dead, yet it stood there before him, patiently waiting to get inside his cabin. Behind it he heard other sounds, saw more movement, and he quickly closed the door, lit his lantern, then reopened the door. With the area in front of the cabin illuminated more fully, he spotted a bobcat and a fawn, several small squirrels and a javelina. All of them had been grievously maimed, and a few of the squirrels looked like they were rotting. The lantern created a semicircle of light directly before him, but it made the area beyond that semicircle even darker, and he stepped forward, swinging the lantern first one way then the other as he saw that there were other animals here as well, animals that had been dead but resurrected. They seemed to be guarding the entrance to a path that led into a section of woods that Marshall would have sworn had not been there when he'd left two months ago.

Guarding it or pointing him toward it?

He didn't know, didn't care. Walking back inside, he got his rifle and a handful of shells that he shoved into the pocket of a coat he put on. Carrying the lantern and the rifle, he strode past, through, over the resurrected animals and down the path. There were trees and bushes that should not have been growing here, that had no business being in California, and Marshall remembered some of the stories he'd heard.

Creatures more beast than man, more devil than beast, that had only to look at bushes to make them grow or touch eggs to make them hatch.

He knew it would be smarter to wake someone from the fort, have a party of men come with him, but he'd always been a man who listened to his gut rather than his head, and he walked boldly into the woods alone, rifle at the ready, prepared for anything.

Or so he thought.

For it was mere moments later when he came across the building. Nearly half as long as the fort itself, the structure seemed to rise out of the forest. Whether it had been constructed in an existing meadow or whether standing timber had been felled in order to provide the site, there was no free space, no ground left over. The large leafy trees grew right next to the front wall, against the sides, leaving no open area.

Marshall had not seen this building before and

doubted that many others knew of its existence. It was new—it had to be—and it was built not of wood but adobe, like some of the Indians used. It reminded him of the hut he had encountered on the trip out to California—

bag of bones

—although it was much, much larger and actually had a door. No windows, though, and he wondered what was the reasoning behind that.

Marshall thought of knocking, decided against it, and alert for any sign that others were about, he carefully placed his lantern on the ground. Still clutching the rifle and ready to use it at a second's notice if necessary, he tried the door. It was unlatched, and he pulled it open as quietly as possible.

From within, he heard a familiar mewling sound that made his blood run cold. No, not a sound. *Sounds.* There was more than one in there, and he shifted the rifle in his arm before picking up the lantern and peering inside.

Within was an antechamber from whose walls hung scythes and swords, knives and shears. The light from the lantern revealed dried blood everywhere. There was an open doorway at the other end of the small room, but the light did not penetrate that far and the space beyond the doorway was black.

It was from here that the sounds emerged.

Marshall was aware that whatever waited in that darkness could see him, but it was too late now for him to hide, and if he put out the flame he would not be able to see. He could turn around and leave, but that was not an option he even considered. Figuring that it would be better for him to move quickly, that it would make him less of a target, Marshall strode through the antechamber holding up his lantern and walked through the doorway into the gloom.

The room in which he found himself was so big that

he could not see the end of it. A cloying odor of musk hit his nostrils the second he passed through the doorway, and it was all he could do not to gag and throw up. The light from his lantern seemed dimmer here and shone not very far, but that didn't matter. Even with his limited range of vision, he could see the luxurious grasses growing on the floor . . . and the tall female monsters chained to thick pitch-covered posts. They blinked against the light, these terrible amalgams of bear and snake and pig and devil, their grimacing mouths filled with too many teeth, their spread legs ready and willing.

Sutter had had this building constructed as a prison.

Or a brothel.

On top of the mewling was another sound, a low rhythmic grunting. Marshall, sickened and disgusted, knew exactly what that sound was.

He held the lantern higher.

And it shone upon the bare back and buttocks of John Sutter.

Sweaty, muscles straining, Sutter was on his knees between the open thighs of one of the creatures, determinedly coupling with it. He turned briefly as the light touched upon him, and there was a crazed gleam in his eyes that reminded Marshall of the way he had looked when they'd captured the thing in the bear trap.

Let's fuck it.

No wonder the fort was in such disarray. Sutter was out here, doing this, spending all of his time *consorting.* Even now, caught in the light, the captain was not embarrassed, did not stop. He turned back around and continued thrusting, making those awful, obscene grunts, eliciting from his monstrous lover that maddening mewling, a sound echoed by the chained captives all about them.

His instinct was to turn tail and run, but he needed

to know what else was in here, so instead Marshall moved to the left and, holding the light aloft, stepped forward and peered into the darker recesses of the huge room. There were more females shackled to walls and posts, over a dozen altogether. He wondered where and how Sutter had captured them. The captain had to have had help, and with a sinking feeling in his stomach, Marshall thought about all of those new men at the fort. It suddenly occurred to him that maybe the old residents, the men he'd known, had not quit and left but had died trying to capture these monsters for Sutter.

He continued forward across the spongy grass, moving deeper into the building. The cloying, musky odor had given way to a far worse and infinitely more overpowering stench, a mixture of shit and piss and rot. He held his breath and stopped, gagging, unable to go farther. Ahead was a large jumbled pile comprised of bodies and bones. Dead open eyes glittered in the lantern light.

He thought he saw Jameson's bruised and bloodied face.

And Big Reese's.

On top of the pile was one of the monsters, male, its oversized penis partially severed and hanging down. Another lay on the right side of the mass of bodies, its ridged shiny skin in marked contrast to the dullness of surrounding work shirts.

But that was not the worst of it. For the pile appeared to be moving, and in the dim yellow light it took his mind a moment to realize that what he was seeing were smaller creatures, some the size of rats, some the size of cats, scuttling about over the dead bodies, crawling over heads, pulling themselves up over arms, sliding down sections of broken skeleton leg. They were slimy and scaly and hairy and spiky, and he knew exactly what they were: babies. The offspring of Sutter and his demonic concubines.

He also knew what they were doing with those dead bodies.

The infants were feeding.

He must have made some sort of shocked noise because, as one, the small creatures paused, stopped, looked at him, many with bloody mouths, one still chewing on the finger from a hand. They began whistling at him, a high-pitched sound that hurt his ears and turned all of the skin on his body to gooseflesh.

This time he did run. Trying to block out all sounds and smells, trying to look only at the ground so he would not trip, Marshall fled back through the building the way he'd come, over the grass, past the shackled females and Sutter, now crying out in ecstasy, through the door to the antechamber with its bloody tools on the walls.

He rushed outside, exhaling heavily, gulping in huge breaths of cool night air as he stumbled away from the building into the trees. The rifle felt heavy under his right arm and the swinging lantern in his left hand banged against its handle so hard as he ran that he thought it was going to break. But he dared not stop or even look back, and he raced through the woods toward the fort until he realized that he'd been running for far too long. He stopped, looked about, but nothing seemed familiar. He'd been running in the wrong direction, and now he was lost.

He saw movement out of the corner of his eye to the right, and he whirled in that direction, the lantern hitting his elbow and causing a flash of pain to shoot up his left arm.

It was one of them.

A male.

There were several trees between the monster and himself, but he could see it clearly in a shaft of moonlight, and it could obviously see him. With a wave of clawed hand, the creature created a miniature tree out of nothing, making it sprout up from a pile of dead leaves on the ground and then branch off until it was as high as Marshall's stomach. Before his eyes, the small tree bloomed, then died, its leaves falling off, its branches and trunk withering to brown stumps that in the end resembled a burned man. The creature grinned at him, a sly, evil grin that he did not understand but that frightened him.

There were others, he saw. Large dark shapes too far away to be seen, which glinted in scraps of moonlight between the trees and could only be one thing.

He understood now why these woods had not seemed familiar to him. They had been changed, added to, made into something else. His mother had told him stories of Jack in the Green, a woodland sprite from the Old Country who shepherded through the winter months all things that grew and who was responsible for making plants flower in the spring. He had not believed those stories, but she had, and he wondered if that was what was happening here. Were these creatures responsible for the growth of plants in the new land? They seemed angered by the intrusion of men into their country, and though in his mother's stories Jack in the Green had coexisted with people, these beings did not seem so benign.

The dark shapes passed between trees, bushes growing in their wake.

What were they doing now? What was their plan? Were they attempting to create a forest so thick that Sutter would get lost in it? Were they planning to rescue those of their kind imprisoned in the building? They were here for a reason, but he remembered their attempt on the fort and doubted that they would try such an attack again. Whatever they were, they weren't dumb.

He had heard no noise, but the one that had been grinning at him from behind the burnt-man stump must have communicated to its brethren somehow, because in the seconds that had passed, those dark shapes had grown closer. Not close enough to be illuminated by his lantern but close enough for him to make out horns on heads, spines on backs, forked tails.

The air was suddenly shattered by the explosion of rifle fire, and one of the creatures fell to the ground with a whistling screech. There was the crack of another rifle, and Marshall hit the dirt, pushing the lantern away and lying flat as he stretched his own weapon out in front of him, ready to fire. "Who's there?" he called.

"Who's *there*?" someone called back.

More rifles fired and two of the creatures fell screaming to the ground.

"James Marshall!" he yelled.

"Stay where you are!"

The grinning creature stopped grinning as watery liquid gushed out from a hole that had suddenly appeared in its head. Within moments, the woods were silent save for the stomping of boots on leaves and the snickering conversation of rough men. The monsters that weren't dead had fled, and though the forest still seemed strange to him, it no longer seemed threatening.

Marshall stood. "Don't shoot!" he called. He saw a group of men heading toward him through the trees.

"You really Mr. Marshall?" one of the men said. Marshall recognized him as one of the new fellows he'd seen at the fort.

"Yes. Who are you?"

"Patrol," he said, and explained that Sutter had commanded them to guard the section of woods around the periphery of what he called his "storehouse." What he had in there acted as an enticement to those monsters, and it was their charge to not only protect the building but kill as many of the creatures as possible while doing so. The man grinned when he said the word "storehouse," and Marshall could tell from his demeanor that the fellow knew exactly what was going on in there.

He could see in his mind the bare back and buttocks of John Sutter as he *consorted* with one of those things.

Was the captain going to share that with these men? *Let's fuck it.*

Maybe Sutter had finally found a way to make his fortune. Marshall himself had been tempted initially, and he recalled before the attack on the fort that most of those with him had seemed ready to jump on the shackled female without hesitation. Matthew had already done so and finished by the time they heard the screams of his wife from outside.

Marshall looked around at the motley collection of fighters before him, knowing that they would gladly pay for some time with one of the females.

But what of the offspring? What would be done with them? And what of those outside of Sutter's purview, like the baby in the canyon? Who knew how many of *them* were out there, fathered by men or monsters out of mothers from both stripes?

"Which way back?" Marshall said.

One of the other guards pointed in a direction opposite to the one he would have expected, and Marshall nodded his thanks, setting off. He walked around the dead body of one of the monsters, flowers blooming around the edge of the gut-shot corpse, and wondered if the men were going to take it and the others back to that building and throw them upon the pile—before partaking of one of the chained females.

He hurried faster, desperate to get out of these woods.

Reaching his cabin, Marshall started packing his belongings, intending to set out at dawn. He was not only through with John Sutter, he was through with California. He wanted to get far away from this horror as quickly as he possibly could, and he recalled hearing talk of silver strikes in Utah and New Mexico territories that . . .

No, he thought. He was through chasing riches. It had brought nothing but heartache and death to everyone he knew.

He didn't know what he was going to do next. But he did know that he wasn't going to work for Sutter, wasn't going to remain here, was going to go to a city where no one knew him and start afresh.

This part of his life was done.

Twenty-seven

Follow the money, Wilson had said.

Research was—*had been?*—the man's watchword, whereas Brian was more of an interviewer. Which was why they'd made such a good team, even if they hadn't actually collaborated on anything. But with the background information provided by Phillip Emmons and with Carrie helping him, he was sure he'd be able to piece together a pretty accurate picture of what was going on.

This morning, the two of them had split up. She'd gone to the main branch of the San Francisco Public Library and he'd headed over to the Office of Public Records, each of them attempting to trace back the family roots of Tom Lowry, Bill Devine, Stephen Stewart, Wesley Fields and Lew Haskell, to look for any indication of personal or business dealings between them and, not incidentally, search for any evidence of unusual encounters or incidents the families may have had in the past.

Brian didn't know how she was faring, but he had struck gold.

Literally.

All of the families—*all* of them—had made their initial money in gold. They'd since diversified and many of them had gone on to make their fortunes in businesses entirely unrelated, but the founders of the dynasties had been forty-niners, and the grubstakes for future generations had been collected in the rivers and diggings of the Sierra gold fields. It was a connection that could not be coincidence, and it implied that those original prospectors had all met with something in the California backcountry that continued to exert its destructive influence on their descendants today.

Phillip Emmons had said that those monsters encountered by Lewis and Clark were known to have mated with humans, and the more Brian thought about it, the more likely that seemed. He didn't buy the writer's theory that the creatures had disguised themselves and somehow infiltrated American society. It seemed far more logical that they had interbred with people and it was the descendants of those unions that were now flipping out and becoming violent, and that, if pure creatures did still exist, they lived outside of society, in those areas of vanishing wilderness far away from cities and towns.

Like the section of clear-cut forest that had been restored to its former glory.

Brian also looked for his own last name in the papers and microfiche through which he dug. After the meeting with Emmons last night, he'd been forced to confront the reasons for his growing obsession with this story, and of course, no matter which thought path he took, it always came down to one thing: his dad.

He wanted to find his father.

Even if his old man was a killer.

STOP ME. The words of the note he had found were never very far from his conscious thoughts, and though they were an admission of guilt, they also revealed a desire to change, to escape, to . . . stop. That wouldn't be enough for the law, but it might be enough for him, and in his more optimistic fantasies, his dad ended up incarcerated while he visited him on weekends and the two of them reconnected.

He hadn't called his mom or his sister in several days, and the obligatory conversations with his editor had been evasive at best. He was using his job as a pretext for conducting a private investigation, and though he had enough information to write several articles, Emmons had been right: The *Times* wouldn't publish the real story. Or at least not all of it.

He wasn't here for his family, though, or his job. He was here for himself. And if that meant burning bridges, then he needed some gasoline and matches because he wasn't about to let anything stand between himself and his goal.

They met for lunch at Carrie's house, a pleasant bungalow on the edge of a historic district. She provided iced tea while he picked up some tacos, and they ate in the well-lit kitchen while, outside, neighborhood children played tag in the street, their excited, happy voices an ironic counterpoint to their own grim discussion indoors.

Carrie went first, and her findings pretty much mirrored his own. She hadn't been able to trace genealogies as cleanly, but she'd found several articles about gruesome murders in the past that had been committed by members of so-called high society. Probably the same articles Wilson had discovered. "What we should do," she suggested, "is see if any of *their* descendants are around today. Those are the ones we should be watching. Maybe we could even give the police a heads-up.

"It's in their blood," she conjectured. "We might not know what triggers it, but like Huntington's Chorea, it's a time bomb waiting to go off."

"It's worth a try," Brian admitted.

She'd also found reference to "Indian gold demons"

in the index of a self-published biography of John Sutter that she'd happened upon by chance while looking for another book that had been checked out. There were no actual descriptions of the demons, but mention was made of them mating with miners desperate for female contact. Pursuing that thread, she had found two other books that alluded to such congress, and like him, she had come to the conclusion that it was the offspring of these unions . . . and *their* offspring . . . and *their* offspring . . . that were the perpetrators of violence over the decades.

But did that explain everything?

They both agreed that the genetic component had validity, but science and magic did not sit well together, and they each concurred that what was going on went far beyond anything biology could account for.

"Money's involved, too," Brian said, and he described what he'd found at the Office of Public Records, including the fact that it was not only tremendous wealth but the original source of that wealth that they all had in common. "There was a study published a year or two ago that said the presence of money changes people. Even playing Monopoly or seeing *pictures* of money made test subjects feel more self-sufficient and thus behave more antisocially. Who's to say that the vast amounts of money possessed by these men and their families didn't contribute to what happened or have some influence on their behavior?"

Carrie leaned over the kitchen table. "We're tiptoeing around the most important thing."

"What's that?"

"Everything's happening at once."

He looked at her.

"Doesn't it seem to you that it's all coming to a boiling point? I mean the timing of everything: those children like Juan, those rich men suddenly snapping and going on killing sprees, that forest that popped up out of nowhere. They're all happening now. It's like it's all leading up to something . . . big."

Brian nodded slowly. "Boiling point. That's exactly what Wilson said. And, yeah, I've felt it, too." He took a drink of his iced tea. "The question is, what is it building toward? What *is* the big event?"

"I've been thinking about that," she said. "Something Phillip Emmons said last night stuck with me: 'They slaughtered invaders in order to preserve and defend the vanishing wilderness in which they lived. It was a protective measure.' When I was doing my research at the library this morning, I looked at everything through that lens, and I have to admit, it made a kind of weird sense. What if whoever—or *whatever*—is left of this dying breed is trying to fight back, retake the land that was stolen from them, come out from whatever small corner of the wilderness they've been pushed into and strike against the now dominant species that stole their spot on the food chain: us?"

He looked at her skeptically. "So we're involved in some kind of ecological horror story?"

"I don't think it's a coincidence that that forest grew back the day—the *day*—after the last stand of old growth trees was cut down.

"Not only that," she added. "Besides their money, what do Lew and Stephen Stewart and all of those other men have in common? Oil, gas, construction, development, real estate. They all make money off the land, through its exploitation or the theft of its natural resources. Sure some of them give back and do good and try to help others, but that's only because deep inside they feel guilty and know they've done wrong."

"So what are you saying? That they're killing their families and committing suicide in order to stop themselves from drilling for oil or building more homes? That's pretty ridiculous."

"Is there anything about this that isn't ridiculous?"

"Yeah, but liberal guilt turning millionaires into murderers? Come on."

"Okay," she said. "Forget that part. But just look at what's happening from an objective standpoint. Doesn't it seem like they're fighting for their own, trying to reclaim their land? When cities expand and encroach on wilderness areas, the animals that live there are either removed or exterminated, forced to coexist or, as is usually the case, pushed even farther out into whatever open country remains. Why should this be any different? Besides, the defense and pursuit of land has caused even more wars than religion."

"So we're at war?"

"Aren't we?"

His cell phone rang, and Brian picked it up, looking down at the displayed number. It was an LA call, but he didn't recognize who it was from. Still, he decided to take it, and answered on the fourth ring. "Hello?"

"Brian? Brian Howells?"

"Yes," he said cautiously.

"This is Lisa LaMunyon!" The linguist's voice sounded excited. "I've done it! I've cracked the code!"

Brian's palm was sweating, and he switched the phone to his other hand so it wouldn't slip out. Instead of excitement, he was filled with dread. "So what do the messages say?"

"They're all over the map. What do you want me to start with? Your father's?"

"Wait. Let me write this down." Brian mimed writing a message on the table, and Carrie grabbed a pen and notepad from the counter next to her wall phone. "Go ahead," he said.

"I've put these in chronological order. The first letter from your father is to your mother. It addresses her as 'Bitch,' then says, 'I love her more than I loved you. I love her body. I love everything about her. I love sex. But I cannot love the children. I love *our* children. Give them back to me. I do not want to do this anymore.' "

Brian was silent, not knowing what to say. He felt as though he'd been punched in the stomach.

"I know it doesn't make much sense. None of them do, really. But the translation's accurate."

Brian reread the words he had written down.

"Do you want me to go on?" the professor asked.

"Yes," he managed to get out.

"The second letter. 'Bitch,' again. 'I am going back. I do not want to go back. The children must be with me. All will be gone. All will be gone.' He repeats that eight times."

"What about the other messages?" Brian asked quietly. "The ones from the crime scenes, the ones written on the walls?"

"Here's where it gets really interesting," the linguist said. "These ones are . . . Wait a minute." She paused, mumbled something incoherent. "Oh my God, I never noticed this before. But seeing them all written down like this in front of me . . ." Brian heard her sharp intake of breath. "They're all different parts of the same message. They're directions to someplace."

"Where? Read them to me."

"The Black Mountain."

Brian felt suddenly cold. He recalled the dream he'd had in his mother's house, in which he'd been walking down a winding yellow brick road, like Dorothy in *The Wizard of Oz*, toward a black mountain crawling with huge white slugs. From somewhere deep within the mountain he had heard his father's screams.

"I don't have these pages identified, so I can't tell you which is which—"

"It doesn't matter."

"Okay, one of them says, 'We live past the big trees,

east of the cities, between the rivers where you stole our
gold.' Another says, 'All homes lead to the Black
Mountain.' "

Brian sucked in his breath.

"The next one seems more modern, although of
course it's in the same language. It says, 'The golden
path leads east and north from Oak Draw.' And the last
one I can't make out because the picture is too blurry.
I can see only a couple of words. 'Gold' again. And
'south.' And 'death.' "

"So they want us to find them. They want us to know
where they are."

"Maybe not us. Or maybe not all of us. Maybe only
those who can read their language." She paused. "Or
maybe you."

Brian took a deep breath. "Remember when you said
that language scared you?"

"Yes."

"Does it still?"

There was a brief hesitation. "Yes."

"Good."

"I'm going to share this with the police," Dr. LaMunyon said.

"That's fine," Brian told her.

"I hope this helps you."

"It does. Thanks. I'll talk to you later." He clicked
off the phone.

"What is it?" Carrie asked.

"That was Dr. LaMunyon, the linguistics professor.
She translated those messages. My dad—" His voice
caught in his throat. "My dad came home because he
wanted me and my sister to go with him. Back to
their . . . village, I guess. The place where they live."

"So that's where we need to go?"

"Yeah. That's where I need to go."

"We."

"Okay. *We.*"

"But how do we know where that is?"

"It's complicated," Brian said, "and it doesn't make any sense. But you know those messages scrawled in blood at the sites of the murders? Those were directions."

"They'd better be pretty specific. Because you saw that new forest. Where would we even start looking? There's probably dozens of scientists and government researchers crawling all over the area. If *they* can't find anything . . ."

He shook his head. "That's not where we're going. Do you have a map of Northern California?"

"Yes." She frowned. "But—"

"Can I see it?"

Carrie left the kitchen and returned a moment later with an Automobile Club map of California. She unfolded it, then turned it over on the table from the Southern California side to the Northern California side.

He traced a line east from San Francisco.

"So where are we going?" she asked.

"A town called Oak Draw."

Carrie paled. She picked up the newspaper and pointed to a headline just below the fold: PRESIDENT RESCINDS WILDERNESS PROTECTION FOR FEDERAL LAND. The dateline was Oak Draw.

Brian felt as though he were rushing down a tunnel made of ice. He was suddenly cold and his head was spinning. "Boiling point," he said.

Carrie nodded.

"Let's go."

Twenty-eight

1880

James Marshall walked up to the St. Millard Hotel, marveling at how much the city had changed. This was not the San Francisco he had first encountered those many years ago. This was a city to rival those in the East, proof if anyone needed it that the West was no longer wild and that culture no longer stopped at the banks of the Mississippi. Of course, he was an old man now, and almost everything amazed him. Sights like this, with well-dressed gentlemen and ladies in their finery streaming into a six-story hotel where every window blazed with gaslight, inevitably made him feel useless and out of his time. The future belonged to the young. *This* was *his* future. And it would be *their* past. The world moved on.

He had been summoned here by the man who'd hired the man who'd hired him to smith. Ordinarily, that would not have meant anything, would not have been enough to tear him away from his bottle and his home. Hell, he'd quit jobs for less. But this was a name he recognized, a name from the past, and even though his memories of that time weren't good, they still had a hold on him, and he wanted to find out what the son of Whit

Fields was doing with his life, wanted to learn how he had turned out.

Wanted to know what he looked like.

That was a big part of it, as sordid and base as it might be, and over the past week, leading up to this, he'd found himself wondering if there would be any sign of what the younger Fields really was.

Pulling his coat tighter against the increasing night chill, Marshall followed the crowd into the hotel, wondering not for the first time exactly why he had been summoned. The lobby was luxurious, floor and pillars marble, walls hung with expensive tapestry. A confident young man sporting tails and a top hat somehow picked him out of the crowd. "Mr. Marshall?" the man asked.

"Yes," he said.

"I am Carson Fields. Very pleased to make your acquaintance."

Now he could see the resemblance. The beard was trimmed neatly, as was the mustache, but the broad nose was the same, as were the deep-set eyes. This was Whit Fields' son.

Still, he kept shaking the proffered hand, looking hard at the face, looking for evidence of . . . something else.

Carson laughed easily, breaking the handshake and motioning Marshall toward the restaurant adjoining the lobby. "I'll bet you're curious as to why we wished to meet you."

Marshall frowned. *"We?"*

"You're a living legend. My father, all of our fathers in fact, made their money in gold, but it was not something they liked to talk about. You are the one who *discovered* gold. You also knew many of our parents. At least that is what you wrote in your autobiography."

"I didn't write that," he demurred. "I didn't even read it. It's probably a load of horseshit."

"Nevertheless, we would like to speak with you and learn what we can. Did you, for instance, know my father? Whit Fields?"

Marshall nodded. "I knew him."

"Splendid! Then we do have a lot to talk about." They had reached the restaurant, and Carson led him to a large round table where close to a dozen young men were smoking cigars, drinking brandy and talking among themselves.

He looked at the men seated at the table, the rich young scions of the Gold Rush generation. Their fathers had earned the money—or, in most cases, *found* it—but it was their responsibility to make it grow and pass it on, build for their families a foundation. And that they had done, starting companies, buying land, putting up buildings.

It was remarkable, he thought, how human they all looked.

Well, some of them probably were. And the others were at least half human. But there was no indication he could see that any of them were . . . anything else. He thought of that night he'd come upon Sutter in his "storehouse," naked, sweaty and straining as he mated with that . . . thing. It was a sight he had never forgotten, one that still haunted his dreams to this day, and it was because of that that he had kept track of Sutter and his men throughout the years, sifting through rumor and story from far away and piecing together what was probably a pretty accurate account of what had gone on after his departure.

Carson made the introductions.

He sat down.

They talked.

Nearly all of them, he soon realized, were ignorant of their origins. Their fathers had married women, their mothers had married men, and whatever acts of monstrous miscegenation had produced these offspring were buried in the past, the knowledge left in the vanishing wilderness, and now no one was the wiser.

He knew, though, and his skin felt cold and clammy just being this close to them. More than anything else, he wanted a drink, a real drink, but he was afraid to imbibe in case he might need his wits about him. They claimed to desire only knowledge of their parents and the old days, but perhaps this was a test, a way to determine how much he knew and was willing to talk about.

A way to find out if he should be allowed to live.

He should not have come. He was nervous and sweaty, and each time the conversation veered too close to the truth for his comfort, Marshall deflected it, bringing up something new. He almost had the impression that some of them *suspected*, that they had questions about themselves and were hoping he would be able to shed some light. But he had no way of knowing if that was the case, and he was not willing to put himself on the line.

These men were all young, rich and successful. They had big plans for the future and the wherewithal to make those dreams a reality. Yet he discovered in the course of the evening that one of their ranks, Porter James— *Teagarden's son?*—had recently killed not only himself but the two prostitutes with whom he'd been consorting as well as one of the prostitutes' daughters. Although, Carson quickly assured him, Porter hadn't really been *one* of them. They had known for quite some time that there was something more than a little off about the man.

Marshall found himself wondering if that was the type of occurrence that from here on out might be happening more and more often. He thought of the old Indian prophecy that removal of the gold would bring about the death and downfall of those who stole it and those who possessed it after, and he looked around at the rich, happy young men seated around the table.

Where will this lead? he wondered.

He was not sure he wanted to know.

Twenty-nine

Oak Draw was a sleepy little tourist trap in the Sierra foothills that was centrally located for easy access to most of the big Gold Rush sites but had no real historical significance itself.

At least not that anyone had known.

Brian and Carrie stopped at the visitors' center, a rustic A-frame adjacent to a *Twin Peaks*-ish coffeeshop. Carrie collected pamphlets from the wall display, while Brian questioned the old lady behind the counter about local legends, particularly anything to do with gold or Bigfoot-type monsters. Back at the car, the two of them sorted through brochures. "So," Brian asked, "where do we start?" He felt anxious, frightened, overwhelmed.

Carrie held up a pamphlet about public hiking trails, pointing to a small, not very clear photo of what the caption said were Native American pictographs. A thin black line led from the photo square to a dotted red line labeled "Ridge Trail A."

"Those aren't 'Native American pictographs,' " Brian said.

"No."

"I guess we've found our starting point."

They were completely unprepared for any sort of hike, so they stopped off first at a camping supply store. The brochure ranked the trail as "moderate" in difficulty and suggested that hikers bring comfortable shoes and plenty of water. They were okay on the shoes, but they had neither water nor anything to carry it in, and they each bought an overpriced backpack into which they loaded containers of sports drinks and bottled water from the grocery store. Brian also bought a first-aid kit, just in case.

"How long are we going to be gone?" Carrie asked.

"If it's more than two or three hours, we'll have to turn back because it'll be getting dark. Then, I guess, we'll just start again in the morning."

"What are we going to do when we get there, wherever 'there' is?"

"I have no idea," he admitted.

There were two military-style Humvees parked in the small dirt lot at the trailhead. That seemed a little odd, but he didn't think much of it until he saw six men dressed in combat fatigues stand at attention when he and Carrie passed their vehicles.

"Are you Brian Howells?" one of them asked.

Frowning, Brian nodded.

"Move out!" someone called, and all six men marched straight over to the cattle guard fence that blocked the entrance to the hiking trail, each of them wearing a pack strapped to his back and carrying what looked like an automatic weapon in some sort of shoulder holster. One man held open the gate as they approached.

"Who the hell are you?" Brian asked.

"Your escort." The one who seemed to be in charge, an older man with a walrus mustache, handed him a cell phone. "Press redial."

Carrie held on to his arm, frightened. Brian was nervous, too, as well as confused, but he was curious more than anything else, and he pressed the redial button on the phone.

"Hello?" The voice on the other end was soft, hard to hear.

"Hello," Brian answered. "Who's this?"

"Mr. Howells?" It was Kirk Stewart. Brian didn't know how he recognized him but he did. He still sounded weak, but there was a determination in his voice that belied his condition.

"How did you find us?" Brian asked.

"Avis car rental. One night at the Best Western in Sonora, two rooms charged to your account. You were easy to track." Kirk chuckled weakly. "Money has its advantages."

Follow the money.

"Yeah, but how did you know to look? What made you even think that we might be heading here?"

"I know where you need to go."

"How—?"

"They're *calling* me," Kirk said, and of everything he'd heard so far, Brian thought that was the most chilling. For he could hear the struggle in the other man's voice to maintain control, to keep the monsters at bay. "My dad was one of them. *I'm* one of them."

Brian didn't know what to say to that.

"I wish I could go with you," Kirk said.

"No," Brian said. "You don't."

"You need me."

"Who are these . . . men?" Brian asked. "What are they doing here? And what do you have to do with it?"

"I hired them for your protection."

"Who are they?"

"Do you know what you're doing?" Kirk asked.

Brian was getting annoyed. He felt sorry for Kirk after everything that had happened to him, but time was wasting and he didn't want to engage in verbal sparring that led nowhere. "I have to go," he said.

"You've figured out what my father is, and the others, and you've traced them to that part of California. Now you're going after them. But you don't know what you're up against. I do." He coughed weakly. "That's why I'm stuck here in this fucking hospital."

"I do know," Brian said quietly.

"But you didn't experience it. Let me ask you. What kind of weapons did you bring? None, right?"

Brian was silent.

"What did you think you were going to do when you found them? Interview them for a story? You're a reporter and you think like a reporter, but that's not what you're going into here. This is a nest of vipers, monsters, ghouls. These things will kill you and eat your head for breakfast. Do you understand me? They'll gut you like a fucking fish." There was a hint of steel in his weakened voice, and Brian recalled the crime scene photos he'd seen, the savage brutality of the attacks.

Kirk sighed. "I don't know what your plan is, why you're going there in the first place, but I'll tell you why I'm sending these men with you: to exterminate them. They're evil, they're dangerous, and someone has to put a stop to them. They tried to kill me. Now it's my turn. Whatever doesn't kill you makes you stronger and all that."

"You can't just . . . slaughter them."

"Why not? It's what they'd do to us. Listen, I don't know you from a hole in the ground. I don't know if you're some bleeding heart or Harvey Hardass. But I do know that I hired these men to accompany you and protect you and kill whatever you find. I'm not arguing with you about it; I'm not discussing it with you; I'm just letting you know." Even in his ailing state, Kirk had the imperious attitude of the extremely wealthy.

"Who are they?" Brian asked.

"My father had occasion to use them in his business. They're men who know what they're doing."

"Are they mercenaries?"

"Of a sort."

Brian didn't know what to say. There was no point in arguing. These men were going to shadow him and Carrie, follow them wherever they went, and there wasn't a damn thing they could do about it.

Except back off.

But that wasn't going to happen. As Carrie said, everything was coming to a head. The stars were aligned, wheels set in motion, whatever cliché one cared to use. Their reason for attempting this trek in the first place was to head off whatever looming disaster lay ahead. Although Kirk was right—they'd had no plan whatsoever. And it *would* be much easier to accomplish their goals with an armed militia at their side.

What about their shoot-to-kill orders, though?

What about his dad?

He and Carrie would have time to work on them while on the trail, explain things more in detail. Things were always different on the ground than they were in the command post, and he was sure that these men were used to using their own judgment as circumstances arose and not automatically following every order to the letter. And if not . . . well, he and Carrie could always turn back depending on how *they* read the situation.

But at the moment, he felt safer with the mercenaries accompanying them.

"Another thing," Kirk said. "I think they like poems. Or . . . not poems exactly. Rhymes. Like nursery rhymes. I don't know how you can use that or if it'll help, but you can never have too much information, right?"

"Right," Brian agreed.

Some of the imperiousness was gone, but Kirk's voice

sounded tired and weaker than ever. "I'd say 'break a leg,' but they may do that for you. Be careful."

"We will," Brian said. He clicked off the phone and handed it back to the man in charge. The name sewn into the breast of his fatigues was *Todd*.

"What's going on?" Carrie asked.

"Kirk Stewart hired these men to accompany us. In case there's danger." He left it at that.

"I don't like this," she whispered into his ear.

"You will when we save your bacon," one of the men said, overhearing.

"I guess we'd better start," Brian said.

Todd nodded crisply. "You heard 'em, boys! Move out!"

Thirty

"Follow the yellow brick road."

They were all thinking it, but it was Carrie who said it, and Brian smiled at her, though that was the last thing in the world he felt like doing. They stood in the center of a shaded glade, staring down at the spot where the dirt trail they'd been following turned into a pathway paved with real gold. It was proof positive that they were on the right track, yet for the first time Brian felt like turning back, heading home and not ever returning or even thinking of this place again. He had never been so scared in his life, and he didn't know what sort of insane hubris had led him to come out here in the first place. Whatever lived here was old, as old perhaps as the red-woods they had passed on the way or the rocks that lined the walls of the canyons through which they'd hiked, and that left him feeling not only intimidated but frightened.

His dream now seemed more like prophecy than anything else, and while Bakersfield and Los Angeles were not to either side of him as they had been in the vision, he understood the symbolism. One was his future and one was his past. Except that the dream had not really been about him, and the path between the future and the past clearly applied to these descendants of men and monsters. They were caught between both worlds, and neither of them could be reconciled.

The mercenaries Kirk Stewart had hired were hard men and doubtless had seen a lot, but they were in awe at the sight of the golden path, and several of them crouched down to touch it with their fingers and make sure it was real. He and Carrie did the same, and the cold feel of the metal caused Brian's heart rate to soar. It was the matter-of-factness of the gold bricks embedded in the ground that made this seem even more terrifying, that gave everything such tangible immediacy.

Even the fun house way they'd reached this point had not scared him quite so much, although it too was plenty frightening. They'd spent the better part of two hours on a winding trail that led to the top of a high ridge. Along the way, they had seen those rocks with the 'Native American pictographs' shown on the brochure. There were a lot more of them than he'd been led to believe—at one point, a series of boulders lining both sides of the trail had been covered with the alien writing—and he couldn't help thinking that they were signposts placed there for anyone attempting this journey. Even Todd and his men seemed to sense the strangeness of those half-scribbled hieroglyphics, and they were silent as they passed by those faded carved messages.

At the crest of the ridge, smaller unmarked paths had split off from the main trail, but they had continued forward until Carrie pointed out an adobe hut at the end of one of the shorter side tracks. The hut had been almost completely hidden from view behind a copse of unfamiliar-looking trees, and it was only Carrie's sharp eyes and a stray shaft of sunlight that had let her see the structure.

Todd had taken the lead, weapon drawn, and Brian and Carrie had quickly been surrounded like the president in the center of a Secret Service detail. The hut had one small door and no windows. They'd called out, announcing their presence, but there'd been no answer, and Todd and Raul, his second in command, had flanked the open doorway, then rushed in, weapons drawn. "All clear!" Todd announced seconds later, and though the building had barely looked large enough to hold them all, they'd gone in anyway. The single room was devoid of furniture, the floor was dirt, the walls undecorated. Only a torn and tattered strip of leather in one of the corners indicated that anyone other than themselves had ever been in there.

Feeling claustrophobic, Carrie had retreated back outside. Brian followed her—

—and they were not in the same location from which they'd started. The copse of trees was gone, as was the small path leading to it from the main trail. They were not even on a ridge anymore. Instead, they were deep in the center of a miles-wide canyon, amid a meadow of dried grasses nearly as high as their waists. A trail did lead from the door of the hut out of the canyon, but it didn't seem to intersect with any others, and he had the creepy feeling that it existed only to lead them to a specific destination.

"Todd!" he'd called. "You'd better get out here!"

They'd been following that same trail ever since, out of the canyon, over a series of hills, through miles of ever-changing forest, until they'd reached this point.

And the golden trail.

Follow the yellow brick road.

"Do you know how much this is worth?" Raul said, gesturing toward the winding path before them. "Millions! Just one of these bricks apiece, and we'd be set."

"Later," Todd said. "First we have a job to do."

At that, Carrie looked at Brian. But he ignored her. They'd been hiking for nearly four hours by his watch, and there'd been a lot of time to talk. He, Carrie and "the team," as Todd called them, had gone over everything. He'd held nothing back—what was the point at this late date?—and while he hadn't received a commitment from any of the men, he was confident enough in the fact that they'd gotten to know each other, and that they now knew him a hell of a lot better than they knew Kirk, who might be footing the bill but was little more than a voice on the phone to them, that he didn't think they were going to blow away his dad on sight.

He was counting on it, in fact.

The golden path led between trees of fantastic shape and astonishing lushness, and he was reminded for some reason of that children's game Candyland.

Where the hell were they?

And would they be able to get back?

Those were questions all of them had been asking and debating ever since emerging from that hut. And they were questions for which none of them had a satisfactory answer. Brian had been filled with an overwhelming sense of dread ever since they'd started on this golden trail, and he had the terrible feeling that the question of how to return was not one they were actually going to have to address.

The sun was sinking behind the mountains to their backs, and though the sky above remained bluish white with only a creeping influx of orange, here on the ground they were walking in shadow. It was exactly what he'd vowed would not happen, and though the team all had powerful handheld searchlights with faces big enough to cut huge swaths through the darkness, he did not like the idea of being out here after nightfall.

Night, he had the feeling, was *their* world.

Still, he made no effort to turn around, and indeed something compelled him to hurry up and get this over with, as though if they were to succeed, they needed to do so quickly.

Or as though dawdling would only prolong the inevitable.

"Look," Carrie said, pointing.

He followed her finger, and it was then that he saw the Black Mountain. It was a mere shape above the tree-tops, a jagged silhouette against the darkening eastern sky, but he knew what it was instantly. Its contours had been seared into his brain more deeply than he'd realized, and its every crag and outcropping was familiar. The mountain was indeed solid black, and the setting sun was unable to shed its light on any part of the peak.

"We're almost there," Brian said, and he was surprised to hear such calmness as he spoke. None of the fear he felt was reflected in the even tone of his voice.

The others were looking up, too, and he could tell from their hushed response that they knew exactly what they were seeing.

"All right, men. This is it," Todd said. He looked meaningfully at Brian. "What do you want us to do?"

Brian breathed an inward sigh of relief. "Just be ready for anything. We don't know what we're going to find." He paused, took a deep breath. "And if my father's there, I'd like to talk to him. We need to find out what's going on before we take any action."

Todd nodded. "You got it. Raul? Me and you. Out front. The rest of you? Behind Brian and Carrie. Let's do this right."

They continued down the path, past trees of wondrous beauty whose tiny leaves glowed in the shadows like jewels, past trees of horrible ugliness whose knotted trunks and branches resembled the bodies of angry, deformed men. A light wind blew through here that carried with it scents of sadness and loss, not recognizable odors but smells that corresponded to nothing, chimerical fragrances able to evoke melancholic memories.

It was a defense mechanism, Brian realized, a way to break down the will of intruders before they had even arrived. Such power seemed impossible, and was definitely not something they could hope to match in any way, shape or form, yet if they knew about it, they could guard against it, and Brian halted the company and told them all what he was thinking. Nearly all of them had come to the same conclusion themselves—he was not the only one with time to think while he walked—and forewarned and forearmed, they continued on.

"I'm not leavin' here without some of this gold," Raul said, looking down at the path.

"First things first," Todd reminded him.

They rounded a corner.

And saw the dead bear.

It stood in the center of the path, nine feet tall if it was an inch, huge clawed paws raised, mouth open and roaring.

Only . . .

No sound was coming out.

And the massive body was riddled with bullet holes, although the blood had long since dried.

Brian knew nothing about bears, only what he'd seen in movies and on TV, but he was pretty sure this was a grizzly. It advanced on them, snarling furiously, silently, its dead milky eyes staring blankly, and Todd and Raul opened fire. Their automatic rifles cut the bear in half, flesh tearing raggedly, bone shattering, as the bloodless top half of the beast fell to the side of the still-standing feet.

And kept moving.

The two men stopped shooting, and Brian took an involuntary step backward. The two halves of the bear's corpse made no attempt to reconcile, but both were still moving and both seemed intent on stopping anyone from going any farther along the trail. The giant clawed feet stomped on the gold bricks, bloodless organs visibly jiggling within the open abdominal cavity exposed behind the jagged clumps of flesh and hair. The top half of the body actually attempted to pull itself forward with its heavy arms, as the open mouth continued to roar silently.

Carrie grabbed Brian's arm, held it, and the other mercenaries looked to Todd for direction. Brian glanced around. They could have possibly gone around the bear, but there were other dead animals as well, he saw, positioned in the spaces between the trees, standing sentry around what was apparently some sort of perimeter. Bobcat and mountain lion, bighorn sheep and elk. Beyond the trees and the dead animals, the forest opened out. It was getting too dark to see exactly what was going on back there, but it was obviously an exposed area because the trees ended in a straight even line, just like the regrown forest they'd visited in the helicopter.

He jumped at the sound of gunfire, and saw Raul and Todd firing again at what was left of the bear. The other men—Garth, Christian, Antonio and Isaiah—moved into position and started shooting as well until there was nothing left of the bear but chunks of hairy flesh and bone. The men remained tense, weapons at the ready, prepared for one or more of the other animals to take the bear's place, but the beasts remained where they were.

"Let's go!" Todd yelled, motioning for everyone to follow him down the—

yellow brick road

—path, and the rest of them hurried past the remains of the bear before the other dead animals got their marching orders.

They rushed between two identical yellow trees that reminded him of something he'd seen in a book as a child—*Go, Dog. Go!*—and stopped.

They'd reached their destination.

They emerged from the trees into the open. The Black Mountain loomed before them, not part of a range but alone, rising above the land like an angry god, massive and implacable. Brian stared up at it. What was it made out of, he wondered? It didn't look like rock, exactly, but neither did it appear to be dirt or sand. What it resembled most was rot or mold, and though he couldn't be sure without getting closer, he thought that it might be nothing more than a gigantic compost pile, reaching its current height only after hundreds, perhaps thousands, of years of accretion.

At the foot of the mountain was the village. Although it was more than that. And less. Dotting the sloping ground were huts of the kind they had entered earlier, dozens of them by his count. These structures had neither doors nor windows, though, and in the adobe with which they'd been constructed he could see large pieces of bone and skull. They were not arranged in any kind of order but appeared to have been set down at random amid a land littered with holes that looked not dug but blasted.

What is in those buildings? Brian wondered. He thought of what had happened when they'd entered the adobe hut on the ridge and saw them not as homes but little powerhouses, energy sources that could be tapped by the monsters that lived here.

And there *were* monsters.

They were all over the place, standing for the most part, doing nothing, as though waiting for something to happen or someone to tell them what to do. A few wandered aimlessly about, but they weren't behaving like actual villagers: mingling, working, performing tasks.

This was their home, he was sure of it, but they seemed to have no real need for community, and where they actually slept—or *whether* they slept—he had no idea. He would not have been surprised to learn that they lived in the holes rather than the buildings or that they simply stood about like this all day long. He looked from one to another, noting the differences in their horrific forms.

All of the females were sexy.

It was not something he had expected or that he would have even believed before this moment. Their faces were indeed monstrous to behold, no two of them the same. Some had big eyes; some had small eyes. Some had noses; some had snouts; some had slits. The shape of the mouths varied, but all seemed to be possessed of the same small sharp teeth.

The bodies were uniform only in their height. They were all nearly as tall as the grizzly. But a multitude of body types were on display: thin, fat, long arms, short arms, clawed hands, fingers, cloven hooves, toes, tails, horns, even antlers. The various figures were covered with a jumble of hair, fur, scales and skin that could be either snake-slick shiny or rough and dull like rhinoceros hide.

Yet they were sexy.

He could not explain it, but as he watched, one of the females closest to them, her pubic area smooth and hairless, her single breast furry, began to sway and dance in place like some primitive stripper, and he was filled with a lust like he had never known. The other men felt it, too. He could see it in the way they stared at the monster and then tried to look away, pressing down on the growing bulges in their pants. He glanced over at Carrie and saw that she had her eyes on one of the males, watching as it stroked its enormous slimy penis and grinned at her.

Brian forced himself to take his eyes off the dancer and saw that the other creatures in the village no longer seemed so aimless or inactive. The monsters had moved closer and were watching their little group carefully, like people trying to circle in and trap an escaped pet. The male and female were distractions, their seductive movements an attempt to keep attentions away from the encroaching horde. He counted eight already that were within easy striking distance, and the expressions on their horrible faces were sly and crafty.

There were piles of human remains on the ground, he saw now, half-eaten carcasses and bones that were not the clean white of movie skeletons but yellowed and dirty, many of them with pieces of rotten flesh still clinging to them.

He yanked Carrie's arm to get her attention and shouted, "Todd! Guys!"

At once they were on alert again and, almost as though it hadn't happened, the monsters in the village were standing dumbly about, staring at nothing, shambling around.

But they were closer.

The female was still swaying to unheard music, the male was still stroking his oversized organ.

"They're trying to hypnotize us!" Brian said. "I saw the rest of them moving closer while we were distracted by those two!" He pointed.

"What should we do?" Todd asked, and once again Brian was filled with gratitude that the man was not so gung ho as to follow Kirk's orders to the letter.

A trail of green—either moss or grass—led between the huts and up the Black Mountain. He could see, in the quickly fading light, where the solid emerald ribbon turned into a multicolored tapestry of the most vibrant hues imaginable. More monsters were coming down from the mountain along that trail, moving from half-light into shadow, having not gotten the message to play possum, and Brian knew that they would have to act fast.

"I want to find my dad," he said.

Todd nodded. "Lights on!" he ordered.

The mercenaries switched on their portable search-lights, and the area in front of them was illuminated almost as brightly as day. Brian would have expected the creatures to shy away from the light, like vampires avoiding a cross, but they didn't seem to mind, didn't even seem to notice, and he grimaced as he saw how truly ugly they were in the bright halogen beams. One of them with horns and a tail looked almost exactly like the traditional conception of the devil, and it stared at him with beetle-browed eyes and grinned knowingly until he was forced to turn away.

Back in Carrie's pleasant kitchen, over iced tea and tacos, the idea that these beings were like some sort of endangered species of animal seemed a reasonable assumption. In that environment, under those circum-stances, many of the harsher truths got stripped away. But Native Americans had considered these creatures demons, and for the first time Brian understood why. Because it was not some fundamental incompatibility be-tween their genes and those of humans that had caused members of the moneyed elite to go on psychotic ram-pages. Such a predilection was a part of the very nature of these things. Coexisting with their enticing sexuality was a wild need for violence that was visible on every face and that could be described only as evil.

"Look," Isaiah said. "Over there."

Brian looked at where the man was shining his light. It was an adobe building much bigger than the others, and Brian couldn't believe he hadn't noticed it before. It was to their right, away from the other huts and just inside the line of trees. It also had a doorway, and when he said, "Let's check it out," Todd snapped his fingers, made a few hand gestures, and he and Carrie were once again ensconced in that presidential security detail as their whole party made its way toward the building.

The smell hit them even before they reached the structure, a sickening stench of rotted food and feces. They were all breathing through their mouths, trying not to gag, and Todd stood several yards back from the entrance and shone his light into the open doorway. Inside were what looked like crudely constructed pens, and Brian was reminded of Lew Haskell's barn. Indeed, a bed of straw could be seen in the closest pen, and lying on that straw was a person.

A human being.

Brian glanced up the slope, and though it was getting so dark that it was hard to see without the aid of the lights, it appeared as though the monsters were hanging back, staying away.

He turned his attention back to the building.

"Come out!" Todd announced in his loudest, most authoritative voice.

The person on the straw stood and faced them, squinting against the bright light and trying to wave it away.

"Go in there and bring them out," Todd ordered Garth and Christian. "Him and anyone else you can find."

"Jesus," Garth breathed, taking a deep breath and trying to hold it. The two of them rushed in, weapons at the ready, and emerged a moment later with the man from the first pen. They went back in, came out with another man. And did it again. And again.

Finally, there were twelve of them lined up outside the building, all with lights and guns trained on them. Christian was off to the side, puking in the grass, and Brian didn't blame him. Even this far away, the stench was nearly overpowering.

An old man with tangled gray hair and a massive matted beard, wearing filthy, raggedy clothes, separated himself from the others. He staggered when he walked, and looked up at an odd angle so as not to be blinded by the lights. The man was sinewy and stoop-shouldered, and though he couldn't see it beneath the dirt and hair and years, Brian knew instantly and instinctively that this was his dad.

Next to his father stood another man, and he too came forward, although he quickly held up his hands in surrender and ran to Todd. He didn't appear to be in as bad a shape as the others, and his clothes, while a little dirty, looked fairly new. "My name's Andrew," he said in a voice that threatened to break down into tears at every syllable. "Andrew Bledsoe. I'm vacationing with my family in Oak Draw. I don't . . . I don't know why . . ." And then he did break down. Brian could tell that they were all wary of the man, unsure if he was a rescued prisoner or some sort of decoy, but he had no time to devote attention to that.

His dad stood before him.

As he stared at the wreck of a man, Brian remembered the last time he'd seen him, when his dad—hair short and neatly combed, buttoned down in his business suit—had given him a hug in front of the empty junior high school—

"I love you, Brian."

—and then driven him to the printer to drop off the page dummies. He was filled with an overwhelming sadness as he thought of all those lost years, all the times he wished he could have talked to his father and asked his advice but had had to make do with a memory and a hypothetical what-would-Dad-do?

Had his father missed him? Or his mom? Or his sister? He looked into that wrinkled, dirty face, those blank, unreadable eyes, and as much as he wanted to believe that their abandoned family had never been far from the old man's thoughts, he could not make himself buy it.

Brian walked forward slowly, and the others walked with him, Carrie holding tightly to his arm, two of the men shining their lights, two stepping forward with their guns raised and ready. Only Todd remained in place, speaking to the man who'd called himself Andrew.

"Dad?" After all these years, it felt strange actually using that word to address someone, and Brian choked up as he did so. He cleared his throat. "It's me. Brian."

The old man said nothing, but he saw recognition in those eyes, a softening, and for the first time there seemed something familiar beneath all of the hair and grime. Brian quickened his pace, arms extended, ready to embrace his dad and—

"He has a knife!" Carrie screamed.

Before the team could even raise their weapons, Brian was jumping in front of his father, waving his hands wildly. "Wait! Don't shoot! Don't shoot!" He turned around to face his dad, and there was indeed a knife in his right hand, an intricately carved blade that looked like it had been made from bone. That hand was gripping the blade so tightly the filthy skin was almost as white as the blade, and the expression on the old man's face was one of shame and despair.

"Don't, Dad," Brian said softly.

His father looked at him, tried to speak, but managed only an incoherent croak.

"I got your letter. You said, 'Stop me.' That's what I'm trying to do."

"Stop me," he repeated awkwardly.

"I miss you, Dad. We all do." Brian took a step forward. He heard clicks and rattles as the men behind him retrained their weapons. "Don't do this. Please. You don't have to do this."

"I do."

"No." Brian was still walking forward, hands extended.

"She's . . . my . . . wife," he got out.

"What about Mom? What about me? What about Jillian?"

The old man's grip on the knife loosened, and Brian took the last step forward and gently removed it from his hand. The moment he did so, there was a shiver in the ground beneath their feet, and puffs of foul-smelling dust flew up from the holes in the earth as though the land itself had exhaled. He didn't know how it had happened, but the monsters were suddenly everywhere, taking a much more threatening stance, and there were cries in an alien language, strange mewling and odd whistles, followed by screams so harsh and dissonant that it hurt their ears. Vegetation was growing wildly all about, dark, menacing plants that threatened to cut them off from everything around them. Vines whipped around crazily like hyperkinetic snakes, and flowers with mouths, like bastard hybrids of Venus flytraps and the monster plant from *Little Shop of Horrors*, pushed up from the dirt and wiggled their way into the world.

The creatures actually seemed to be moving with purpose now, picking things up off the ground, touching their hands to the walls of the huts, walking about in precise ordered steps almost like a ritualized dance. No one knew *what* they were doing—but they were doing something.

Between the trees that formed the boundary to the village appeared more dead animals, big ones, as well as living plants more than capable of doing serious harm to a human being.

"What are they doing?" Brian asked his dad. "What's happening?"

The old man started to speak, then stopped, frowning,

as though he'd suddenly forgotten what he was going
to say.

Or how to say it, Brian thought, and he remembered
those letters with their earnest attempts at simple English. Perhaps his dad had forgotten how to write *and*
speak after all this time.

Twenty years, he told himself.

But *he* would not have forgotten how to speak and
write after twenty years, or even after eighty. He'd
learned the English language, it was imprinted on his
brain, a part of who he was, and he didn't understand
how his father could forget such a basic fundamental
thing after *any* amount of time.

Then Brian looked around at the plants that were
sprouting up between the doorless, windowless huts; at
the monsters doing God knew what; at the holes in the
earth that appeared to be breathing; at Black Mountain,
which loomed over it all, and realized that he had no
idea what his dad had gone through. In all likelihood,
he would never know, and the horrors to which his father had been submitted would remain forever a mystery, unable to be translated or explained.

One of the females began shimmying toward them
down the slight slope. It looked like a partially shaved
Bigfoot with the tail of a rat and the face of a gargoyle,
but damn it, the thing was still sexy, and though Brian
knew it was wrong, he was filled with lust. The reaction
was instinctive, involuntary, and he could tell from the
suddenly still postures of the men around him that they
felt it too.

Todd shot the monster.

"Kill them all!" the man named Andrew yelled hyster-
ically. "The women first!"

There seemed to be no reaction among the creatures
to this killing of one of their own, but seconds later,
another female started toward them, her pink pubic area

distended, hair that looked like rope hanging down from the top of her white head and from the sides of her leathery body. In the light of the halogens, she looked grotesque.

But sensuous.

Brian felt more than saw his dad's tension, and when his father let out a painful, guttural yell, Brian somehow knew what was coming next.

"My . . . wife."

Even before he had finished saying that, Raul had opened fire and blown her away, thin gruelish liquid spurting out from her mortal wounds like water from a fountain.

Brian reached for his father, but he had already darted away, screaming, and though Garth tried to keep track of him with his light, the old man disappeared into the vegetative darkness almost instantly. Brian started after him, but Carrie grabbed his arm, holding tight. "No," she said.

He pulled away from her—

And Todd grabbed him by the shoulders, turning to face him. "No."

The other men were gone as well, Brian noticed, having taken the chance to escape, although Andrew remained behind. He was the only one who didn't seem fully acculturated, and though no one was willing to entirely trust the man yet, the lost and frightened expression on his face told Brian that he was safe, that he wanted only to get out of there and go home.

But not before killing the monsters.

"Shoot them all!" Andrew screamed crazily. "Shoot them down!"

A top-heavy creature with a lionlike face and gazellelike legs jumped through a bush toward them, and someone shot it down in midstride.

"Practice run," Todd said. "They're testing us."

"We don't have enough ammunition to take out all of them," Raul noted.

"Off with your packs," Todd said softly. "Get your explosives."

As the two civilians, neither he nor Carrie were involved in this tactical discussion, and he looked into her face, a hazy alabaster in the darkness. Even without light, he saw worry there and concern. "Don't even think about it," she told him.

"I can't let them kill him."

"You might get killed, too."

"I might anyway. We all might." He turned away from her. "Dad!" he cried.

"Shut up!" Isaiah hissed. "They'll know your weakness. They'll exploit it."

"They know it already," Brian said. "Dad!" he called.

Something hit him on the back of the head.

When he came to, he was lying on the ground and Carrie was crouched worriedly next to him, bending over and touching her cool hand to his forehead. His skull felt as though it had been pierced with an ice pick, but when he felt around he could find no blood. He sat up. He had probably been out only a couple of minutes, but somehow several of the mercenaries were gone. All of them, in fact, save Isaiah, who stood behind Carrie, his light dimmed and pointing at the ground.

"Sorry I had to do that," Isaiah said. "But I did." He motioned toward the threatening vegetation that surrounded them and already blocked off several views of the village. "Let's go. We need to get you up and get past that, out in the open so we can see what we're doing."

"Are Todd and—"

"Already out there," Isaiah told him.

But when they moved past the still-growing plants,

Isaiah shooting one of the whipping vines and using a knife to slice through a writhing sinewy stalk that dripped blood when he cut it, they saw that the rest of the men had not progressed any farther, but were standing together, facing a virtual wall of creatures, several dozen thick, training their lights and weapons on the monsters in what looked like an impasse.

"What's this?" Isaiah asked.

"Custer's Last Stand," Christian said.

No one commented. The comparison hit a little too close to home.

"They're watching us," Todd said. "We can't get past them." He shone his light to the right, at the bodies of three dead monsters lying on the ground amid thick blades of waving grass. "Garth tried to go around and they attacked. We took them out and regrouped." He looked at Brian. "Any ideas?"

"Rhymes," Brian told him. "Nursery rhymes."

"What?" Raul said incredulously.

"Kirk said that they like nursery rhymes. I'm thinking we could use that to maybe distract them, hold their attention while the rest of you go out and . . . do what you're going to do." He met Todd's gaze. "What *are* you going to do?"

Todd lowered his voice. "We're dropping explosives in the holes and slapping some on the buildings. Best-case scenario? We kill a whole bunch of them and scare the rest enough that they're running around like chickens with their heads cut off, so we can pick them off in the chaos. Worst case? We can't even get out there and they kill us here where we stand. In case you haven't noticed, we are slightly outnumbered." He took a deep breath. "Nursery rhymes, huh?"

Brian nodded.

"Any ideas what kind?"

Brian shook his head.

It was Andrew who began chanting, "Fee fie foe fum. I smell the blood of an Englishman." He repeated it over and over again at the top of his lungs. Brian had not known what to expect, but the line of creatures suddenly shrunk as it closed in around them, moving into the beams of the searchlights, hundreds of misshapen eyes focused directly on Andrew. Behind them, those creatures still working at whatever tasks they were trying to complete stopped what they were doing and came forward. A stray beam shone over the heads of the monsters and over the village, its last dim traces hitting Black Mountain, revealing more creatures still coming down.

How many of them were there? Hundreds?

Custer's Last Stand.

Andrew was screaming. "Fee fie foe fum! I smell the blood of an Englishman!"

All of them took up the mantra, and the monsters seemed to move as one, dazed and mesmerized.

"It's working!" Brian said quickly between lines.

Todd nodded, grabbing Garth, the first man scheduled to go out. "You know how to time it, right?"

Garth nodded.

"Set it for ten. Go!"

The rest of them continued to chant.

"Fee fie foe fum! I smell the blood of an Englishman!"

With a few quick instructions, Todd sent out the next man, Isaiah, who ran to the left, past the edge of the line of monsters, then dashed forward into the village unmolested.

"Fee fie foe fum! I smell the blood of an Englishman!"

Christian screwed up. He was not paying attention to what he was saying or his mind was wandering somewhere else, but instead of "fum" he said "fuck," and the change was instantaneous. *All* of the monsters stopped where they were, and the air was suddenly filled with a strange keening sound. In the light of the overlapping beams, the females started dancing in place, gyrating to unheard music, while the males stood where they were and began mindlessly playing with themselves.

"Quick!" Brian yelled. "What rhymes with 'fuck'?"

"Suck!" Carrie said.

"Fee fie foe fuck. On a cock you like to suck." He raised his hands as if directing a chorus, and they all started chanting. "Fee fie foe fuck! On a cock you like to suck!"

The creatures seemed pacified momentarily, but they also appeared to be building themselves into a frenzy, and Brian saw a few of them looking furtively around as though searching for something to . . . fuck.

Yes, that was it exactly, and he was about to tell Todd, but the team leader must have figured it out for himself, because now all of the mercenaries were running out, crouching low as they spread out to different parts of the scattered village, explosives in hand. They had gone without lights, leaving their handheld halogens on the ground, pointing outward in a semicircle. Only three of them were left—Carrie, Andrew and himself—and they chanted the rhyme in unison as loudly as they could.

"Fee fie foe fuck! On a cock you like to suck!"

Illuminated by the static beams in what was now the darkness of true night, the rising moon providing a blue-tinged backdrop, the monsters appeared even more grotesque, their terrifying faces and hideous physical attributes combining with the lurid sexuality of their movements to create a repulsive tableau.

And yet . . .

Brian pressed down on his erection as he chanted.

Garth was the first one to return. "There was gold in

those holes," he said breathlessly. "I could see it in the moonlight as I set my explosives. Must be millions of dollars' worth in there."

Raul followed almost immediately on his heels. "That place is a fucking gold mine."

Brian waved his arms, encouraging them to chant, and they joined in.

Todd and Isaiah made it back safely, but as Christian ran around the gathered creatures who now seemed numerous enough to populate a high school football stadium, one of the females jumped him. It was screeching, shrieking, in that harsh, guttural and unbelievably loud way that Brian was now starting to think was their language, and it grabbed him, shoving his head against its pink fleshy vulva and grinding its crotch into his face as it cried out frenziedly. Christian's arms were flailing, but he couldn't shoot and neither could anyone else, for fear of hitting him.

An explosion rocked the village with a flash as bright as the sun, and one of the huts blasted apart, chunks of bone and dried mud flying into the air so far that some of them hit the crowd of monsters.

With a horrible cry almost as loud as the explosion, the female dropped Christian and began screaming, running in circles like a robot that had short-circuited. Dozens of others were doing the same, and the creatures surrounding them or close by them were staggering in different directions as though drunk.

In quick succession, three more explosions went off. Then a fourth and a fifth. The mercenaries had grabbed their lights again and were standing with automatic weapons at the ready.

The guns weren't needed.

As explosion after explosion detonated in hole and hut, the ground shaking, phosphorescent light flashing in the darkness, hunks of dirt and rock and plant and bone flying up and falling down, the ranks of monsters were decimated. They seemed connected to this place somehow, their very existence intertwined with the fate of this land, and as the village was destroyed, they began to self-destruct.

It was a terrible thing to see. Some of them fell to the ground, thrashing furiously about until they expired. Others ran around crazily, bumping into trees or one another or even getting caught in the last of the explosions before finally dropping dead. Still others appeared to decompose before their very eyes, *melting* into the ground as though they were made of wax.

But that wasn't the most remarkable consequence of the bombing campaign. It was enough, and far more than Brian or any of them had expected, but what happened next was enormous.

Black Mountain disappeared.

The final explosion went off in one of the holes, and with a rumble that seemed to shake the world, the mountain sank in on itself. The air was filled with the overpowering stench of rot and decay. In the moonlight, Brian saw the peak drop, felt the hard quaking of the ground as the mountain seemed to deflate and collapse, and he braced himself, waiting for the end, expecting to be engulfed by a tsunami of rock and dirt—or whatever the mountain was made out of.

But it didn't happen.

The mountain subsided into the earth with a final massive *whomp*, and then it was gone, an entire half of the sky suddenly visible from where they stood. Within seconds, all of the holes in the ground, even the expanded ones made by the explosives, were filled from within, blackness welling up inside each of the cavities and rising until there *were* no holes, only slightly darkened sections of ground.

That smelled like sewage.

Maybe it *had* been a compost pile, Brian thought.

He remained where he was, as did Carrie, as did the mercenaries, as did Andrew. All of them were too stunned to move, too overwhelmed by the enormity of what had just occurred to react, their brains still unable to process all of the information they had been fed.

Carrie spoke first. "Is it over?"

None of them answered.

"I think it is," she said a few moments later.

Brian looked from her to Todd and watched as a grin slowly spread across the face of the dazed mercenary. "We did it," Todd said wonderingly, then said it again, louder and with more confidence. "We did it!"

"I don't know what *it* is," Raul responded, "but you're fuckin' A right. We goddamn did it."

A cheer went up from the men, and as though some spell had been broken, they were laughing and shouting and high-fiving each other. It made sense, Brian thought. This was what they did. It was what they'd come here to do. But he and Carrie and poor bewildered Andrew were still reeling from the events of the past twenty minutes, and it was taking them longer to decompress.

With the mountain gone, the night seemed lighter, the moon and stars making the sky seem almost as bright as it did in the city, and Brian looked slowly about what was now a massive expanse of seriously damaged ground. He could see for miles, all the way to what looked like another forest, but it was movement closer in that caught his attention.

For stumbling about the smoking land, moving through the adobe rubble, the bodies of monsters and the burned pieces of plant, were men.

One of them was his dad.

Brian ran forward, past a burned apelike monster with cloven feet and a too-small head, around a filled hole whose odor made him gag, to where his father stood looking dumbly up at the stars. He grabbed his dad's shoulders, was surprised to feel bone so close to the skin, then hugged the old man to him, ignoring the stench of *them* that permeated his father's coarse wild hair. "Dad," he said through his tears. "Dad."

A tentative hand reached around his back and patted it. "Brian," the slow voice said thickly.

The mercenaries rounded up all six of the men who remained alive, placing them together against the still-standing building near the trees that they had apparently called home. Andrew, talking to Carrie and explaining for the third time about his family vacationing in Oak Draw, seemed to be getting better and more coherent by the minute, but the other six, his father included, stood docilely where they had been led.

"What do we do with them?" Brian asked Todd. "Take them back with us? I'm not sure they're in any shape—"

"Call it in." Todd tossed him a cell phone. "The authorities can use the signal to find you."

"Are we even . . . in a real place?" he asked, thinking of what had happened in the hut on the ridge.

"Only one way to find out," Todd told him.

Brian dialed 911, got an answer but immediately lost the signal. He moved, changed direction, and tried again. This time he got through. It was a Calaveras County sheriff's office that he reached, and when the dispatcher asked him what the emergency was, he hesitated. He had no idea where to start, and if he gave an honest account of what had just occurred, the dispatcher would probably think it was a prank call and hang up. So he simply said that he was one of fourteen people lost in the woods somewhere east or northeast of Oak Draw. He had no idea of the exact location, so if there was some way to trace the phone signal, the authorities could find them that way and send rescuers out. "Some of us are injured," he said. "About six of us."

"Fourteen hikers?" the dispatcher said in disbelief. "Six injured?"

"That's right."

He kept the line open for several minutes, and the sheriff's office was able to track the signal.

"Keep the line open," the dispatcher said.

"Can't," Brian told him. "Batteries are low. I'll keep it on, though. Call when you're getting close."

The truth was, he didn't want to keep the line open, didn't want the sheriff's office to hear what they were talking about and then think he was bullshitting them, so he pressed the button to end the call.

"I want to get some of that gold," Raul was saying. "I'm not digging through one of those shit holes for it, but we got miles of that yellow brick road we could pry a few bars apiece out of."

"Don't do it," Andrew said. He stared flatly at Raul. "That gold is . . . cursed."

Brian would have expected at least a couple of the men to laugh, but none of them did.

"I believe that, too," Carrie said quietly. "As does Brian."

He nodded in agreement.

"Okay," Todd said simply. "That's good enough for me."

Raul blinked. "You're going to give up all that money? Millions of fucking dollars?"

Todd nodded toward Brian's father and the other men. "Are you really willing to take a chance?"

Raul was silent for a moment, then finally shook his head.

"Me neither."

Brian and Carrie walked a little ways away, exploring.

He had put the cell phone in his pocket and taken one of the lights. "We did it," he said.

"But that's not the end," Carrie told him. "What about other people like Lew who we don't know about, who are still out there, ready to go off?"

"The police will just have to take those incidents as they come. Maybe they'll even be ready this time and know what to look for."

"Maybe," she said in a voice that implied exactly the opposite.

Brian frowned.

She nodded toward the mercenaries, who were smoking cigarettes and laughing, already turning what had happened into battle stories. "Look what they did here. They wiped out everyone and everything. That was their mission. Your buddy Kirk Stewart hired them for just that reason."

Realization dawned on him.

"Who's to say he hasn't hired them to also go after friends or business associates of his father, men he suspects of being corrupted?" she said. "Or other rich men he's heard about? Maybe he's hired other 'teams.' I keep thinking about the end of *The Godfather*, where Michael's attending the baptism of his child while killers are carrying out his orders and murdering his enemies at the same time."

Brian remembered the steel he'd heard in Kirk's weakened voice and thought that her comparison was probably very apt.

How did he feel about that?

He wasn't sure. But his part in all this was done. He was not going to keep chasing this for the rest of his life. He'd found his father and that was good enough for him.

"Well, kids, gotta go." Todd was waving at them. "You can keep the light."

"What?" Brian looked over and saw that the other members of the team were packing up their guns and strapping on their packs.

"Hey!" he said, hurrying over. "Where are you guys going? The helicopter'll be here pretty soon."

"We're not waiting for any helicopter," Todd said simply. "We don't exist." He pointed. "And you never saw us. You either," he said to Carrie.

Brian nodded slowly, as did she.

The men had secured their gear and were ready to go.

Todd smiled, and the others gave various high signs and salutes. "See you around."

"Thanks . . ." Brian started to say.

"Move out!" Todd ordered. And then they were gone, disappearing into the trees as though they had never been there.

"What do we do now?" Andrew asked fearfully.

"Wait," Brian said, and looked around to make sure his dad had not moved.

The helicopters arrived sometime later, with phone calls announcing their arrival a half hour, fifteen minutes and then five minutes before the landing, and it was not only a local sheriff's detail that came to rescue them but state and federal agents as well, which made Brian think that someone somewhere had some idea of what was going on.

The next several hours were a blur. They were flown to Sacramento, questioned alone and in pairs. Andrew kept demanding to be returned to his family, and when Brian asked about the fate of his rental car, he was told not to worry, everything would be taken care of. They spoke to police and state and federal agents, and even a woman who seemed like some sort of psychiatrist. "Don't talk to any reporters," he remembered telling Carrie at one point.

She smiled. "My story's exclusive to the *Los Angeles Times*."

His father had been arrested for the murder of Reverend Charles, and Brian thought that at least some of the others had been placed into custody as well, but he didn't want to think about that right now, didn't want to deal with it, and he gave Jillian a quick call and a bowdlerized version of what had happened and asked her to find a lawyer and take charge of the situation until he returned to Los Angeles and got everything straightened out.

It was early evening when they were finally allowed to go. Andrew had gotten lost in the shuffle, but he and Carrie were still together, and they were both given plane tickets and a ride to the airport. Both of them were dirty, their clothes wrinkled, stained and torn, and they looked so much like homeless people that others in the terminal made a special effort to avoid them or take a wide walk around them. Both he and Carrie laughed about that, although afterward she said soberly that now she knew how some of her clients felt when they were out in public.

Neither of them had anything to check, and they sat alone near a window, staring out at the night as they waited for announcement of their flights.

"Did we do the right thing?" Carrie asked. She was looking at him intently, the expression on her face one of worry and concern. Her eyes had gained a haunted look over the past few days, and he wondered if he looked the same.

"I don't know," Brian admitted.

"I've been thinking about that forest. The one that regrew overnight. Don't you think that such power could have been harnessed somehow? I mean, with so much deforestation and global warming and all of these environmental problems we're facing, doesn't it seem like we had a solution at our fingertips that we could have used? And we just wiped it out? Bam! A few explosions and a whole species, extinct."

Brian thought of that species, the evil expressions on those hideous faces, the piles of bones and rotting human carcasses. He recalled Lisa LaMunyon's translation of one of his dad's letters.

All will be gone. All will be gone.

"You said one time that this was a war," he told her. "Well, maybe it was. And maybe we did what we had to do. What did Phillip Emmons say when he was referring to those things? They were committing defensive acts? I think we did, too."

"But we'll never know."

"We shouldn't have been the ones to find them," Brian admitted. "And especially not with Kirk Stewart's army. It should have been scientists or the government or . . . somebody."

They were both silent for a moment.

"So what about your dad?" she asked finally.

Brian sighed, feeling tired, realizing suddenly that he had been up for forty-some hours straight. "I'm letting my sister handle that now. I'm pulling a Scarlett O'Hara. I'll think about it tomorrow."

Carrie smiled. "A man who knows his *Gone with the Wind*. I'm impressed."

"Oh, I'm a font of interesting attributes once you get to know me."

They were on different flights going in different directions, and when the boarding of Carrie's plane was announced first, the two of them looked at each other like lovers reluctant to part. They *weren't* lovers, there hadn't been even a spark between them, but what they had shared made them closer than many couples who had been together a lot longer, and he thought that under different circumstances they might have had a chance at romance.

"Call me if you're ever in San Francisco," she told him.

"Or if you're ever in LA."

They hugged awkwardly, and he watched her walk down the long hallway to her plane. Ten minutes later, his own flight was called, and he showed his pass to the crisply uniformed woman, and walked wearily down the corridor, where an attendant helped him find his seat, making no mention of his unkempt appearance or obnoxious odor, treating him as though he were a regular passenger, and for that he was grateful.

He still had notes and supplies at the hotel in San Francisco, he realized as he stared out the window at the terminal building. And clothes. Were the law enforcement officials going to take care of that?

He closed his eyes. He'd think about it later. If he had to, he could call Carrie and have her pick up his stuff and ship it. Right now, he was tired.

Thinking about his belongings made him consider what type of article to write and how much he should tell Jimmy and whether or not he should pull his own experiences into it or go strictly objective.

He was still trying to think of how to write his story when he fell asleep.

"Please fasten your seat belts. We will be landing shortly."

The announcement woke him up, and Brian opened his eyes, stretched and straightened.

"We will be arriving at Los Angeles International Airport in approximately twenty minutes. Please make sure you have all of your belongings."

Brian smiled, feeling relaxed and peaceful for the first time in a long while. Northern California was beautiful, and San Francisco was a wonderful city.

But Southern California was home.

He looked out the window as the plane descended through the clouds and was gratified to see, spread out below him, the twinkling lights of Los Angeles, like jewels on black velvet, stretching westward across the conquered land all the way to the infinite darkness of the vast Pacific Ocean.

Epilogue

Dexter and Pam waited by the grammar school swings for Tony and the others to come, but when the full moon rose high enough to cast their shadows on the sand, it became pretty clear that none of their friends was brave enough to show up.

No matter. They didn't need anyone else anyway.

The Place no longer worked, but Dexter had found the new location. The two of them cut through the trailer park, walked past the old house that had been converted into Aunt Edna's Beauty Parlor, then continued down the street to its end, where two unfinished luxury homes sat at opposite sides of the cul-de-sac.

People had started using the empty lot between the two unfinished houses as a dump, throwing unused concrete, yard waste, cans and bottles, even the frame of an old motorcycle onto the cleared section of ground. Dexter led the way around the back of the piled refuse and stopped.

"Here it is," he told her.

The two of them found a place to hide behind a jumble of cut branches.

They waited.

A woman arrived alone. She immediately kicked off her shoes and pulled down her pants. After taking off her top and bra, she rolled down her panties and pissed in the dirt, stirring it into mud and applying it to her face with her fingers. She got on her hands and knees and chanted: "Engine, engine number nine. Take me quickly from behind."

It came from the culvert this time, shambling forth from the darkness, a thing of hair and snakeskin, with deep eyes that could not be seen and sharp small teeth that could.

As Dexter and Pam watched, it took the woman roughly, rudely, in a way that made her scream.

And around them the flowers bloomed.